LOVE AND OTHER POISONS

By Lesley McDowell

FICTION

The Picnic
Unfashioned Creatures
Clairmont
Love and Other Poisons

NON-FICTION

Between the Sheets: The Literary Liaisons of Nine 20th-Century Women Writers

Love and Other Poisons

Lesley McDowell

WILDFIRE

Copyright © Lesley McDowell 2025

The right of Lesley McDowell to be identified as the Author of
the Work has been asserted by her in accordance with the
Copyright, Designs and Patents Act 1988.

First published in 2025 by
WILDFIRE
an imprint of HEADLINE PUBLISHING GROUP

1

Apart from any use permitted under UK copyright law, this publication
may only be reproduced, stored, or transmitted, in any form, or by any means,
with prior permission in writing of the publishers or, in the case of
reprographic production, in accordance with the terms of licences issued
by the Copyright Licensing Agency.

All characters – apart from the obvious historical figures – in this
publication are fictitious and any resemblance to real persons,
living or dead, is purely coincidental.

Every effort has been made to fulfil requirements with regard to
reproducing copyright material. The author and publisher will be glad
to rectify any omissions at the earliest opportunity.

Cataloguing in Publication Data is available from the British Library

Hardback ISBN 978 1 0354 1169 6
Trade paperback ISBN 978 1 0354 1170 2

Typeset in Scala by CC Book Production

Printed and bound in Great Britain by Clays Ltd, Elcograf S.p.A.

MIX
Paper | Supporting
responsible forestry
FSC
www.fsc.org **FSC® C104740**

Headline's policy is to use papers that are natural, renewable and
recyclable products and made from wood grown in well-managed forests
and other controlled sources. The logging and manufacturing processes
are expected to conform to the environmental regulations
of the country of origin.

HEADLINE PUBLISHING GROUP
an Hachette UK Company
Carmelite House
50 Victoria Embankment
London EC4Y 0DZ

The authorised representative in the EEA is Hachette Ireland,
8 Castlecourt Centre, Dublin 15, D15 XTP3, Ireland (email: info@hbgi.ie)

www.headline.co.uk
www.hachette.co.uk

With gratitude
Emma Tennant 1937–2017

I tell my secret? No indeed, not I;
Perhaps some day, who knows?
But not today; it froze, and blows and snows,
And you're too curious: fie!
You want to hear it? well:
Only, my secret's mine, and I won't tell . . .

Or, after all, perhaps there's none:
Suppose there is no secret after all,
But only just my fun.

– 'Winter: My Secret',
Christina Rossetti (1857)

Prologue: Rowaleyn, 1857

I open the window and lift my skirts, take a step over the windowsill and ease myself down on to the lawn. It's like escaping from a prison; the clouds part as I run over the wet grass, granting me an unlikely moment of morning sunshine.

The long drive down to where our carriage stands, in front of the coach house, curves past the woods. I want a walk in the fresh air, but not in that direction. Not yet.

Then a cacophony of voices, like the screeching of crows, stops me.

I squint in the direction of the noise, hand above my eyes. I must be mishearing. But no – someone – people – are shouting my name. *It's her! Madeleine! This way, Madeleine!*

Down at the gate at the end of the drive stand a group of men, their caps raised as they wave in my direction. There's a huddle of at least six of them, before a few women dressed in smocks and headscarves appear beside them. *There she is! It must be her! Madeleine!*

They jostle each other at the gate as I stand, frozen and staring. One of the men begins to climb it; behind me, Papa shouts for Mr Blane the coachman.

The man on the gate is almost over; he's stretching out his

arms to me like a lover. Then, *bang!* A gun goes off, the women scream, and the man falls backwards on to the ground.

I turn round; both Papa and Mr Blane are carrying hunting rifles.

The end of Papa's is smoking.

I.

'With regard to the prisoner's statement to the chancellor of the French Consulate, that the deceased had never been in the house, his Lordship remarked, "Now really, gentlemen, the statement of the Dean of Faculty that this girl starts into a heroine at this moment is an exaggeration which I did not think to hear from my learned friend."'

– The Lord Justice-Clerk charge to the jury in the trial of Madeleine Smith, 8 July 1857, Edinburgh

New York, 1927

After you've gone and left me cryin', After you've gone, there's no denyin'...

Though it was spring, the parlour was dark in the mornings, facing northwards as it did, which suited my mood. I sniffed at my favourite song playing on the gramophone and took out my handkerchief, the one with the initials 'LS' woven into a corner where lace touched the edges. Then Marion Harris's sweet voice got me singing along with her instead, swaying in the gloom.

You'll feel blue, you'll feel sad, You'll miss the dearest pal you—

'Mrs Sheehy! Mrs Sheehy!'

The shouting of my name outside gave me a nasty start, and I cursed out loud. But I recognised his voice: the same man had been calling on me three mornings in a row. I seized the gramophone arm but it slipped, and the needle scored across the record.

'Damn him!' I said again. I'd sworn twice already, and it wasn't even noon.

'Mrs Sheehy!'

His voice was deep, and carried through my open window like an actor's. Spring was chilly, but I liked to hear noise from the street. It was all I invited in now. Noise – and dust. Dust I could hardly help, for it got everywhere in the Bronx, especially with Park Avenue being so close to the Grand Concourse. The city was shooting up so quickly this far north even the tiniest birds had to shake it off their wings. Little warblers, coughing up grit and soot. A breeze would pick up, and leaves from the trees – the few left after they'd dug up enough for the Concourse – would shower you with it, like icing sugar scattered over cake. Uninvited, it blew through my window, settling as far indoors as the mantelpiece.

This suited my mood, too, with its filth and darkness. It suited the presentiment that had set up home in my head ever since the New Year rang in four months ago. Every day was a bleak wondering, with my fears of discovery only growing, and my feelings flitting about like a flock of starlings, giving my heart strange beats and skips.

No: I wouldn't open the door to folk I didn't know. Dust couldn't be kept out, but strangers could. And anyone who did call – wearisome salesmen mostly, by the cards they left in the mailbox – soon left me alone when they got no answer.

This one seemed more persistent. But I hadn't answered him in three mornings so far, and I wasn't about to do differently today.

'Mrs Sheehy! You at home, ma'am? Your window's open!'

Arms held out for balance, I tiptoed in stockinged feet over the parlour floor, moving past my paintings, which were propped up on either side of the fireplace or set on the mantelpiece. One or two ancient gowns that doubled for painting smocks trailed down the backs of dining chairs I'd brought here from Eighth Avenue. Just this parlour, with a single bedroom at the back, and a tiny kitchen and washroom: it was all I needed now.

The gauze curtain at the parlour's bay window trembled

in the breeze. I'd not looked out the last three days he'd come calling in case he saw me, but this morning I was cross after my record got scored, and crossness made me bold, had me peeping out for a glimpse of him. He was bending low on the stoop, gazing through the frosted glass door into the hallway, as though he had a right to know what was inside.

He was no salesman. He carried no wares, and besides, his oxfords gleamed and his white baggy pants dazzled. Angled sideways on his head so that his face was hidden from me, sat a spotless white boater. There wasn't a single speck of dust about him at all. The brand-new, dirt-free Chrysler parked by the sidewalk had to be his, then, too. No hopping on trolley cars or driving some old jalopy for him. Like the times, he was, flashy and drunk on credit. But the downturn would come soon enough.

I let my breathing slow; my fingers, arthritic and swollen, twitched at the curtain. And that was when he raised his fist and rapped at the glass door so hard it gave me another fright, causing me to stumble backwards. The rug caught my ankle and pulled me down, making me yell, though more from panic than pain.

The noise gave him his chance.

'Mrs Sheehy! Are you hurt? Mrs Sheehy!'

I waited in a heap on the floor, hand at my mouth. Then someone else ran up the stoop and let him into the building.

'Damn old age and its traps,' I muttered, my third curse of the day, but it was my granddaughter, Violet, who called from the hallway, not the stranger.

'Grandma? Grandma, are you OK?' She sounded so stricken, I was ashamed.

'Oh, Violet, thank goodness it's you! I'm fine, I tripped, that's all—'

'I'm coming in, don't you move!' In she flew as though I were on fire, running in her too-high Mary Janes and pulling off her scarlet coat. 'Oh Lord, Grandma,' she cried, blue eyes wide and blond hair bobbing. 'Here, let me get you up—'

But just as she was bending down to help me, something too bright and white crossed my vision and I fell back down again. For *he* had followed her in, of course, and my gnarled old hands flailed uselessly, my voice high-pitched and insistent as a child's. 'Whoever you are, you'll get nothing from me! Get out of my home! Get out, I tell you!'

'Grandma!'

The shock in Violet's voice didn't stop me, though. 'Get out!' I said again, though more weakly, as the stranger removed his boater and set it on the dining table. I put up my hands to shield my face, for fear of some absurd recognition by him.

But his face caused the only absurdity, for absurdly beautiful it was, his feline eyes shining like coffee, with thick black eyelashes no decent man should have. Almost made-up, they seemed, mascara-smudged and mesmerising. Violet was pressing her hand to her chest as if to keep her heart from breaking through it. But his gaze was turned on me and slowed my own heart down so I was sure I must have died, and he and I were both ghosts.

'Who – who are you?' I stammered.

My eyelids fluttered and Violet said, 'Grandma! Grandma!' I heard the stranger urge Violet to take me by the elbow, and together they heaved me gently off the floor and on to the daybed, which was set against the wall.

'You don't understand,' I said to Violet, gasping and blinking hard. 'This man's been calling on me every day—'

'I hope you don't think I mean you harm, Mrs Sheehy,' he said. He'd put out his hand for me to shake but I wouldn't touch it.

'But you *have* – been calling on me, I mean. Who are you?'

'Name's Harry Townsend. And I'm very pleased to meet you at last.'

Violet said, eagerly, 'I'm Violet Wardle – *Miss* Violet Wardle. And this here is my grandmother, Mrs Lena Sheehy – oh, but you know that!'

He smiled. 'You never answered me, Mrs Sheehy, not once all these days. You're a hard nut to crack!'

'Then take a telling,' I said. 'Mr – *Townsend*. I don't speak with strangers.'

I sat trembling, my dry, wispy hair suspended in front of my face. I tried to pin it up, but it just fell back down. Even that little action had me out of breath. My hands shook, too, for I knew what was surely coming. He'd say he was a reporter, and had found me out. I wanted Violet to be gone so she wouldn't hear what he'd have to say, but she was too blinded by his looks to notice any warning signals from me.

'I'm no stranger, not really,' he said in that rich, low voice, drawing one of the dining chairs towards him and settling himself in front of me. 'I thought you might recognise the surname.'

'I don't know any Townsends,' I said, rudely.

'Ah, my mother's a Conti, though – Angela? Daughter of your friend, Teresa Conti.'

Surprise had me clutching at my chest, the breath I took

in was so great, and I pitched forward as if to get up. Violet squeezed on to the daybed to steady me.

'Teresa's grandson? You're not – a newspaperman?' It burst out of me before I could stop it.

He only laughed, though, and looked at Violet with a comical expression on his face. 'Now, why would you think—'

'No, I meant – oh my, you're *Teresa's grandson*,' I said again, as if repeating it would divert his attention from my slip-up. Even so, relief was coursing through me, for Teresa was indeed my good friend, my old neighbour from Eighth Avenue. I'd not seen her since my move uptown.

Then a thought struck me. 'Teresa's all right, isn't she? Oh my, is Teresa in trouble?'

'No, she's fine, don't worry,' he said. 'Did she never mention me to you? Harry?' He grinned more widely, showing two front teeth that were slightly crooked.

Teresa had twelve children in all, and God knew how many grandchildren, more than twenty at least, so their names were forever lost on me. But there was one called Enrico, which was Italian for Henry, and I thought that must be him. 'Are you the one who lives out west?' I said, testing him a little first. There was something else at the back of my mind, a sad story, I thought, but I couldn't remember what it was.

'That's right,' he said. 'I'm Harry, the one out west!'

Maybe I smiled then, just for a second, before my rudeness hit me, making me ashamed of how I'd treated him. 'Well, I *am* very sorry,' I said. 'Had I known who you were, of course I'd have answered—'

He shook his head and proffered a strong, sunburned hand

to lay on my pale, wrinkled one. I gulped at the kindness in the touch. Violet let out a sigh of envy.

'There's no apology necessary, the fault is mine,' he said. 'I frightened you in my eagerness to speak with you. Might I offer my condolences, too, for the loss of your husband last year? My nonna told me. She was sorry to see you move uptown.'

My feelings tumbled about. Grief and suspicion and fear had been grappling for a hold, but his taking of my hand, and the revelation of who he was, banished them all.

'I remember Teresa talking about you now,' I said, eagerly. 'Enrico, she calls you. She thinks you're the bee's knees. She should have warned me you looked just like a movie star!'

He laughed, and so did Violet. 'You're too kind,' he said, 'but I prefer being behind the camera—'

'You're a movie director?' Violet interrupted, breathy and excited. I didn't mind her being here, now that I knew he wasn't any danger. He seemed confused by her interruption, though, and the brief alteration in his expression alerted me to something else about him, a kind of guilelessness, I thought.

'That's why I'm here,' he said. 'I run my own film company. Newly set up.'

I was confused. 'That's why you've been so persistent?'

'*So persistent*,' he said, imitating me. 'Gotta love that accent.'

'Grandma lived in England a long time,' Violet said, before I could stop her.

'My nonna mentioned that. And, well, it's why I'm here. The two of you went to see a play together last year, *Pygmalion*.'

'Yes,' I said, but slowly, for I was still in the dark. 'At the Guild Theatre on 52nd Street.'

'Well, there's a revolution coming in movies – "speakies".

They're making a film with actors speaking, see, and when it hits, there's gonna be the biggest fight for movie rights to all the best-selling plays. *Pygmalion* would make a fortune as a "speakie". And my nonna – well, she told me you knew its author, Mrs Sheehy. George Bernard Shaw himself.' He pushed a forefinger towards me, and I shrank back a little.

Violet nudged me. 'Grandma! You never said.'

'Oh, no, I think Teresa must have misunderstood,' I said. But my heart had quickened.

'Are you sure?' Harry asked. The expression on his face was as plain as the meaning in his words; he wasn't a man for misunderstanding. 'He'd take tea with you, she said, when you lived in London.'

I shrugged, trying to recall that night at the theatre. Maybe I'd had a whisky tonic beforehand; maybe I'd wanted to impress Teresa. Maybe I really did say it, and then forgot it just like that. How could I have made such a blunder? What else did I give away?

'So I was thinking,' Harry said casually, taking out a gold cigarette case and lighting a cigarette with a gold lighter, 'you might help me meet him. Something like that?'

'It would have been such a long time ago, in the years before Grandma came out here,' Violet said to Harry, in a kind of whisper. 'But she's shy about it. When she was just a girl they had a big house in the country, with servants, and she went to balls, too. Later on in London she was married to my daddy's father, and then she came here, and a long time after, she married Grandpa Willy.'

Violet was so enjoying reminiscing, she was going to do more of it. That focused me at last.

'Shaw? Oh, I knew lots of people then who wrote plays and poetry,' I said, waving my hand. 'Someone was always doing something that looked like it might be important. And for a moment or two it was, and then it wasn't, and then it just – disappeared.'

'He's a famous socialist,' said Harry, rubbing his chin. 'How'd that sit with your servants and country houses?'

It wasn't a question I wanted to answer. What I wanted was something for a dry throat. 'I haven't even offered you any tea,' I said, getting to my feet. But I'd moved too quickly, and found myself swaying and tipping forward. Harry jumped up to catch me.

'Let me get that tea, Grandma,' Violet said, and she scurried off to the kitchen, leaving Harry and me alone together.

My eyes closed as everything spun, but Harry held my arm and said, 'Settle yourself now,' as I eased myself down on to the daybed. I leaned back and his lips brushed my ear as he whispered, '*Mimi.*'

Just that. A single word.

Mimi.

It was more than enough to force my eyes wide open, make me blink in alarm. 'What – what did you – what did you say?'

But just then Violet came back into the parlour with the tea tray, and he went to help her. I was still amazed at what I'd heard – or thought I'd heard, for I must have got it wrong. *Mimi.* No, he couldn't have said that. Was I starting to hear things? I couldn't afford to make those kinds of mistakes. Like so many who came to this city looking to live their lives over again, it didn't do to make mistakes.

Mimi.

Sudden tears bubbled up, to my shame, and Violet poured me a cup of tea, patted me gently. 'It's been too much for one day, I think. She's ninety-two, you know,' she said to Harry. 'Why don't you come back tomorrow? Talk a bit more with her then?'

'Of course,' he said, taking up his boater.

'There's really no need—' I began, but Violet was already ushering him to the door.

'Nonna'd never forgive me if I made her ill,' was all I heard him say, as they passed out into the hallway.

My hand shook as I put down my cup. When Harry called out, 'See you tomorrow, Mrs Sheehy, take care of yourself,' I could only murmur a reply. Then the front door slammed, and he was gone.

'I don't see how I can help Harry,' I said when Violet returned to the parlour. But she had a dreamy look on her face. How quickly we fall for a smile. My late husband's smile had been wide open, causing me to tumble into it the first time I met him, all those years ago. But I wasn't so keen to see Violet fall. She put an arm around me and squeezed my shoulders. 'He's so cute, though,' she said, and gave me a wink.

'I think I need a little sleep,' I said, though it wasn't much past noon. Violet fixed me some lunch, which she left in the kitchen for me, before picking up her packages and kissing me goodbye.

After supper, another record on the gramophone had me sitting on the daybed, singing along.

It's a story that's never been told, I'll be carried to the new jail tomorrow . . .

'The Prisoner's Song'.

'Well, that was a foolish choice,' I muttered to myself, and I was about to lift up the gramophone arm and change the record, when there was a sharp knock at the front door. I thought to check through the window first to see who was calling on me, then his voice rang out.

'Mrs Sheehy!'

Harry. Had he forgotten something? The sun was setting and rays of crimson and peach cut across the frosted glass of the front door.

'Did you leave something behind, Harry?' I said, opening the door to him. He didn't reply, but stepped inside the hallway and headed straight for the parlour, without waiting for an invitation. I stumbled after him. 'What are you doing here?' I said. 'Do you want – is it about Violet—?'

It occurred to me that maybe he wanted her address to call on her, given how sweet on him she'd shown she was already, and I was thinking how to manage that request when he removed his boater and showed his face more clearly. Perhaps he'd spent the last few hours in a speakeasy; perhaps it was something other than liquor. Whatever it was, his face looked different from that morning, less friendly, less handsome, somehow. His words gave me no doubt about his true intention.

'I know who you are, Mrs Sheehy. Who you really are, I mean. *Mimi*. That's who I want to talk to you about.'

His voice was so calm, I felt the need to match it. 'You don't want to talk about Mr Shaw?' I said, and tried to smile. But my smile wobbled, and as it did, so my resolve disappeared and my shoulders sagged. It had finally arrived, then – the very thing I'd been dreading for years. And delivered not by a stranger, but by a dear friend's grandson.

Harry grinned his film-star grin, notwithstanding his crooked front teeth, and I realised, too, what had changed about his expression.

It wasn't guilelessness, as I'd thought that morning, or a lack of nuance. No; it was stronger than that. There was a crudeness to him, a kind of vulgar simplicity I'd glimpsed in some silent movies I'd been to see. But those were harmlessly vulgar, childish in their simplicity.

His crudeness lacked that innocence.

I waited as he strolled around behind me and shut the parlour door. I knew now exactly what he was going to say, for he was nothing if not a hostage to that crudeness in his expression and in his character. And so, of course, he said it right out.

'Let's talk about the murder.'

Glasgow, 1855

'He spoke of her by her first name, "Madeleine", and by "Mimi". He gave me to understand that there was a mutual attraction between him and this lady.'
— Witness Mrs Clark at the trial of Madeleine Smith,
2 July 1857, Edinburgh

When Mama is ill, I remove the stopper to her little bottle, and the aroma that escapes stings my eyes and seizes my throat. My brain fizzes for a few moments, and then I sigh, become a ghostly girl gliding from her room to mine and back again.

When Mama is ill, dust and soot collect under my fingernails. They settle on my scalp, hide inside my nostrils, dig down into my lungs. Turn my insides black as a witch's heart.

When Mama is ill, our house on Bedford Place is darker than the deepest forest. No light gets in through the velvet drapes. Parties and dinners must stop, and every step is silent. We speak in whispers and take our meals in the kitchen at the back of the house, for the dining room is just beneath Mama's room, and even the scraping of a fork on a plate might reach her above and make her screech.

And so the windows outside turn sooty from St Rollox, the

giant smoking chimney in the east. Dust balls in corners. The sound of a brush sweeping is too much for Mama. From my books I blow grit, dirty my fingers with the pages.

Her illnesses always take place at the end of winter, when Christmas is long past but March days are still cold. Papa escapes out to his architect's office on St Vincent Street as often as possible, which leaves me trapped indoors with Mama, unable to accept invitations or call on my friends or even visit the shops nearby on Sauchiehall Street.

Only I can attend Mama in her delicate state upstairs. Too many servants might talk.

So occasionally I snap at the small, bony boys delivering different medicines from local apothecaries. Sometimes, they call at the back door, if Mama has procured something she thinks Papa might disapprove of. Of everyone in the family, I have it worst. 'Stay by my side,' Mama murmurs through the stench of illness, of unbrushed teeth and unwashed hair, for nobody can lay a finger on her to wash her but me, not even our housemaid, Christina, when she removes the bedpan.

All of this I must do as penance, for when I came back from Mrs Gorton's Academy for Young Ladies in London last summer, Mama and Papa both made their disappointment in their eldest daughter very clear.

I'd received no offers of marriage. No rich man's son had pledged himself to me. My failure meant a round of parties, which was fun, at first. Dinners, and introductions, most of them to as many of my brother Jack's new friends as he could produce, and countless outings – even a balloon ride.

But few of those boys marked my card at balls or delivered

glasses of punch or whispered promises. Even though I smiled and nodded and agreed with whatever they had to say.

'What do you think is the *point* of you?' Mama had said to me, before my departure for London. After I returned and the *point* of me proved no reason to celebrate, I smiled harder at a duke's son who was hosting a dinner party in Edinburgh. We removed to a dark corner of the dining room hidden by the drapes. He bade me follow him to the stables behind the house, where no one would see us. My heart beat very hard as I lingered at the servants' entrance, watching him stride across the cobbles of the horses' yard. My parents would be proud of me yet.

The duke's son did write after our encounter. He was very passionate towards me and I thought that at last I could prove myself, so even though I was reluctant at first and he had to prevail on me with perhaps less gentleness than I'd expected, I believed that was the true *point* of me. And when he demanded a lock of my hair, it seemed that my *point* had been won. I sent it, along with the words of intimacy that he'd used towards me at the time. I believed it would secure his proposal. How could it not?

But his next letter told me that he'd been pledged to another all the while, and then, only a few months after this, Mama told me he'd sickened suddenly and died. It seemed that a door, although closing, was now locked tight. That night upstairs, in front of my bedroom fire, I distracted myself with thoughts of Cathy's ghost returning to Heathcliff to tap, tap, tap at the window for her love. Would the Edinburgh boy do the same for me, even after disappointing me so much?

I waited and waited for that tapping at my window. For his ghost to say how sorry he was, that he loved me after all.

It never came.

But the parties continued until Mama's illness, which meant my smiles did, too, and they grew ever more desperate. My hunger for a fiancé. Mama and Papa surrounded me with boys and parties, but like a child in a sweetshop warned not to eat a single one lest it spoil her supper, I wasn't to taste their pink-tongued, blond-haired, sugary sweetness.

How it hurts never to taste, never to be full.

'There must be something wrong in how I look, or talk, or behave,' I said to Christina just before Mama took to her bed and the shutters came down. 'I am the wrong shape; I have the wrong face.'

'Perhaps you just *want* too badly,' Christina replied. She'd found me weeping in the kitchen, staring at cream puddings and baked scones that I couldn't eat.

No: wanting too badly only makes me devour *myself*. All through winter and the start of spring, I spend nights in bed pulling at the collar of my nightdress, scratching at my neck until blood appears, then sucking whatever smudges my fingertips. I rip the membrane on the inside of my mouth so many times and swallow it; I chew my fingernails to the pink and swallow those, too.

I'll be like one of Macbeth's witches soon, for I even chew the ends of my hair. When I was bent over the washing bowl one morning, as Christina soaped my curls, she chided me for ruining them.

But on this March morning when she's done brushing my hair dry, I'm more desperate than usual for some reason, and say, 'I'm going out. It's been *weeks*. I don't care what Mama wants anymore.'

Christina begins to tidy my bedroom in silence, picking up the lace drawers left on the floor, the pairs of calfskin boots scattered around the bed. She plumps velvet cushions, dabs at something in the washstand, straightens my silver jewellery boxes. A tuft of hair escapes from under her cap and a few grey strands show amongst the black, though she's little older than me.

I may have silk skirts and fox-fur capes, but Christina has a fiancé, which makes her the richer one.

'Did you hear me?' I say. 'I'm going out.'

'If your mother wakes up she'll need you, and I'm on my own with Agnes being ill,' she grumbles.

'You'll have to be enough for her. I won't stay indoors another minute.' My voice trembles.

'You're nineteen years old, Maddie, not *nine*.'

'Don't be so mean—'

'Who am I to say you can't go? I won't answer for you, though, I mean it.'

But I'm too delighted, and now she's bending down to help me pull the buttons through on my boots and tie my too-tight new jacket, and carefully set my flat bonnet.

'I want to see and be seen,' I say. 'I want—'

Ah, but what do I want, when no one wants me? A *wolf* of a man is the only kind to devour *me*. Milk-teethed boys who make empty promises and die too soon of silly illnesses haven't the stomach for me.

'You want to watch yourself,' Christina says. 'It's too plain on your face, that's your problem. They read you like a book.'

'Then I'll be a difficult book,' I say. 'A foreign book. A French book!'

She snorts. 'A French book. Aye, so you will.'

'You just don't want me married and leaving you,' I say.

'I'll be leaving you before you leave me,' she huffs, so I give her a hug. Christina blows hot and cold with me; she's my only confidante, but sometimes she resents it, tells me I take liberties with her position, and that I should remember that Papa is the one who employs her. Other times, like this, she's soft and yielding like a true friend, and I can forget she's a servant – but then Mama's bell rings and she has to pat her grey skirts and run in to her.

In the glass, my cheeks aren't pink enough, so I splash them with water before hurrying downstairs to the gloomy entrance hall.

A heavy black curtain is drawn across the front door. *Fortress Mama*. But it's easily pulled away, and the door is lighter than it looks, so in a second or two, I'm breathing in all of Bedford Place and the shops and the coffee houses and the carriages just beyond it, along with the horse muck and the smoke and the grime that a rare westward wind's blowing from the St Rollox chimney.

How incredible that it's over four weeks since I last stepped outside! Maybe that's what has me hesitating, behaving like that lady writer trapped inside her father's house until a poet came to rescue her. *But there's no poet coming for you, Madeleine – hurry!*

By the time I've crossed Renfrew Street and Sauchiehall Street both, I'm dizzy with my new freedom and have to stop for a moment to catch my breath.

And that's when the rain starts to fall, of course, stopping my escape. I tsk, but up on Bath Street, the entrance of a new coffee house offers shelter, so I hurry there to wait for the rain to stop, shaking my skirts and smiling still for getting away.

I'm so happy to be free of Bedford Place that at first I don't notice the bearded gentleman sitting in the coffee house bay window. Only when something makes me turn does he come into view, and then he raises his hat to me as if he knows me, and I freeze and blush, hot and cold both, because I know him, too.

We have met before. On the street, alone together. Without so much as an introduction.

I'd no notion I could behave so boldly when I came out of Paterson's one afternoon two months ago, just before Mama took ill. My friend Mary Buchanan was inside, taking an age over some silks, and I wanted fresh air. The last of the winter sun was only a dribble on my face, but I lifted my chin up towards it just the same, and closed my eyes.

A cough nearby made me open them again. A bearded man was standing barely a foot away, his long necktie and open shirt collar just visible beneath a striking Inverness cape the colour of rowan berries. He tapped a silver-topped cane at the ground. In his other hand, his gloved fingers held a lit cigarillo.

The tip of it briefly glowed.

'As fine as any in Paris,' he said to me with a slight accent, not waiting for an introduction. A rude foreigner, the kind that Papa's newspaper was forever warning young ladies against, who had been 'flooding' into the city lately. I gazed down at my plaid skirts and he nodded at the shop.

'Oh,' I said, feeling like a fool.

'Oh, indeed. *Très beau*,' he said, then looked back at me again.

I blushed; my eyelids fluttered. 'Do you – do you know Paris well, sir?' I was brave enough to ask.

'I do. Though I am no Parisian, alas.'

'You *are* French, though? Your accent is—'

'I am from Jersey, but my parents are French. French was all I spoke as a child.'

'How fascin—'

'And I lived in Paris, during the revolutions. I served in the military there.'

We'd learned about the revolutions at Mrs Gorton's Academy. The thought that seven years ago, when I was a child playing with dolls, he might have been killing men with his bare hands, almost made me swoon. I wobbled on my heels, and he stepped over to steady me, his hand firm at my elbow.

'The sun – it's warm,' I said, as he let go.

'You think so? I find it very cold here.'

'Perhaps you're not used to—'

But that was when Mary appeared, her mouth falling open at my speaking to a strange man, and she pulled me away before we could exchange another word. It seemed afterwards, though, that I must have conjured him out of my dreams somehow, for back at home I struggled to picture him, and then I forgot about him, because running after Mama took over every thought, every action.

But perhaps I never forgot him entirely, just buried him deep inside instead. Because my heart's bounding now at the coffee house entrance, and in a way it never does with any of those pink-cheeked boys. Not even with a duke's dead son.

And so I bob a tiny curtsey at his raised hat in the bay window, even as my legs tremble and my mouth dries.

He responds immediately, getting to his feet and gesturing to the empty chair beside him.

It's much too daring of us both; but maybe this is how things are done in Paris, I think, so I don't hurry, but I don't dawdle, either. Breathing softly, I lift my skirts and, unchaperoned, step over the threshold of the coffee house to meet him in the dark interior beyond.

Only it's not quite so dark in the window. We can be seen by those passing on the street, and my breath catches in my throat lest Papa should walk by, or one of his associates.

'Emile L'Angelier,' he says, bowing; when he straightens up, his face is every bit as handsome as it was two months ago. His tanned cheeks are softly lined, for he's older than me, perhaps as old as thirty. His whiskers are thick and dark; his long hair is wavy and loose, not oiled or tied.

His eyes are as sad as a poet's, but his lips are full, and they glisten wet and red as a wolf's tongue. I'm suddenly aware of my own lips, so dry, and wet them. His eyes rest there, and my heart swells too huge for a breath. Suddenly it's as though I've let go of my dress, my underclothes, in front of him, and that's such an appalling, thrilling thought that I shiver all over, and he says, 'Are you well? Mam'selle—?'

'*Madeleine*,' I stammer. 'Madeleine Smith. I am very well, thank you, sir.'

He lifts my gloved hand and kisses it.

'So you got away, Maddie,' says a voice behind us, startling me into pulling away my hand. My brother Jack appears suddenly out of the darkness of the coffee house; he grins and winks at my shock. 'Is Mama fully recovered then?'

'I didn't know – you are here? But how do you know—?'

Flustered, I bump down on to the empty seat beside Emile as Jack takes the one on his other side.

'Oh, I was here for a while, then Emile passed by and

recognised me,' says Jack. 'He knows the Bairds.' The Bairds are business associates of Papa's, and the youngest son, Robert, is friends with Jack. I gasp, but not at his news; Emile is pressing his leg against mine beneath the coffee table.

'I know the Bairds through a work colleague,' Emile explains. His dark blue irises are almost black, and when I look into them it's as though I'm falling, somehow. Jack orders more coffee, but when it arrives I don't dare lift the cup for the trembling in my hands.

'What work do you do, Monsieur L'Angelier?' I manage to ask.

'Emile works for the merchants' house, Huggins and Company, on Bothwell Street,' says Jack, before Emile can answer. My brother's acting very boldly, pretending to be worldlier than he is. A small smile plays on Emile's lips; his leg presses harder. 'You know – Robert's been advising there. You are a – what do you call it, Emile?'

'I have a *commercial position* within the company,' he says.

'The Bairds have a very fine place not far from there – on Royal Crescent. Perhaps you know it?' Jack says.

Emile's eyes grow a little more melancholy, even as his leg presses, which makes my heart soften with sympathy for him. My annoyance at Jack increases.

'I've not yet been invited to dinner there,' Emile says. 'But perhaps one day soon.'

'Our house in Bedford Place isn't so fine as theirs,' continues Jack. 'But Papa has put everything into Rowaleyn, our country house down the river. The Bairds don't have nearly as fine a place in the country as we do.'

'No, I am sure not. But any house in the country must be a

wonderful thing, no matter how fine it is. I should very much like a house in the country myself one day.'

Jack raises his eyebrows as if someone with a mere *commercial position* couldn't possibly hope to own such a thing. For myself, I can't help noticing the frayed edges of Emile's dandyish hat, the scuff of his boots. His faded kidskin gloves on the table; the yellowed cuffs of his shirt. Papa has no time for those who cannot better themselves, despite his own financial troubles when we were small. He dug himself out of that hole, Mama said once, the only time we ever discussed it, when she was mentioning possible matches for me before I went to London. 'Your Papa admires a man who has made his own fortune,' she said. 'Though we would both be happy for you to find a man who has inherited his.'

Papa would rather I married a Moor with a fortune, than a working man like Emile. But I don't care about wealth, and I blush for Jack's snobbery.

'Papa designed Rowaleyn all himself,' I say, quietly. 'He works very hard.'

'Oh, it's quite spectacular, Rowaleyn. Everybody wants to be invited there,' Jack insists, then lists the names of the titled folk that Papa has coming for shooting in the summer. I worry that Emile will find Jack's boasting vulgar, but his eyes light up at the mention of dukes and lords, and he teases his long hair into resting about his shoulders. He might be an exiled French prince banished by the Emperor, and I think of him being presented to Papa's friends.

'Tell me more about the fine people who attend your parties,' Emile says. 'I like to know how they dress and talk, how they *conduct* themselves.'

'Really, whatever for?' Jack says, raising an eyebrow. 'Shooting parties are mostly a drunken affair anyway.'

I frown at him; he says, 'It's true, Maddie,' and I frown again at his use of that childish name.

But Emile's eyes glitter, and he leans forward, stroking his moustache. 'I want to know – I like to – make a *study* of the conduct of nobility. You see, I have an ancestry that is noble—'

I knew he must have, but Jack looks highly sceptical. 'No one cares about *conduct* after a shoot,' he says, 'nobility or not. After all, who's there to check us?'

I can see he dislikes Emile asking these questions; they're not understanding one another, which makes me squirm a little. When the waiter arrives again and Jack's attention is diverted at last, I intervene and murmur, 'I believe we met outside Paterson's once, Monsieur L'Angelier. I – I am often to be found there.'

'Call me Emile, please. And I know where to find *you*, Madeleine,' he says, leaning towards me.

I can't reply for the feeling bubbling up inside; a few minutes later, when Emile takes his leave of us, he kisses my hand again, now ungloved, and my blood heats as his whiskers brush my bare skin. Then he strolls out of the coffee house without as much as a backward glance.

'How could you be so *vulgar*?' I say to Jack, because it must be his fault Emile didn't turn round. My face says it all, as Christina has warned me. 'All that talk about drink—'

'He's the vulgar one – wanting to know about "conduct",' Jack says, and snorts. 'Well, perhaps he would – he's just a clerk at Huggins. "Commercial position", indeed. He hasn't got a penny to his name. And the *showy* way he dresses, in that cape! The colour of it. Imagine him turning up at Rowaleyn like that.'

'But he has ancestry. And he's been a soldier. He's *lived*. And in Paris. During the revolutions! He told me,' I add, when Jack looks surprised, 'when you were talking with the waiter.'

'You'd have Papa invite him to bring his "ancestry" to the shoot in summer, then?' Jack laughs; suddenly, I want to slap him. 'And his soldier's gun? Maybe he'll aim it at Lord Hamilton's son—'

'Don't mock him like that. He'd beat every lord at a shooting party.' My hands tingle again at the thought of him amongst Papa's friends. A true man; a military man.

'Maybe. But you can't set your cap at him. Even if he does know the Bairds. And don't tell Papa you spoke with him. Not without an introduction. A country house, indeed! As if *he'll* ever have that.'

Back at Bedford Place, I make for the drawing room just off the hallway, and in my rage at everything Jack has said, I pull on the curtain rope and open the drapes to the street. Spring light reflects in puddles after the rain and makes the gold clock on the mantelpiece glisten. Everything in the room glitters, for all the dust that's gathered here: the rosewood sofa and armchairs; the cut glass of the decanters left on the table; the oil paintings of my grandfather and the Duke of Hamilton; Mama's silver boxes and china figurines in the brass cabinet. The semi-grand piano in the corner; the embroidered screen in the corner opposite. The rosewood card table and the embroidered stools beside it. The two enormous vases on the mantelpiece, which will remain empty of lilies or roses, because now that spring has come, we'll be leaving here for Rowaleyn as soon as Mama is better.

It all calms me, though. I know Jack's wrong about Emile. He belongs here amongst fine things, with his elegant whiskers and his sad poet's eyes and his 'ancestry', whatever it is. Yes, his cape is very bright – garish, even – and his way of adjusting his hair would infuriate Papa, who loathes vanity in a man. My spirits sink a little. But then I remember his *I know where to find you*, and I make a deep curtsey and say out loud, 'Mama – Monsieur L'Angelier,' and nod to the empty chair. I picture Emile bowing low to her, and kissing her hand very lightly, like a true gentleman. My French prince.

'What are you doing?' It's Christina, standing in the doorway. 'Who's Monsieur L'Angelier?'

I tell her about the meeting at the coffee house. 'And oh' – I seize her by the arm as she closes the drawing-room door behind her – 'his leg was pressed against mine the whole time.'

She frowns. 'You want to be careful,' she says. 'You're the eldest daughter, you're worth something, you know.'

I'm suddenly brought low again by the recollection of empty calling cards.

'I'm not worth anything to anyone. Not to any man I've met so far. But he is different – he's a grown man. At least thirty.'

Her eyebrows shoot up. 'You don't want any offers from a thirty-year-old clerk—'

'Were you not just saying this morning that I was nineteen, not nine? Mama wasn't much older than that when she married Papa.'

'You're already thinking of *marrying* him, are you?'

Christina marches over to the drapes, pulls on the cord to

close them again. Darkness returns to the drawing room. 'I'd like to see the look on your papa's face when you tell him that.'

'I'm making a point, is all.'

'Then I'll make a point, too. The master was no clerk.'

'He wasn't rich when he was young—'

'He worked for your mama's papa; he was in training as an architect. And he wasn't *French*, either. You know what they say about French men.'

I have no idea what 'they' say about French men. 'None of the boys of my age have been French. Maybe that's only to their detriment.'

Christina opens the drawing-room door and pushes me out into the dim hallway, its paintings in shadow, for all it's so bright outside. Immediately, I feel smothered in dust. Only Emile can blow it all away, free me from it!

'You're wrong,' I say, 'Once Papa meets him—'

'Don't be ridiculous. Your Papa won't meet a man like that. And he's no prince.'

'He has a poet's face – he's – he's like a wolfish poet – in a prince's clothes.'

Christina only laughs at my confusion, though. 'Aye, I'll bet he's all that. He'll be used to a certain kind of woman, then. And that's not *you*.'

'It never is me, though, is it?'

Christina's look softens; she takes my hand. 'It will be, Maddie, one day. Just be patient.'

But how to be patient now that I've met him, spoken with him, learned his name and given him my own?

I'll not be an old maid, trapped with Mama for ever, I think in bed later, lying awake to gnaw at the skin on my wrists, nip the flesh on my arms, for I'm so very hungry. And when I finally fall asleep near dawn, my dreams are full of wolves and boys that try to hide from them, before they're ripped apart to dissolve in pools of blood.

'I don't know where he lives, only where he works,' I complain to Christina the following evening in the kitchen. It's the first occasion we've had all day to speak, because of running after Mama's wants, and we're both tired, flopped over the kitchen table. 'It's not as if I can wait about on the street for him. And I can't send a note, either. What if he never got it, and someone found out, and told Papa?'

Papa's tempers are legendary. I chew the tender part of my lower lip, which stings. Rub my eyes too fiercely, as though I'll see something different when I'm done.

'You look like you've escaped from Bethlem,' Christina says, and gets up from the table to come and smooth down my hair, which has gone without brushing all day. Her firm strokes against my head are soothing, make my eyes close, and she hums a soft tune, her fingers pulling gently through my curls, as my head rests on my arms.

'Bethlem would be an easier place than *here*,' I murmur, but inside something nags, making me regret not looking after my appearance better. My neck nips; when Christina lifts my hair a little, she tsks at the scratches underneath.

'I'll give you a cream for that,' she says. Christina is good at making all sorts of poultices and mixtures from stuff she stores in the kitchen. She fetches a small jar from high above the grate and dabs a little on my neck. 'Look at your wrists, too,' she says.

'D'you think that would ruin it between us?' I say.

'Ruin what?'

'Perhaps he'd not care for me to write first. Emile.'

She sighs, almost annoyed-sounding, but just then someone knocks lightly at the back door. Three quick, short raps. It's late now, almost ten o'clock. Upstairs, everything is as silent as ever. Mama is in bed, of course; Papa is in his study.

The gas lamps on the street outside don't carry light to the back of the house, which remains in darkness. The only light in the kitchen now is the fire, flickering in the grate of the range. Christina hurries to the back door, then waltzes in, leading her fiancé, McKenzie, by the hand.

He's a slinking, thin man, thin as gruel, but wiry under his jacket and shirt, which shows when he walks, for there's power in his step. He has black eyebrows and tiny eyes that don't meet mine. His jaw is straight, at least, but he smells of the street, all smoke and unwashed bodies. When he touches his sooty cap with dirty fingers, he still doesn't meet my gaze. He never does. What does she like about him, I wonder, as Christina takes him through to her little bedroom, just off the kitchen, a lit candle in her hand. There's only a narrow bed in there, and a washstand, and a small cupboard for her clothes.

Before she closes the door, she sets the candlestick on the floor, and gives me an odd look from the doorway. I stand up, ready for her to shoo me away.

But she doesn't.

I hesitate. The kitchen darkens as the fire goes down. Far away, a horse and cab sound as a couple of rowdy gentleman arrive at a house nearby, full of drink, by the sound of their fighting talk. I get up and go to the door to the scullery, which leads to the back door through which McKenzie entered, and close it gently.

From Christina's room come strange noises. It's wrong to eavesdrop; I should go back to my bedroom, of course. Yet I find myself tiptoeing over to her closed bedroom door.

The keyhole is large. I hold my breath and get down on my knees as the drunken gentlemen's arguing outside sounds increasingly foolish, and urgent. But the urgency that interests me is coming from behind the bedroom door.

I put my eye to the keyhole, my heart thrumming so hard the pair behind it must surely hear.

But they don't, and at first there's nothing to see, for Christina's room is windowless and the candlelight so very low. Some flashes of white cross my vision; the grey of her skirts. Then suddenly the iron bedframe strikes the wall, once, twice, three times, startling me into a loud 'Oh!'

And I flee the kitchen for my room upstairs.

My back's against the bedroom door, one hand over my mouth. The duke's dead son had pushed my back up against the stable door and rummaged about my skirts. Then promised we would be wed, before his letters told me no.

Tears spurt out of me like a cough. The easy sway in Christina's hips as she waltzed across the floor to her room, leading McKenzie by the hand, tells me *she* has never been jilted.

More tears follow, stinging and bitter, so it's some time before I'm calm enough to go to bed, and hours before sleep comes.

Downstairs in the kitchen early the next morning, McKenzie's sitting at the table, his brown hair almost falling into his bowl of porridge, his shirt partly unbuttoned and his bare arms white.

Such thin arms he has, hard as horses' bones and just as strong. From the doorway, I watch in my nightgown, biting my lip. I've had very little sleep, and none of it easeful. I start when Christina bangs a spoon against a pot. Her hair's undone and her cheeks are flushed, as if she's only just come from her bed, too. When McKenzie finishes his porridge he gets to his feet slowly, but before he makes for the back door, he plants a kiss on Christina's cheek, and squeezes her behind until she squeals. And then he's gone.

'If Papa knew what you were doing, you'd be out on the street,' I say, wiping suddenly damp hands on my nightgown.

Christina stares, then slowly licks the spoon McKenzie has left behind.

'Slattern,' I say, and she slams a bowl down on the table, and marches over to grab my hands and twist them behind my back until I cry out, 'I'm sorry, I'm sorry!'

'You'll not say a single word to him,' she hisses in my ear, lips pressed against my hair, digging her fingers in hard. 'Or I'll tell your papa who you met in the coffee house.'

My cheeks burn. 'You wouldn't—'

'*Slattern*,' she says back to me, then Mama's bell rings and she lets go, pushes me out of the kitchen. I stumble up the stairs to Mama's room, struggling to get my breath. *Slattern – me?* How dare she; how dare she?

Hours later, long after I'm washed and dressed and have seen to Mama, the word is still spinning round in my head. *Slattern*. Perhaps that's what Emile thinks of me, too. After all, I *was* forward; I *was* bold, letting him press his leg against mine. Perhaps that's why he hasn't written. He can't call without an introduction, but he could write.

And he hasn't. So perhaps he's like those other boys I've met, after all.

I know where to find you, Madeleine.

All he made me was another empty promise. Later, outside Mama's bedroom door again, the familiar putrid whiff of the bedpan gathers in my nostrils and makes me almost retch, along with the sound of Mama's moaning. But in I must go to her, for there's no one else who wants or needs me.

'I wish I was Christina; I wish for a fiancé to lead into a little room with a narrow bed,' I whisper over and over by Mama's bedside. 'Whoever he is, make him come soon. Make *him* write to me.'

But time drags on until supper. The house twitches and moans along with Mama; noises from the kitchen below scarcely reach us in the bedroom above the drawing room, and only occasionally does the front door bang shut. But there's a ghostly kind of whine coming from the pipes, and behind the walls, too. The only other sound is the ticking of the grand French clock on the mantelpiece; I'm too morose, and fancy its dreary beats counting away the hours of my girlhood.

When Christina finally taps at the bedroom door to relieve me of my duties, I'm listless and yawning. Jack and Papa are both still out, though it's dark by now. On my way downstairs, I hesitate at the pile of the day's letters on the silver platter on the hallway dresser.

'Send me a letter, send me a letter,' I murmur over and over, eyes shut and hands clasped in prayer. 'I'll do anything. I'll be a good girl from now on. Just send me a letter.'

But when my eyes open, the letters are all addressed to Papa, of course. It's enough to make me curse – though I hardly know any curses beyond *damn* – and promise never to be good again.

And that's when a sliver of white pokes out from the floor at the side of the dresser. An envelope.

The house groans; the pipes whistle as I pick it up and turn it over to read the address there, and gasp out loud.

Miss Madeleine Smith, of 164 Bedford Place.

His hand is florid, but proud and masculine, too. My poet-soldier-prince. *Oh, I'll be a good girl*, I murmur, but the envelope smells of his cigar smoke and suddenly the urge to cram the paper into my mouth and swallow it, letter and envelope both, has me kissing it, licking along the edges, my eyes closed tight.

Somehow he discovered my address. I hurry back upstairs to my bedroom, forgetting all about supper. On the bed, I spread out his words before me. They are few, but perfect.

Dear Miss Smith,

It was a great pleasure to meet with you – should you care to respond to this note, I am at ____ on Great Western Road, near the Botanic Gardens.

Yours,
M. Emile L'Angelier

Never did my heart grow so large. To crush every bone, every muscle.

'Yes,' I whisper. 'Yes, I *care* to respond.'

The letter smells even more strongly of his cigar. That urge comes over me again, and this time, I ball up the paper and put it in my mouth.

'What are you eating, Maddie? You haven't touched your supper.' Christina's voice; she's standing in the doorway, staring at me.

'Nothing,' I mutter, and swallow the chewed paper.

'You've got a look on your face—'

'What look?'

She cocks her head; a smile grows on her lips. 'I've come to tell you – your mama's feeling all better suddenly. She's even sitting up and taking some soup, bright-eyed as anything. So you know what this means – time to go to Rowaleyn. As soon as next week, she's saying.' Christina crosses her arms.

'Already? No. It's too soon—'

'You won't have very long to catch your poet. You won't see him till October at least.'

'I won't go! I can't. I'll stay here – I can manage by myself.'

'Your papa won't let you stay on in town alone.' Christina sounds shocked, but she appears to be enjoying herself, and a thought occurs to me.

'It'll mean you have to go, too,' I say, slyly. 'No more visits from your *fiancé*.'

She looks downcast at that, which pleases me. 'I'll just suggest to your mama she hires someone from the village instead,' she mutters.

'Oh, no, she much prefers to take you with us! You know that.'

We look at one another. 'I have a fiancé now. It's different,' Christina says, lifting her chin.

'Well, I have—'

'You have nothing.'

I have an envelope. *His* envelope. I ease it out from where I've hidden it under my skirts and show it to her.

'I have to write back. I have to meet with him. I can't go to Rowaleyn. Ah, how do I stop Mama taking me away?'

Christina sits down beside me on the bed. 'There might be a way,' she says. 'But if I do it, you're not to say a word to anyone, right?'

'Do what? What can you do?' I seize her hands.

'Nothing *bad*, honest. It's just, we want a delay, don't we? I'll do it for you, Maddie, but only once. Mind and remember that.'

I nod. 'Thank you, thank you,' I say.

We have a common purpose now, and that sudden moment when Mama's illnesses fall away and the house is full of activity and is opened up again – when she wants everything done immediately, and which is worse than when she's ill, for there's an unreal brightness to it, brittle and shifting and demanding we humour it lest it snap, and which makes us pretend and plan and do whatever she asks – ah, that sudden moment will be different this time.

For into the kitchen we go, Christina and I, where she takes down one or two of Mama's special bottles from the shelf in the scullery, and mixes a few spoonfuls together in a saucer. Then she takes some other ingredients from unmarked jars and mixes them in, too. Then she boils some water for a hot toddy, and carefully pours in the mixture, which disappears in the heat. We don't speak as she stirs; it's wrong, what we're doing.

But we want to stay.

Later, back in my bedroom, I write a reply to Emile.

Dear M. Emile L'Angelier,

It was a pleasure to meet with you again, monsieur. I long to know more about la belle France *from one who has lived there. It is my dearest wish to improve my knowledge of the language, and to visit the country a* bientot.

Yours,
Madeleine Smith

Will he like my French learning, the language of lovers?

All the rest of that evening I pace about in a state; after I persuade Christina to run through darkening streets to deliver my letter herself because tomorrow's post is too far away, I picture Emile reading it, and seizing his pen to reply.

No, we cannot possibly leave for Rowaleyn yet. We mustn't.

When Christina gets back, it's almost ten o'clock. She takes another of her special 'hot toddies' to Mama. We won't know until tomorrow, she says, if it has worked.

In the morning, Mama is indeed laid low with a terrible headache and cannot get out of bed.

Rowaleyn, Papa announces at supper, is postponed until the end of the month after all.

I would feel bad about what we have done, only the whole day passes without a reply to my note from yesterday, and that's all I can think about. In the dining room next to the drawing room – for Papa has said suppers may begin there again and we won't eat in the kitchen anymore – my meat and potatoes sit untouched. At bedtime, my waist, my breasts, my belly, seem ever more shrunken. I'm still hungry, still starving, but food repulses me. In the dark later, I dream of choking on mounds of paper, and clouds of cigar smoke that bring tears to my eyes.

The next evening, tired and cross, Christina and I are alone again in the kitchen when McKenzie calls, but this time, I get up from the table straightaway, head down, and make for the door. Somehow he catches my eye for the first time and says, with a grin that shows surprisingly clean, large teeth, 'No peeking now, lass.' Christina gives me a warning shake of the head which makes me even more furious.

In my bedroom upstairs just half an hour later, though, she appears with an envelope in her hand.

'This has come for you,' she says, dropping it on the bed. A bruise is blossoming on her neck. She doesn't say another word, but shuts the bedroom door after her.

Dear Miss Smith,

It would be my great pleasure to talk more of France and its beauty to one as beautiful as you. *I will teach you everything I know. My lodgings are far from you, but* you *are no distance to me, should you wish it.*

Yours
Emile L'Angelier

'To one as beautiful as *you*'. 'No distance to me, should you wish it.' He thinks I am beautiful and means to come to me. To Bedford Place . . .

It's all I could have wanted him to say, but it's impossible; Papa would never admit him as my guest, not without an introduction. What to do? I want to gobble up this letter, too, but there's another kind of ache inside me, one that heats my chest, has me pulling at my collar to try and cool it down.

Nights at Mrs Gorton's. A girl in our dormitory with a forbidden book. We'd pass it back and forth between our beds, searching for what we wanted.

Dear M. L'Angelier,
    I would so prefer une leçon privée, away from the house. Perhaps we may meet outside Paterson's to discuss it.

Sincerely,
Madeleine

My hand's trembling; my fingers slip and blotch the paper.
Les Liaisons Dangereuses was the book.
McKenzie's jeering face makes me lift the pen again. Another blot of ink. Beneath my signature, I write:

    'My love frightens you, you find it violent, unbridled!'
                                    – Pierre Choderlos De Laclos

The thought of him reading it is terrifying and delicious all at once; I bring the finished letter to my lips before my nerve fails, then seal it, and pull the bell for Christina to deliver it.

All the next day, my feelings gallop like a runaway horse, have me snapping at everyone. By evening there's still no response from him.

'He's a working man,' Christina says, 'so he'll not be back at his lodgings till late.'

I drop a plate and a cup and break both.

'I'm not paying for those,' she grumbles. 'You can explain it to your mother.'

'Who cares about a plate, when there's no answer from Emile?' I say, miserably.

Sleep is impossible until nearly dawn. I scratch my hands almost to ribbons, bite my lips until they bleed.

'He's going to think you're a madwoman,' Christina says when I wander into the kitchen the next morning, with my skin pale as gruel and my hair askew and the backs of my hands covered in red marks. She hesitates, then pulls something out of her pocket. 'This came for you – Christ, don't go running to him, Maddie, wait! You're going to your ruin, I'm telling you.'

But I won't listen. I snatch the letter from her and run to my room to read it in peace.

Madeleine,
   Outside Paterson's – at 2.

Emile

I reach Paterson's just as it starts to rain. I pace back and forth, panting, for I've taken too long to make myself presentable since receiving his note and, as a result, have had to run all the way to make it on time. After a short while, a dressmaker comes out to usher me in from the wet, but I refuse.

Fifteen minutes pass, then twenty, and he doesn't show.

Thirty minutes pass.

He doesn't show at all.

I'm furious and desperate and near to tears, but there's no other choice for me but to go back to Bedford Place. In the warm kitchen, Christina forgives my rudeness of before, and helps pull off my sodden boots, my soaking cape.

'Is he making a fool of me?' I say. 'Why would he do this?' Thoughts of the Edinburgh boy make me sob; am I never to be right, never to be wanted?

'He wants you to beg for him,' Christina says, sighing, as she sets my wet boots by the kitchen fire.

'I don't understand, why would he—?'

'He wants you doubting, like this.'

'But he said I was beautiful. So why did he not show?'

'Ah, Maddie. Will you listen to me now, if I tell you?' she says, stroking my clenched fists softly until they uncurl.

And what else is there for me to do but nod, and listen, as she whispers in the gloom of the kitchen all the things she knows about grown men and what they are and how to act with them.

'Don't ever show you're giving chase. Always hold something of yourself back. And never, ever let them lay a finger on you,' she says. 'Remember that when you meet the "gentlemanly" sort, for they're all of a muchness. Never believe them, Maddie. They'll lead you into ruin, every one of them.' And I nod, and promise to forget my soldier-poet, as I snuggle in her arms in the warmth of the kitchen, my empty belly rumbling.

But when another note arrives the next morning, all her advice disappears.

My dearest Miss Smith,

I waited for you and you did not come. I will assume you do not care to meet.

Yours, E.

'How did I miss him when I waited so long for him?' I say to Christina, waving the note in front of her face. We're in her little bedroom, sitting on the hard, narrow bed.

'Did you miss him, though?' she says, slowly. Christina cannot read quickly; she stares at the letters, makes me repeat what he's written. 'I think he's toying with you.'

'No – I have to apologise – *beg* him to forgive me. Convince him I made a terrible mistake—'

She lays her hand on mine. 'I'll bet a month's wages he was watching you all the time. Seeing how long you'd wait for him.'

Her voice is disgusted, but there's a thrill running through me at the thought of him in the shadows, looking on me, saying nothing. I lick my lips.

'I want him, Christina. More than anything else I've ever wanted.'

She strokes the hair back from my face; she looks sad, for some reason. 'You're love-sick already and you've only met him twice,' she says. 'You're going to learn the hard way, Maddie.'

'But I've listened to you – I know what to do, you told me. What's the point of me knowing it all, if I can't put it into practice?'

She knows when she's caught.

'So tell me what to do. Please – tell me.'

And so she does.

Dear Emile,

I did wait for you. But if you do not care to meet my interest with yours, it is better that we do not meet again.

Madeleine

Every part of me objects to it. What if he believes I really mean never to see him again? Perhaps Christina wants that for me, to spoil my fun. Yet I do what she says, because I don't know what else to do, and when I'm done, she snatches the letter from me and heads out to deliver it to his lodgings.

There's no answer all day, though. I'm cursing her advice, and by the next morning I'm determined to write another letter, begging him after all, if begging is indeed what he wants. But Christina drops a note into my lap just as I'm forcing down some coffee for breakfast.

'Told you,' she says.

The Coffee House 2pm

There's no signature, but it's his hand. I read out loud what he's written, clutching my nightgown.

'If you had any sense, you'd not turn up,' she says. 'Give him a taste of his own medicine. Cocky so-and-so.'

'He's replied, and that's all I want!'

'You want a lot more than that – but you can't go alone. I'll follow—'

But I'm dancing out of the room, too delighted that it's worked, and too delighted to thank her, for she scowls and grumbles when she helps curl my hair and choose the best dress. But she does kiss me for luck, at least, even though I know she's hoping that he won't show again.

Which is indeed how it seems, for he's not appeared by two o'clock, and I'm despairing all over again, not knowing what to do, pacing back and forth past the windows of the coffee house, ever more conscious with each step of how I must look to anyone inside, and praying silently that nobody who knows my parents will pass along the street and notice me.

And just as I'm ready to weep furious tears, to run home yet again, a voice at my ear says, 'Madeleine,' and there he is.

His melancholy eyes stare deeply into mine; his moustache bristles against my ungloved hand. The jaw of his arm traps my fingers as we walk. I've been dreaming every night of this wolfish danger, and now it's arrived.

'You have not introduced me to your papa,' is how he begins, though, a little too plaintively.

I'm a little disappointed, too, that he hasn't noticed my dress, how well I've made myself look for him.

'You must at least have spoken with him about me. Haven't you?'

'No, I – not yet. I—'

'But surely you wouldn't reply to my notes without doing so?'

He sounds so shocked, I'm taken aback.

'I – I thought that you wouldn't want—'

'Really, Madeleine! That *I* would not want? What could make you think that?'

We turn into a side street. There's an alleyway on the left. He continues, oddly fretful and even scolding.

'A respectable young woman would not *dare* reply unless you had spoken with your papa first – I assumed that you would have – you must.' With stern disapproval, he withdraws his arm from mine.

I'm so dispirited by his words that I can't help what I say next. 'Well, I *do* dare. Mama and Papa do not *rule* me—'

He's shaking his head like a disapproving churchman, not the wolf-man of my dreams. 'That's very disappointing, Madeleine. I don't care for it—'

But I interrupt, suddenly annoyed at his keeping me waiting, only to chastise me in this way. 'Well, your *disappointment* is very disappointing to *me*, Emile. And not at all what I thought you were about.'

I bite my lip, for it sounds so very high-handed and criticising, but it's too late now. Saying the wrong thing, doing the wrong thing, as always; ah, for Christina to advise me again, just for a moment . . .

But Emile only raises an eyebrow, before glancing down the alleyway to our left. Then he seizes my wrist and pulls me towards it.

Perhaps I haven't ruined things after all. The tiniest of shivers returns as he says, gruffly, 'Perhaps you are right. *Disappointing* is no good.'

'Where are we?'

'Your *leçon privée*.'

Embers that have lain inside me, black and cold, begin to glow. My blood warms as the sky above darkens from the buildings on either side of us. They close over us like towering trees in a forest as he hurries me along the cobbles past shut doorways, discarded boxes, rotting vegetables.

The darkness only grows as the voices of folk on the street

behind us fade away. I slip and stumble a little in the slime; he yanks me on, as though I'm a child.

Which almost makes me cross, except he halts just in time. Then he pushes me ahead of him towards the scratched black of a doorway which is set back so deeply from the lane it's almost impossible to make it out.

My legs turn to water. He must mean to *kiss* me, out of sight of the street. I bite my bottom lip again, but this time to bid the blood come and redden it, and I wish for a mirror to show how it makes me look.

'Here,' he says, pushing more.

The door in front of me doesn't budge, though. From behind, he presses on, as I object, 'But it won't open.' The full length of his body is now crushed against mine and I cannot move. I protest again, 'Emile, I can't breathe. What are you—'

Then, to my great shock, he shoves his hand at my mouth, squeezing tight till I'm wincing in pain and can't say a word. His body moves heavily against mine as he whispers in my ear, 'Quiet now, my *daring* girl.'

It's all my fault, what is about to happen. What he's doing now, pushing at my skirts, his thighs against my behind, his free hand at my back. Yes, it's my fault, as his finger probes my lips, pushes its way hard into my mouth so that tears spurt from my eyes. It's too awful, what he means to do; and it's my fault.

My fault.

The cage of my crinoline creaks. I whimper a protest.

My fault.

'Mimi,' he whispers, and I close my eyes. But all of a sudden, he wrenches his finger out of my mouth and steps back. I sink to my knees, appalled, my hand over my bruised lips.

And then I hear it – a laugh.

A laugh, and from him. Harsh and bitter.

When I twist round to look up, though, he's frowning, not smiling, and certainly not laughing. He looks as though he hates me.

'"A love violent and frightening", did you not say in your note?' he says.

The scorn in his voice has me stammering, 'What – what—'

'Only my fun,' he says, stepping up close so that I shrink back against the door, but this time with my fists clenched. He shakes his head, waggles a finger. 'After all, you had your fun with me.'

'What do you mean, *my fun with you*?' My voice scratches in my dry throat; my fists are on the cobbles.

'I'm not a *game* for rich young ladies to play. So learn your leçon privée, Madeleine. I won't be caught like that.'

There's no mistaking the contempt in his voice. I scramble to my feet; he doesn't offer a hand to help me up but heads along the alleyway, and suddenly I'm so furious at how he's dared to treat me, so humiliated by his easy scorn, that I run after him and seize his arm and demand that he stop immediately and explain himself.

Highhandedness returns to me; he spins round, though, to match it with real anger, shaking my hand off his arm, and making me pull back, fearful of more violence. When he speaks, it's in a low voice.

'We meet on the street, with no introduction. And you are very friendly to me, a complete stranger,' he says. 'Then we meet in the coffee house. And you don't refuse, you don't *behave*. Oh no – you are *very* friendly again, very friendly indeed.'

Suddenly I'm blushing, remembering his leg pressed against mine. I knew it; he's spoken my fear. I did not refuse. I did not *behave*.

Slattern.

'I – I—'

'What else am I to think of your behaviour, Madeleine? That you want me to write to you; you make it very clear that is what you want from me.'

'I – I did. But—'

'And then you write *those* words to me. Those words!'

The crudeness of the quotation I used appals me now. Of course: how wrong of me, how stupid. Tears come into my eyes again, but this time, his anger has gone. He looks at me with pity in his expression.

'You have no idea what those words mean,' he says.

'I – I do. I mean, I thought—'

'And now, of course, you regret writing them at all. So we will say goodbye. As I said, I will not be a game for you to play.'

He turns his back on me again. It's the worst jilting, the worst refusal, and I have only myself to blame.

'Please!' I say. 'You're right, I shouldn't have behaved so – I am sorry. I only wanted—'

But I can hardly say what it is I do want. Shame runs down my cheeks, out of my nose, has me sniffing, unable to say any more. He hesitates, then turns round, and this time his look is more kindly.

'You are sorry, you say?'

'Yes – I'm sorry. I wasn't playing a game,' I say, dabbing my nose with my handkerchief. 'I wasn't. I didn't know what to say to you, is all. Our housemaid, Christina, she told me—'

His shoulders ease. 'Ah!' he says. '*She* told you what to write to me, that is it?'

'Not all – some, yes, most of it—'

'Madeleine.' He puts his hand gently on mine, holding the handkerchief at my eyes, so gently and softly that I lean without thinking, and rest my palm on his coat for a moment. He touches my hand, and murmurs, 'What nonsense has she told you? I understand – you were not mocking me after all—'

'No – I would *never*—'

'Then I understand you better. Ah, my dear Madeleine. You have been – *misused*, I think.'

Misused. I think of the duke's dead son. 'Yes,' I say. 'Yes, I have been.'

He pulls me closer to him. 'And by a common housemaid.'

'I – she has more – oh, experience than me. She has a *fiancé*—'

He pulls away, but he's smiling. I've never felt such a fool.

'I know. I know,' I say. 'I was stupid to listen to her. I get things wrong, all the time.'

But he tilts my chin, and his eyes lock with mine to make me blink hard, and he says, 'You are neither stupid nor wrong. I won't let you think that. But you must let *me* show you. Let *me* guide you. Not some *housemaid*.'

His face is so gentle and handsome that the urge to cram him in my mouth, beard and fingers and chest and all, comes back like a ravenous hunger, and I remember how starving I am.

'And you must tell your papa, of course. You must introduce me. Understand?'

I'm so delighted he hasn't abandoned me, hasn't thrown me

aside after all I've done wrong, that I promise rashly, quickly; seize his hand and press it to my still-bruised mouth.

'Your *leçon privée*,' he says. 'Your *first* one.'

Back on the street, in the light of the day, my heart trips and runs as he talks about Paris, about Edinburgh, where he has some friends, about a job he used to have in the Botanic Gardens. I hardly hear him; the memory of his body crushing mine is like one of Mama's forbidden potions, making me feel light and ghostly. At the corner of Bedford Place, shaded by trees, he stops and says, 'Remember to speak with your papa about me?'

'Yes, Emile.'

'Good girl.'

He kisses me chastely on the cheek; my mouth turns to his.

'Ah – no, not yet,' he says, and smiles. 'Take instruction only from me, yes? My Madeleine. My *Mimi*.'

It sounds as though he's eating my name. He taps my mouth with his finger.

'Yes.' I breathe out the word. 'Yes.'

Melancholy eyes look over me from my head to my toes. 'Mimi,' he says, again, and then suddenly he's gone towards Renfrew Street, leaving me standing alone, patting my thrumming lips.

II.

'The letters continued on her part in the same strain of passionate love for a very considerable time – I say passionate love because, unhappily, they are written without any sense of decency, and in most licentious terms.'

– The Lord Justice-Clerk charge to the jury in the trial of Madeleine Smith, 9 July 1857, Edinburgh

New York, 1927

Let's talk about the murder.

It was true that I'd always expected to hear those words, even though I'd long pretended to myself that I didn't. Not just these last few months, because it was almost exactly seventy years since the trial, but from the first moment that I arrived in this city over thirty years ago. Every day, I expected a form of them to confront me somehow. As the years went on, the urgency behind that expectation lessened, though, and so I eased into a kind of patient preparedness. I knew how I'd respond, or so I thought. How I'd conduct myself. It would be with quiet dignity. A polite refusal to say a single word.

But now that the time had come, it wasn't at all how I expected it, and neither was I. The trembling that slipped through me began quietly enough, with a tingling in my toes. In a few seconds, however, it had wormed its way up to my fingers and my arms, and then it seemed to burrow inside me, to make my veins prickle with dread. I knew then that my body wouldn't accept the news, so I sat down on the daybed, my hand over my heart, waiting for the prickling to stop. Harry didn't seem alarmed; he was too busy fishing about inside his pockets for something to notice my stricken state.

In the end, it was that word that stilled me, and saved me,

too. 'Murder.' There was something about it; its darkness was too cheap, too easy. The images it conjured up were cartoonish; even the sound of it was melodramatic, with those two heavy syllables, that almost-rhyme inside them.

Those aspects of the word slid an odd sort of calm over me as I sat, letting me breathe more easily at last. And as the evening outside my apartment grew livelier and noisier, and party sounds from the street drifted up through the window, I took more comfort in the absurdity of the word 'murder' than I'd ever imagined I could.

Harry lifted one of the dining chairs for himself, just as he had some hours earlier, and set it opposite the daybed like before. His approach hadn't grown any subtler since the morning. He'd not make a good poker player, that was certain. His face still had that odd, boiled look, as though he'd spent too long in the sun, or in a speakeasy, but there was a flicker at the edge of his mouth betraying just for a second that he wasn't entirely sure of himself. And so he shored himself up the only way he knew how, believing his crudeness to be his best weapon.

'You poisoned a man to death,' he said. 'Emile L'Angelier. Seventy years ago. Arsenic. Says so, right here.'

He'd taken two objects from inside his blazer. One was a book, the other a newspaper page, and he placed them both beside me on the daybed. It was the newspaper headline that caught my attention first, though, lurid as it was.

Madeleine Smith in America! Scandalous Murder Case 70 years old!

I'd been used to seeing plenty of headlines like this over the years. The public fascination with the case meant it was never out of the newspapers for long, and every time a story came up, Willy would comfort me, tell me I was safe with him, and there was no way I'd be found out.

But it was always alarming, no matter how much trash they printed – and trash it always was. They never even researched it properly – and the New York Public Library carried all the details they needed, for once upon a time it was reported on from Canada to Calcutta.

What a fool I'd been, believing Harry's ruse about meeting Shaw. Most likely it was something he'd thought of on the spur of the moment because Violet had showed up, and he hadn't been expecting that. Or maybe it was a reason he'd had ready all along, in case I wasn't alone when he called. Yes: the newspaper article proved Harry had been planning to confront me from the start.

'I don't even know what to say to something like that—' I began, but he interrupted me.

'Go on.' He nodded at the single sheet of paper. 'See what they have to say about you.'

I shook my head but picked up the page. My apartment wasn't large and its new-fangled electric light system was bright – too bright for me, really. I preferred soft lamps, sometimes even just candles, for they reminded me of when I was a child, and that gave me comfort when I needed it most.

However, they were not the best for reading by, so I leaned behind me for the switch on the wall, and on came the ceiling light, illuminating the whole room. Harry looked up, blinking at its beam, and I thought again about movies and movie-making, and what he'd said about being better behind a camera.

Tucked beneath a cushion was my spectacles case. I took plenty of time getting them out and fixing them on my nose. Then I picked up the page with my fingertips as though it might be something vile, and read, slowly as I could. The *Sunday Chronicle* wasn't a newspaper I took in.

> Seventy years ago this summer, beautiful heiress Madeleine Hamilton Smith stood trial in Edinburgh, Scotland, in a case that shocked the world!
>
> Accused of murdering her secret French lover, Pierre Angler, she was the sensation of the age.
>
> When poor Mr Angler was found dead in his apartment one morning, it was to the wealthy young socialite that authorities looked. Had she poisoned him the night before his death with a cup of hot cocoa, which the pair would drink on their many clandestine meetings?
>
> For it was after Mr Angler threatened to show his lover's letters to her father, that he died suddenly.

The newspaper account was full of errors, of course, the most obvious being the dead man's name. But I wouldn't let on I knew that. Not yet.

Instead, I glanced at Harry as casually as possible and said, frowning in a disapproving manner, 'Well, this is a very sordid tale.'

'You better believe it,' he said. He sat back and took out that gold cigarette case of his. He offered me one this time and I accepted, concentrating on my fingers not shaking. The nicotine hit me with my first draw, but it had been a while and it made me cough. 'I'd call it sordid. Beautiful young woman who's unmarried, carrying on like that under her family's nose? *Clandestine meetings.* Would have been a real shocker if they'd found her out. No wonder she wanted to kill her boyfriend, threatening to expose her to her father like that.'

He looked amused.

I stubbed out the cigarette. My throat was burning. 'This *story* simply tells me that blackmail doesn't pay, Mr Townsend,' I said, though my voice croaked from the nicotine, poisoning my lungs.

'Because you killed the blackmailer? It's one way to deal with it. But carry on reading – let me know what you think.'

I looked at the page again.

Post-mortem examinations showed over a hundred grains of arsenic in the dead man's body. Miss Smith had purchased arsenic on *three* occasions before the unfortunate victim's death.

But the prosecution was unable to prove that the lovers had met the night before Mr Angler died. And so, a verdict of 'Not Proven' was given, and thus, the accused woman walked free!

'Over a hundred grains of arsenic!' he said. 'I read it takes only four or five grains to kill a man. You really wanted to make sure he was dead, didn't you?'

I leaned over for the beaker of water sitting on the dining table. He handed it to me, and as he did so, I thought I heard it again, that whispered *Mimi*.

But he was saying instead, 'And just think: if they didn't have that special verdict in your homeland, you know, that "Not

Proven" one – well, then, you might have hung. You might not be sitting here in front of me at all. What a shame that would have been.'

He seemed to enjoy the effect of his words, fixing his eyes on me as he did.

I bristled, unwilling to show fear. 'We live in a world that's very keen to see women suffer and even die,' I said. 'No matter how innocent they are.'

'You saying you were innocent of that charge, then?'

'How can I, when this person is not me?'

He wiped his forehead. Night-time had arrived with the coming of darkness outside, but already there was a change in the temperature, in the breeze that came through my open window. The spring coolness had gone; we were plunged into a deep summer warmth, as sudden as that, and sweat was glistening on Harry's brow. A little dust blew in with the breeze and settled on his white boater. Somebody turned up a wireless in another apartment, and a melancholy jazz tune filtered through the gritty air.

'Read on,' he said. 'It gets more interesting, I promise.'

I wanted him out of my apartment, but how to manage it was the problem. All I could do for now was carry on, deny his accusations. So I read as he bade me.

Now living in Milwaukee, Madeleine Smith is bony and grey-haired, a God-fearing woman of ninety-two years.

Does she have regrets about the affair? 'Mostly of the shame it caused my family,' she says. Her home is cold and spare and there are no pictures on the walls or photographs of family back home.

She came to America, she says, 'because my native country dealt so harshly with me, I could not bear to live there'.

It is said that some still believe her guilty of the crime. No one else has ever been accused of the murder of Mr Angler.

'I am innocent of the accusations against me,' she says. 'And I thank God every day for His support. To that end, I pay for prayers to be said for poor Mr Angler's soul in my local church.'

A blurry picture of an elderly woman dressed in black and wearing a lace cap accompanied the article. I squinted, trying to make out her face. She could have been anyone.

'I wondered who she was, too,' said Harry, drily. 'That reporter didn't do his research. Well, of course he didn't; not when I'm looking right at her here in this apartment in the Bronx. Nowhere near *Milwaukee*.'

He said it as though that city had no right to claim possession. 'I don't know anything about this woman – or this man, whoever he is,' I said. 'I have no idea about any of it at all. A murder case? Do you have any idea how absurd this sounds to me?' And I tsked, shook my head again.

He just smiled. 'I can play this game as long as you want, Mrs Sheehy. Madeleine. *Mimi*.'

So he said it a third time; perhaps he was worried he hadn't unsettled me enough before. I let the newspaper page float from my arthritic fingers down on to the daybed.

'Who on earth is this "Mimi" you keep mentioning?' I said, and even affected a yawn. 'She sounds like some kind of French dancer.'

But he'd lured me into a little trap. That was when he indicated the book on the daybed: *The Trial of Madeleine Smith* by F. Tennyson Jesse.

'I bought it just a week or so ago,' he said. 'It was his pet name for you, Pierre Emile's. "Mimi", he'd call you. But you know that, of course. I think you'll like her, this writer; she's mostly on your side. Thinks you're the Eloise to his Abelard.' He chuckled a little. 'Says if only you'd been born into the modern era we have now, you'd never have done what you did. But I wonder if that's true. Seems like a timeless story to me.'

I needed to think much faster. Who knew how much more the writer of this book had discovered? Harry was crude in his thinking, but he wasn't fool enough to show his whole hand yet. A fluttering returned to my fingers, and inside my chest. Like a tiny bird was trapped inside my ribcage.

Harry licked his lips, hungry as a cat.

'Tell you what,' he said, getting to his feet. 'I'll leave you to read it.'

He was saving his prey for another time, then. I found myself standing up, too. He was a full foot or two taller than me, of course, even standing as straight as I possibly could.

'I'm not reading some trash-filled book about a person I've never heard of,' I said.

'You'll be better off telling me the truth, in the end. This act of yours can't go on for ever.'

'It's no "act" – I simply have no idea what you mean by any of it. I've never heard of this Madeleine woman – or this "trial"—'

'Yes, yes,' he interrupted. 'You keep saying that. So you're not ninety-two, just like Madeleine Smith would be now? Violet says that's your age. And you didn't go on to marry George Wardle a few years after the trial, like Madeleine Smith did, according to this book? Wardle is Violet's surname – and she said you had been married to her grandfather before you became Mrs Sheehy.'

He was putting it all together so fast it made my brain freeze.

'I can get more proof, believe me, Mrs Sheehy. But it's easier just to work with me, not against me. I'll come back in a day or two and you can tell me all about it then, just the two of us.'

'I'm not letting you back in here!' I said, hot and cold all at once. 'I'll speak to Teresa about you! Your grandmother will be appalled to hear what you're doing to a friend of hers.'

He just laughed at that. 'You think that's gonna stop me? My nonna's a doll, but I've got too much riding on this to be scared by a telling-off, Mrs Sheehy.'

He didn't explain what he meant by that. What could he possibly have 'riding' on it? Again, though, I wasn't quick enough to ask, and he left the parlour quite abruptly with a phony friendly sounding 'Don't be going anywhere now!' as he strolled down the hallway.

I found myself alone with the newspaper page and the book he'd brought. I switched off the light and sat in the dark of the parlour for a while. It had been so much easier when my husband, Willy, was alive. His presence kept the past at bay. I'd never known exactly what to do with the past, beyond painting it. Not *my* past, but an idealised one that never belonged to anyone. It felt safer, that way. My paintings held no clues to what I was, once; copies I made of red-haired princesses in medieval gowns by painters like Rossetti didn't give me away.

The past was paper, and paper burned, much to my relief. But the present was all manner of machines that kept things alive when you wanted them dead. It wouldn't take Harry long to trace more of Violet's heritage, if he chose to.

I got up eventually and went to my little back bedroom to lie down and calm my thumping heart. To my surprise, I dozed off, despite being sure I'd never sleep again. But terrible dreams soon woke me, ones that had me calling out in the dark. Strangely, though, I couldn't move a muscle, not even to go and boil the kettle for some tea, and later, after I'd fallen asleep again, I wondered if that had been only another dream, trapping me in a mess of my own making.

Sleep might push me over the edge, tumbling into nightmares, but wakefulness could be worse.

By the time sleep, such as it was, had had its fun with me, it was late the next morning. My hands shook from the moment I rose, and my breath kept coming in fast little bursts that had me pressing on my heart to try and slow it all through the day. By sunset, I was no better, so I took the newspaper page Harry had left behind for me into the little kitchen, lit a match and burned it in a pot, before shaking the charred flakes out into the backyard. Then I forced down a supper of bread and cheese before taking up Mrs Tennyson Jesse's book. In the electric light of the parlour as the sun slowly set, I started to read.

It was as bad as anything else they'd written over the years. Every time I thought it couldn't touch me, what they said in news reports or in books, there would be a line, just a single line, of judgement. And I'd fall for it, work myself into a state over it.

Mrs Jesse's book had just such a line.

In those days there was nothing for Madeleine Smith to do but to get engaged, a very tame state of affairs for a character like hers.

'A character like hers.' Of course. There was never any real understanding from any of these vultures, never any real compassion. How it angered and disgusted me. I dropped the book on to the daybed, promised myself I'd not give Mrs Jesse the satisfaction of reading a single word more of her ridiculous book.

The sun had fully set by now; this time yesterday Harry had shown up for the second time, and I had a bad presentiment about him appearing again, even though he'd said 'a day or two'. I wanted to put out the light and sit quietly in the dark before heading to bed, but something drew me to the kitchen first, to make a pot of tea.

And sure enough, just as it finished brewing, the doorbell rang.

To my relief, though, it was Violet's voice that came through the apartment from the hallway outside, not Harry's.

'Let yourself in, my dear!' I called. I felt for a moment like the grandmother in the tale of Red Riding Hood, especially with Violet in her scarlet coat.

Which made Harry the wolf.

'Grandma,' she said, sighing and sitting down on the daybed as if out of breath. 'Guess where I've been all day?'

She smelled of roses, and the circle of light the parlour lamp gave off shone on hair that was newly waved. She was wearing a dress I hadn't seen before, too, a shade of fuchsia that set off her pink mouth and blond hair. She noticed my look and shrugged, smiling.

'Promise you won't be sore – but Harry called on me this morning and took me out for lunch! He said you gave him my address. You are naughty, Grandma!'

I laid down my cup of tea with difficulty, such was my

indignation. 'I certainly did no such thing – how dare he tell you that!'

She looked surprised, and a little shameful. 'Oh – perhaps I got it wrong. Maybe I did—'

'And what do you mean, took you out for lunch?'

How quickly Harry had dug down into her heart. Those Hollywood eyes of his were nothing but poison.

Violet giggled and sighed again. 'He took me to the Waldorf, can you imagine? Harry's got a whole suite! We sat downstairs in the bar for hours; we drank old-fashioneds all afternoon. Oh, the splendour of it, it was magnificent.' She burped, and giggled, covered her mouth. 'I'm still a little tight, I think,' she said. 'What time is it? After ten already? Oh my, I need a black coffee.'

I waited, silent and fuming, until she was back from the kitchen.

'I'm sorry to call on you so late, but I was on the way back from Daddy's, then saw your light was on,' she said as I seated myself on the daybed.

'How is Tom? Is his cold any better?'

'Oh, a little—'

But I couldn't hold it in any longer. 'Harry's staying at the Waldorf, is he?' It was only the most expensive place in town. So he was making money, out west. That troubled me, too, as much as his wooing of my granddaughter. How much to confide in Violet now she'd had her head turned? 'What did you two talk about all afternoon?'

Violet took a dining chair, so her face was in shadow, which suited me. I was afraid to see her adoration of the man threatening me.

'Oh, we talked about ourselves. His business is going so well, and he's met Ronald Colman! And he asked a lot about you, too. Well, I told him to go to the gallery; remember how you took me there when I was little and we saw it together, the Rossetti painting?'

My eyes narrowed and my fingernails, ragged as they were, dug painfully into the loose skin of my palms. 'Why would he care to see that?' I said.

'It's because – oh, Grandma, can you believe this? – he thinks a film about *you* would be a real draw!'

'What—'

'Because of you living so well when you were young, and knowing folk like George Bernard Shaw, and sitting for Rossetti for that painting.'

Found. That was the name of the unfinished painting Rossetti had spent years on. A sudden flash of a dark cloak, of a bent body leaning in to a wall, crossed my mind. He'd begun the painting of what was supposed to be a prostitute who'd been found by a former lover, and who was staggering against a brick wall, her face turned away in shame. His mistress at the time, Fanny Cornforth, had been the model for it. But he hadn't finished it, and when he went back to try, Fanny was no longer the slim, shapely girl he'd started with. He'd needed another body to stand in for her.

I'd told so few stories about the past to Violet. But I'd told her that one, one day, many years ago. Never thinking that it mattered, ever would matter. How wrong I was.

'That's a ridiculous idea,' I said, but my trembling had started up again and my voice shook.

I couldn't hide my upset from Violet; even in her inebriated state, she noticed it, and her concern made her hug me gently, say, 'What is it, Grandma? There's something eating you, and I don't think it's just Harry wanting to film you. What's the matter? You can tell me.'

The Tennyson Jesse book was on the table; I couldn't keep my gaze from wandering to it and, to my alarm, her gaze followed. I had to stop her seeing what I'd not been smart enough to hide away, and so I pointed instead, with a shaking finger, at the day's newspaper, which lay beside it.

'It's that poor woman,' I said. 'I've been thinking about her all day and it's upset me so.'

'Ruth Snyder?' Violet said, reaching for the newspaper. 'I haven't seen the latest yet.'

The headline was splashed across the front page.

Sash Weight Murder Trial Begins!

The whole of New York was talking about it. Just as the world had talked once before about a woman accused of killing a man. It should have been the last thing I'd want to discuss, or even think about, but I needed to distract Violet and we'd both been following the story, from the moment Ruth Snyder and her lover, Judd Gray, were arrested.

'They're calling her "Momsie" and "Ruthless Ruth",' I said, shuddering. 'How horrible to call her those names.'

'Well, she's done a horrible thing, Grandma, smashing her husband's skull in like that. With a sash weight, of all things!'

'But she says it was her lover, Judd Gray, who hit her husband.'

'And he's saying she planned it and talked him into doing it!' said Violet, a little triumphantly. I didn't want to push back too much, especially as Violet continued, 'Just listen to what this reporter says about her. I don't think there's much doubt about her character. "She is not bad-looking, I have seen much worse. Her life is full of illicit love, mystery, booze, and jazz. But she is a shallow-brained pleasure-seeker, accustomed to unlimited self-indulgence."'

'Oh, Violet,' I said, shaking my head. 'Character doesn't lie in one's appearance.' Then I remembered my own assessment of Harry, judging his character reflected in that crude manner of his. I coughed. 'What does the reporter say about Judd Gray's looks?'

But the reporter had written nothing about those. The 'Roaring Twenties' everybody talked about was too busy roaring at women, and women only.

Violet shrugged. 'I think she's the real killer, Grandma. And I think she deserves what she gets.'

I felt a stab of panic at her refusal to understand what I was trying to say, and it caused me to be reckless.

'I can't help wondering if her greater crime in the eyes of the world is fooling a man into helping her do it. *If* she did. She has a daughter, after all. A daughter who will be missing her mama.' My voice broke a little, startling Violet. I swallowed and pointed to a headline on the facing page.

Mae West jailed with 2 producers; Leading Lady in 'Sex', Timony and Morgenstern Get 10 Days – $500 fines for first two. Suspension for 19 IN CAST Court Sees Trial as Vindication of City's Morals – Jurors Ask Clemency.

Teresa and I had gone to see her play on Broadway last year, about the same time we saw *Pygmalion*. Violet came with us.

'I agree, that's ridiculous,' Violet said.

I settled back down a little; I hadn't realised I'd been clenching my fists. 'They're making her work in the kitchen. Giving her the grubbiest jobs, to take some of that shine out of her. It's what they do to women who shine too brightly, Violet. That's what they do.'

Violet took out a handkerchief to dab my eyes, for they were wet, suddenly. 'Mae West will be just fine,' she said. 'Don't take on others' pain so, Grandma. You feel too much.'

I nodded and leaned my head against her shoulder. But I was only allowed to rest it there for a moment or two, for a motor had pulled up outside the apartment, its lights blazing.

The Chrysler.

Harry.

Violet jumped up off the daybed before I could stop her, and ran out into the hallway to let him in. I heard her giggle as he came in through the front door, and then into the parlour he strolled, as though he owned the place. I bit my lip; it seemed arranged between them, this meeting. On her way home from Tom's, indeed! I was annoyed with her now, my darling Violet. That was what Harry had done already.

'Good to see you looking so well, Mrs Sheehy,' he said. That boiled look had vanished, but the harsh line his crude character had drawn about the jawline was still there. Again, though, I thought about how Ruth Snyder's looks had been described, and tried not to fall into the trap of easy judgement. It vexed me that I hadn't written to Teresa about him first thing that morning. Neither of us had the new telephone system; a wire was the best I could do, or the post. Teresa would surely stop him when she heard what he was doing.

Violet was gushing. 'I told Grandma what you said this

afternoon, Harry, about being so interested in her life, maybe making a film.'

So she *had* called on me to talk me round before he got here. I folded my arms, as he stood looking down at me on the daybed.

'Well, what d'you think, Mrs Sheehy?' he said. 'Would you make for a good movie?'

'Hardly,' I managed to say. I was considering pretending to have written to Teresa anyway; I could call his bluff on that and see how he really felt about his grandmother's disapproval.

But the look on his face stopped me. He was staring hard, not at me, but at the mantelpiece. Violet noticed his staring, too, and asked what the matter was, but he ignored her and made straight for one of the photographs framed there.

In my confusion about his accusations, I'd forgotten all about it.

The woman pictured was middle-aged, wearing an old-fashioned black bombazine dress, and a lace-trimmed bonnet that tied under the chin. Her smile was a little vacant, but her eyes were large and kind.

'Who's this?' he said, but I wouldn't answer.

'Why, that's Grandma's younger sister, Janet,' said Violet, brightly. I signalled to her to say no more, shaking my head, but it was too late. 'She died a few years back.'

'Janet,' he said, turning slowly to face me before coming up close and leaning down to whisper in my ear. 'Madeleine had a sister called Janet. She's dead now, too.'

My mouth opened, but no words came.

He stepped back, saying loudly, 'What a crazy coincidence that is; don't you think, Mrs Sheehy?'

He'd caught me like a rat in a trap.

Rowaleyn, 1855

'Miss Janet looks like a girl of thirteen. Miss Janet always slept with Miss Madeleine – in the same room and in the same bed.'
  – Witness William Murray, servant, 2 July 1857, at the trial of Madeleine Smith, Edinburgh

Now that Mama is well.

Now that Mama is well, our house is full of light and air. Windows are flung open, floors are swept. Invitations are issued and dinners attended, all in a flurry before we pack up our belongings and head upriver to Rowaleyn next week, out of the city.

Now that Mama is well, Janet can return from our cousins' house, for she's too excitable and noisy to stay with us during the silent months Mama lies moaning and in pain. I always resent her being sent away, for she's my only ally even though there's nine years between us.

I don't keep secrets from my girl, not even Emile, though he's the biggest secret I've ever had. He writes me every day now since our *understanding* in the alleyway, makes declarations of feeling so intense that I can't not dance every step, sing every word.

I'm being thoroughly irritating, Christina says. 'It's better Janet'll soon be here. You're lost to his attention.'

She's right; I am. But how not to be, when three or four notes a day arrive? I hug them all in disbelief, because no man has ever been so attentive, so open with how he feels, what he thinks. *How beautiful you are, Mimi*, he writes. *How irresistible! How desirable!*

He writes other things too, that make me blush for daring, but at the same time, I'm afraid those parts of me he thinks will be *so alluring, so divine*, will only disappoint him. I have no full *embonpoint* like Christina, being so very flat-chested; my hips are wide and bony, my legs too stocky. My complexion is sallow, my shoulders are narrow and my neck is too squat, I complain to her in the kitchen, where it's hot, full of steam from the many supper pots on the range.

'Maybe he likes a squat-necked girl,' Christina says, cheering up, so I smack her lightly with a spoon for being so cheeky.

'But even my *hair* is unremarkable,' I say, staring gloomily into my hand mirror after wiping it clear. 'What if I'm not worthy of him?'

As she ladles out the soup, Christina mutters, 'You're giving him everything he wants, talking like that. So be careful what you do tonight. You know what I think of him sneaking in here by the back door.'

'McKenzie does it—'

'He's my fiancé,' she snaps, banging down the ladle to make me jump. 'And he's not pretending to be a gentleman, thank God.'

'Emile's not pretending, he *is* a gentleman—'

'He's a working man, no better than that,' she says, hurrying away upstairs with the tray of soup bowls too fast for me to answer her back.

Emile is a gentleman, I tell myself again. Even if he can't yet come to the front door, for I haven't worked up the courage to tell Papa. He's to tap at the back door for me instead; *I can't bear to be away from my Mimi any longer.* And all today I've been on ninepins, forcing down a little beef and vegetables at lunch, though they churned in my stomach from nerves, so that Mama wouldn't notice, or Papa, or Jack, that I'm not myself.

Not myself, because I cannot be, must not be, Madeleine. *I am Mimi now.* Madeleine is the short-legged, thin-ankled, bony-hipped daughter whose card no boy will fill. *Mimi's different*, I tell myself after supper, when the pots are cleaned and put away, and the kitchen's empty of Christina, who's sulking in her little room just off it, for she's not getting to see McKenzie tonight.

And by the time I emerge from my bedroom, I truly am Mimi, tiptoeing down to the kitchen through a house that's silent except for the clock in the entrance hall striking eleven. My transformation is complete: curls brushed loose over my shoulders until they lie shining and glossy; my best ivory night-dress, softly silk, unbuttoned from the neck but only to the beginning of my breastbone; velvet slippers that lighten my step; my glittering eyes and my thrumming lips.

Down the stairs Mimi goes like a beautiful wraith. A drowned Ophelia, a tired Mariana. Millais is my favourite painter; I saw his work when I stayed at Mrs Gorton's. The beautiful, slender Isabella in silver was my aim, so my nightdress in white and my dark hair long and loose is a good match. I think of women with soft red mouths and lovelorn expressions, ready for a wolf-man and a poet, and part my lips just so, widening my eyes. Gently adjust the nightgown's neckline; swing my way across the kitchen floor, but more elegantly than Christina did when she led McKenzie to her room.

Down here, the only light is the glow of the kitchen fire through the grate, which warms my complexion. I pinch my cheeks just a little, bite my lower lip and pace back and forth over the kitchen floor, because Mimi is impatient for her darling.

It's just before midnight when a faint tap sounds at the door beyond the scullery. I run over and open the back door slowly and with care, in case it's not him.

But it is him!

Alas, though, he is soaking from the rain, and so furious. I'd not thought of the weather, and how he might get here on foot, not even take a cab.

'Let me in, Mimi, for God's sake,' he says, pushing past and shaking off his hat. He stomps over to the grate, and takes up the poker to stir the fire, get the flames jumping. Without another word, he peels off the dripping cloak and scarf, then sits down and heaves off his boots.

He's dressed now in only his trousers and a shirt, which clings to his damp chest. I'm staring, unsure what to do, as he doesn't seem to have noticed my transformation at all. *I am Mimi*, I remind myself, though, and approach him more confidently this time to make him see her.

And now it seems that he does. 'My beautiful Mimi!' he says, pulling me to him. 'And in only a nightgown?'

'For my beloved,' I say.

He brings me to his chest, hugs my body with his knees. I set my hands on his shoulders, stare into his eyes, a bold Mimi.

'Like a bride on her wedding night,' he murmurs. 'Ah, how I *need* my Mimi, it overwhelms everything.' He pushes up my sleeve, kisses the bare skin of my arm. 'I need every inch of you, every day, Mimi,' he mutters, which reminds me of Christina's words. *Don't give him everything.* But he's so handsome, and so desperate. My fingers stroke his wet hair; he nuzzles against the flatness of my chest. 'Ah, how I need you!'

We look like a painting, I think. Millais would surely call us *The Lovers.*

His lips reach the gap in my collar and my legs tremble as he pulls me on to his lap. 'Do you need me as much as I need you? Do you, Mimi, do you?' he says, his fingers digging a little into my thigh. 'Tell me, Mimi. Tell me you need me, too.'

'I do . . . I do,' I say.

'Do you, Mimi? Tell me.' His beard brushes against my breast, his lips kissing there as he slowly lifts the hems of my nightgown.

'Yes, Emile,' I gasp. 'Mimi needs you so—'

A loud cough barks through the darkness.

My hems fall; his head jerks back. I pull the collar of my nightgown together.

'*Miss* Madeleine – what are you doing so late?'

Christina. I can't speak, don't dare look round.

Emile whispers, 'Send her away,' but she's crossing the kitchen to us and it's too late now.

'It's very late, *miss*,' Christina says.

I still can't speak.

'And who are you?' Emile sighs and lifts me from his lap to stand up, pushing the bulk of his fringe back from his forehead.

I can scarcely breathe, and grip the back of the chair.

'You'll wake up the whole household,' she says, sharply, approaching us.

But he's not afraid of her. 'I asked who you are,' he says, 'to interrupt us so rudely.'

'Never mind who I am. I know who you are, all right, and that's enough. I know your *kind*.'

'You are just a *housemaid*. And *she*' – he nods towards me – 'is the mistress of *you*. How dare you interrupt us?'

'Oh, I dare all right. But let's see what the master says to it, will we?' Christina goes to stand by the kitchen door. 'I can call him down right now. Get his opinion on his daughter meeting with Frenchmen after midnight—'

He murmurs something I can't hear, but it's a threat of some sort, I know that, and Christina understands it, too, judging by the look on her face. The thought of Papa being called down and finding us here, like this, with me in my nightgown, and Emile's shirt open, is so terrible, so appalling, that my legs weaken suddenly. Neither of them seem to grasp fully what discovery would mean; an image spikes in me of Papa, furious, a poker in his hand, striking Emile over and over, striking me . . .

'You have to go, Emile,' I urge him. 'It's too dangerous. If Papa should find you – I think – I think he would murder us both.'

He thinks I'm making a joke of it, chides me a little with, 'Nothing frightens me, not your Papa, and certainly not a *housemaid*.'

Just the same, he fastens his shirt, bends down to pull on his boots. 'That's right, on your way,' Christina says, opening the kitchen door that leads to the hall.

'I'll go the way I came,' he says.

'I wasn't holding this open for *you*,' says Christina, contemptuously.

I can't stand it anymore, this game they're playing, as though there's nothing more at stake than a correct exit to the street. 'Be quiet, Christina. Oh, how dare you, how dare you!'

Emile takes up his coat, his hat, and before I can even say goodbye, he's across the kitchen floor and through the scullery and the back door, out into the lane.

I fly at Christina, my fists raised. 'How could you threaten to call Papa! How could you!'

Christina seizes my arms, her grip too strong for me to fight. 'Jesus Christ, Maddie. What you were letting him do—'

'Only what I *wanted*—'

'Are you that simple? And what more would he have done if I hadn't come in?'

'What I wanted!'

'Fool!'

'Slattern!'

She lets go of my arms, but only to strike me on the cheek at my remark. It's a weak slap, though, making me cry out more from surprise than pain, before she marches over to her little room and shuts the door.

'Slattern,' I mutter again at her closed door before hurrying upstairs to my room to pen a letter to Emile full of apologies – apologies and longing. For as the wick burns down, the memory of his touch and his kisses, all while Mama and Papa slept overhead, mixes with that threat of our discovery and what Papa would do if he came upon us, and blood and desire mingle so much I can barely tell fear from delight, and it seems to me now that they are both the same.

Fear and delight. Fear and delight. When I wake the next morning, the first thing I do is to send John the houseboy with my note to Emile; Christina will only refuse. Emile's speedy reply only an hour or so later makes me gasp, so full is it of his *burning need* for his Mimi, to *fondle and kiss her.*

But the day is slow apart from more notes from him, and I'm moping about, longing to see him, when a carriage arrives in the square: Janet is home. Last night made me forget her coming; I wave from the drawing-room window and rush out to see her.

Her girlish face is plumper and less vacant than it was when she left us, all nerves and fainting from a too-busy Christmas season.

'I'm looking forward to going to Rowaleyn, Mama,' she says carefully in the drawing room, sitting close by Mama, who is watching her closely.

I go over and hug her; Mama says, 'Enough, Maddie, don't excite her.'

'I had such a very quiet time, though,' Janet says, and sighs.

'You are like me, my dear – we are great engines who run out of steam sometimes,' Mama says, before telling me to take Janet upstairs. 'And tuck her in well, Maddie; I don't want her tired out too much.'

Sitting up in our enormous bed, she looks a little lost and forlorn. 'Did you miss me?' she says. 'I missed you – and now you look so different. Your hair is looser. You're altered.'

'No, I'm not at all,' I say hurriedly.

'But you *are* very different.' My dear girl looks so stricken I hug her again. 'I don't think I like it – has something happened while I was away?'

'You're only eleven,' I say, tutting. 'You're not supposed to see—'

'See?'

'What nobody else has—'

John knocks at the door; it's another note from Emile.

'Tell me who it's from,' Janet begs.

'From a great magician – who has changed me so much for the better,' I say, teasing her, but that won't stop her being curious. Not Janet. Not my adorable, nosy sister, who watches everything her Maddie does so closely.

Rowaleyn is so new, so full of Papa's dreams. So sparkling and shiny, like a great palace of light. If Lancelot and Guinevere had wanted light on their affair – for it's all turrets and round towers and spiral stone staircases made bare by a central cupola over the main stairway – they'd find it perfect. But if they preferred some medieval darkness for their love, then they would be sorely disappointed. Mama, at least, is never ill under this light, this newness, this bright endless summer in huge rooms with bay windows. I've given Emile a very exact description of those, as they are the public rooms he may enter once I've introduced him to Papa.

But not straightaway. My bedroom's upstairs, which I must share with Janet, as though it's indecent for me to have my own room at the age of twenty. But no amount of arguing with Mama about it has changed anything. She and Papa are next door, and Jack is along the hall, just as in Bedford Place.

Downstairs, Christina shares a big room with the new cook Mama has taken on for a few days a week, and the new laundry girl, for all the summer parties we have create a great deal of work.

All of this is new and fresh and clean and bright. It's as far from the city as we can get in a day; the river beyond ripples and reflects like a pretty mirror, and we can look there and forget the ugliness of the smoke and the dust and dirt.

But I think it might be a little too well-ordered, a little too open-roomed and clear of shadowy corners for me now. I want the secret places where lovers go, not the polite rooms that Mama and Papa prefer. Where might I meet with my lover, if he's not permitted to enter the great white hallway?

Emile's friend, Monsieur Auguste de Mean, the French consul, is holidaying nearby in Helensburgh, at least, so he can stay there from time to time. He cannot be apart from his Mimi for the summer. And I can't be apart from him.

So we take the steamer, Mama, Papa, Christina, Janet and I – Jack, as the son, is free to come when he wants, of course – a week after Emile kissed me in the kitchen in Bedford Place. Our clothes and books and furnishings follow by rail, as we sail quickly past warehouses and workers' cottages to glide below green hills. The river will carry on upstream towards the low mountains beyond, but we disembark long before that happens, then take a boat across to Papa's carriage, which is waiting on the quay.

It's hard not to be excited by all that's ahead, even if it is time without Emile, for there will be dinners and parties and lunches and games of tennis and evening billiards and even some horse-riding, and Papa has promised I may learn to shoot this summer, too. Janet wants a dog; I should learn to run a household better, says Mama.

But when we climb down from the carriage after the ride up from the riverbank, Janet and I escape Mama as soon as possible to survey our newly furnished bedroom and decide it's very fine. Perhaps that's why I forget – unforgiveable to forget! – about the note Emile sent me just before we left. Only after supper in the dining room do I remember and head for the library to read it alone under candlelight. Janet's in bed, exhausted; Mama and Papa are sitting in the drawing room.

His need of me will be the *death* of him, he writes. He cannot live without his love; he cannot live without his *wife*.

His wife.

Can it be, so soon? When I'm so short of stature and my colour's so poor, because I still feel that way, for all his compliments? Yet the words are there, written in ink on the page, and in his own handwriting, so I must believe it.

We will be married, he says, as soon as my Papa permits, and that's how he'll refer to me from now on, as he is my *husband*. For a moment I think he means it as a joke; then I read on, and learn what he wants in a wife.

You must not go out so often as you have in the past, for I know what temptations there are for you at Rowaleyn. Do not attend so many parties, my love, and do not talk with so many young men. Remember you will be married to me. I want my Mimi to practise her music and her drawing. To read useful books and not reprobates like Byron . . .

But I can't *not* go out – and I can't *not* read Byron, which he must know. His passion for me makes my heart quicken; his jealousy fires me. Life as Emile's wife will be full of passion!

My beloved husband, I respond the next day, all the while expecting him to mock me for it. But he doesn't: ah, *this* is truly who Mimi is. A *wife*, Emile's wife, and that emboldens me at last to speak with Mama at breakfast the morning after.

'This may well be your last season, Maddie,' Mama is saying. The dining room is bright, facing south as it does, and the window is open to the birdsong outside. Janet cocks her head, munching some toast; Papa has gone to inspect the gardens. 'Next year, you will be *twenty-one*. You must make more of an effort, if you're not to be outdone by younger girls coming up.'

The evening before, I'd been surrounded by a dull crop of gangling youths, scratching at their necks and speaking to me as though I were a doll.

'There is – there has been – attention from—' I struggle to get the words out; I don't know how to begin.

But Mama is beaming. 'One of the young men last night? I saw how Mr McAdam's boy was talking with you.'

'No, no, none of them,' I say. 'The gentleman is not here – he is in Glasgow.'

She frowns, thinking of all our acquaintance in the city.

'He is a gentleman, although he works for a living – just like Papa,' I add, quickly.

Mama's frown deepens. 'He is an *architect*?'

'No, no – he is – in *commerce*. He knows the Bairds—'

'Ah! A friend of Sir James – well, then, he would be very welcome, of course.'

'No,' I say, colouring. I can't lie to her. 'He's not a *friend* of

Sir James, exactly – he's employed by him – at his company, Huggins and Co.'

Mama goes very quiet. She looks thoughtful. 'I see. I see. What else?' she says.

I judge that her thoughtfulness might be a good sign. 'He's older than me, which means he is very responsible and serious—'

'How much *older?*'

'Well, he is thirty-two. And he is from good French parents—'

'He is *French?*'

I'm just about to explain better, as Mama is looking very ill, when Jack bursts into the room with, 'He's a clerk. You're talking about Emile, aren't you? You're not *still* thinking about him, Maddie?'

I'd forgotten Jack was joining us this morning from town. He's all in a flap, sweating and panting as though he's run all the way. He grabs the toast rack and munches his toast as loudly as Janet, who's watching us anxiously. She starts to bite her nails.

'A *clerk*,' says Mama. 'He is thirty-two years old, French, and a clerk?'

'And penniless as they come,' says Jack, cheerfully. 'He's got a room on Great Western Road, up by the Botanics. He's a real dandy – you should see how he dresses, Mama. Red tweed cape and a fancy silver walking stick. I might get one; I hear all the women are swooning for him.' He winks at me.

'*Jack!*' I say, horrified by the effect he's having on Mama, whose face is pale as porridge.

'But it's true – he has an eye for a rich young lady. He's been engaged twice already, heiresses each time! Didn't you know that, Maddie? Did he not tell you that day in the coffee house?'

About his previous engagements to rich young women? No, I didn't know.

But Mama's up on her feet. 'What day in the coffee house?' she demands.

'Didn't Maddie tell you, Mama?' Jack says, innocently.

Mama pulls the bell for the houseboy, who arrives before I can say anything more. 'Get the master, now!' she says. 'Janet – go to your room immediately, this business is not for your ears. And Jack – how disappointing, to let your sister, your own sister, speak with such a man.'

She goes on and on until Papa arrives. I'm in despair, in tears, and Jack's trying and failing to argue back. When Papa enters, after hearing what they have to say first, he dismisses Jack, then suggests Mama leaves for her own room to calm herself.

He motions me to sit, while he stands at the fireplace, hands behind his back. It's a pose we all know, and dread, for it's the prelude to a storm. But he begins quietly enough.

'I don't like that he insinuated himself into your company before he knew *me*,' he says, and my heart sinks. 'My family are not opportunities for men like that. And I don't like that he's got *you* asking for him. It's not decent behaviour, not gentlemanly.'

'But he *is* decent,' I say, even as I colour at the memory of him coming to the kitchen in Bedford Place. 'He knows he can only get an introduction through me—'

It's the wrong thing to say. Papa colours, too. His voice rises in volume. 'Exactly my point, Maddie! Encouraging my eldest daughter into behaviour that's not respectable. I won't stand for it!'

'But, Papa, I would never not be respectable.' I don't know

how I dare challenge him, for I've never dared do so before, and it seems to take Papa by surprise, for he quietens. I take another breath and say, 'And Mama is arranging all these endless, awful parties for me.'

And to *my* surprise this time, his expression even softens. 'Ah, Maddie. It's your Mama making you hurry, making you see possibilities in the wrong place. I understand. So none of the boys she brings are catching your eye,' he says, and his hands release. He even looks a little amused. 'Well, I don't blame you for that – they're a lot of weak-looking fools. But that doesn't mean this older fellow who's got nothing to his name is for you, either. Be patient. The right one will come along.'

'But I'm twenty years old already.' The whine in my voice only makes him frown again, though, and his face reddens once more.

'And you will have only the best of men, not some foreigner whose family we don't know, who's a clerk at Huggins. He's been engaged twice, Jack said? To rich young women? That's an adventurer and nothing more.' He smacks the table with his fist; I shrink back a little. 'For heaven's sake, Maddie! No, I'd not be doing my duty as a father. I'm right about this. I'll not waver, d'you hear me? Do you hear me?'

I nod, having no other choice, and say, meekly, 'Of course, Papa.'

The storm is averted, but only just. 'Then I give you permission to write to this – *man*. But only to tell him to cease his attentions *immediately*.'

'Yes, Papa.'

And so, in utter misery that afternoon, I write to him.

I must banish your image from my heart. My papa will not give his consent. It almost breaks my heart. Burn all my letters. Be happy. Forget me.

In truth, I've been stung as much by the news that Emile has been engaged twice before, as I am by Papa's refusal to admit him.

It's a day later that Emile's response arrives. He's refusing to accept what I say, and will come to Rowaleyn that very night, he says. I'm to wait for him in the kitchen, just like in Bedford Place.

He won't give me up, but he has an explanation to give me, on which everything hangs. Little wonder I'm now trembling with anticipation in the dark of the kitchen, as the rest of the household sleeps. Not least because I'm disobeying Papa, which none of us ever do, if we can help it. I shudder, thinking of Papa's fury were he to discover me doing the very thing that he's forbidden. It was bad enough before, when he didn't know about Emile. But now that he does, and he's expressly forbidden I see him – ah, Mama couldn't save me from his wrath, from the objects he'd throw at my head, like he does when Jack displeases him.

He might even disown me. I'd be a fallen woman, homeless, like Nancy in *Oliver Twist* or Little Emily in *David Copperfield*. Thoughts of dark nights under bridges, alone and unprotected, are terrifying; but Emile would never let that happen. He'd scoop me up, defend me against Papa. For he's refused to give me up.

Yes; that's what I must remember as I pace back and forth between the windows that look down over the driveway on one side, and down to the river on the other, watching for a light. He's coming through the woods beyond the house. I'm leaving the kitchen window open so that he'll find the correct room.

Christina's in the servants' bedroom with the cook, Mrs McGregor, and the laundry maid, Agnes, far away down the corridor. Upstairs, the clock strikes midnight.

Janet was snoring when I left her; I was naughty, slipping a little draught into her cocoa so that she wouldn't wake and see I'm gone. But she's been asking so many questions lately, and I can't risk her seeing him.

The clock in the kitchen ticks away the minutes as I wait, breathing hard, in my nightgown and slippers, my hair loose once more. It feels strange this time, though, and I'm tapping my foot nervously. Perhaps not only from my fear of Papa, but because those two fiancées of Emile's are playing about my head. Did he call them *Mimi*, too, I wonder. Did he visit them in the dark, and do the things he did with me, with them, too? Did he *need* them as much as he needs me?

Jealousy makes me uneasy and desperate both; it makes me unsure, suddenly, of Emile, of who he is.

What, I think, if Papa is right?

But then Emile's face appears at the window, peering through the gloom. I give a tiny cry; he taps for me to open the window further. In he climbs over the windowsill; the night is still and humid. His hair is damp and sticks to his cheeks; his shirt drips with sweat. It has been a long walk from Helensburgh, he says, taking a chair. 'Pour me something to drink, my lovely *wife*.'

I pour some red wine into a glass for him; he drinks it all down in one, then asks for another. When he presses my hand to his lips, I'm cold to it, though, and he feels the coldness, for he says, 'Have you fallen out of love with me so soon? Just because your Papa forbids it? Mimi – surely not.'

'Who were they?' I ask, blurting it out. 'You had two fiancées – what happened? My Papa says you are – an *adventurer*.'

I turn away, heartsick, but he laughs. Then he says, 'Ah, you think I'm false, too, then,' and gets to his feet as if to leave.

'Wait – you can't go without giving me an explanation!'

My highhandedness stops him, just like it did in the alleyway. We're facing each other; I shiver suddenly as he rubs his chin.

'Another test for us – and you fail this one, too,' he says. 'Listening to gossip – falsehoods about me.'

'Are they false? Were you engaged to them or not? Tell me!' I'm near tears; he's frowning at me as though he loathes me.

'Ah, Mimi,' he says, shaking his head. 'How you are disappointing me. I have been engaged before, that is true. First to a lady who broke with me, and broke my heart in doing so. And then to another, whom I loved very dearly, as she loved me. She fell sick after her family refused to let us see one another.' His voice grows quiet; the frown has gone. 'They made her heartsick, and she died from it. *Died*. Did your *informers* mention any of that? No? I did not think so. For shame, Mimi – you do not trust me at all—' His voice breaks with pain.

I burst into tears, for I, too, will surely sicken and die if they keep Emile from me.

'Save your tears,' he murmurs. 'She does not need your weeping.'

But *I* need it. 'I'm just so very sorry for her. For you. Ah – for *me*, too! Because I didn't know,' I say, dabbing my eyes. 'My Papa has you wrong, calling you an adventurer—'

He buries his face in his hands. I don't know what to do, am unsure whether he'll let me comfort him. When he looks up, his cheeks are wet, too. 'Christina *says* – your Papa *says* – what did *I* say about you being misused? That you must listen only to me? Don't you trust me? Or will you break my heart as she did, too?'

Misused.

Of course; but that's because I am just poor, weak, Madeleine, after all. Mimi would never let herself be misused. Mimi would not let her papa forbid, or Christina insist. Emile turns again to leave, but this time I run to him and wrap my arms about him.

'Don't go,' I say. 'Make me your Mimi again.'

He sighs but he does sit down, and, after a kiss or two, pulls me on to his lap and dabs my cheeks with a handkerchief from his pocket. Then he kisses my forehead, my nose, my lips, and I smile as his hands travel over my stomach, my breasts, up to my neck.

But it's leaving me cold, still. Not because of his poor, dead, heartsick fiancée. No, because I'm still Madeleine.

'Make me Mimi,' I whisper. 'Please, Emile. Make me Mimi again.'

He pulls away to study my face. I wonder if he understands, but then he says, softly, 'I know what you need. Remember that, Mimi. I always know.'

'Yes, yes, I will,' I murmur. Madeleine obeys housemaids and fathers. Mimi defies them all.

'Be a good girl, then, and trust me, yes?'

I nod.

'Then stand in front, here, and turn around for me.'

The only light in the kitchen is from the moon outside and the single candle flickering on the table. I get up off his lap and stand, facing away from him, as he bids me to lean gently against the kitchen table. I hold my breath and close my eyes, wait for the feelings to surge through me, that passion I felt before and which gives me all the courage I could ever need.

Below, the hems of my nightgown start to lift, tickling the backs of my bare calves. I breathe out; his fingers tap up the backs of my knees to my thighs, making me giggle a little. And then they reach the rump of my behind.

I hold my breath again; those dead, black embers inside me are flickering, just like they did in the alleyway.

Mimi.

Behind me, Emile shifts off the chair. I twist round a little: he's getting down on his knees.

'Do you trust me, Mimi?' he says, looking up at me.

'Yes, Emile,' I say, and he pushes my nightgown up even further, all the way to my waist. I let out a gasp. 'Trust me, Mimi,' he says, and a tremor, light as electricity, passes along my spine as he holds firm my naked hips, and his beard bristles against the small of my back, and then his serpent tongue snakes its way deep, deep down and between the cheeks of my behind.

He brings her back: Mimi. That's who I am again, and how delicious it is to be her, to feel that irresistible fire, that gushing of heat that simmers inside long after he's gone and I'm back in bed beside a sleeping Janet, full of confused delight. My heart beats so hard that I think it'll never soften again and perhaps its beating will kill me.

Love. I lick my lips, the backs of my hands, trace my tongue along my arms just as he did.

Love.

But it takes an age for the fire he's set in me to dampen down.

Dreams of smoking cottages and dark paths full of watchful eyes have me twisting and turning when I do fall asleep, so much that Janet wakes in the early hours and murmurs, 'Be still, Maddie, be still.'

Or is that him speaking, and I'm dreaming, asleep after all? *Be still, Mimi, be still.*

When Janet shakes me awake in the morning, there's alarm on her face. 'You were having a nightmare,' she says.

'Was I?' I say, rubbing my eyes.

'You were being murdered, Maddie. A bad man was killing you.'

I only laugh, and hug her until she settles.

In the kitchen later that morning, Christina is silent until it's just the two of us, alone at the table, she kneading some bread, me playing with my hair, unable to do any sensible thing. I'm lost to everything but my body's recollection of last night.

But her hushed voice is urgent enough to alert me when she finally speaks. 'Maddie, you shouldn't have done it – let *him* do it – what he did last night.'

'You mean you *saw* us?' The truth dawns, dazzling me. 'You mean you *spied* on us?'

'I'm telling you, it's not right what he did – it's not right. Are you mad to let him? He's mad too, I tell you. I don't like him. No, I don't like him at all – he's not right in the head, if you ask me.'

'Don't be so simple. It's not for you to have an opinion on us,' I say, getting up from the table. How dare she say these things? '*Emile* says that he—'

'I don't care what Emile says. He'll say whatever he wants if it makes you do – *that*. But I'll not be party to what you're doing,' she says, wiping her hands on her apron.

I'm furious, and so is she, but for some reason, she's blinking back tears, too.

'I mean it, Maddie,' she says. 'If he comes back to the house, I'll fetch your papa—'

That's why she's near weeping. She's afraid of my papa, too. 'I'll tell him about McKenzie if you do,' I mutter.

'Do it,' she says, but she bites her lip then, and I know she's bluffing. 'I'll get another post. I don't care. But Emile is – well, he's *bad*, Maddie. He's wrong.'

'He's my *husband*—'

But just then Mama appears at the kitchen door. 'Maddie, where have you been? Don't you know the party is to start in less than an hour? Look at the state of you! Hurry up!'

I start, and Christina wipes her eyes with her apron. We can't say more to one another now, which is as well, for I don't want to care about her weeping. I only want that fiery tingling back; I need that gush of heat more than anything. I hurry as Mama bids me, and by night-time, after a boring party of card-playing, I'm parched and dry as dust, and desperate for that feeling, for him.

He sends a note the next morning that Christina delivers to me in my bedroom without a word. But it's terrible news for me: he must go back to Glasgow immediately. I cannot see him for a whole week.

Never have my spirits plunged so low; never has such desperation taken me over. *What am I to do, what am I to do? How can I wait all that time without you? With nothing to help me?* I write.

He only tells me, *Be patient, Mimi.*

For the rest of that week I'm wretched, but eventually some entertainments do start to distract me a little. I decide to tell

Emile about my lace gown for a particular dinner, meaning to arouse him, but he writes back, annoyed and criticising: *I insist you only wear brown. No bright colours, Mimi. No lace. No pretty collars.*

But I cannot only wear brown, Emile, I reply. *And I must dress appropriately for parties.*

I'm a little cross that he doesn't seem to understand at all what's expected of me here, or how frustrating it is to be without him for so long.

His answer a few mornings later is harsh.

I expected better of you than this. I wanted better than this from my wife. You are shaming me, Mimi. How you are shaming me. You are my own, mine alone to kiss and fondle. I will not have others touch you. It is unbearable to me.

It's horrific to me that he could think I might be intimate with other men. I don't know how he could have such a notion, and feverishly, I write back, refuting it all. But I must ready myself for lunch with Mama, and end up rushing my words.

It's while I'm out with Mama that Christina steals Emile's letter to me. I don't discover what she's done until later that evening in the kitchen after supper, when she waves it in front of my face, before threatening to toss it into the kitchen fire.

'Wee dictator,' she says. 'How can you stand him telling you what to do all the time? And what's this about others touching you? Is he mad?'

'He's jealous. He just loves me so much,' I say, grabbing for my letter. But she's holding it too high for me to reach it, and I stumble as she flicks her hand away.

'Damn you!' I say, losing my temper. 'Give me back my letter, you witch!'

'What on earth are you doing?' says Janet, running into the kitchen as Christina and I shriek and grapple with one another. She pulls me away and I shake my head at Christina, daring her to say a word. But she does worse – she hands the letter to Janet before I can stop her.

'You mustn't read it, it's private,' I say, but it's too late, for she's caught enough words already.

'"Mine alone to kiss and fondle" – what is this, Maddie?'

She sounds so shocked I can barely look at her. Christina smirks, hands on her hips.

'Janet,' I say, then take a deep breath. 'You were there when I mentioned him to Mama, do you remember? She didn't understand that he's a – very *great* gentleman, my *admirer*. He's a – a *poet*. And of very *warm* expression. Like – oh, like Byron, perhaps. His ancestry is very noble – he has lived in Paris, and—'

'Your sister's fallen for a French adventurer who likes to paw her,' interrupts Christina, addressing Janet crudely. 'Your Papa was right to try and stop it but she's been meeting him here at night, nonetheless.'

Janet gasps in horror; I press my palms together. 'Please, Janet, he's not at all like Christina says. We are – we are *in love*, do you see? So please – don't say a word to anyone. Not a single word.'

'But he comes here – into the house?' Janet whispers. 'Papa will kill him if he catches him.'

'Which is why Papa mustn't ever know – promise you won't say a word. Promise me, Janet, or I don't know what will happen.'

* * *

It takes more persuasion to bring Janet to my side: a great many warnings of how Papa will punish me; a claim that he might banish me, even from her, which is what works best, for she wants me never to leave her.

But now, at last, he's coming again tonight.

I warn Christina to be in her room, because the kitchen is the only place we can meet, and tell Janet to stay in our bedroom and not make a sound. I won't have either of them spying, or stopping me, or doing anything to spite us.

It's a balmy July night of humid air; flies flicker just outside the kitchen window. The river a mile or so below the house sends many of them fluttering up in search of the lights that make them throw themselves desperately against the windowpane, over and over again.

In the morning, little spots of dried blood from dead flies will have to be washed from the windows. The tiny black dots on the sills outside that look as though the soot from St Rollox has followed us all this way must be swept up.

For now, though, I must blow a few early dead flies away. Then I push up the window sash with eager fingers, careful not to make too much noise. The moon is full tonight, and lights up the room. The house is quiet after the bustle and noise of the day, the visiting boys that still come and go all the time, for ever since our terrible confrontation, Mama has been more determined than ever that I make a good match, and that's what I must explain to Emile.

Ah, my love, my true husband. I'm almost leaning out of the window in my keenness, when there's a noise behind me, pulling me back in.

Christina steps out of the shadows just as Emile appears and starts to climb in through the window. I'm caught between them both as Christina says, boldly, 'Enough of this.'

Emile stops and stares, one foot over the windowsill.

'You're not setting another foot in here,' she says to him. 'Filthy gold-digger. Get going or I'll tell the master—'

'*I'll* tell Papa about *you*,' I say. 'Leave us alone!'

Emile lifts his other leg over the sill, nevertheless, and comes to my side, puts an arm around my waist.

'We are used to folk against us, aren't we, Mimi?'

'Oh, is that right?' says Christina before I can reply. 'The master'll be more against you than he'll be against me. So I wouldn't bother telling on me if I were you, Maddie. He'll have *him* arrested for breaking and entering – and serve him right. Let him spend a night in the cells.'

But I won't be shaken, not with Emile by my side. 'The more you fight us, the more you push us together.'

'Indeed,' Emile says. 'For we are husband and wife.'

I nod. 'Yes, yes, we are.'

Christina scoffs. 'You're not even married—'

'No,' I say, hesitantly. Emile's hand grips my waist more tightly. 'But in our eyes, we are husband and wife. So leave us in peace—'

'I'll not do that. Not while *he's* in the master's house. A fox in the henhouse is what he is.'

'And you have carried my letters to him,' I say. 'So you're in as much trouble with Papa if you tell him.'

'I don't care about that; I told you,' she says.

Emile is looking her up and down, though. Suddenly, he says, 'What is your price, Christina? You are engaged, too, yes? You will need new shoes' – he points to the clogs on her feet, then looks at the top of her head – 'or a new hat perhaps. A new dress?'

'You think you can buy me?' she says. 'Well, I won't be bought!'

But I know what she wants for her trousseau, and she can't afford it; she told me weeks ago.

'A new crinoline,' I mutter. 'That's her price.'

She bites her lip, glares at me for the betrayal.

Emile nods. 'A new crinoline it is, then. Whichever one you want.'

'Like you can afford it.'

'To keep my Mimi safe, I will pay any price.'

My heart swells at that.

Christina shakes her head; I think she's refusing, but she isn't. She's only bargaining, for she says, 'I might keep quiet about the two of you – but you're not meeting in the house. Not anymore. That's my condition, and I'll not waver on it.'

Emile pushes a little but she won't give on that. After agreeing, to my great frustration he climbs back out of the window.

'Not yet! You can't leave, I've waited two weeks for you.' I'm almost ready to weep, but he only kisses me a chaste goodnight before whispering, 'Another night, Mimi.'

And then he's gone.

I tell Christina what I think of her, but she shrugs. 'The master's going to find you both out, I mean it,' she says. 'And I won't have it laid at my door.'

'You'll still take a new crinoline from Emile, though,' I say, miserably.

Where are we to meet, with her eyes on me all the time? I trudge back to bed and get in to lie beside Janet, too wakeful with disappointment to do anything but stare at the ceiling and wish for my wolf-man.

It's another ten agonising days before Emile sends me a note about his plan for us. He includes more strictures about my behaviour. I've explained to him more carefully about the young men Mama insists I meet with, and how she insists I must dress for them. But it only makes him more furious, for he writes, *I will have to show you what a good wife is*, and tells me, *You must take that lesson into yourself.*

I remember my *leçon privée*. That shivering fear in the alleyway; ah, I may wonder what he means by *You must take that lesson into yourself*. Part of me – the Madeleine part – fears it, of course, for Madeleine is a trussed-up coward. But the Mimi part, the bold part of me, only longs for it.

He has divided me in two, it seems indeed, and they are not friends. I will have to banish one of them for good: I want to be only Mimi. I want Madeleine forgotten, and it's tonight, when he's coming for me a third time, that I intend it to happen.

And so I follow his plan, and wait downstairs in the quiet of the kitchen. After a while, at the right time, I open the window. I pause for Christina's breathing, in case she's nearby, watching. Then, in a flash, I'm over the windowsill and running across the grass as fast as I can to the woods beyond. When I stop at last to look back, it's too gloomy a night to make out if she's following, but she doesn't seem to be. On into the woods I go, bold Mimi, wife of Emile, panting my way to the little clearing beyond the bramble bushes and rhododendrons.

My slippers are soon wet, even though the leaves and blooms keep much of the ground drier than the grass. Midges buzz about. Something rustles in the bushes beyond, and twigs crack, making me pause, but it's only an animal of some sort: a rabbit, most likely. Owls hoot and there's more scrambling; they've caught a mouse and a shriek goes out, or maybe it's something bigger.

The woods get darker the deeper I go, and I sniff the mossy air; it's thicker here, filling my throat. The tiny clearing should be only a little beyond. The Madeleine part of me isn't gone yet – her voice in my head tells me this is a terrible plan in such darkness, that I should turn back to the house, but I am Mimi and so I ignore her voice, and hurry on.

A moment later, to my great relief, Emile steps out from behind a tree. I cry out and reach for him, but he brushes me off him.

'I have heard even more reports about you recently,' he says, holding out his palm as if to ward me off. 'So many reports. About your behaviour at parties, your flirting with every boy and man in sight—'

'It's not true!' I say. 'Please, Emile. I've been longing for this – how can you? I've explained about what Mama expects—'

'What about what *I* expect?' he says, rubbing his face. He seems tearful, which makes me think again that he must love me so much, and I only have to show him that I love him, too. 'You are supposed to respect a husband. *Obey* a husband. I am your husband. Not any of those boys. But you prefer them—'

'I love *you*, Emile.'

'Is it not bad enough that I have to skulk about the woods, that I cannot go through the front door of your Papa's house?' he says. 'Ah, you *enjoy* it, Mimi. You *like* my humiliation.'

I fling myself at him, not caring about his coldness, wanting only that heat he can bring me. And suddenly I know how to bring it about. *Mimi* knows.

'And if I do?' I whisper, my hands at his face, his neck, his hair. 'If I do like it? How will you punish me, husband? For flirting with all those boys Mama brings me? For shaming you?'

He catches his breath. 'Ah, Mimi,' he murmurs. I press myself to him, and he doesn't resist or push me away. Slowly, I lift the hems of my nightgown.

'You only mean to use me,' he mutters, but he doesn't move.

'Yes,' I murmur in his ear. Then I turn away, face the tree. Will he do it, I wonder, trembling with my nightgown in my hands, caught beyond my hips.

Mimi knows.

For then he's on his knees behind me. He does as I urge him to, as Mimi urges him. And in the end, it's Mimi who cries out his name, and who sinks, exhausted, on to the mossy ground, elated still, to have got what she wanted from him.

'Emile,' I murmur, closing my eyes.

'Those boys do not get on their knees for you,' he says. 'They do not humiliate themselves—'

'No,' I say, stretching my arms behind me on the grass, smiling at him. 'They do not.'

Suddenly, he's getting to his feet, pulling me up with him.

'Time, then, for your lesson,' he says. 'Show me what a good wife you are.'

I remember his letter. *Take that lesson into yourself.* My hand flies to my neck. 'I'm ready,' I say.

I know how babies are made; my dormitory bedfellows at Mrs Gorton's Academy at least whispered that. So I know what he has, what he keeps between his legs, and I shiver in delight, before he pulls me round behind him, wrapping my arms around his hips, to place my hands on his front, where he's hard. I gasp to feel it.

'I'm ready,' I say again.

'Then give me the very same I gave you. *Good* wife of mine,' he says.

I start, confused. He can't mean *that*. Christina's voice whispers in my head – *it isn't right, what he does* – and I pull away a little.

'No, no,' he says. 'You must, Mimi, you must do it. Exactly what I did for you. Take your lesson. I said I would show you.'

Is this what he intended all along? For it's not what I had thought at all, and suddenly, I'm furious at the trick he's pulled, feel cheated, because I wanted what husbands and wives do together. Not this.

I fight to free my hands but he's holding them tightly.

'Get on your knees as I did,' he mutters, pushing my arms down behind him so that I have no choice but to get down on the earth at his feet. Only then does he free my hands, but it's to loosen his long shirt and the waistband of his trousers.

His breath quickens; his own hands are on his hardness.

'Hurry, Mimi,' he says.

I could run away. Madeleine would run back up to the house, never see him again.

But Mimi would not run away. So Mimi crouches down on the mossy ground as he instructs, as tiny animals twitch and cry all around her. Mimi lets a different kind of urge push through her as she holds his hips with both hands and presses her face to him. Mimi is not afraid to lick and suck and push her tongue between; Mimi knows what to do.

Mimi knows.

Only after I'm done and he's lying on the ground beside me do I notice that raindrops have been falling all this while, and I'm soaked through.

'I think you are too much, Mimi,' he's saying. 'You are a savage; look how you hurt me.'

He shows me his buttock cheek where I bit him; but Mimi isn't ashamed and I say, 'I only did what you told me to.'

'You may dress up for a drawing room. But underneath it, you are a savage. You want controlling,' he says.

All the way back through the wet woods, he scolds me for *enjoying myself too much*, for enjoying my hurt of him. I'm too astonished, and become cross with him. By the time we near the house, he is still scolding – 'Control, restraint, is what you want, Mimi' – and he won't even kiss me goodbye.

As I make my way over to the house across the wet grass, it occurs to me that he wanted me to feel ashamed; he wanted me to resent my humiliation. Is that what *he* feels when he is on his knees behind me? But I'm Mimi now; I cannot let her go and feel what I do not feel. I won't pretend otherwise and he must understand that, savage or not.

And for the first time in these past few months, I wonder if *my husband* truly knows his wife, after all.

A few mornings later I'm in the kitchen alone when Christina comes in and glances at me, the scissors in my hand. 'Emile wants a lock of my hair,' I say, 'and it's as good an engagement ring as any – Ah, no, what are you doing?'

For she's gripping my shoulders, squeezing hard.

'*Someone* has to wake you up, Maddie!' she urges in my ear.

'What he's doing to you isn't right. He's – he's making a *slavey* out of you, poisoning you—'

'Don't be so ridiculous,' I say. My head hurts a little; I haven't been sleeping so very well since all that passed between Emile and me in the woods at night, have been puzzling over my feelings.

'I'm afraid for you, I don't recognise you anymore. Sneaking out to the woods—'

'So you *were* watching, I knew it.'

She releases me. Her face is flushed. 'Yes, I followed you. All that way. And what he made you do— '

'I only did what I *wanted* to.'

'I don't believe you. I think he's *bewitching* you, you're not Maddie anymore—'

'No, I'm not her, and I don't want to be her. I am – *savage*. I am Mimi.'

To my surprise, though, I find that I'm weeping, and Christina has wrapped her arms around me. 'He's making you into his own creature,' she's saying, 'and you're losing who you are.'

'You're wrong,' I say. 'I'm becoming *me*. This is my nature. I am—'

'He's destroying you, because you'll not give him what he wants.'

'What he wants is Mimi, and I give him all of her. It's Madeleine he doesn't want—'

There's a sound at the door, a sob. We stop and turn to look there.

Janet.

She has heard every word.

III.

'And here it is that the correspondence comes to be of the utmost importance, to show that the writer was a person quite capable of compassing any end by which she could avoid exposure and disgrace, and of cherishing any feeling of revenge which such treatment might excite in her mind, driven nearly to madness by the thought of what might follow the revelation of this correspondence . . .'

– The Lord Justice-Clerk charge to the jury in the trial of Madeleine Smith, 9 July 1857, Edinburgh

New York, 1927

'What "crazy coincidence" are you talking about, Harry?' Violet asked. She might have spent an afternoon drinking old-fashioneds with him, but she was a girl after my own heart and she could sense danger when it was present. The air in my apartment had changed so subtly since his arrival, she hadn't noticed it at first. But Harry's presence said something different, and she was looking at me, not at him, even while she directed her question at him. There was concern in her eyes.

I knew she saw me as vulnerable, and had done ever since Willy's death, in spite of my good health and my independent ways. It would be cruel of me to play on that concern of hers, but Harry was threatening me with that reference to Janet, and I didn't know what else to do.

'I think – oh, I think he must be mixing me up with someone else, my dear, and it's very unsettling,' I said. I even made my voice wobble a little.

Harry just raised his eyebrows at me. 'Really?' he said. 'You sure about that, Mrs Sheehy? Maybe Violet can help us figure it out, then – what do you think? Violet – isn't your father Tom Wardle, and your grandfather in England George Wardle? Mrs Sheehy's first husband? Because I was reading this book—'

I had no choice. I'd tried calling his bluff but he was

answering me with one of his own, and I couldn't take the risk. Thank goodness I'd at least had the sense to burn that newspaper page.

'All right, Harry,' I said, quickly. 'I'll do your film. Whatever you want.'

Triumph spread across his features. 'Well, now,' he said, rubbing his hands, 'isn't that just grand?'

I folded my arms, clasping my elbows.

Violet looked at me and said, 'You sure about this, Grandma? You don't seem too happy about it.'

How I wanted to take her into my confidence. But to break it to her that all these years had been a lie was more than I could bear. When I'd talked it over with Willy in the past, he'd say that she'd forgive me, that she'd understand why I couldn't tell folk, not even some of those I loved best in the world. But just the thought of Violet, confused by my lack of faith in her – maybe even broken-hearted – was unbearable to me.

Over the years, not-confiding had become my habit, until finally it was my preference, and for more reason than not wanting to hurt Violet. I'd simply become a different person. I wasn't the same young woman I'd once been, and leaving her in the past was more than a necessity; it felt utterly natural.

Perhaps it was no wonder that I'd ended up in the New World. It was where folk went to live new lives, after all. Meeting Willy was the best thing that ever happened to me, and my new life truly began with him. The old me was long dead and gone. I wouldn't have her resurrected now.

So I simply smiled at Violet's concern and said, 'Yes, yes, I am. It's fine, it's just a lot to think about.'

'I'll be with you all through it,' Violet said. Then she turned to Harry and said, 'That's all right, isn't it? I can help – she's ninety-two, after all.'

A little shade crossed his face, making it clear to me that he didn't want her there either.

I said, hurriedly, 'Doesn't Tom need you, with that cold he has getting worse? You know your father takes them so badly now, they really lay him low. Truly, I'll be fine with just Harry.'

'And more folk in the room only means more noise gets picked up,' Harry said. 'I'm sorry, Violet, I have to be strict. The microphone is just too sensitive.' She looked downcast at that, but then he said, winking, 'After we're done, I'll treat you both to drinks at the Waldorf, that a deal?' and as I said, 'That's a great idea, Harry,' and made myself smile brighter, she had no choice but to agree.

I yawned then, making out I needed my rest so that they'd leave me in peace. Which they did, albeit only after a few more questions from Violet, and Harry insisting that he'd call for me in the morning just before ten, to take me to the Waldorf.

At least Violet had forgotten all about Harry's 'coincidence' remark by then. What I needed most, though, was to stop and think about what I'd agreed to, and how I was going to manage it.

Once they'd gone, I put a record on the gramophone to try and calm my beating heart.

> *Some day he'll come along, the man I love,*
> *And he'll be big and strong, the man I love.*

'Oh, Willy,' I murmured. For the first time in nearly thirty years, I felt truly alone without my husband by my side. My bones ached and my muscles cried out for rest from worry. My ankles had swollen, and through the window, dust mingled with the humidity to hamper my breathing. A sudden thirst had me drinking all the milk there was in the cool box in the kitchen, and afterwards, I lay down fully dressed on the daybed.

For hours I drifted in and out of sleep. In the pale dawn light, as the cranes clanked on and the street began to wake up, I got up to change and lie down in my proper bed. It seemed I'd only just closed my eyes, though, when it was time to get up and prepare myself for what the day was bringing, and still I'd resolved nothing.

The first thing the day brought me was another newspaper headline. I was sitting by the window enjoying my morning cup of tea when a paperboy came by, shouting out the first news of the day as he passed. I called for him to come up the stoop and gave him a couple of nickels for a copy of the paper.

The headline was chilling in its finality.

Ruth Snyder and Judd Gray Found Guilty In The First Degree In Swift Verdict. Both To Get Death Sentence Monday. Mrs Snyder Unconscious an Hour in Cell. Symptoms Resemble Epilepsy, Doctors Say.

'They're really going to *execute* her?' I said to the boy, but he was back down on the sidewalk already. Inside the parlour, I searched the paper for mention of a petition being got up in Mrs Snyder's favour maybe, or some such thing, but there was nothing.

'This is where women-hating gets us,' I muttered. Not a single voice was raised to save her, not after all those reports about her morals, her dyed hair, and her cheap, too-fancy clothes.

'Mind your own business and the world will mind its own,' Willy would say, whenever those phony interviews appeared over the years and had me scouring the letters pages afterwards. Always some women-hater would be calling for 'justice' – by which they meant the death sentence.

'Some of them would like to do the executing themselves; I swear they would,' I'd say back at him. 'The world doesn't always want to mind its own business, not when there's a chance to put a few women in the ground.'

But he didn't like that kind of bitter talk, did Willy, so I kept those thoughts mostly to myself. Now, though, living alone, I could give full vent to them, and so I did, tottering round and round my parlour, arguing with myself about whether to write a letter to the newspaper in question or not.

I wondered about Ruth Snyder in her cell, recovering from her fit. Stuck in a tiny room, overheating in the sun but unable to get shade or any kind of coolness. They'd torture her until the end, and that image was what did it, what made me sit down, pen in hand, to express my thoughts on the matter to the newspaper editor.

Before I could write a word, though, a low whistle below the window made me look up.

Harry, flashy as ever and waving up from the sidewalk. Sure enough, the clock on the mantelpiece said it was almost ten. At least he was punctual.

'Your carriage awaits, ma'am,' he called up from the sidewalk, opening the door to his Chrysler. 'The Waldorf beckons!'

A couple of flappers had stopped to admire the motor and

were giggling, exchanging a few words with him, so I took my time fetching my hat and shawl. Petty victories like making him wait passed too quickly, though, as I said goodbye to the parlour and shut the front door, shuffling like I was going to my own execution, though I bet Ruth Snyder would have given anything to be getting into Harry's motor in my place. It seemed I couldn't get rid of the woman, haunting my thoughts as she did these days.

Harry ran up the stoop to take my elbow and help me down to the sidewalk, like a good grandson might.

'You're right to be in movies,' I grumbled at him. 'You know how to put on a show, don't you?'

'Oh, I ain't got nothing on you,' he said, winking then helping me on to the spotless running board. I didn't care to know what he meant by that remark. It was easier than I expected, though, to get in and sit down; the leather seat was plush and the dashboard a shining walnut. Behind me ran a long seat for more passengers, and a hood that could be pulled over in bad weather.

For a moment, I wished Willy was with me, for he'd have loved a drive in such a stylish motor, but then I swallowed down thoughts of him; they would only soften me when I needed to be hard. Harry shut the little door, and walked round to the driver's side. I held myself still while he got in and started up the engine, and then we were off.

The summer breeze nearly blew my hat right off my head, pinned though it was, and I gripped my shawl. Every bone in me was jostled, though somehow the fancy seat made it better. I held on as tightly to the leather seat as my arthritic fingers would let me, as on Harry drove, block after block, across the bridge, and down to the corner of Fifth Avenue and 33rd Street until we reached the Waldorf Astoria.

I got out reluctantly, recalling how Willy had known some of the builders who'd worked on the other half of the building after the Waldorf part was done. Twenty years ago, the city had gotten over calling it 'Astor's Folly', but the men who'd sweated and slaved building it never did. Two friends of Willy's were killed during its construction. All that marble and steel and stone and glass – not to mention the blood and bones of those who perished – and not a single part of it affordable to the men who broke their backs for it.

We'd both sworn we'd never set foot inside it. So I silently sent Willy an apology as the uniformed doorman opened the double plate-glass doors and tipped his hat to us, and in I went.

What a sight that interior was. More palatial than any king's residence and richer than an emperor's. I couldn't help gasping out loud that it was beyond anything I'd ever experienced.

Harry looked surprised. 'You had that grand country estate, and those town houses you lived in when you were a girl—'

'They're nothing to this,' I said. 'This would make, oh, I don't know – the Ritz in Mayfair look shabby.'

The foyer was big as a ballroom, pillared and panelled and resplendent with rugs and mahogany chairs and soft covered couches. An enormous glass chandelier hung down, electric and fully lit, and velvet drapes tall as trees framed the windows. The reception up ahead was a curved marble desk as long as the rail on an ocean liner, and engraved in gold. I trod carefully over the spotless tiles, anxious about slipping, while all around me gleamed pink and green and cream.

I had to lean on Harry's arm. He guided me over to the

elevators; he was on the first floor, he said. The bellhop looked young enough to be a schoolboy, and tapped his hat as Harry gave his room number. When the elevator doors opened to a corridor every bit as plush as downstairs, with more pillars and palm trees and lush carpeting, I hesitated.

'I got a great view of the street,' he said. After we passed a couple of doors, Harry stopped and unlocked one. 'So whaddya think?'

The suite was L-shaped, with a ceiling at least three times higher than those in my apartment. The bed up ahead of us was set behind two pillars and looked the size of a tennis court. The windows, high and wide, faced the late morning sun, which was already heating the room. Several Louis XIV-type armchairs, as well as a chaise longue, were arranged in the second arm of the room, facing more windows, and I made for one of those.

Everything in the too-large hotel room was designed to prise something out of you; there wasn't a single dark corner, not a cupboard that didn't advertise itself with glamour and gold. There was nowhere to keep a secret, so I sat with my arms folded, intent on keeping my story to myself, not trusting for a minute the opulence that working men had paid for in blood, or this showman who was only after fame.

'See, here's how it works,' he was saying, gesturing to the part of the suite that was behind me. I twisted round in my chair and gasped again. A large carbon microphone that looked just like a telephone was set on a stand, and a big electric light was set up on a black tripod. Beside the light was a kind of elaborate steel box.

He'd had it all planned; this equipment would have taken

time to transport with him from his film company in Los Angeles.

'You knew before you read that newspaper,' I said. 'Before you read that book—'

He nodded, opened his palms. 'I'll come clean with you,' he said, sitting down. 'Let me order some tea first.' I waited while he placed the order, and a waiter in black and white soon delivered a silver tea set to us. I wanted to refuse to take anything from him, but my throat was scratchy with dust from the drive.

'You can't blame my grandmother,' he said. 'It was just before your husband died—'

'Teresa knew nothing!' It burst out of me before I could stop it.

'She heard you,' he said, quietly. 'You were having a disagreement, you and your husband. Last summer, it was. Arguing about telling folk. He wanted you to come clean, but you wouldn't. Said you'd hurt those you loved the most. You shouted it – my grandmother was out on the fire escape, having a smoke. She heard it all.'

My mouth fell open. Willy and I had indeed had that row. *Tell Violet the truth*, he'd said, for the hundredth time, *before she finds out*. But she didn't have to know, I'd said. *And how you going to explain it*, Willy said, *when you're a hundred years old?*

I'll be gone long before then, I'd replied. I hadn't realised I'd been shouting. But we'd been in the kitchen. The window was open for the heat; Teresa's kitchen looked out back, too. If she was indeed on the fire escape that night, she'd have heard us.

'It means nothing,' I said, but I swallowed, too, and he heard my gulp of fear.

'Your husband said, "How many more stories like these are

you going to endure? They'll find you out, one day, among all these phony Madeleine Smiths." My grandmother and you got the same newspaper delivered every day. She looked through her copy and there it was – a story about Madeleine Smith. Seems like they were building up to your anniversary year, don't you think?'

It felt wretched to be caught like this. 'Why would she think that person was *me*? She never said anything to me about it,' I said, but it was a last feeble attempt to wriggle out of his trap, and my stricken voice shook with the effort.

'My grandmother thinks the world of you,' Harry said, opening his gold cigarette case and taking one out to light. 'You're her best friend. She'd never have confronted you. But it was obvious from the row you'd had with your husband who you were. And it kinda startled her, too, you know – she told my mother when she was visiting Christmastime, and my mother told me. It's not every day you find your friend of twenty, thirty years could be a murderer.'

I opened my mouth to object to the word he'd used. But he hurried on, 'I just had to come and – well, make sure a few things checked out first, before I got you here. Your Violet was a stroke of luck.'

A real hard shiver ran through me when he said that. Violet would be devastated to think she'd played some part in Harry's extortion – and it was extortion, there was no other name for it.

He finished his smoke, then nodded at the equipment. 'Sound on film,' he was saying. '"Vitaphone". When you speak, it records you on this phonograph right here.' He pointed at two great black discs, also set on a tripod. 'Each reel of film will correspond to each disc. That way, your voice will sound at the same time you appear on film, see?'

The camera was a Mitchell Standard Studio Camera, he said, proudly, as though that would make a difference to me. It was enormous and black, with two cylinders that held the film reels, and it dwarfed him.

'Warner Brothers are gonna change the business for ever,' he said. 'And by the end of the year. Gotta get ahead fast if I want a piece of it.'

'Extortion.' I said it out loud, what I'd been thinking.

'Don't call it that – I only want you to tell the truth, Lena. It's OK if I call you Lena? Mrs Sheehy just confuses things,' he said. 'That's all you gotta do – just tell the truth, in your own words.'

'What makes you think the trial wasn't the truth?' I said, then bit my lip, for I'd tripped right up, mentioning the trial like that.

He couldn't hide his delight. 'Why, that's exactly it!' he said, grinning again. 'Glad you're admitting it now. We know that trial wasn't the *whole* truth. But let's start at the beginning, shall we? You know, where you met him, L'Angelier. How often you saw him, that kind of thing. I want the audience to get a real clear picture of you both when you were young. It's a big journey, from young love to *arsenic poisoning*.'

He smirked a little, and I pursed my lips. I couldn't have hated him more at that moment if I'd tried. 'There's a problem,' I said, not moving from my chair. As long as I was out of reach of that equipment, he couldn't film me. Nothing would get me out of it; I was determined. And so I said, 'And the problem is your *tone*. I find it very offensive. This isn't a joke, Harry, but you're treating it like one. This story isn't for fun.'

A flash of concern crossed his features. He was no reporter; he was no policeman, or lawyer. He didn't know the right questions to ask, or even how to ask them. That crudeness of his was like being swung at with a cudgel – he had no idea how to tease out from someone what he wanted. And suddenly, it seemed that he knew it, too. I'd found his Achilles' heel, and he had just enough self-awareness to know it existed.

'I don't mean any disrespect, I assure you,' he said, quietly. 'I'm just asking for a few details, what you remember—'

'And what if I can't? I'm ninety-two years of age,' I said. 'The past is a long time ago, and you want me to recall events from seventy years back, when I can barely remember what I had for lunch yesterday.'

I knew perfectly well what I'd eaten for lunch, but he didn't know that.

He looked really worried now. 'Maybe I could use a better tone, like you say. Help spark the memories that way,' he said, getting to his feet and removing his blazer. The boater was gone, too. I watched, amazed, as in all seriousness he bowed low in front of me and extended his hand. 'Miss Smith – may I escort you?' he said in a strange attempt at an English accent. 'I would very much care to take your picture.'

He wasn't making fun of me; he really thought talking to me like he imagined a suitor from seventy years ago might, would change things. But I'd sworn to myself I wouldn't get out of my seat, and I held fast to the arms of the chair.

'You need to tell me first what it is you want, Harry. That's what I don't understand.'

'I just want you to tell your story.'

'Yes, yes, you said all that. But why? The story of an old

woman who was once accused of doing something dreadful, and who was *acquitted*—'

'Were you, though? It was controversial, what they said.'

'I'm innocent,' I said, vehemently. 'I'm not at all what you think I am. And I'll not perform for whatever court you think you can create in this hotel room.'

He rubbed his chin.

'You want to film me because you think I'm guilty,' I said, and it was like a light switching on. 'That's it, isn't it? You think that I'm – that I'm *like her.*'

He frowned. I pointed at the newspaper that was lying on his bed. I'd caught sight of it when we first came into the room.

'You think you've got another Ruth Snyder on your hands – that's it, isn't it?' Contempt and excitement mingled in my address to him. 'Well, I'm sorry to disappoint you, Harry, but that is ridiculous.'

Stiffness in my joints made getting to my feet a slow job, but I wanted to take my time, to smooth down my dress. Show I wasn't afraid. He watched as I picked up my hat and my shawl.

'I don't think it's so ridiculous,' he said slowly. 'Ruth Snyder and her lover murdered her husband, got him out of the way.'

I sighed. 'Yes, they did,' I said. 'And it has nothing to do with anything else.'

'I think it has,' he said, getting to his feet and taking my hat and shawl out of my hands. I didn't have a grip strong enough to resist it. 'I think it's a mirror image of it.'

Suddenly, I felt furious. Did he never listen to anything anyone else said?

'It's no "mirror image", Harry. For I had no husband. My "lover" was the man who died, not the man who did it, like Judd

Gray here. This is simply preposterous. And insulting. I'm tired now; I want to go home. Give me back my things.'

He wouldn't, so I made for the door without them, but he caught my arm as I did so.

'Wait a minute,' he said, and gestured towards the newspaper. Its headline was just as horrible as the one I'd read only an hour or so ago. 'Let me tell you—'

I shook Harry's hand from my arm. 'You have nothing to tell me; this is harassment. Do I have to call out, or scream or something, to make you let me go?'

'He was your "husband"; Emile was,' Harry said, coming right up to me.

I swallowed hard.

'That's what you called each other in your letters. So the book says.'

'Not a real husband – he was – he was a *lover*, not a husband.'

'No, he wasn't.'

There was a strange look on his face, as though he'd just seen the truth.

'He wasn't your lover at all. Not by the time you killed him. Because you had a different lover by then. William Minnoch. The man you got engaged to for real.

'And what I'm thinking is, that you did it together. Just like Ruth Snyder and Judd Gray. You and William Minnoch. You poisoned Emile together.'

Rowaleyn, 1856

'I had no idea she was engaged to any other. I was not aware of any attachment or peculiar intimacy between her and any other man.'
— Witness William Harper Minnoch, merchant and partner in the firm of John Houldsworth and Co, at the trial of Madeleine Smith, 2 July 1857, Edinburgh

'You're too nosy,' I whisper to Janet in the dark. She wants to see the book Emile has given me for my twenty-first birthday.

It took an age for me all through last summer, and beyond it, to assure Janet that Emile hadn't changed me, that I was no 'slavey' to him, and that he was my love who didn't mean me harm. She was so very upset by what she heard between Christina and me in the kitchen that day. Even now, twelve months later, she won't like him, she says, and never will.

Outside, in the woods beyond the house, an owl hoots. A fox shrieks, caught by his mate. I imagine voles, mice, all sorts of creatures running along the paths I took with Emile last year. Pigeons and doves, sparrows rustling in the dark away from a predator.

'You promised you'd let me see it,' Janet says crossly, and kicks her feet under the blanket.

'That was before I knew what was in it,' I say, and nudge her. 'It's not for lambs like you.'

Everything is under darkness, has been so, all this year past. My words with him, our meetings, our kisses, our *loving each other*, as we call it now, what we do, on the rare occasions we can meet for any length of time. Our loving takes place in an underworld beneath drawing-room mores – quite literally, for the kitchen in our new house in town is in the basement, the drawing room directly above, on the ground floor.

Beneath the drawing room is where devils roam and bad fairies play tricks.

Beneath the drawing room is where eldest daughters kneel to become savages.

Beneath the drawing room is where I nip and bite and scratch, but not myself any longer. No; I don't need to turn on myself now. I have Emile for that.

What he disliked at first last summer he has since grown to demand through winter to spring. I am *his* savage, he says. I am what *he* has made me, he says, and I think about what Christina said that night in the kitchen, but I have decided that I am happy to be 'his creature'. He alone has discovered my true self, the one hidden beneath a crinoline. He alone controls her, for I bite and scratch only where he directs.

Christina hates him. Though she still took *her* crinoline, the one he bought for her.

'He'll make you ill,' she said to me one night, after I sneaked him into our new house in India Street. Mama wanted a change from Bedford Place, and Papa hoped that new surroundings might put a halt to her winter ailments. But they didn't, and so I had to get used to a new set of rooms, and a new outlook on to Elmbank Place, which is mercifully only a little further away from the coffee houses and shops that I love. It's also a very little nearer Emile's new lodgings on Franklin Place. Christina's room is in the basement beside the kitchen here; in Bedford Place, the kitchen was on the ground floor, alongside the drawing room. I like this arrangement much better; we can make use of her room, even her bed, Emile and I, without the risk of being heard or discovered.

Her hatred of him is only making her sad, though, I told her.

'He's draining you of the pink in your cheeks,' she said one morning, after Emile stayed very late and I got little sleep. 'You look like the devil's mistress.'

'The devil's *wife*,' I said, 'if you're going to see us in simple terms.'

She mooches about now, like a sulky child. How much the situation between us has turned these last months, when once upon a time she knew everything and I was her student. She enjoyed that power over me, being the admonishing friend. She doesn't understand how all great loves are life-altering, must be so; that all great loves must change a person. So she reads her Penny Dreadfuls and tries to scare me with stories of women led astray by men; women found on riverbanks, with ropes around their necks, or weights tied to their feet.

'How do you know what Emile's fiancée died of?' she said to me. 'Maybe he killed her!'

'His last fiancée was no *savage*, then,' I replied. Not like me. Savage Mimi.

I embrace my transformation now; now I lick my lips like a wolf-girl after tearing flesh off an animal's bones. When he says I am 'too much' for him and must calm my savagery, I only laugh. And when I wrote to him once of a party I attended and the man I spoke with there, before Mama shut down all social gatherings with her winter illness, he was the one to respond in a frenzy.

Do not flirt. Do not go to a ball without my consent. Do not go out more than twice a week. Do not go to the shops on Sauchiehall Street.

Do not go out with your friend when you are in town. Write every day to me, and to me alone.

Now I'm the one making him jealous. Now I'm the one tutting at his loss of control.

He cannot come to me so often, though, for his work keeps him too busy, he says. That's why he's given me the book. It's full of pictures to make me gasp; drawings of women naked and open, in all positions, being kissed and fondled by more hands than can be real. He found it in Paris years ago, he says, and it's mine now, for when he cannot see me, for when he's too exhausted by work or ill from all the poppy seeds he likes to crunch, the laudanum he likes to take.

I showed the pictures to Christina one night in the kitchen. 'Depraved is what he is,' she said, horrified, but even so she giggled with me over some of them, as much as we gasped. There's a particular picture he has marked; another present will follow, he said in his note when he gave it to me.

He'll deliver it here to Rowaleyn tomorrow night, when we meet at last. It has been some weeks since we last saw one another because we are still in secret, even after all this time. I know Papa will not admit him, will never admit him, but

Emile still refuses to believe it. And I've never asked Papa again, though I've told Emile that I do ask, and often. I wouldn't dare mention him to Papa, after he forbade me to see him. I did mention his name once again to Mama, just before Christmas, and it did not go well.

You have changed, Mama said. *You are kind only with Janet.* I was very rude when she said Emile could never be admitted to our home, and to my astonishment, she burst into tears and retired to her bed for the day.

Papa is saying now that it's high time I had a husband. He's forgotten what he said to me last year about taking time to find someone suitable.

He wants me off his hands. He's fearful of me, I think. He can see what I've become: a fully grown woman. I don't scratch my neck or rip the inside of my mouth with my teeth anymore, or worry that I'm too short, or too flat-chested. No; I've spent the winter smoothing buttercream over my thighs, oiling my hair, enjoying my food to satisfy my stomach and let my breasts and shoulders grow plump and firm.

Christina can hardly bear it. I think perhaps she loves me, Christina, for all she waltzes off with McKenzie like that when he calls. She's jealous, and angry that she was wrong when she said Emile would ruin me. On the contrary, Emile has turned me into a *queen* of a woman, with my full bosom, my rounded hips, my soft belly, my rosy cheeks. I devour cream and cakes now, not my own *self*; I'm always eating, more and more, for my aim is to fill myself so full as Mimi that Madeleine cannot find any room inside me at all.

Mama calls me fat, for my dresses are forever being let out. But I like fat, savage Mimi, and I like her power.

Papa, Mama, Christina do not, of course. I might bring what is beneath the drawing room to the surface one day. The fullness of savagery, hidden beneath my crinoline.

How it makes me smile; yet I can still lose my temper with Emile when he defies me and withholds himself from me. That's his true punishment. Just before we left for Rowaleyn, he made his familiar complaints about wanting to tell Papa we were engaged. I was ready on my knees, my mouth open, but he would not permit me, and when he left, I raged about the kitchen as loudly as I dared, in the quiet of night-time.

Later, I woke up Janet in our bedroom. I wrote a letter to him, saying that I'd not see him ever again, which pleased her at first, because she thought I was throwing him over.

'Not at all – he'll come running back now, with his tail between his legs!' I said, to her dismay. 'This is how to deal with men who don't give women what we demand when we demand it!'

He replied just before we set out on our journey from the city to Rowaleyn for the summer season.

> *I warned you repeatedly not to be rash in your engagement and vows to me, Mimi, but you persisted in that false and deceitful flirtation, playing with affections which you knew to be pure and undivided.*
>
> *You have deceived your father as you have deceived me. You have never told him how solemnly you bound yourself to me.*
>
> *You have truly acted wrong. May this be a lesson to you: never trifle with anyone again.*
>
> *Think what your father would say if I sent him your letters*

for perusal. Do you think he could sanction your breaking your promises?

One last time, Mimi. I give you all my trust in this matter.

I showed his letter to Christina on the morning of our departure.

'How can you be so calm?' she said. 'With what he's threatening to do?'

I licked some of the cream she'd left in a bowl the night before. 'He makes threats like this all the time. He means to excite me – he likes to do that.'

'He hasn't threatened to show your letters to your father before,' said Christina, pulling the bowl out of my hands. 'If he gets me in trouble, I'll—'

'You'll what?'

Her face was white. 'I'll not hold back, Maddie. You need to understand that. If he betrays you—'

'You will, too?' I say, suddenly furious.

'You don't have a living to earn. See yourself thrown into the gutter if you will, but I'll not join you there. I mean it.'

Christina's words did shake me, and more than Emile's. So I made myself write back in a gentle, meek tone, begging him to forgive me.

When his reply came, demanding to meet, I assumed it would be at our usual place in the woods at Rowaleyn.

'And that,' I said to Christina, 'is when I will get him to give me what I want!'

But he's told me that he's coming to the kitchen tonight, and in defiance of Christina's threat last year. And he's bringing my present, so he cannot be so very annoyed after all. I slip downstairs in the dark, with a single candle, for my first time with him this summer, my heartbeat light and quick. In the kitchen, I open the window; to my delight, he's already waiting outside for me.

Once he's inside, I kiss him hard and keen, my arms about his neck, but he's tired, it seems, for he pushes me away with a weary sigh. That makes me cross; I'd even rather he was angry than sad, for sadness lacks passion.

'You were very wrong calling a halt to things like you did,' he says.

'And your letter was very mean to me – but I am sorry,' I say, looking down, but then glancing up at him through my eyelashes so that he knows I'm not sorry at all. 'But you keep on insisting on what I cannot do. I can't *make* Papa do what he will not.'

He has poppy seeds with him; he reaches into his jacket pocket and munches on them. There's something else odd about him, though, and I ask what it is.

'Arsenic,' he says.

'Poison?' I say, shocked, for it's what the gardener lays down to get rid of pests.

'Only a couple of grains. It upsets my stomach, but it's necessary to keep up with *you*, my dear, the way you have me running about the countryside, coming to you at all hours—'

'I don't understand.'

'They give it to horses, to keep them in the race for longer.' He sits down as if suddenly exhausted and shuts his eyes. He sounds bored, dulled by something. For the first time in a long while, I am anxious about his feelings for me, and it occurs to me that I wanted him to show up tonight because I needed to know that everything was right between us after his threat to show my letters to Papa. That I'd indeed got what I wanted: him, but also his commitment to silence. For him to take back his threat.

But now that he's here and like this, so despondent and listless, I'm not happy at all. I wait, worried and biting my lip. After a few moments, his eyes open.

'Your present!' he says. 'I have not forgotten it.' This brightens him a little; there's a sheen on his face, and his eyes glitter like silver. I brighten, too; this is better, I think. Now we will have our fun.

He reaches into his coat pocket and takes out a varnished mahogany box. Wind makes the trees outside flutter and bristle; the wind whistles, too. It's a night when ships anchored in the city will rock, their stores pitching and rolling, and our neighbours will worry about profits and losses.

'Open it,' he says, handing the box to me.

I set it on the table first. The box is oblong with catches at either side.

'You must be very quiet with it, though,' he says, smirking oddly. I fear he has bought me some dull musical instrument like a flute.

Inside the box are folds of red velvet. It *is* a flute; a present from dull boys, and my heart shrivels. Reluctantly, I fold back the velvet, which reveals a white object beneath.

It is certainly long like a flute, though made of ivory. A flute it is *not*. I lift it out and gasp.

Veins like tendrils wind along its trunk, all the way to the bulging, round tip. It's heavy, and almost as thick as my wrist.

'See how well it resembles the real thing? See how carefully the carving is done – feel how smooth it is,' he says, taking it from me and stroking it. The tip of it, he rests at my lips. 'Open,' he says, and so I part my lips, touch the tip with my tongue. 'Many wives have them,' he says. 'Army wives. So that they will not forget the pleasure their husbands give them, when they are away on campaigns.'

I don't understand.

'Like the book,' he says, 'it is from Paris, too.' He traces the object down my neck and over my shoulders towards my belly, tickling me.

'I told you that you were *my* savage,' he says, softly, 'but this will tame you whenever I want. So lift up your dress, there's a good girl.'

I'm too confused to refuse.

He nods at the kitchen table behind me. 'Pass me that dish,' he says. He rubs the tip of the object with a smudge of butter. 'I know what you want, Mimi,' he says, and his eyes glint in the candlelight. 'Yes, I know what you want.'

But this is not what I want, though he arouses me first with kisses and fingers that press until I gasp. When the object touches my skin, warm and smeared with butter, I close my eyes as he bids me, but he's more given to the thing than me, and as he nudges it between my thighs, my moans become more false than true, for it's uncomfortable to be pressed so against the kitchen table, to have something so ungiving and not of him enter me, even if it is only a little bit, as far as a thumb might go.

'I don't think I care for it,' I say, when I can no longer pretend. He ceases and pulls my nightgown hems down with a tug.

'Don't be such a fool,' he murmurs. His face is in shadow

but there's a growing sense in me that he might have enjoyed my discomfort more than he liked arousing me. 'Think – if you were to get with a child. You are always at me, wanting more from me that I cannot give. Just as you cannot give me what *I* want. Tell your father that we are engaged! I have to be accepted into your family – your Papa has to accept me. I'll not be sneaking about when I am his son-in-law, why can't you understand that, Mimi? I want to be able to hold my head up! Be acknowledged as a gentleman, not a clerk!'

'*I* acknowledge you as a gentleman,' I protest.

'*You* are not everyone. Dear God, do you have any idea of what it is like for me? I cannot go to the Bairds' – I cannot go to the dinners and the parties, because I am *nobody*. They have to know that I am *your* husband. I am the son-in-law of Mr James Smith, and I will not be overlooked!'

The air sours as the candle dwindles; something is changed between us. He's looking at me with resentment – and disgust.

'I thought you loved me for who I am,' I whisper.

'You are rich; you are spoilt. You think that *love* is all that matters, and when it's a secret, it's exciting to you. You don't know what a torture it is to *me*. You have no idea how hard the world is, or what it is to work every day in a miserable post and never have what you need to make life bearable.'

'I thought *I* made life bearable—'

'How like you, to imagine that you, alone, are enough.'

I'm too horrified even to cry. He's pulling on his coat; this is all I am to get tonight, and I rush at him, say, 'Papa would *have* to let us marry if I were to get with a child.'

But he holds me off. 'And that would be the most stupid mistake of our lives,' he mutters. 'If he were to cast you off—'

'He wouldn't – Papa would not.' But my voice falters even as I say it, because I cannot be sure that Papa would not do exactly that. The thought of telling him that his eldest daughter is with child – unwed, by the man he forbade her to meet with – ah, it's impossible. 'Even if he did – I don't care about money and parties and country houses. We would be together every day, in the open, like you want—'

'Where? In my lodgings? In a single room? You, me, and a child? That would be madness. You say you don't care about money, but that's because you have never been without it. You would care quickly enough if you didn't have enough to eat. No, Mimi. Until you tell your Papa that we are engaged and you *make* him accept us, accept *me* – then this is all we will do together.' He points at the object on the table. 'Now make me some cocoa quickly before I head back to Helensburgh. You can do *that* for me.'

My legs wobble as he pushes me towards the stove. The pot and the milk are on the table. The cocoa jar is on the shelf.

'Why would we risk a future of poverty?' he's saying. 'So think on what I'm saying, Mimi, and see the sense in it. After all, you may use *it* yourself in the meantime – I give you permission. It will keep you happy when *I* am not here. Take the edge off your endless wanting. Such a spoilt Mimi you are. Always begging. Always exhausting me.'

The milk boils; I stir in the cocoa. He's speaking quietly but his tone is not gentle, not kind.

'*I* am to use – that. On *myself*?' I say.

'Just as I told you – like an army wife. You will soon enjoy it.'

I won't, I want to say, but again, that suspicion that he might like my lack of enthusiasm plays in my mind. He sips the cocoa when it's ready, says, 'Too many particles, Mimi. You must stir it better as it boils. No; I will instruct you how to get on with it, and you will tell me how you get on, in your letters. Write to me *exactly* how you get on.'

He drinks the rest of the cocoa quickly, seeming eager to be away, and then he is gone.

My confidence is quite gone, too. I head upstairs and hide the box under the bed before sliding in beside Janet. But sleep is impossible, and eventually I get up, retrieve the box and sneak down to Christina's room, where she's sleeping alone. I wake her gently and show her the object.

'That's not for a woman's pleasure,' Christina says, shocked. 'Army wives, indeed! Your head buttons up the back, Maddie, if you believe that.'

I'm on the verge of tears. 'He says I mustn't get a child by him. Not until Papa approves.'

'He's right about that, at least.'

'But perhaps the truth is – his desire for *me* is not so strong now. Perhaps he's not *tired*, as he says, but bored of me, of my – *form*. So he's given me this instead,' I say, desperately.

'You don't make him hard anymore, you mean,' says Christina, crudely.

'Oh, but what if he has other women who do? He's always talking in his letters about the women he meets when he's out in town.'

Christina snorts and says, 'You're a fool, Maddie, and he's playing you like a fiddle.'

And just like that, the balance shifts towards her, as it did with Emile only a short while ago. Power slips away from me completely; how easily I lose it. I begin to tear at my fingernails, chew the ends of my hair.

'There's plenty of other ways not to get with a child, and that book has shown you most of them. No – this is about his own wants – and putting you down,' Christina continues. She pulls at my hair to stop me chewing it. 'Oh, for heaven's sake, when are you going to wake up to what he's about?'

'You don't understand – he *knows* me better than anyone.'

But for the first time in months, I think it may not be true. Christina takes the box for me and agrees to hide it under her bed, in case Janet should find it under ours. I'll not use it, no matter what Emile wants.

He writes the next day that he has to go back to Glasgow and cannot say when he will come again to Helensburgh, as his work is very busy, and so I must write and tell him how I get on with *it*.

A week later, another letter arrives, asking for such a description. I show it to Christina. Late that night, after we have drunk some of Papa's best wine, we sit up in the kitchen by the light of a candle and write the most outrageous things we can think of, giggling all the while. I'm sure Emile will know the letter is false, but when he replies, he doesn't seem to think so, and even asks for more.

But this doesn't reassure me, not at all. I seem to have lost something more than Emile's attention; I've lost Mimi, who liked her food and stroked her body.

Instead, Madeleine has returned, and now I pick at my supper, pick at my skin. I spend a listless day late in May, fretting about the endless summer ahead with so few of Emile's visits, while he's likely visiting someone in Edinburgh after all. I snap at Christina, and annoy Janet, too.

When I come in from a walk in the woods late that afternoon, brooding and cross, Mama is waiting for me.

'There will be new faces at supper this evening,' she says. 'So hurry, and put on your best lace dress. Get Christina to help you. What a state you look! Really, Madeleine.'

I walk away from her, wander up to my room and consider staying there all evening instead, telling Mama I have a headache.

But Mama insists, and so Christina helps dress me in as much lace as possible, and in the brightest silk I can find, with my hair curled perfectly. I'm sorry for Emile not seeing me like this, just for a moment, as Christina smooths cream on my hands, pats perfume gently behind my ears, and places a light, soft kiss at my neck.

'You're too good for him. For any man,' she says, but I can only think of his last warning to me of a young woman he lately met, who was so ladylike in her manners. *You could learn a great deal from her, Mimi*, he wrote.

'I hate him sometimes,' I whisper, and she nods.

'I know,' she says.

'But I can't give him up,' I say, and she nods at that, too, and squeezes my hand before I go out on to the landing.

It's a late supper, but as Janet has recently turned twelve years old, she's allowed to attend, too. She meets me on the stairs beneath the great cupola, where the sunset sends a pink glow about us, and we go downstairs together, hand in hand. The dining room is lit up for a party, not supper, and there are at least twenty folk gathered at the table. Mrs McGregor has had help from the village all day to cook and now to serve, Christina said earlier, though I spent too much of the day out walking by myself to be aware of anything in the kitchen.

Papa gets up to greet us as we enter. 'My beautiful girls! Madeleine, come and sit here,' he says. He sits at the head of the table; Mama is at the bottom, already beckoning to Janet. I spy Lady M— and her daughter, too. A quick glance tells me there are more ladies then men, and most of them are Mama's age.

So this will be a very dull dinner, and I have no idea why Mama made such a fuss of how I was to dress. But then Papa beams and says, 'And this is a new acquaintance of mine, from the city – William Minnoch. Please, my eldest daughter, Madeleine.'

A gentleman with black curly hair is sitting with his back to me. He gets to his feet – he's very tall, at least a head above Papa – and bows so I don't see his face straightaway. When he kisses my hand, though, something makes me pause for the pressure of his lips there, and when he straightens, I am more surprised than I thought I would be.

His mouth catches my attention first – a pinkish, smudged mouth that any woman would choose for herself. His eyes are large and soft powdery blue, like a woman's, too, but his nose is straight and his jaw is square, and his black curls are sleek and shining. The mingling of these features produces a strange sort of fluttering inside me that's part allure, part detachment, and I find myself stammering a little as I make my introduction.

It's an elegant stammering, though, even I know that. I smile demurely, wondering if he will be dull, despite the odd mix of him, but his voice is deep while his gestures are light, and so that mix carries on fascinating me, even if his talk on actuary work is not at all interesting at first. But he likes opera and plays, and even a few of the novels I like, too, though he mentions writers I've never read, Edgar Allan Poe and Nathaniel Hawthorne.

'I'm thinking of taking a balloon ride next week,' he says, during dessert, when Papa's attention is diverted. 'Would you like to accompany me?'

I've never been up in a balloon before. 'How exciting!' I reply. He gives me a look that I find even more curious.

When Papa eventually takes him and the two other gentlemen in attendance to the library for cigars and brandy, and Mama sends Janet to bed, the rest of us women go to the drawing room, where Mama leads me to the window.

'You seemed to enjoy speaking with Mr Minnoch,' she says, slyly. 'I think he enjoyed speaking with *you*.'

I don't want to give Mama what she wants, but I'm feeling so pleased with myself, I can't help it. 'Yes, he has something about him, I cannot put my finger on it—'

'He is *extremely* wealthy,' Mama whispers, 'and there's talk of him going into the political sphere one day.'

'So he may not be born a lord, but one day he might become one?' I say, teasing her.

She raises her eyebrows. 'I would say *will*, not *might*.'

I like William Minnoch. He has a hinterland, I tell Christina later, when she comes up to my room. Janet is still awake and listening.

'There is something more to him,' I say. 'Something secret. I want to find out what it is.'

'You'll have to *marry* him to find that out,' Christina says. 'But your Mama and Papa mean it to happen.'

Marry him.

I'm already 'married'. My 'husband' is Emile. Long after Christina goes back downstairs and Janet falls asleep, I'm still awake, hot and bothered by that phrase ringing in my head.

Marry him.

Eventually, I get up to write to Emile. But something's shifting under me, like a carpet sliding beneath my feet, and I have to grip the pen to steady my hand, and to search for words that secure, that do not wobble.

> *Darling, there is an absurd report in town at present – I have heard it from many – that I am to be married to Mr Minnoch, junior partner of Houldsworth and Co. He tried to get a house at Row but could not. I suppose it is these circumstances which have given rise to it. You, darling, may hear it . . .*

I give it to be posted first thing in the morning, but that slipping feeling hasn't gone away, and there's a change in the air, too, a lightness that unsettles me. When I go down for breakfast, Mama's tone with me is softer, encouraging; Papa even smiles, which he never does in the mornings.

I'm jittery all day, and can't make up my mind about anything, from what hat to wear to which flowers to pick in the garden. Nothing eases me until Emile writes back.

When he does, it's to say that he is coming to me, straightaway.

For *he* is my husband and no other.

Another thought has been niggling at me since I wrote my letter to him. A plan to prove to myself how we really do love one another after all. To return us to what we were before he brought me the object and complained about Papa accepting him. I want that feeling of power back.

I want to be Mimi again.

It's just before midnight only a week after the supper party that I slip out for the woods, light on my feet, without a lamp, for I know the way so well now. And when I reach the clearing, there he is, by *our* tree.

He's ill-looking though, and I can't help but compare him to well-groomed William Minnoch. His hair is grown far too long and is straggly; his face has thinned; he seems smaller, somehow, than I remember. Perhaps that, too, is a comparison with Mr Minnoch. I feel impatient, suddenly, as though he's let me down in some way.

He scuffs at the ground like a child, without looking at me. 'I'm very cross with you, Mimi,' he says. 'To write me that letter.'

I bristle, but must pretend meekness, apologise. The wind dies as the moon rises; the rain has stopped, the skies are clear. The woods are dark, for all the moonlight. It feels *dangerous* tonight, I say, to try and arouse him. But he holds me off, and under the light of the moon his face is pale.

'Are you well?' I ask him, anxiously. 'Are you eating enough? You must take better care of yourself.'

That helps his mood a little. He sniffs, rubs his sleeve against his nose. 'My stomach complaint – and a summer cold, I think.'

My spirits sink; we'll have no fun tonight. And he is here to admonish me, anyway – which he does.

'Where is your sense of control?' he says. 'Where is your sense of what is *right*? Aggravating me with rumours of engagements! When you are engaged to *me* – but this wouldn't happen if you were honest, and told your Papa. It has been months since you promised to tell him – months! I'll not keep on like this, I told you—'

'Why do you never think how hard it is for *me*?' I burst out.

'Ah, Emile – don't go—'

For he's striding away at my show of temper, but I run after him, and grab his coat, his arm. We grapple in the dark, clawing and grabbing at one another, then suddenly we are tangled together on the ground, and I'm grasping at his trouser waistband as he pulls at my nightgown. We are like two foxes, snapping and biting, before somehow, for the first time ever, I am astride him, and I'm panting and grasping, my nightgown up around my waist.

He is fully inside me, for the first time. I cannot stop, so delirious I am with it, and he cannot either. We move together even as he murmurs protest, but it excites him, too, what we are doing. He cannot help but thrust and spill inside me, inside Mimi. No; he cannot resist her, or how she makes him howl.

Ah, but how furious he is afterwards. Pushing me off him and ordering me to wipe myself clean of him, before scrambling to his feet as though I'm a poisoned creature he mustn't touch.

'Emile,' I say, reaching out for him to pull me up.

But he's too busy worrying his hands through his hair, muttering, 'Dear God, we should never have done it, I would not have done it but you—'

'But we have only done what two people who love one another do. When they are husband and wife as we are.'

'And if it's done? If you are now with a child? Oh God, Mimi.'

'I suppose we did wrong,' I say, getting unsteadily to my feet and leaning against a tree, for my heart's still thrumming. He's distraught, nearly weeping. 'But I only wanted what every wife wants—'

'And what of the consequences of it? If your Papa does not accept me? If he throws you out? *What if I do not marry you after all* – have you thought of that?'

'What on earth do you mean?' I say, but then he catches at my nightgown, rummaging about it as if he's looking for something. 'Emile! We are married! Oh, not in the eyes of the law, I know, but – what are you doing? Leave my nightdress alone!'

'There's no sign of your bleeding. You are a virgin, so where is it?' he says, thrusting my nightgown at me. 'Or have you been lying to me? How careful I have been with you – never to go so far—'

I think of the object, nudging; his fingers, probing. 'Perhaps you went further than you think—'

'Oh, so now I am too stupid to know? You mean to humiliate me, into the bargain?'

Without another word, he bolts through the woods into the darkness, leaving me to find my way back to the house alone, shaking and tired and utterly confused. I make for Christina's room and kneel by her bedside, to shake her gently and whisper what has happened.

'What if I'm with a child already? He says he'll not marry me – but we *are* married, we are,' I say, and begin to cry.

Christina gets out of bed. Without another word, she leads me into the kitchen, and takes out a cloth. 'Go to the bathroom upstairs,' she says at last. 'I'll bring a pail of water. It's not ideal, but a *douche* is all you can try.'

Upstairs in the large tub, the room lit by a single candle, she orders me to remove my nightgown, and pours in the pail of warmish water as I sit and shiver. Two minutes later, she returns with another pailful of water, which she tips in beside me. 'Now, soak this cloth, and wash *up inside* – as far as you can,' she says.

I start to weep again, though, so she takes the cloth from me, and wipes gently between my legs.

'Lift up your knees,' she says, and so I do, sniffing and leaning back a little, as she works the cloth between my thighs at first, and then further up inside, her fingers brushing gently where Emile had been so rough.

'He was looking for a sign – of bleeding,' I whisper. 'But there isn't one and now he thinks I'm mocking him. Or that he isn't my first—'

'That's all they care about,' Christina says, sharply. 'Being first. Making their mark.'

'But I wanted it so much—'

'Christ, Maddie. Sometimes I think you don't even know what a "reputation" is.'

'I don't care about that—'

'I don't know what you learned at that Mrs Gorton's, but it hasn't helped you one bit,' says Christina. 'It never ceases to astonish me how rich mothers think keeping them ignorant will help their daughters. My mother made sure I knew what was what, the minute I could understand it.'

'You don't make this mistake ever with McKenzie?'

'No, I don't, and I have my mother to thank for it. All your mother's made sure of is what colour dress you wear to what dinner party. I tell you, if I ever have a daughter, she'll not be as ignorant as you are, Maddie. She might not have a penny to her name, but she'll not be meat to some man the way you are.'

I'm quiet as she says all of this.

'Perhaps I should educate Janet better then,' I murmur. 'If Mama will not do it.'

'Be quick about it, then, for Janet's growing up and they'll be sniffing round her soon.'

I swallow. All I've shown Janet so far is how to bait Emile, to rouse and rile him. I must do better.

At last, I say, 'Is that not enough? Is it done yet?'

Christina murmurs, 'Just a little more, to be safe', her free hand resting on my thigh. Her breath mingles with mine in the candlelight as I think of how I shall teach Janet never to meet with wolf-men in the woods.

It's the day of the balloon ride. My friend, Mary Buchanan, has come to Helensburgh for the event. Mary is my most discreet childhood friend. She knows my secret about the Edinburgh duke's son and knows a little about Emile, though not that I meet with him at night or that I am his 'wife'. She disappointed me when I told her who I'd met in the coffee house with Jack last year, and that he had pressed against my leg there; she called him 'low-born'. And so I haven't cared to mention him again. Christina would no doubt call Mary ignorant for being as ill-informed about the world as I am, and say I should find more *knowledgeable* women friends. But Mary makes me laugh, for all her snobbery about Emile, and sometimes that's as necessary as knowledge.

Jack is accompanying us today, as well as Mr Minnoch. *William*, as I am to call him. To my relief, my menses have arrived, so I know I'm not with child; I have Christina to thank for that.

It seems that all of Helensburgh has turned out on this bright June day; there is a fair on, and the street along the pier overlooking the Clyde is covered with stalls of all kinds, and a band plays in the bandstand beyond. I haven't felt so happy or excited in ages; Emile's behaviour in the woods has made me so miserable, and it's freeing to shake him out of my head and into the winds. The balloon is set up in the gardens towards the hill where the winds are strong, but it is huge enough to resist them, and we all gasp when we see it.

William's carriage takes me and Jack and Mary the short trip from Rowaleyn to the village, and onwards up to the balloon and its basket. A small crowd has gathered by the gardens; only a few of us will have the privilege of a ride, though.

Jack's almost beside himself with anticipation; Mary looks terrified, her blond hair coming undone below her hat already, but she's too sweet on my brother not to join in. We get down from the carriage, and William leads us through the crowd towards the giant basket, where some men in hats are standing. They tip their heads towards him, and it occurs to me that this is more than just part of the fair.

'Did *you* arrange for this, William?' I ask.

'You've found me out,' he says, and smiles. 'I have always wanted to go on a balloon ride, ever since I was a boy.'

'So this is a dream of yours?'

'Yes – but I think it more exciting because you are with me.'

I blush, but already the men are guiding us towards the basket. The ropes are enormous, holding it down as the great balloon creaks and groans against them, but still the basket, large as it is, looks too light, too unsafe for the balloon itself. 'Will we not be carried away?' I say. 'The winds are very strong—'

'The gas will make sure it does not lose us,' he says, pointing to the stream of fire that burns away above the basket into the balloon. Mary and I are helped in first, with many squeals from Mary, then Jack and William get in after us. Then the men release the ropes.

'And up we go!' cries William, taking off his hat to wave it in the air. Two men scramble into the basket alongside us to work the gas, as Mary screams and the basket tilts and bumps and rocks us from one side to the other. Twice I fall into William's arms; twice he steadies me; then we are up, climbing higher and higher above the houses, above the trees, and on past churches and farms, higher up into the blue sky, and I cannot help but squeal, too. William pulls me closer to him as our excitement builds together.

Mary's in hysterics in a corner of the basket, being comforted by Jack. I can't hear what William is saying in my ear for the wind bellowing in my hair, so I take a risk, and, while Jack's attention is given to Mary, seize his hand and press it to my bosom. The basket lurches with the wind and tips him further into me, pinning me against the side of it, my face crushed against his neck.

And that's when I see it: the tiny tattoo of a black bird – a crow, possibly – hidden beneath his collar. I can't quite make it out, but it must mean something, and I'm reminded of Emile and his dead fiancée, and the dead duke's son, and I wonder if William, too, has a past love and this is his mark for her.

When we right ourselves, laughing, we are still hand in hand, and I'm more captivated than ever. As the basket descends towards the site of Dumbarton Castle, just beneath the great rock itself atop which the ruins sit, it jostles us again, so I'm robbed of the chance to ask him about his tattoo. When we land, Mary, weeping loudly, has to be helped first, lifted by Jack over the edge of the basket and into the arms of William's coachman. Jack raises his eyebrows at me as if to say it's my fault his trip has been ruined, but William's at my back, edging me forward, and saying, 'Allow me.'

He lifts me to pass me over the side. I'm thinking of protesting that I can manage very well myself, but as it turns out, my legs are shaky from the experience, and I'm grateful to be set down carefully in the carriage. Mary's still weeping and shaking but I'm too elated, and when Jack and William join us, I cannot stop voicing my feelings about the flight.

At Rowaleyn, Mama and Janet are desperate to hear about it, and it's some time before I'm alone with William.

'You did enjoy the ride?' he says. 'You did seem to.'

'It was perhaps the most exciting experience of my life – if only because we might all have died – so Mary must have thought,' I say, and laugh.

'Ah, but death is the greatest adventure, don't you think?' he says, lifting my hand to his lips.

'Not really—'

'*Death* is the most exciting experience of our lives,' he says. His look is intense.

I cough, and say, 'On your neck – the tattoo, I saw it. Is it a memento of a sort?'

We are in the conservatory, as it's begun to rain. Papa has had delivered all sorts of new plants, and the leaves of a great cheese plant are spread wide above us.

'It looks like a crow.'

William's lips pout, even as his jaw clenches. He blushes;

his eyelashes flutter. His voice, when he speaks, is both grave and excitable at once.

'If I tell you, Madeleine, it must not go any further.'

'It is a secret, then?'

'It *is* a secret. And you'll know it soon, I promise, but not today—'

'Ah, you're teasing me, William,' I say. 'But I'll find it out.' I can pout as well as he can, and do so, and that's when he surprises me very much, and plants a quick kiss on my cheek. My fingers touch the spot; I think about how to match his many contradictions, if to match them is the best response or if it would not do.

And then he whispers, 'It is the sign of a special *band* of brothers,' and puts a finger to his lips.

Later that night, after the house is quiet and I'm unable to sleep for thinking over William's words, I tiptoe down to the kitchen. Christina is sitting there, alone, drinking some cocoa. It's just after midnight; we've hardly spoken at all the last few days. She doesn't turn round when I enter, says only, 'I take it *he's* written to you again? You down here to meet him?'

I'd forgotten all about Emile. I sit down and tell her about my day with William, about the tattoo on his neck, hidden low. 'I said there was something about him,' I say.

'But he kissed you?'

I shrug. 'It was a very little kiss, but I think there will be more.'

She raises her eyebrows. 'And the tattoo – what "special band of brothers"?'

We speculate as she makes some cocoa for me, our coolness towards one another over the last few days forgotten. 'Maybe he'll get his "brothers" to pay back Emile for how he's treated you,' she says. 'If ever a man needed a good kicking, it's him.'

It should alarm me, should distress me, the thought of harm coming to him. But it doesn't. I am a savage, after all. I sigh, and say, 'They're probably a group of men who do something quite harmless. Watch birds. Trains, perhaps.' We both giggle.

Then she says, 'Why hide it, then?'

Why hide it, indeed?

In the weeks that follow, my scratching and nipping, which had begun again lately with Emile's change towards me, his accusations and dismissals of me, disappear. I enjoy teasing William with questions about his 'secret', which he seems to enjoy refusing to answer, and the game between us intensifies, as our encounters increase in number, much to Mama and Papa's delight. I hear so little from Emile at all now, that he might be a figment of my imagination were it not for occasional harsh notes, telling me how I have betrayed him, and how I do not love him as a 'wife' should.

But it seems to me now that we have never been a husband and a wife, not as we should be. I don't think William would ever speak to me in this hot, accusing way. William only ever compliments me on how I look; he never tells me what to wear. He doesn't surprise me with sudden meetings, or arrive in a state of drunkenness, or delirium. I don't wonder what he thinks of me, for he tells me all the time how well I impress him, or how touched he is by my friendship. He doesn't question whom I speak with at dinner parties he hasn't attended; he doesn't grab my wrist, or pull my hair.

But he doesn't get down on his knees in the woods, either; he doesn't stroke my legs, or lap at me in the most intimate way. I miss all of that so much sometimes I think I cannot bear it. But I do not miss the object; I do not miss rough fingers. My wolf-man is no longer the man I want, for he no longer exists. Emile is only an angry accuser, full of jibes and orders; I see that better now, what he has become, now that I have William by my side. My once-husband.

By the time of our last week at Rowaleyn, I've been in William's company more times than I have been in Emile's this past year.

September's leaves seem to turn yellow around us as we take a stroll through the woods. Daringly, I lead him towards the little clearing that is my old spot with Emile. I want to see what ghosts of our encounters exist there, now that I'm free of him. I want to see William in the place that was once Emile's.

My longing for a certain kind of fun, too, has been plaguing me a little more these past few days. William won't get on his knees; I don't want him to. But I think we can have our own fun, perhaps.

So I say, 'It's so very pretty at this time of year,' and lift my skirts to step over the branch lying across our path.

'As are you,' William says, just as I knew he would. He takes my hand and stops in the path, a high kind of colour in his cheeks and a little perspiration on his neatly trimmed black moustache. He presses my hand to his lips.

'Dearest William,' I murmur, but suddenly he kisses me on the mouth, his lips closed.

'I want to walk this path with you again, dear Madeleine,' he says when we pull apart, 'and every summer. If you would make me so happy – if you would accept my proposal—'

It's as though Emile is a ghost indeed; there's a gust of wind behind William, shaking some damp leaves from the trees above, and they fall on his head.

He laughs. 'This is not the moment,' he says, and I think Emile must have called the wind to stop us, and so I kiss him back as passionately as I can, my mouth open and my tongue pushing against his pressed lips until he opens his mouth, too.

He gives a surprised little moan; so this will be my fun. But then he pulls away, looking a little shocked, so I gasp, quickly, 'Yes, William, yes. I will accept you, I will; I do.' Then I pout and press myself against him, and he wraps his arm protectively around me. Our loving will be very respectable. But if I am just a little disappointed – if Mimi has been well and truly banished by William's gentlemanly ways, banished by a man who will never know her – then I will temper that disappointment with the knowledge that I am, finally, behaving wisely.

I am *Madeleine*, not Mimi, and I am making a success of being who I am at last.

William chastely kisses the top of my head. Then he holds me from him with a worried look. 'I did hear – forgive me for mentioning it, Madeleine – but there was talk – of your affections elsewhere.'

That does surprise me. Who has been gossiping? 'I can't imagine – who else could I have seen when I only see you—?'

'I thought it was gossip – no, I knew it,' he says, tucking my arm under his as we make our way back to the house. 'It was so vague, I'm sorry. I listened to servants talking once—'

'Servants here?'

He shakes his head. 'In the city – you see why young women must be careful.'

I laugh, though I'm nervous to hear this. 'Yet you took me up in a balloon!' I say, and he laughs, too.

Back at the house, we give Mama and Papa the good news that they have been working towards all summer. How simple; how easy it is. Champagne is poured; Janet hugs me, makes me promise not to leave her. William disappears to Papa's study with him and Jack, and the three of them emerge hours later, very drunk. William's barely able to get into the carriage to go to his residence here, but kisses me messily before he leaves.

Mama exhausts me with talk of dresses and venues and bridesmaids; Janet is giddy and too full of excitement to go to bed until she faints clean away, causing much alarm.

But I am happy, at last, I think; *this* is where I am supposed to arrive. *This* has been my destination all these months past. Emile is no more; it is over between us.

The next day, I write to tell him so, without mentioning William, or our engagement, though he'll hear of it soon enough when the banns are announced next year. Mama wants a summer wedding: a June date is favoured. When we return to the city, it will not be to our place on India Street, she tells us at breakfast, but to a grand, new building on the very fashionable Blythswood Square.

I find out when I see William later that he has taken the apartments next door. So I'll not be leaving Janet when I marry him, I tell her in bed that night. She'll be right next door for as long as she wants to be, and we hug one another and promise we'll never be apart.

At Blythswood Square on the very day we move in, I insist on a bedroom in the basement, for it has a fireplace, and I must have a fire through the winter months. Janet will share it with me, of course. The house is very grand but very cold, too, with such enormous windows, and long corridors, and a great staircase. The enormous drawing room at the corner of the building looks out over the square in front and on to the street that runs along the left-hand side. Upstairs is Mama's room, and Papa's, and Jack's. We have a small library upstairs too, and Papa has a study. In the basement is my room with Janet, then Christina's room, and the kitchen and scullery, with the back lane beyond.

It's by far the biggest, grandest house that we've ever occupied in the city; Papa is bursting with pride, for it tells the world how important he is. Buildings he has designed are being built only a street away; this city, he says, is becoming his in all but name.

But my insistence on the bedroom in the basement isn't just because it has a fireplace and I so hate the cold. It's also because it will be easier for me to meet with Emile, as Christina only has to leave the back door off the latch before she goes to bed, for it makes a terrible noise to unlock. Then I can hurry along the corridor to the kitchen without anyone hearing a thing.

For he has demanded a meeting and I have agreed – a last, final meeting, but only to prove to myself, and to him, that I'm no savage Mimi but a new Madeleine. It was as Madeleine that I won William. William with the delicious dark secret he'll not yet reveal. God forgive me, but I still warm when I think of those times with Emile in the woods at Rowaleyn. But the object – the object in the mahogany box which Christina keeps hidden for me among her things – ah, the object is what has ended it. That, and his assertion *if I did not marry you*. When I had thought for so long that we already were; that he meant it when he called me 'wife' all those times.

So I prepare myself one cool, misty October night. I've sent him directions to the back door in the lane that leads to the kitchen. I wait alone there in the unfamiliar room – for we are only days moved in – with unfamiliar sounds reaching me: the march of a policeman walking along the street; some rabble-rousers from a tavern. Christina's gone to bed, but she'll come if I call on her.

I shiver just a little as the minutes tick by. It's just after midnight by the time Emile arrives. I hear the latch on the back door lifting, and in he comes, shuffling over to me as I sit by the kitchen range. The change in him since I last saw him is remarkable. He's even thinner than he was in the woods that summer night months ago; his beautiful hair is quite raggedy and thick. Pale and shivering, he gives off a strange whiff of something chemical, and I wonder about his lodgings at Franklin Place.

'So – *wife*,' he says, mockingly. There's a dizzy look about him, though, with his eyes wide and his breathing rapid and hard. 'What do you mean by all of it?'

I stand up, the better to remain strong. But he surprises me; he sits down and begins to weep, covering his face with his hands.

'I cannot bear it, I cannot bear it,' he says, over and over. It's such a distressing sight that even though I don't want to go near him, I have to comfort him, must put my arms around him as he sobs.

'I did not think,' I say, 'that it would matter to you so much. We have seen each other so rarely—'

'Caused by you. If you had told your Papa by now, I'd not be at Huggins, I'd not be working every hour of every day—'

The moment he says this, I let him go. 'The purpose of our engagement was to get you away from your work, it seems.'

He rubs his eyes, squints at me in the gloom. 'Your Papa can hardly have a son-in-law in a clerk's position. Look how grand he is now.'

I back away from him, my heart banging at my bones. 'Christina said – she warned me. "A little gold-digger", she called you—'

'Do not be so crude, Mimi. Don't be so simple—'

'Don't call me that!' I say. I want to shout, but even in a house as large as this one, my voice might carry too far. 'I'm not "Mimi". And Christina is right.'

Surely it cannot all have been a lie? I start to shake.

Emile gets to his feet and grips my shoulders. 'I have given you *all* of me – every last part of me – but it has never been enough for you. You wouldn't care if you destroyed me completely. You would not care. You have consumed me entirely, and now you think to throw me away like rubbish, but I will not let you.'

He strokes my hair, roughly at first, pulling my head back. There are tears on his cheeks; suddenly, tears spurt from my own eyes, too. He starts to kiss my cheeks, our tears mingling, and then he kisses me, hard on the mouth, pushing his tongue down deep into my throat.

That heat he always fires up isn't gone from me yet; between my legs that spark lights, and in spite of everything he has said, I kiss him back, more urgently. His hands slide over my hips, down beneath my nightgown. He knows too well how to arouse me; he knows what I've been without these past months.

On to his knees he goes. His fingers, then his mouth between my thighs. In the moment I lose myself, forget William, forget weddings, forget it all; I am Mimi again. I've failed already at what I meant to do. Emile knows what works on me, what makes me savage indeed.

Afterwards, when I'm gasping and draped across him, he whispers, 'Fetch the box, *dearest wife*! Hurry!'

Though I don't want to, I find myself obeying him as before. I go to Christina's room where she snores, alone and asleep, and feel under her bed for the box's hiding place.

Back in the kitchen, Emile is loosening his clothing. I set the box down.

'Open it,' he says.

I do so, then wait, gloomy and sullen at the thought of what he wants to do to me.

But it's not that at all.

'Now – be loving *me*, wife,' he murmurs. He turns and stretches, face and chest down, across the kitchen table. I must ease his clothing down all the way, he says, and in a kind of dream, I do so, and follow his instructions to smooth the object with the goose fat sitting on a dish on the table. I must press the tip between his thighs, then carefully edge it into him, only pushing further when he tells me to.

I'm hesitant, which he likes at first. Then he demands that I push more, in and out, slowly, but deeper. He has never made with me the sounds he makes now; guttural groans, the pitch of which he must muffle, until there's nothing coming from him but a whimper and a sigh.

And for all the time it lasts, I feel nothing at his pleasure. I'm not meant to, that's clear; I am excluded entirely from what he needs. Though I remind myself throughout it all that I am the future Mrs William Minnoch, I have never felt more like a servant to a master I loathe than I do now. And all I can think is, *I will never escape him.*

But *he* is feeling much better. He's fastening his trousers, pulling on his boots, asking for cocoa. He's strengthened by our renewed commitment, he says, though I have made no such promises to him. He smirks a little at my silence, and says, 'But you are so very good with it, Mimi. You should feel proud of yourself. I have trained you to be a very good wife after all.'

I can't wait for him to leave; when he kisses me good night, he pushes his tongue into my mouth, grabs between my legs and squeezes until I cry out.

'You are *my* wife, only,' is the last thing he says before he leaves.

After he's gone, I rush to the kitchen sink to cough and bring up every last loathsome drop of him. I'm so distraught, I don't notice who has come into the kitchen.

Janet.

'I hate him,' she says.

I've never seen such a look on her face; such an appalled and frightened look.

'No, no, he just loves me too much, that is all,' I say. 'What – ah, Janet, what did you see? I told you not to leave the bedroom when he calls.'

'I *heard* – but it sounded so bad, Maddie. I did wait, and then I came. I saw – his goodbye. I think he likes hurting you.'

I start to weep at the kitchen table, my head in my hands. Janet sits beside me.

'Don't speak of it to anyone,' I say. 'Promise me.'

'I won't, Maddie. But what are you going to do?'

'I don't know,' I say. 'How to be rid of him when he'll never leave me alone? Papa will only get richer – that's all he wants, not me, not me.'

It's some time before we go back along the corridor together to our bedroom. I lie in bed for hours, long after Janet has fallen asleep, shivering and biting my lips, my fingernails, tearing the inside of my mouth, searching for a way out. But there's nothing. There is no way out.

The next day I cannot get out of bed and plead my menses for an excuse, though Christina knows it's not true when she comes to collect my nightgown, and Janet knows it, too, of course. They whisper together, but I don't even ask what they're saying.

But I must eventually make myself presentable, for I'm meeting with William, and we are going to the opera. He will tell me his secret soon, he says.

I try not to be dull. Alas, I have a secret, too. Can I trust him with it? Would he see off Emile, chase him from the city, if I told him what he makes me do, will make me do for ever if I have to marry him instead?

All through the performance I wonder, as William's hand lays with mine, his fingernails polished and pink and rounded to perfection, what kind of man he is. What kind of fiancé he will prove to be. If he will fight for me, and win me.

Later, in my room in Blythswood Square, with Janet sleeping peacefully in our bed, I decide to light a candle and write to Emile. This time *will* be the very last; I'll not waver a second time. Not for a man who only wants relief from a dull employment, who only wants my Papa's money.

So I take my time, and explain myself fully; I will make

him understand what this final breach means. He might be taken by surprise, I write, by the sudden change after our 'renewed commitment', but he must have noticed a coolness in me. Oh, I did once love him, truly, fondly, but much of that love has gone.

Even if I had become his wife, I say, *I still could not love him as I ought.* As he wants me to. Surely, I think, he will know what I refer to.

At the end, I ask him to return my letters: *Be at the gate in the lane, and Christina will take the parcel from you. On Friday, I shall send you all your letters.*

Christina has to see him; I cannot. No more proving anything to myself; the risk is not worth it. In the morning, I send John the houseboy to deliver the letter to Emile, and at least I do not have long to wait, for his reply to me is almost immediate, and it reaches me that evening, just as I'm getting ready for another night out with William.

We are to play cards with Mary Buchanan and Jack, in a smart new members' house not far from the square. William has given me a beautiful gold locket, which I'm just clasping together as I dress alone, when John knocks on the bedroom door.

I take the letter from him, close the door, and begin to read.

It is Emile's worst threat yet.

He'll not return my letters at all, he says. Instead, he is going to send them directly to Papa. He has kept every note, every letter, for that very purpose, he says.

It has always been in his mind to do it.

It has always been his intention.

And unless I break off my engagement to William

Minnoch – for he knows about it, everyone in town knows, he writes – then he will destroy me.

I will tell your Papa all that we have done together.
I will ruin you for any man. It is my promise.

'Maddie! William's upstairs,' Janet gushes, as she bursts into the room. I'm wiping my eyes; she sees the letter and snatches it up to read what Emile has written.

'Oh, Maddie, he can't do this. "*Ruin* you"? I must fetch Papa—'

'No, no, Janet, wait!'

She stops by the open bedroom door, and I hurry to close it.

'You cannot say a word to Papa! You must not! My letters are very – oh, they are very *intimate*, do you see? I have said things, described things – what we—. Ah, Papa will throw me out on the street if he reads a word. I tell you, Janet, he will.'

'Papa would not – would he?' And I see in Janet's eyes that terrible doubt she has, too, for we have all seen Papa in one of his tempers when his plans are spoiled. And his plans for me are too good for that; his house on Blythswood Square is too grand.

'My letters are . . . Nobody else can ever see them, Janet. I mean it. They are – very *bad*. Very wrong.'

She understands what I mean now. I have educated my little sister, at last. I have given her the kind of knowledge that Christina said her mother gave her, but it is a terrible thing, to destroy that innocence, even in the name of protection, for I see the way her face changes, and how she grows up, in a single moment. And it is my fault.

'Maddie, you have to stop him,' she says, quietly. At least I need not fear a fit or a convulsion or a faint from her now; not now that she is so grown and so responsible.

'I know I do,' I say, 'but the question is how to do it—'

I'm interrupted by Mama calling down for me, as I'm keeping William waiting upstairs. I pinch my cheeks, stuff Emile's letter into my purse.

'But you must say nothing – especially not to Papa – or to William.'

'Of course,' she says, and her cheeks flush a little. 'I'm not a fool, Maddie.'

I take her hand and squeeze it a little. 'No – I'm the fool. You'll not be like me, Janet. Don't ever be like me.'

She hugs me, suddenly, but I might weep, and William would wonder, so I push her gently away, and upstairs we go, hand in hand.

My only option after his terrible threat is to write endless promises to Emile, which I do all the way to Christmas. Only after that do I have some respite, for he goes to Edinburgh for the festivities, insisting on an announcement about our engagement in the New Year. This year, for the first time, Mama's winter ailments don't appear – she attributes this to her excitement about my wedding in June.

And then William tells me his 'secret'.

It is mid-January and we are leaving the theatre, after seeing *The Enemy's Notebook*, a play that William was most keen about, for it is full of ghosts and the supernatural, and the Theatre Royal made the stage suitably dark and frightening. During the carriage ride home, I clutch William's hand, and he whispers, 'What think you of ghosts, Madeleine? Do you believe in them or not?'

I say I do; back at the square, he comes in for a whisky in the drawing room. Mama and Papa allow us to be alone now that we are engaged and our wedding is only a few months away.

William looks most mysterious and dark, in his black suit with his black curls and black moustache. I pour him a whisky and we stand by the fire; he kisses my cheek, then whispers again, 'Can I trust you with it, my dear?'

I tell him that of course he can. He pulls down his collar to show me the crow tattoo.

'Your special band of brothers,' I say, and touch it lightly. He smiles, a little hungrily, I think, and so I stand closer, press myself against him.

'We are the followers of Allan Kardec,' he says. 'You'll not know the name,' he adds, for I am shaking my head. 'He believes in reincarnation and the science of spiritism. Where the spirit of a person may return after death to a new body.' He grips me, suddenly, and his face is close to mine. 'There is an old spirit in us all,' he says, 'and I think that the spirit within you is one that knew my spirit once. Don't you feel it, Madeleine? That connection we have?'

'Yes, William,' I say. 'But why – why is it a secret?'

'Because some refuse to believe it – mock us. We use a thing called a spirit board to contact the departed, and some think it goes against God. But it is the very *principle* of God, do you see?'

I recall then his comment in the balloon. 'You said "death is the greatest adventure".'

'And it is, for it is never-ending in returning us to other bodies—'

'So no one ever really dies?'

'You could think of it that way, yes. Only the old body rots, once the spirit leaves for a new one.'

I grip his arms, suddenly cold throughout. 'Make me warm, William,' I say, and kiss him. His moustache bristles against my lips; I whisper, 'I think I was once a woman called Mimi.' He shivers at that, and when I bring his hand to my breast and press it there, he moans a little, and closes his eyes.

To my surprise, though, he soon breaks away. 'A secret for a secret,' he says, holding my hand, his powder-blue eyes wide. 'What is yours, Madeleine?'

I don't know how to tell him, can only murmur, 'I don't have a secret.'

'Yes, you do. I have thought about asking you – when we went to the theatre a few weeks ago, just before Christmas.'

I frown, confused.

'You had a letter in your purse,' he says.

Silence.

'I read it – I should not have, I know, but when you left for a moment, it was there.'

There's a strange sort of noise in my ears.

'I asked you once before, about gossip, about another gentleman,' he says.

'There is none—'

He shakes his head. He's not angry, or even sad. He has a different kind of look altogether. 'What is he to you? I think you have to tell me.'

'It was not to *me*; he was nothing to me. He was everything to *Mimi*.'

And I tremble as I whisper what little I can.

* * *

There are to be over a hundred people at my wedding. It will be the social event of the year, which only heightens my fears about Emile's behaviour.

I pick up the bills and the satins and the drawings that lie scattered on the bedroom floor about me. It's a morning in February, two weeks after William told me his 'secret' and I told him mine, or a part of it.

In our carriage rides since, he has been protective, but eager, too, with kisses and discreet fondling; he calls me Mimi, my 'spirit name'. He forgives me, he says, for whatever encouragement I gave this man, for I was too young when I met him to know better, and had no real guidance. He knows that Jack is not a wise brother; he knows Papa is fearsome in his temper.

It means a great deal to have a man *not* be angry with me, like Papa, or Emile. William never raises his voice or loses his temper. He obeys a gentlemanly code all of his own, and with him, I can breathe and be my best self, the kind of self I want to be.

He has another streak in him, though, that I did not expect. For he has suggested *vengeance* against the *verminous man* who thought he could wrong me. I have told him – God forgive me – that Emile deceived me; that he told me lies about his station in life, his prospects. That we met once or twice in town, and that was enough for him to imagine a closer connection than was possible, or likely.

'I think he was a wolf in his past life,' I said to William, when I was done with my tale.

'And I am an expert shot at vermin,' he said, holding me gently.

'You make a terrible joker,' I said, to tease him, but I did not care for his use of that word, *vermin*. Emile is many things, but he's not that.

But William looked very serious, and it struck me that he was someone who might take pleasure in killing a man. *Death is the greatest adventure.*

I shivered a little more then, and he drew me closer. 'No proper gentleman would allow his wife-to-be to be threatened in such a way,' he said. 'There is a code of conduct to follow.'

Emile wants to be a *proper gentleman*, thinks to use me to acquire that status. William knows what a *proper gentleman* is, doesn't need me to make it so.

What exactly would his code of conduct permit, I wonder, and throughout my dreams at night there come visions of a bloodied Emile, his body dragged before a group of hounds and torn apart, his entrails dripping and his bones smashed.

Emile has returned from Edinburgh, as he promised he would. His threats have returned, too; this time, he insists in his note on coming to the square at noon the next day with all of my letters to show Papa.

I think about William Minnoch, his rifle cocked and pointing, as the great front door opens to reveal Emile standing there before him. I picture the gun going off.

Would William be foolish enough to go so far? I won't believe it; I think I am the one who must save *him* from doing something he believes to be honourable.

'He has threatened it before, Maddie,' Christina says. She's come to my room at my calling out. Janet has come, too. The three of us read his latest letter. Christina looks exhausted; Janet stricken. 'Put him off again.'

'It's different now he's given a time, though. Noon tomorrow!' I say. Panic fills me. 'What do I do? Tell me, what do I do? Everything I've tried has failed. Even William – ah, he thinks Emile is a poor man who's too fascinated with me, that he can chase him off, or maybe worse—'

But William must not, cannot, do anything that will cause himself harm. I've not always been good at caring for others' fates. I did not care to think about Emile's hurt when I threw him over; I did not think about Papa's shame beyond fearing his reaction.

I care for Janet's fate, and for mine. But William, I must care about, too.

I pace back and forth while Janet, wide-eyed and white-faced, bites her fingernails. Christina frowns.

'I might only have a few hours,' I say. 'He means it. I've delayed too often. He means to do it. By noon, he said.'

'Papa cannot throw you out, he would not,' Janet cries. But I can't reassure her with false words anymore.

'Yes, he will; he will. I have to accept it. I have to tell Papa I'm engaged to Emile, or he will show Papa my letters. Either way, I am ruined. That's the only end for me.'

'And what is the end for *him*?' says Christina. 'He's getting too old for rich daughters to consider him. His looks are fading.'

I stare at her.

'He thinks you're his last chance at an easy life,' Christina says. 'He thinks your Papa won't throw you out because it'd mean too terrible a scandal, as if throwing over William Minnoch for him wouldn't be scandal enough. No – he wants something he can't have.'

'So what am I to do?' I say. 'It's making him mad. He won't listen to reason.'

'We have to remember that,' says Christina. 'Consider what *he* has to lose, if you do go to your Papa and tell him about the *other* man you're engaged to.'

I wait for her to smirk at that, but she's too serious. We are all too serious.

'If your Papa throws you out,' she continues, 'then that's a bad end for *him*. At best, he'll end up with a wife who has no money. At worst, he'll be shown up for abandoning you, for all the world would know he'd done so, and he'd probably lose his job at Huggins. So he knows he's taking a risk. You can hold him off a bit more. He'll go to the brink with it, is my guess. Whether he's mad enough to jump over the edge and take you with him – well, that's another matter.'

The full horror of what she's saying dawns slowly. 'Then he will do that,' I murmur. 'He'll take me with him – over that edge. I believe – that he *wants* to. He wants to ruin us both.'

'Then hurry up and write to him. And I'll try and think what to do.'

Christina heads out as Mama's bell rings from upstairs. Janet sits while I write.

Emile, for the love you once had for me, do nothing till I see you. For God's sake, do not bring your once-loved Mimi to an open shame.

Oh do not till I see you on Wednesday night. Come to the gate – I shall see you.

Oh Emile, be not harsh to me. I am the most guilty,

miserable wretch on the face of the earth. Emile, do not drive me to death.

When I ceased to love you, believe me, it was not to love another. I am free from all engagement at present.

Emile, for God's sake do not send my letters to Papa. It will be an open rupture. I will leave the house.

I will die.

I would not again ask you to love me, for I know you could not. But oh Emile, do not make me go mad.

Pray for me – for a guilty wretch. But do nothing. Oh, Emile, do nothing.

I ring for John, the houseboy, with instructions for him to deliver my letter immediately and to wait for a response. 'You must not come back without a response, do you understand?' I say, and he nods, alarmed.

It's some hours before Emile's reply arrives. I must announce our engagement by noon tomorrow, he says again.

Or you will be on the street, where you belong. You will be at the mercy of every man to use as he wants. You will die a sick, diseased creature in squalor and misery.

I can smell his desperation, the whiff of sweat rising from his letter to sour in my nostrils. I shove the paper into my mouth, but cannot swallow it. I gag and choke it up instead, coughing until the tears pour down. Janet cannot comfort me, nor can Christina suggest yet what to do. I postpone my night out with William, feigning a headache, and go to bed. As Janet sleeps on beside me later that night, I sneak into the kitchen for one of Mama's old bottles, the kind that doctors don't prescribe.

It makes me feel as light as air. Like a wraith, I drift up and down the dark corridor outside our bedroom, searching for another answer, until dawn breaks and the house begins to wake.

After some lukewarm coffee alone in the empty kitchen, I return to the bedroom, where my hand shakes so much writing my letter to him that the ink blots the paper over and over.

Emile, my father's wrath would kill me – you little know his temper. Emile, for the love you once had for me, do not denounce me to Papa. Emile, if he should read my letters to you – he will put me from him. He will hate me as a guilty wretch.

I put on paper what I should not. I was free, because I loved you with my heart. If Papa or any other saw those fond letters to you, what would not be said of me? On my bended knee I write to you and ask you: as you hope for mercy on Judgement Day, do not inform on me. Do not make me a public shame.

For the love you once had for me, do not bring my father's wrath down on me. It will kill my mother.

I grow mad. I have been ill, very ill, all day. I have had what has given me a false spirit. I had to resort to what I should not have taken, but my brain is on fire. I feel as if death would indeed be sweet.

Janet is still sleeping in our bed; Christina will be asleep still, too. In the grey dawn, I have never felt so alone, so small in this enormous house. Eventually, I ring for John, who appears, sleepy-eyed and in his nightclothes.

'Deliver this as soon as you're ready,' I whisper at the bedroom door. Janet stirs but doesn't wake up. 'Then I want you to go to the apothecary on Sauchiehall Street. I want you to make a special purchase.'

He nods, pockets the letter.

'Ask for a vial of prussic acid. It's a cosmetic aid,' I add. 'I must look my best for my wedding. But don't tell anyone.'

He doesn't understand, but he's happy to get away from me, and he wanders back along to the kitchen.

Silent in the bedroom as Janet sleeps, I look out my finest dress.

Prussic acid is quick and painless, they say. I want to look my best when I take the poison.

Perhaps then Emile will be sorry at what he has done.

Perhaps Papa will be sorry.

And I think of William and of my spirit passing into another body after death, that we are never truly dead, and I hope that he is right.

IV.

'Probably, though none of you may think for a moment that he did go out that night, and that, without seeing her, and without knowing what she wanted to see him about, he swallowed above 200 grains of arsenic on the street; on the other hand, gentlemen, if he did not commit suicide, keep in view that that will not of itself establish that the prisoner administered the arsenic. The matter may have remained most mysterious – wholly unexplained.'

– The Lord Justice-Clerk charge to the jury in the trial of Madeleine Smith, 9 July 1857, Edinburgh

New York, 1927

'I told you my story wasn't for *fun*,' I said. 'You're making a mockery of it, and I won't have that. Be serious, or I won't do this at all. You can tell Violet whatever you like; I don't care. In fact, tell Violet your theory that William Minnoch and I did it together! Yes, do that. She enjoys a good joke, and she'll laugh in your face.'

I balled my fists as best I could, given that my fingers were hardly able to bend these days at all. My contempt was genuine, though; he knew I wasn't calling his bluff this time. His suggestion – a joint murder! – really was the greatest nonsense I had ever heard.

'I think you've been reading too many crime novels, Harry,' I said as he stood there, my shawl and hat in his hands. 'Now give me those, please.'

He had the grace to hand them back to me. 'At least you're not denying you knew Minnoch,' he said.

'You want to be careful about who you accuse, Harry. That's defamation of character. Have you thought about that, with your filming and recording? Accusing innocent folk of terrible crimes – Mr Minnoch and his family might not be so keen to have his name dragged through the mud like this.'

For the second time, I thought I had him, and wished for a

moment that he'd been filming me after all. That would have been a reel of film he'd only have to destroy.

'Can't libel the dead,' he murmured.

'But Mr Minnoch might not be dead. *I'm* not.'

I wasn't sure when the exact moment had come that I'd confirmed his beliefs about my identity, but whenever it was, we were past that moment now – that was certain. He narrowed his eyes as if the pressure of thinking harder was too much.

'But Emile L'Angelier is dead, and seventy years dead now, too,' he said. 'D'you never think of him, Lena? Does he never haunt you? Not even in your dreams?'

His words were meant to chill me, and they did. But I wouldn't tell him what ghosts there were waiting in the night for me, sometimes even in the day. 'Which of us isn't haunted by our past?' I said, at last. 'We each have one, after all. You can't live and not have a past.'

'Let's talk about living then, Lena. Let's talk about those living after Emile was murdered. About his family – his mother, for instance. Newspapers said she was devastated by his death. By his *murder*, I should say.'

'If "murder" is indeed what it was,' I said, narrowing my eyes at him. 'You're so keen to compare him to that poor husband of Ruth Snyder – well, there's no doubt Mr Snyder was murdered. Nobody bashes in their own head with a sash weight. And it's no accident, unless you think it dropped on his head somehow.'

Harry rubbed his chin, a habit I was noticing more and more, like he was practising for something. 'So you're saying Emile overdosed himself? Well, I guess enough of your supporters have said it over the years.'

'He was a man who took all sorts of things! Laudanum,

opium from poppy seeds – even arsenic. He took it to ease a stomach complaint. They still recommend it, you know, for easing the pain of diverticulitis—'

But Harry waved a hand at me 'An overdose – accidental or otherwise – is a possibility, sure. But only you and he know the real truth of it.'

I shook my head. 'That's just where you're wrong, Harry. I have no idea what happened to him, or how. You have to believe that. I have nothing else to tell you.' My pleading made me realise how exhausted I was, all of a sudden. 'I really have to go home,' I said. 'This has been quite enough for one day.' I put my hand to my heart and wobbled a bit to emphasise the point. 'But you want to think over what I said. I can't tell you what I don't know, and I don't know what happened to him the night before he died.'

He agreed, if reluctantly, and to my great relief, we left the suite and took the elevator down to the ground floor. When he dropped me back at my apartment, he said he'd be there first thing in the morning to pick me up again, and I didn't doubt it. He was enjoying it too much, it seemed to me. Not the baiting of me, as I'd first thought. But that worrying-out of the manner of Emile and his death – that had him hooked all right, and he thought I was the key to the mystery. I wasn't just a way for him to make money, to get attention. He wanted to *solve* it, too.

What made folk want to do it – *men* want to do it, I wondered as I got myself ready for bed later. Why couldn't they let a mystery just *be*? Why did they need a solution, an answer? But then I needed an answer, too – although to a different question.

How could I persuade him to leave me alone? To give up

on solving his 'mystery', and go back west, forgetting me and forgetting Violet?

Violet. Violet was my most precious thing in this world, more so even than Tom, and I'd do everything I could to protect her.

And so it was that too early the next morning, I forced my old, aching bones out of bed, hours before I expected Harry would call. I dressed quickly, had a small breakfast and then I was outside, stepping down on to Park Avenue, my breathing hard, as worry quickened my steps. More than once I had to stop for a short rest by the railings of a dusty but new apartment building. 'Remember your age,' I muttered, though in truth that was getting harder to do as the years passed. It was anxiety rather than exertion that had me breathing so hard, though, as I passed uptown folk years younger than me, a seemingly never-ending bustle of suited young cake-eaters and cloche-hatted flappers, treating the working daytime like it was a night-time party.

The cranes clanged further uptown, and the motor cars rumbled and tooted along the street all the way to the Grand Concourse. Always it shocked me, how wide open and never-ending the Concourse was, like a dusty ocean lined with townhouses instead of ships, each a dozen or more storeys high. It ran so far north you couldn't see where it petered out and the countryside began. Like a view of the ocean as you sailed out of harbour, that had you feeling you were at the very edge of the earth itself. When I'd sailed on the *Arizona* from the Old World to the New all those years ago, squinting at the tip of the horizon, I was fearful of falling right into it, ship and all. Giddy and spinning, I was on the deck that September day almost thirty years ago, my fingers tight around the ship's rails.

The times and the city weren't right for slow-thinking old women, though, forever looking back over their shoulders. On my way to the trolley-car stop, I passed a queue of young women waiting in plain dresses beneath a sign that said 'Staff Wanted', fanning themselves in the sun and not giving me a second glance, because nobody noticed women of my age. I did wish that I could have joined them. The urge to live my youth over again didn't often rise within me, for it was a lie that I didn't care to think about. But Harry's persistence had forced me to think back over it, and the taste of bitterness in my mouth was there more often than it was not. So I allowed myself a little romancing as I saw those young women, wondered what I might have been doing had I been born in a different time, or had I not believed the lies I was told when I was too young and foolish to question them.

It wasn't until much later in my life that that youthful kind of freedom was mine to enjoy at last. When I first stepped off the ship, the noise and force of this strange new city hit me like a wild wind that threatened to lift me up into the sky. For all it was smaller than London, there was something bigger about it – bigger ambitions, maybe, and certainly taller buildings, reaching up to the heavens. The dockside was teeming with more folk than I'd ever seen in a single place in my life, and I was afraid, in that moment, of what I was doing, what I was about to do, thinking I'd be found out and it would all go horribly wrong. But then Tom's face had appeared amongst the crowd on the dock, the broadest smile on his face. He'd shouted out, 'Mama!' as baby Violet, gathered up in Annita's arms beside him, waved her little hands, and then I knew it was right, what I had done.

What the words *safe harbour* truly meant. I should be grateful that nobody noticed me now. That I was just another unremarkable old woman, of no account to anyone. But I had felt free, in spite of the past, ever since I'd set foot in this city all those years ago. That was what it had meant, coming here. And it was what a new identity had meant, too. *Mrs Sheehy*. For Willy had been part of that freedom the city offered me.

It was only as I got nearer to Eighth Avenue that my worries about confronting Teresa rose up. For she was my intended destination, the answer to my question of how to stop Harry. What exactly had she told her grandson about that conversation with Willy she overheard in my apartment that night? It occurred to me she might try to defend Harry's actions, for she was always very loyal to her family. But for all he said she couldn't railroad him, Teresa was pretty formidable, and I really thought she might be able to put a stop to his pursuit of me.

And so on I ploughed, stumbling down from the trolley car and on along our raggedy street, with the rundown brown tenements from the old century that were never the most fashionable, nor the most expensive. We lived mostly among other working folk, Willy and I; among artisans and artists and shopkeepers and seamstresses. The street's children played together in a jumble in sun or in snow, and every other apartment spoke a different tongue to the one before it. This was where we felt at home.

Oh, how I missed it! Children didn't play up on Park Avenue the way they did down here, not with their uniformed nannies everywhere. I'd moved uptown to be nearer Tom and Violet after Willy died, and to a place with fewer stairs, given the arthritis that was crippling my hands and slowing me down. But the Concourse was too business-smart and serious for artistic types.

'What have I done?' I muttered. 'What have I done?'

I gazed at the long, sooty windows above me, and the early morning sun beat down on my crêpe dress and wool cape, and on my crazy unkempt hair that no hat could keep quiet. For a moment, I half expected to see Willy standing on the fire escape in the sunlight, and the shock of knowing he'd never be there again, that I'd never see him there or any other place, came rolling through me like a terrible wave, and my body sagged and my eyes filled with tears.

Perplexity overtook my sadness soon enough, though, as I approached the main entrance to find a door had been fitted where previously it had been open to the street. I pushed hard at it but it didn't budge.

I wasn't in the wrong place. I wasn't crazy. Our building had never had a 'super', the way new fancy ones did now. There was no new-fangled electric doorbell system that so many buildings like Violet's had had put in either.

I stood, pondering what to do, when the door opened and almost tipped me forward on to the person behind it, and they let out a cry.

It was Nancy, the young woman who had moved into our old apartment. She didn't recognise me at first, too busy brushing herself down after I'd almost knocked her flat. But then she squinted against the sunlight pouring in and said, 'Mrs Sheehy, is that you? My goodness – what're you doing here?'

But my mouth had dried and I could only totter in the doorway.

She caught my arm in a firm, young grasp and said, 'But you don't look so well.'

'I'm just a little tired out is all,' I said. My legs were heavy and sore, and my breath came in little gasps.

'Have you come down all this way from the Bronx?' she said. She had lovely golden hair; I remembered that about her, its close waves. She was dressed for spring, in a light blue satin, and her cloche hat had a pretty little daisy motif on it. She looked a picture, and I said so. She laughed. 'You do know, don't you, that you don't live here anymore—'

'You don't have to worry, Nancy, I'm not losing my wits,' I said. 'I'm only here to see Teresa – but there's a door here. Since when was a door put in?'

But Nancy was already losing interest, now she knew I wasn't dying on her. 'Oh, Mrs Conti's no longer here, didn't you know? She had a fall, about a month or two back. A bad one, on the stairway, because someone was there who shouldn't have been, and she took fright and tumbled. So now we have a front door that locks.' She held up her keys.

'Teresa fell? Is she all right?'

'No, she was in hospital for weeks, and then she and Mr Conti left the building altogether.'

'Oh my goodness – where to?'

'I don't know for sure – somewhere upcountry, I think. I'm so sorry, but I have to run.'

'But she never even wrote to tell me!'

'She broke her arm, in her fall, as well as a few ribs, I think – maybe it was her writing hand?' Nancy said. 'Will you be OK now? I really have to go!'

And then she was gone, just as something else struck me.

'But he said she was fine! Harry, her own grandson. *He said she was fine,*' I called out, but too late. Nancy didn't catch my words, and I was left standing in the doorway, shouting at the street.

He would have known that his grandmother had had a bad accident. His mother would surely have told him. Which left only one other possibility: he had lied. But why?

All I really knew was that he wanted to use me, and to use the trial, to make a film about the murder case. That didn't justify him lying to me about Teresa.

No: it didn't make sense at all, and I had a sinister feeling about it.

By the time I got back up to Eighth Avenue, it was after noon. There was a penned note from him pushed under the door.

Where are you? I'll call again tomorrow and you better be here.

I couldn't decide whether to confront him outright when I saw him the next day, and had a fitful night of sleep, dozing on and off. By the time Harry called the next morning – a good hour before I expected him; he wasn't going to let me get away again – I was tired and irritable.

'Where'd you get to yesterday?' he said, out on the stoop.

'I don't have to tell you everything,' I said, rudely.

'Who's got a problem with their "tone" *now*? I wouldn't try running out on me. You know, I almost paid a visit to Violet yesterday.'

'But your theories are so many and all of them absurd. I don't think she'd listen to you.'

'Wanna chance it?' he said, holding out his arm for me to take.

I scowled at him; he just grinned. Then I remembered my trump card. For the length of the car-ride downtown I didn't say another word, nor did I speak when we were in the elevator going up to his suite. He seemed amused by that, too, and inside his suite, he wasted no time in switching on that big light and his recording machine.

'Sit right here,' he said, 'and speak into this microphone.'

I nodded.

'So—' he began, but I held up my hand.

'Let me speak,' I said. I heard the film rolling, the record, too. 'I have something important to say first.'

He raised an eyebrow, folded his arms.

'I took the trolley car to my old apartment on Eighth Avenue yesterday,' I said.

'You did what?'

I repeated it, right into the microphone. 'I wanted to see my old neighbour, Teresa. Your grandmother.'

The look on his face was ugly, and for a moment I felt afraid. But I was too determined to stop now.

'So imagine my surprise, Harry, when I found she wasn't there. That she'd had an accident, weeks ago. And she's gone to live upcountry. Yet *you* told me that she was fine! Why did you lie to me?'

I spoke with more calmness than I felt, concentrating hard on keeping my voice steady. He didn't reply, but switched off the recording equipment, and went over to the window, opening it, then lighting a cigarette. The breeze was hot already. Some of the dust on the windowsill shifted, and a scent of witch-hazel and lilac drifted over from his hair and his clean-shaven face. I had that flash again of him in his rooms, preparing himself.

Anxiety, I'd thought it then, about making a good impression. Now, it seemed to say something else about how he meant to look.

He stood there a few minutes, blowing cigarette smoke out into the breeze, and I thought perhaps I could just slip away, that maybe I'd done enough to stop him. But then he came over to me, that annoying, amused look back on his face again.

'Oh, Lena,' he said, fixing deep brown eyes on my watery blue ones. I tried not to blink. 'There's no great mystery. My nonna asked me not to tell you, that's all. She didn't want to worry you, not in the midst of your grief. And she was right.'

'I don't believe you,' I said. His new-fangled scent masked a deeper, older kind of maleness, before moving pictures came, or motor cars. The kind of maleness that knew it ran the world through brute force, but liked to pretend it was something other, less primitive – bigger brains, or pioneer spirit, or some eugenics nonsense.

There was something *other* about him that was just Harry's alone, though. It jabbed at me like it was impatient for me to realise it.

'No, I don't believe you at all,' I repeated.

'It's the truth, I promise you that,' he said. His voice was light, but his eyes, which I had at first thought feline, seemed more wolfish, suddenly, with a disc of animal yellow in the centre of coffee-brown irises. A reflection of the light outside, perhaps. 'I tell you what, why don't I give you her new address and you can write her yourself? I've got it somewhere.' And he made a show of patting his pockets as though he kept it about his person at all times. What a phony he was.

'How do I even know you are her grandson?' I said it, right out.

He only smiled. 'How else would I know about your friendship with her? How would I know any of it?'

That was true. I bit my lip a little and my hands twitched.

'Don't you think it's about time you stopped playing these games, Lena?' he said. 'None of this is about me – it's about you, and Emile. The man you murdered.'

'I did no such thing! You think you're getting some kind of confession out of me, so you can say, look, I solved it, this terrible murder.'

'So take your chance!' he said, stubbing out the cigarette and pulling up a chair beside me. 'Tell the world the truth. You didn't say a word at the trial, so say it now! Put the rumours to bed.'

'But I don't *know*, don't you see?' My voice rose as I tried to convince him. 'I keep telling you. I don't *know* anything – not about what happened to him, not even *about* him. Oh, I don't think I ever really knew who he was—'

I had to stop right there, take a breath.

The truth that he'd finally got out of me was a truth that I'd avoided most of my life. It hurt me beyond words, the cruelty of that admission. That I never really knew him. It knocked me sideways, sent my mind reeling, and all I could do was babble, weak and confused.

'He – oh, I mean, that he had to *pretend*, you see – to be something he wasn't. He wasn't a rich man, he wasn't a gentleman; they looked down on him for that—'

I broke off again; I'd said too much. But all the same, I couldn't stop.

'It breaks my heart, how it was. It wasn't how *she* said it was at all—'

'Like who said? Who's *she*?'

Harry was up close, staring at me. I coughed, alarmed at what I was only now understanding, as well as what I was revealing to him. How easily he'd fooled me into talking. His crudeness was producing results, confusing me. I still knew what he wanted, though; I could see it in lights in theatres everywhere.

Madeleine Smith Speaks!

All the lookalikes clustering for photographers. The selling of my voice and my face to strangers all over the country.

Everything I'd always feared.

'Go on,' Harry said. 'Like *who* said?'

I couldn't just sit there. I struggled out of the chair and stood in front of him, looking down as he sat with one ankle resting on the knee opposite, his leg bent.

His leg bent.

And that was when the stopper on my memory popped, just like that. How it bubbled up, before rising into the air like some long-suppressed and powerful scent released from an ancient bottle. I took in that scent, took it deep down inside me, before breathing it back out again, to blow away his wickedness.

'Emile wanted to be someone he wasn't,' I said, slowly. 'Only you – well, you already *are* that, aren't you? Someone you're not.'

He frowned. 'We're going over this again? I told you, my nonna didn't want to worry you, that's all.'

I shook my head. 'I remember it now. Teresa's daughter

Angela went out west and had a little boy. Enrico was his name. I can see why you might shorten it – Henry – to Harry.'

He gave a sigh, said, 'Come on now, Lena—'

But I wanted to take my time, be as clear as possible. 'That's why I didn't make the connection at first. Little Enrico. Not *Harry*. Little Enrico out west. He caught polio when he was five years old. It ruined his legs, Teresa told me, years ago. Yes, I remember it now.

'But your legs, Harry – they seem to be just fine.'

I pointed at his shiny loafers as if to make the point. Motors tooted outside like a kind of applause at my catching him out so. A few hollers even drifted up to the hotel window, high up as we were. I smiled.

He smiled back, muttered, 'Lena, Lena.'

And then he did something strange: he held out his hand to me.

'It was a risk,' he said. 'I figured you were ninety-two, and he told me you'd never actually met him. So there was a good chance you'd not remember that detail, 'specially not with Teresa having all those grandchildren.'

He shrugged at my refusal to take his hand. 'It's no great mystery, and it doesn't alter a thing. Teresa's grandson – Enrico – is my business partner; we run the film company together. He told me about you. See, his grandmother really did overhear you that night, and really did put two and two together, and tell her daughter. But he doesn't know I'm here. Enrico has more – oh, morals, I guess you'd say. A soft touch. I love the guy, but you gotta be tough in this business.'

The truth wasn't always an easy thing in my life. More than once, it had caught me unawares, almost felled me. This time,

I felt that threatening faint, that dizziness before the eyes. But I wouldn't fall in front of him. He was an imposter, and I should have spotted that straightaway, with my history.

Yes; I was more annoyed with myself than I was with him in that moment, because I hadn't realised it sooner. But anger made me strong.

'You're just a liar. A cheap conman. No more Harry Townsend than—'

'Oh, I *am* Harry Townsend,' he interrupted me. 'Enrico and me, both christened Henry. What are the chances? We had fun with it when we first set up the company, you know, trying to figure it into the name of it. Like Metro-Goldwyn-Mayer, or Warner Brothers. But "Two Henrys Pictures" isn't so – catchy. I'm not quite the liar you think I am, Lena. But enough about me, and Teresa's offspring. I think we've got more to talk about.'

'No,' I said. 'We do not. I'm not speaking with a liar and a conman.'

'Oh, you can teach me a thing or two about lying, Lena. Pretend all you like. Pretend you know nothing. But it's plain as day that's not true. There's guilt written all over your face. All these years since the trial, and you can't shake it.'

It was another lie of his, and I knew it, for I was nothing if not practised in my expressions, and knew exactly how I came across.

I was preparing my features to show exactly that when he continued, 'Someone else knew that about you, too. Didn't *she*? You mentioned her before. Come on, Lena, we both know it.'

And my expression changed.

Blythswood Square, 1857

'He (L'Angelier) said, "No, I won't; she shall never marry another man as long as I live." He also said, "It is an infatuation; she'll be the death of me."'
– Testimony of Thomas Fleming Kennedy, cashier to Huggins and Co., Glasgow, at the trial of Madeleine Smith, 2 July 1857, Edinburgh

The February wind blows hard; the February wind blows clean.

The February wind blows soot and dust from our house on the square with ease, it's so grand and wide. Not a single speck dares cling to any sill or step of ours for long.

The February wind blows Emile's words into the fireplace, where they burn. The apothecary wouldn't sell prussic acid to our houseboy, so I'm not a spirit, inhabiting another body. I'm still Madeleine, trapped in this body which Emile may use whenever he wants, because I can't refuse him. The wind can only take *his* words into the fire, not mine.

My words damn me. And so it goes, that *tap, tap, tap* of his cane against my bedroom window, or at the back door.

Tap, tap, tap, Mimi! Let me in!

Did Heathcliff shudder when Cathy's ghost came tapping,

as I do when Emile shows? Would I rather it was his ghost haunting me, and not his living self? Janet lies awake for that tapping, pleads with me not to go to him when it comes. Christina curses it, when he taps at the back door.

'I'd like to smack him with that cane of his,' she complains. 'He'll land us all in the mire, the way he's going on.'

He did not bring my letters to Papa by noon that day after all. But only because a stomach complaint seized him so hard that he was taken ill and could not move from his bed.

I might wish that stomach complaints seize him every day for the rest of his life.

But in a week he's well enough to call on me again. I move like a ghost the minute I hear his tapping; float to the back door, or to the window. I whisper, ghost-like, in Christina's room, where he paws at me to show my love for him, to give him what he wants.

He is thinner than ever, his eyes wild and his hair just as straggly as before. Absurdly, it annoys me that he makes no effort for me, doesn't care to try and arouse me in any way. It strikes me that he much prefers it when he knows I must pretend.

In front of the fire, on his lap, I nevertheless stroke and kiss his whiskered cheek, his dry mouth. He isn't fooled, even though his eyes are wide and staring like a mad person's. I nuzzle his ear, and his hand slips under my nightgown. He knows how to stir me still; even now, after all his threats, against every feeling, my body still betrays me and responds, and my hand pushes down below the waistband of his trousers.

'What would your Papa think, after all, if I did get you with a child?' he says, getting to his feet unsteadily. It is such a mad thing to say after all his objections that I can't reply, but then he presses me against the kitchen table, before pushing up hard into me.

But I'm cold; for when he is done, I know it is for the last time. Somehow, I'll make it so.

I reach for a cloth to wipe myself. A sudden spasm in my belly sparks strange tears; he relents, comforts me a little, even begins to weep himself.

'So now you might be with child – our child,' he says. 'Do not let yourself fall into the gutter, Mimi. Tell your Papa tomorrow. Tell him you are carrying my child.'

'You didn't want that before,' I say.

'Maybe I have come round to your way of thinking,' he says, with bitterness in his voice. 'Maybe a child is the only way to make your Papa pay – look what he has put me through! Yes, maybe I'll enjoy seeing you plump and full with my child, Mimi.'

When he kisses me before he leaves, I think I might be sick there and then. Afterwards, I run back to my room, try to *douche* as best I can at the washstand.

I hate him.

I hate him.

The February wind blows away from our house high on the hill, away down to the filthy-brown, clogged-up river so many streets below, where the great ships sit and unload their packages from the East, from the South, from across the ocean to the great West. And then the river takes them upstream again, sluggish and thick at first, then up towards Rowaleyn, before it starts to flow, free of silt and detritus, past the Cumbraes and the isle of Arran, then into the Irish Sea and up and over to America.

America! The land of prairies and painted men; of cotton fields and runaway slaves; of great mills and railroads; of all walks of life, or so Dickens writes. William's excited by my mention of the New World, 'where all manner of heathen exists', he says, 'though it's not so dreadful as Australia'. He thinks it's a land of spirits born again in primitive bodies, and they're desperate to learn how to transform themselves beyond the restrictions of the flesh.

I want to transform myself into something unrecognisable to Emile; only then might I be free of him. But it's impossible. Ah, to be free of that torturous *tapping*! It fires my brain to think of a place wide open to sunsets and fields, without a tapping on doors. To be a pioneer woman in a homespun dress standing outside a wood-framed hut, or a tragic angel of goodness and liberty, like Evangeline St Clare in *Uncle Tom's Cabin*, which I've lately been reading to Janet at night, to drown out that tapping noise.

'Let the wind send me across oceans,' I murmur at night in bed. Let the wind blow away his tapping.

Let me sail away from Emile.

Tap, tap, tap.

Then one day, when she is tidying up our bedroom, Christina announces that McKenzie has landed a better job down at the docks, which means he can afford a small place for them both soon. She'll not 'live in' anymore, once she's married, she says. It distresses me so much that I grasp her round the waist, and won't let go, even though she tries to push me away.

'I'm sorry,' I say, kissing her cheek before she twists away. 'I'm sorry, please forgive me, don't leave me.'

She softens a moment, sighs. 'I can't save you from him, Maddie. I tried to—'

'I know – you were right, all those times. You said he bewitched me; it was true. He made me a stranger to myself—'

I can't say any more for weeping, and sit on the bed. Christina sits beside me, stroking my hair gently to calm me. She kisses my cheek with soft lips that are so comforting I want more, and kiss her on the mouth, pressing there, opening my lips and pushing in with my tongue. For a second, she responds, and then the moment of frenzy bursts, and she shoves me from her as hard as she can. I slip off the bed and land on the floor with a bump, where I resume weeping.

'Dear God, but his madness is turning you mad, too,' she says, standing up and wiping her mouth with the back of her hand. 'What are you playing at, Maddie? Get your head straight.'

'I'm trying, I'm trying! But I don't know how. What do I do, Christina – what do I do?'

'Stop acting like a mad thing, for one. Your Mama's noticed it – she thinks the wedding is stressing you.'

'What – what has she said?' I wipe my wet face with my sleeve like a street child.

'I heard her tell your Papa that marriage to Minnoch would make you more *stable*, so she must be thinking you're not.'

'I don't believe you, it's not true.'

She slips down to the floor beside me, but not too close. 'I mean it, Maddie,' she says. 'They put you away for it, families like yours, when there's someone can't cope among them. Don't you think your Mama would do it, if you showed her up? Weeping and wailing like this? What if she'd just come in here a minute ago? You have to pull yourself together, and fast. Or they'll put you away.'

It goes round and round my head all the rest of that day and night.

They'll put you away.

If Emile goes to Papa with my letters, perhaps that's what Papa will do. My letters will prove how mad I must be, to have done all the things I have with Emile.

Tap, tap, tap.

When Christina helps me to bed not long after my odd behaviour, with a bed warmer and a cup of cocoa, she tells Mama that it is my menses, to excuse me from dinner. Mama makes my excuses to William, who was to take me out.

They'll put you away.

I've read about women who are put away by their families; stuck in madhouses and left to rot.

'Janet,' I whisper, when she comes down to see me after supper. 'Janet – if anyone should tell you I am mad, and put me away, will you come and find me when you're older?'

Janet snuggles in close, says, 'But why would anyone put you away, Maddie?'

'Because they'll say I was bad, to have been in love with Emile for so long. And they are right. I behaved very badly. Sometimes when women behave badly, they're taken away. You have to promise always to be good, Janet. I couldn't bear it if they took you away one day, too.'

I don't want to frighten her, but I live every moment of every day in a constant state of terror, seeing only harm everywhere. God help me, but I must frighten Janet, too, to save her from what is heading my way. From who is heading my way, with his silver-topped cane and his filthy whiskers and his demands that I cannot satisfy.

At bedtime, at least, I have a little respite. Christina comes in to say good night, and tells me that she will 'see to' Emile, for he has insisted that he will call on me.

I am so relieved that I fall asleep, but he's a devil that won't stop, will never stop, and he's reaching beyond me to harm whoever he can.

Because the next morning I learn that Janet had slipped out of bed and waited in the kitchen for his tapping at the back door, before Christina could get there first.

She told him to leave me alone, as I'm engaged to Mr Minnoch.

She thought she was protecting me, my dearest girl. But she has done it; she has tipped him over that edge, and now he is dragging me with him, and we are tumbling into darkness, for a note arrives from him saying that he will come tonight to Papa with all my letters.

It is over.

'It's all my fault,' says Janet, stricken, when I burst into tears. 'I thought he would leave you alone if he knew.'

Christina tries to calm her, for she's fretting, her breath catching.

'I'll go to Papa,' I say, standing up. 'I'll go right now. I'll take whatever punishment he wants.'

'And lose William? Lose all your prospects? Because this will get out,' Christina says.

But William knows, I say.

'Not about all that you've done – and if your Papa puts you away for madness, because that's a better explanation than his daughter being a *whore*—'

Christina's harshness causes Janet to burst into tears now, too. It's almost comical, how desperate we are, the three of us.

'Your Papa will know I took your letters after he told you to stop it,' she says, and bites her lip. 'I'll not get a position anywhere else, and we need it.' She pats her belly.

My eyes widen. 'You and McKenzie?'

'In seven months,' she says. 'But I'll still need a place, some work somewhere. He's not just threatening your future. This will finish any marriage prospects Janet might have, too, if it gets out, which it will. Ah, if only you'd got that prussic acid, then I'd have put it in his cocoa!'

'He's always got stomach complaints,' I say. 'He takes laudanum and poppy seeds, and arsenic, too.'

Christina stares.

'It's for *stamina*, he says,' I say.

There's silence; the word 'arsenic' hangs in the air. There's a thrumming in the room, though; the blood of the three of us, pulsing through our veins. I know I should dismiss Janet, send her to our room. But I don't. I need her, and clasp her hand. Then put my other hand out for Christina to take.

'Isn't he ill? Isn't he *always* ill? And by his own hand? His stomach complaints,' I say, desperation making my voice climb a little higher.

Christina motions for me to quieten. 'Let me think,' she says, and so we do, we three. We think, and we think, and then, when the thinking is done, and it's time to speak, we do so in low whispers.

Christina takes up a kitchen knife and nicks a tiny cut first in my middle finger, then Janet's, then her own.

'We're bound now,' she says, and Janet and I nod. 'If one falls, we all do.'

We press our bloodied fingertips together.

'Blood sisters,' says Janet.

'Blood sisters,' say Christina and I together.

Later, I scribble a reply to Emile asking him to meet with me tonight, one final time, before he goes to Papa. Then I splash water on my face, pat it dry and smooth my hair as carefully as any woman who's not mad might, and Janet and I dress for the outing we have so recently decided upon. John takes my letter, to deliver it straightaway.

Outside is a chilly but sunny February day. We take the back door out into the lane, because too many callers come to the front door. Dressmakers and florists and masters of ceremonies. Victuallers and vintners; dance masters and milliners. They seek out Mama like hunters stalking deer; as we step into the lane, the front door bell rings, and behind us Christina gives us a shove, says, 'Hurry!'

The February sunlight seems too bright, though, and I almost lose my nerve, wanting only to run back to the shadows of the house. But Janet pulls me towards the gardens opposite in the middle of the square, where buds are showing on the trees and green shoots push through the earth by the railings.

So much new life.

The view down to the river's too bright today as well. Thanks to the wind blowing the fog and the soot from the St Rollox chimney far away to the east, blue skies gleam and the far-off water glitters, making me think of Rowaleyn and summer, and my wedding day.

'Isn't this a pretty colour, Maddie? Will you wear it in June?' Janet says, stopping at a shop window. She points at the pink ribbon there, her breath steaming up the glass.

'Perhaps,' I say. 'Ah, look, what's that there?'

There's another shop sign further along, Murdoch Brothers, the druggists. When we get there, I insist on Janet waiting outside for me. Inside is gloomy, with huge glass bottles with all sorts of horrible things inside them, each with a label on it, sitting on the mahogany shelves behind the counter. I place my order with the chemists' boy, who marks the date.

February 21st.

Once outside again, I take Janet's arm, and we make our way back to the house. I'm worried about how excitable she can be, how talkative, how friendly. As if she's reading my thoughts, she squeezes my hand, says, 'I love you, Maddie.'

Back at the house, I get ready again to go out with William tonight, before Emile comes. In the kitchen, Christina's busy. I place my purchase from Murdoch's in the scullery, under some other boxes.

Janet and I have a quick supper in the kitchen, then when William calls for me, she goes up to Mama in the drawing room. It's a clear night, and the stars sparkle above us as he hands me into the carriage. I'm very chatty, for I'm nervous, and he notices.

'But you know the Middletons well,' he says, thinking it's the company at the reverend's party that is making me jittery.

'Yes,' I say, smiling weakly, 'but this time I'm with my husband-to-be.'

He pats my arm, and doesn't wonder.

It's after ten before I return. I kiss William goodbye by the front door, and he leaves for his own apartments next door, while I slip inside and run down to my bedroom. Janet lies in bed, wide awake. I put my finger to my lips, and she nods.

I think my little sister has the strongest will of the three of us. I try to look more resolute than I feel, change into my nightgown and get into bed beside her. There's an hour before he's due to call, and I hold Janet, and stroke her hair, while the clock ticks.

Tap, tap, tap.

When it's time, I go along the basement corridor to the kitchen, past Christina's bedroom, whose door is shut tight. I tip the contents of my purchase earlier into a saucer, which I place on the high shelf beside the canister of cocoa. Then I sit alone, breathing lightly in front of the kitchen fire as I've done so many times before. When his signal comes, I go to the back door; the gate is left off the latch, as arranged.

As I lead him into the kitchen, he says, 'It's a perishing night. Warm me quickly, Mimi, for God's sake.'

He paws at me a while, his mouth dry and so foul-smelling it almost makes me gag. He lifts up my hems as usual but there's a perfunctory quality to his movements, and I know it's not what he really wants. Not from me, not anymore. I respond half-heartedly, though, which annoys him into stopping.

'Let me make you some cocoa,' I say, pulling down my hems. I must be nicer, be more welcoming. I smooth back his greasy hair, let him settle in a chair by the fire. He's cross, though.

'Now I know about William Minnoch and you, as everybody else does, it seems,' he says. 'But you still haven't told your Papa about us. Time is running out, Mimi dear.'

I swallow. 'It's not true about him – Janet was wrong to tell you. Ah, be patient, Emile, it'll break Papa's heart when I tell him – and he's not been well. I wish you'd understand, it's cruel what you are doing—'

He snatches my hand. 'I wish *you* would understand; I'll not let go. So then *I* will tell him. You said in your letter that you had come to your senses, but it seems not. So – tomorrow will be the right day.'

I plead, 'No, no,' but he says, 'So perhaps this will be our last night together? If you think he will disown you, I will have to fetch my Mimi from the gutter, where her Papa has thrown her. But I think that perhaps I'll not bother, since she has failed me so badly. I prefer to leave her there.'

'No, Emile,' I plead with him again. 'No – please – for your Mimi.'

I shiver; the fire is low, there's only just enough heat to boil some milk. I get the jar from the shelf before he can refuse. As the milk warms, I stir in the cocoa, but he's watching me, and I can't think how to divert his attention and sprinkle in a few grains of what's needed without him seeing what I'm doing.

Just then, though, something clatters in Christina's little room along the corridor. The noise has him out of his chair, heading towards the kitchen door.

I reach up and take a pinch from the saucer that's beside the canister, and sprinkle it quickly into the cup of cocoa before he turns round.

'It was nothing,' he says, shrugging, and sits down. 'Not enough to waken your Papa upstairs, anyway – not yet, that is.'

I don't reply, but hand him the cup of cocoa.

He sips it hungrily, then grimaces. 'I always have to tell you to *stir* it, Mimi. These little particles are worse than usual—'

'I'm sorry you were ill before,' I say, hurriedly. 'But I'll look after you always, you know that.'

'So you say,' he grumbles. 'You won't need your letters from me then, will you?' He finishes the cup of cocoa; I can scarcely breathe. 'Expect me around noon. Prepare your Papa, if you can.'

He doesn't kiss me before he leaves, but hurries out the back door and into the chill of the night. My heart beats loudly; I check his cup, then rinse it out in the kitchen sink. I wash the saucer, too, before making my way back to my bedroom, and getting into bed beside a wakeful Janet.

'It's done,' I whisper.

I sleep fitfully, waking over and over, dreaming that he is already transformed; perhaps is already another being, in another body, somewhere far from here. When it's time to get up the next morning, Janet and I go to the kitchen and wait while Christina finishes with breakfast, and the little maid of all work, Agnes, who always arrives at dawn, continues her cleaning upstairs.

By noon, Emile has not shown. There's no note; there are no demands, no threats.

And every day that passes after and I hear a beautiful nothing, my breath grows and my head lifts. The tapping is no more; my skin softens and bends and pinks.

Life with no Emile in it is a pleasant thing.

The last week of February moves slowly since my purchase at Murdoch Brothers, and my meeting with Emile. Every day I expect to hear something about him, but when March begins, and Mama's energy for wedding plans increases, the hours slip by more quickly and I even start to forget to expect bad news, or any news at all.

Papa announces that we will take a short holiday in Bridge of Allan, starting on the 6th. We will be away for eleven whole days, from the 6th to the 17th of March, he says, and a change away from the basement of Blythswood Square, away from the shops and the coffee houses, does not seem so bad to me or to Janet. William will be joining us at some point, too, and suddenly it seems as though Emile never even existed.

Not long before we depart for Bridge of Allan, though, I am waiting outside a coffee house on Bath Street for my friend, Mary Buchanan, who wants to talk to me about my brother, Jack, and what her hopes might be of him. I'm thinking what to tell her, for Jack is very flighty these days, when the plain, short-sighted Miss Perry stops beside me.

Miss Perry is a friend of Emile's whom he has told about us. I smile and nod and think to pass on by, but she stops me.

'Miss Smith!' she says. 'Why, only the other day I was with your *friend*, Monsieur L'Angelier.' And she gives me a disapproving look. 'He said he thought he might *die*, he was so very ill.'

I can only blink, for my heart has stopped. She's dressed head to toe in black and brown as if in mourning and it confuses me, suddenly, thinking she must be mourning him – but perhaps he's already in another body, and that's what she means when she says she has seen him. I look down at my green velvet skirts, my green gloves. Green, the colour of Mama's little bottles.

'And he looked dreadful, so thin and white,' Miss Perry is saying. 'He'd actually fallen down, he was so badly taken. He couldn't even ring the bell for his landlady to help him.'

Suddenly, I think I might faint, and must lean against the wall of the shop. 'I had no idea,' I murmur. 'How terrible for him.' My heart resumes beating, if only to sink like an anchor in the Clyde. 'But if you've seen him – he's better now?'

She nods, her head bobbing like a blackbird's. 'He's a *little* bit better. But he – has peculiar thoughts. He said – well, I think you must speak with him, my dear.' She stops and considers me, her bird-head cocked and little beak pouting. 'Perhaps the delirium hadn't quite left him; perhaps that is what made him say to me the things that he did. About *you*, I mean,' she says, a little flustered, then purses her thin lips.

'I cannot think why he would. I've not seen him in a long time.'

'Really? But he said he had seen you! Only two weeks ago. I thought that—'

'Oh yes, a few weeks past. But I have been so very busy since.'

'With your engagement – yes, he told me. Ah, such a secret to carry.'

I want to point out her misunderstanding, that it's William, not Emile, I am marrying.

But then she says, 'I do hope you can make him happy, for he doesn't look as a man about to be married should,' and a coil of fear twists so hard in my belly I can't even reply.

When my friend Mary Buchanan arrives, I tell her something has happened at home and I must go back to Blythswood Square. Sure enough, there's a note in the kitchen from Emile. Christina looks furious and petrified.

'You couldn't have used enough,' she says, pointing at the note.

I read it. 'He wants to visit me tonight.'

'No – no, he can't. I won't go through this again,' says Christina. I'm astonished. 'What *you* have to go through? It's me – alone!'

'Alone? *We three*, you've been saying all this time. I'm happy for it to be you alone, believe me.'

But we don't have time to argue like this. I hurry to my room and pen him a reply, hoping to delay him with good wishes for his better health.

On Friday we go to Stirling for almost a fortnight. I am so sorry, my dearest pet, I cannot see you ere we go – but I cannot.

Will you write me for Thursday, at eight o'clock, and I shall get it before I go – which will be a comfort to me – as I shall not hear from you till I come home again.

I will write you – but, sweet pet, it may be only once a week – as I have so many friends in that quarter.

Write me for Thursday, sweet love.

It works; Emile says he is ill again, but not so severe. He must see a doctor, his landlady has said. And so all is quiet until the morning of Friday, March 6th.

The day we leave for Bridge of Allan.

Emile writes that morning that his doctor says *he* must go to Bridge of Allan, too, that a holiday will help cure his stomach complaints.

I must be cool, in spite of his threats, for the mad woman is hovering at the edges once again, just waiting for me to make a mistake. 'They'll put you away,' she sings and sings in my head – and I saw it in Miss Perry's eyes, the way she considered me a few days ago.

Tap, tap, tap.

But we are due to leave for Bridge of Allan in only a few hours.

I give the houseboy, John, a note, telling Mary Buchanan to meet me on Sauchiehall Street in an hour's time. She's to be my bridesmaid, after all; I must get a few things for my trousseau before we leave town, I write. Then I hurry to be ready, before heading out into the sunshine to meet her.

First, though, I tell her, I have an urgent purchase to make at Currie's, a different druggist on Sauchiehall Street. Mary and I make for Paterson's, and I buy more fripperies that I do not need. Then I rush back to Blythswood Square, for we are due to leave so very shortly, and Mama is shouting all over the place.

In the kitchen, I nod at Christina and whisper, 'I will take it to Bridge of Allan, should he come there.'

'And use it *all* this time,' she mutters.

Emile doesn't come to Bridge of Allan after all.

Every day I wait on tenterhooks for a letter; every time the bell rings at the house where we are staying, I start, and wonder how to manage it, should he appear to Papa with my letters. But it seems he will not, for there's been no word from him. I keep my little package close by me at all times, hidden in my purse, for I can't have any of the maids here discover it.

'I've been reading more about America,' I tell William, as we stroll along the main street of the town together, my hand resting on his arm. It's an open view, with the hills so close and the air so clean and fresh. So far from the St Rollox chimney; so far from industrial soot and dirt.

'What's your fascination with that place?' William says. 'You talk about the clean air here, how much you love it, Madeleine – so what do you imagine New York is like?'

He's the only who calls me that; he says 'Maddie' is too childish, and he doesn't care for nicknames at all anymore, so he doesn't use 'Mimi' either.

'I think we might visit at least, and see,' I say.

'But does it have great sights, great monuments and libraries and galleries? I've heard folk say it's to scrub about in and get their hands dirty.'

He stops, and leads me to a bench where we sit in the March sun.

'The package in your purse,' he says, nodding to it. 'I did not mean to look, but—'

'This is the second time, William,' I say, feeling panicked. 'Do you mean to search my purse every day when we are married?' I'm flustered, standing up, gathering my purse to me.

He says, quietly, 'It's a druggist's purchase, Madeleine. What is in it? I have a right to know, as your fiancé.'

'It is – it is for my complexion. It brightens it.'

'It's a poison; I know that from the little skull in the corner.'

I say, 'Another girl told me about it, when I was at Mrs Gorton's Academy. Arsenic calms redness in the skin; it makes it more – translucent. I just don't care to leave it at home – servants do talk, and it's none of their business.'

He gives me a strange look. 'It's not up to me to advise you on beauty methods,' he says, slowly. 'But you must take care with it. One slip and it could be very bad. If a person should take it unawares, for instance . . .'

I can't make out his look, or his words.

'I will take the greatest care, William,' I say.

'And that gentleman – he has not been bothering you again?'

'Monsieur L'Angelier? No, no, not at all. I think it has all been resolved, William.'

'Then I'm glad to hear it.'

But on the very last day of our holiday, on Tuesday, the dreaded note arrives.

Emile writes that he's on his way to us in Bridge of Allan, and he's bringing all my letters to show Papa. I scribble a note back, telling him that we're leaving within the hour, and suggesting that he meet me at Blythswood Square on Thursday night instead, for by the time he arrives here, we will be gone.

I have only a little time. The day after we arrive back at the square, just a little after noon, I send an urgent note to Mary Buchanan to meet with me again, for there are more ribbons to be bought, as a matter of urgency, I say. I go to Currie's a second time, for I'm worried that what I bought last time won't be enough on its own after all.

I must be sure. I must be sure.

I purse my lips first, then smile pleasantly when Mr Currie enters from a back room. 'It's for the gardener at Rowaleyn,' I say, when he asks why I want it. 'He's been having some trouble with pests, rats and mice.'

He shows me the book where I have to sign for it.

'Of course,' I say, and smile again. He notes the date.

Wednesday, 18th March.

He takes down a large china canister and weighs out one and a half ounces on his special scales. I'm used to the colour of it now, but he feels obliged to explain, anyway.

'We must mix it with soot,' he says, 'so that it might not be mistaken for anything else. Flour, and the like.'

'Of course,' I say, nodding. 'How sensible. I imagine people still make mistakes, though.'

He doesn't reply, but merely lets the boy package up what he has measured out.

I'm anxious, suddenly, that it's not enough. One and a half ounces looks like barely anything, and most of it looks dark.

'Will it be enough?' I say. 'What if it is all soot?'

'We use one ounce of soot to a pound of arsenic, Miss Smith,' he says. 'So there's enough for rats, all right. But you only need a pinch. That'll sort a whole nest of them.'

Six shillings' worth doesn't look like so much, I think. But I take the package, small as it is, and thank them both.

I still haven't found another way, I say to Christina later. Cocoa is no good. It must be by another means, but what, I have no idea, and all that evening, I fret about baking cakes, or bread, or some other food.

On Thursday evening, though, Emile doesn't appear as I requested. I send a note, expressing my surprise that he did not show. I'm skittish all of Friday, waiting for a response, but it doesn't come. Mama puts my jumpiness down to wedding nerves.

Finally, on Saturday, I can bear it no longer and write to Emile, asking him to meet me once again, this time *tomorrow night*.

Tomorrow night.

Do come, sweet love, I write. *Come, and we shall be happy.*

I spend Sunday afternoon with William, who is quiet, and for some reason asks again if I have heard from *that gentleman*. I'm too distressed, and so I lie, tell him that he has indeed written, after a long period of silence. He is making himself very ill taking laudanum, poppy seeds, and the like, I say, to which I attribute his writing to me again.

'I wonder he is not dead, he is ill so often,' I say. 'He would come back in another form, as something else – would he not?'

'We do not change our inner selves,' William says. 'Reincarnation does not change the essence of who we are.'

'Then he'll return a wolf,' I say. 'I am sure he will do himself a mischief.'

'Perhaps he will learn in his next life,' William says, and then we talk of other things, the wedding, our honeymoon, his apartments next door where I will live with him.

But our conversation stays in my head. The idea that Emile will return to the world as what he is inside, no matter what form he takes. A wolf.

When I get back to the house, I have a late supper with Mama and Papa and Janet. John announces the news that Christina is laid low with a stomach upset and has retired to her room, just as we have planned it between us, so Janet and I say nothing, but Mama and Papa complain together about servants.

After supper, I go down to Christina's little bedroom, which she will vacate later. I tell her *how* I have decided to do it; the method I've chosen.

She stares, disbelieving, then says, 'I won't stay for that. You're mad.'

'Don't you see?' I say. Tears make me rub my eyes. 'It's not like a – poison to scatter for putting down rats. That was my mistake before.' My teeth start to chatter, though her room isn't cold. 'I have to think differently – like how a hunter would kill a wolf. A bullet that goes deep inside. Or a knife. Some *plunging* thing.'

I scarcely believe it myself.

Christina's eyes are round and fearful. 'You're not going to tell Janet *how*, are you?' she says. I bite my lip. 'You can't, Maddie. She's too young for any of this as it is.'

'How else will she learn the real danger of some men?' I murmur, but Christina seizes my wrist.

'You're not to tell her; don't do it. This is just for us, you and me. We're the only ones who'll ever know the – *how*. Tell her what her part in it is, but don't explain the rest. You'll regret it if you do, Maddie.'

I think of the look on Janet's face. My intention falters. 'All right,' I say, at last. 'Only you and I will know.'

And so much later, at ten o'clock, when Janet goes to bed as we have arranged, I kiss her in silence, and change into my nightgown.

Janet lies under the sheets, eyes wide open. I put a finger to my lips, and blow out the candle.

'Do not come in to the kitchen,' I whisper. 'No matter what you hear. You might cause a – *distraction*, you know? And there can't be anything to disturb – what I'm doing.'

She nods in the gloom.

Along the passage I go once more. A dim candle lights Christina's room, which she has prepared for us. I pass on through the corridor to the kitchen, and through to the back door, where I lift the latch. Then I return to the kitchen, and wait, alone.

When he appears just before midnight, he's hot, dishevelled, his eyes glazed, his face yellow. He's walked all the way from the station, after chasing me to Bridge of Allan as he thought we were still there, and only received my note to meet a few hours ago. 'You exhaust me, Mimi, thinking you can avoid me for ever, but you can't.'

His words are a little slurred but there's no wine on his breath.

'I never want that, I only want—' I say.

'A husband, a child?' He grabs me, suddenly, and pushes me clumsily against the wall of the kitchen. He's fumbling under my nightgown but in a wretched, desperate way. This is not my plan at all.

I mutter, 'Let me be loving you, husband; let me.'

He stops, stands back, swaying. Whatever he's taken – laudanum, poppy seeds, arsenic, perhaps – he's almost delirious with it.

I soothe him as much as I can, kiss and stroke his cheek. 'My dear husband. Christina's room – shall we go there instead? You are too exhausted . . .'

My hands drift down below his waistband; my fingers stroke and fondle him there. His eyes close; he murmurs, 'Yes, yes.' I pull away and hurry into Christina's room. In the low light of the candle she nods, then gets out of bed, and scurries along to the bedroom where Janet lies.

Back in the kitchen, the fire is out. I take Emile by the hand and lead him into Christina's room, guiding him to the bed. We sit, and I continue to stroke and kiss him. Then I get off the bed and reach under it for the box. I take out the object.

'My husband,' I whisper. 'Let me do this for you.'

He sighs and nods, murmurs, 'Hurry, Mimi,' as he loosens his waistband and lies face down on the bed.

I warm the object in my hands first. Under the bed are two dishes. One holds goose fat; the other, sooty powder. I rub some fat over the tip of the object. Then I take some of the powder and press it on to the very tip of the object. Then I apply more goose fat; then more powder.

Emile murmurs as I begin, my fingers coated with goose fat, probing soft and gentle at first, before he's aroused enough to urge me on. Only when he is desperate and begging do I push between his buttocks and gently ease in the tip of the object, thick with fat, powder grains submerged within it. Slowly and with care I work again and again, dabbing more powder on to the tip when I remove it at certain points, before pushing it in once more. Each time I'm ready to stop should he feel the grains, say that something feels wrong.

But he doesn't. He's in a kind of delirium all through it, and only when he reaches a kind of exhausted pitch and spills himself am I able to stop. I have no notion of whether I've used enough, whether it will work. I only want to weep, and go to bed, but I must wipe the object clean first, and put it back into the box before he sees it.

I murmur some soft words as he lies there. 'I can't make cocoa, for the fire has gone out in the kitchen,' I whisper, but he says that's no matter.

'This time, Mimi,' he says, rolling at last on to his back to pull up his trousers, 'at noon.' He slurs a little, sounds woozy. 'Nothing will stop me coming at noon.'

'Yes.' I nod. 'Noon. Papa. I'll be ready. We'll tell him together,' I say, 'about our engagement.'

I help him off the bed, and fetch his coat. He sways in the

darkness for a few moments before I can guide him to the back door. It is just after one.

I go back to the bedroom, where Janet and Christina are sitting up, waiting for me.

'It's done,' I say. 'It's done.'

Christina says nothing, just hurries back to her room. Janet opens her arms to me, and I lie there, shivering for a while, until we both fall asleep.

Janet wakes first that Monday morning, but I lie in bed till it's almost ten o'clock. I cannot face the day, but I must. When William and I are married, we'll not go traipsing about the place so much as Mama and Papa, I think. I'll rest more; will be good and quiet.

When the doorbell rings upstairs, I assume it's for Mama, as Papa is at his office, and I'm not expecting any friends or callers.

Eventually I have to get out of bed and wash. In the kitchen, Christina's making porridge. We don't say much to one another, beyond a nod and a look. Janet chatters about some birds, or kittens, I can't be sure.

'I might go out later,' I say to her, sipping my coffee. 'Do you want to come with me? We can take the air.'

'Yes,' says Christina before Janet can answer. 'Get out from under my feet, the pair of you.'

I don't want to be here when noon comes; Christina doesn't either, I can see that, but she has no choice.

Janet and I return to our bedroom and I take particular care with my dress, my hat, my jacket, for we'll meet so many well-wishers out in town now that the wedding banns have been posted, I say, that I have to give them the best account of myself.

I've just fixed my bonnet and taken up my purse when the front door upstairs bangs hard. Janet looks at me, alarmed; I shrug and make a face.

'Hat-makers, maybe,' I say, and we head out along the basement corridor. 'Hurry,' I add, for Janet drags her heels so, 'before Mama catches us and keeps us indoors!'

But we've only reached the bottom of the stairs when Mama appears at the top of them. Her face is utterly unreadable.

'Maddie, I have to speak with you at once,' she says in a shaking voice.

I look at Janet, whose hands grip her little purse. 'But we are about to go shopping – may it not wait, Mama?'

'It will not wait. Nor should it. I think—' Mama breaks off, and wobbles on her heels, tips forward so that both Janet and I believe she's about to tumble down the stairs. We rush up to catch her, just in time.

'Dear God, Maddie,' she breathes, looking up at me, as I hold her steady. 'How could you? How could you?'

It's Christina who pats Mama's hand and fans her face and tells her to be calm when she collapses on us at the top of the stairs; it's Christina who pulls from her pocket her own little brown bottle and shakes a couple of drops on to Mama's tongue when she can be still enough for it.

'I must have dreamt it – what that woman said—' Mama gasps at last.

I must comfort Janet, who clings to my waist.

'What woman, Mama?' I ask, but Christina gives me a terrible look and Mama only points at me with a trembling finger.

'She came for you. You. Come upstairs with me, now,' Mama

pants, and so Christina heaves her to her feet, and I tell Janet to wait for me in the kitchen.

In Mama's room, she arranges herself on the bed, hand to her forehead.

'Oh, Mama, whatever is the matter?' I say. 'I was about to go shopping with Janet, I need—'

'That woman who just called here,' Mama interrupts, her breath coming short and heavy. 'Her name is Miss Perry. She says that she is a friend of that awful man you once knew. That she met you in the street a few weeks ago.'

I catch myself a moment, then steady my voice and say, 'Why on earth would Miss Perry call—?'

'Oh dear God. I can hardly believe it.' But Mama is fidgeting so badly that she cannot go on, and I have to sit on the end of her bed and wait for her to speak. Finally she says, 'Just tell me, Maddie, that you did not meet with that man. That you kept your promise to me.'

'That man?'

'Please, this is no time for games. The Frenchman, Angelier.'

'You mean Emile? Of course not. I wouldn't disobey you, Mama.'

She stares at me, then blinks hard. 'Miss Perry says otherwise.'

'Miss Perry is a silly woman who says nothing sensible—'

'The man is *dead*, Madeleine! Only this morning. The man is *dead*.'

Mama's bed tilts oddly underneath me then, as though I'm on a boat out at sea. Even when I grip the quilt edge, it doesn't stop tilting. Wave after wave seem to roll the bed back and forth; I close my eyes, but that makes it worse, so I have to keep them open, even though everything is rocking so much I think I might be sick.

'Miss Perry came straight here because of what she says is your *engagement* to him.' Mama is hoarse. 'I told her there was no such thing, but she said *she had it directly from him*, and as lately as only a few days ago! Dear God, what have you been doing? How many people think this, if Miss Perry does? You are engaged to *William*. How can this be true?'

I open my mouth but no words come out. I'm a fish, gasping for air. I need one of Mama's little bottles if I'm not to suffocate here in her too-warm room. But Mama cannot stop talking.

'She says he appears to have died from taking something foul. She said the smell in his room was terrible. His landlady is in a state of shock. She went for the doctor but there was nothing he could do.'

'She was *in his room*?'

'What does that matter? She insisted on seeing him for herself – it is more than I could have done.'

But all I can think of is what I have failed to consider, in my focus on Emile alone: the very existence of my letters. Which will be sitting in a pile, perhaps, on top of his desk, ready for him to bring to Papa today. My letters, which I must retrieve somehow, or all of this will have been for nothing!

How could I have failed to see that he wouldn't have brought them with him last night? I had only one thought: *will it work this time?*

I close my eyes as Mama babbles; all I can see is the object, pushing in, over and over.

Then it occurs to me that Miss Perry might have seen my letters, if they were left on his desk. Why, anyone who goes into his room will see them! A doctor; his landlady. I put my hands over my ears to still my rocking head. Mama smacks her hand on the mattress suddenly, and my heart jumps.

'Are you listening to me? This sordid horror of a story – and *you* are connected to him. People think you are *engaged* to him. Dear God, what will your father say? This will get out. How can we quieten it when the man is dead? Madeleine – Madeleine!'

When I come round from slipping off Mama's bed on to the floor in a faint, it's not Christina's bottle that works for me. No, a little brandy on my lips is enough to do the trick; then a little waft of smelling salts, too, and I'm revived enough for Christina to help me downstairs to my bed, while Mama shouts more questions after me and cries out orders for Papa to be fetched immediately.

In bed, I lie under the covers, breathing as lightly possible. I want to tell Mama that Emile isn't *dead*; if William gave me permission to, I could explain to her about reincarnation, and how he will merely go on to occupy another body.

He is not *dead* as we understand it.

But my letters are a different matter.

I must go now, get them back. I sit up in a rush, grab at my boots and my coat. Janet comes in then and calls for Christina, who runs in and wrestles me back on to the bed when I try to get up.

'You don't understand,' I pant. 'I have to go to Emile's rooms – I have to get my letters.'

'Are you mad?' Christina says. 'You can't just walk into a dead man's rooms and help yourself. Be quiet, Maddie. Don't make me slap you, because I will.'

Janet quivers in the doorway. Suddenly there's a crack on my cheek as Christina slaps me.

'Shut up!' she says. 'Shut up about your letters and get a grip of yourself!'

Janet's staring in wide-eyed horror; I'm thrown back on the bed, with Christina pressing down on my shoulders.

I'm panting, out of breath, but I'm still at last. Upstairs, the front door bangs open and closed. Papa. We all look towards the corridor, as though he might appear at any moment, raving and furious.

Tap, tap, tap.

I shake my head furiously, mutter, 'Stop that sound, stop it,' and Christina stills my face with her rough hands.

'It's just the clock,' she says, 'counting twelve. Just the clock on the mantelpiece, Maddie.'

Noon. The time he was due. So I've been unconscious this long after Mama spoke to me. Time's slipping about, like a drunk man on an icy street. I'm burning all over; Christina soaks a handkerchief in the wash bowl and pats my face.

'You need to prepare yourself better than this,' she says. 'I had no choice, smacking you like that.'

'I'm calm now,' I say, though the heat in my bones says otherwise.

She stops dabbing my cheeks; when I touch them, though, it's like touching flame.

'I sent John to find out what they're saying,' she says under her breath. 'The news is out now – folk are saying that he killed himself.'

'But his connection to me – they'll find that, if anyone reads my letters. And then it's over, Christina. For all of us. *Blood sisters.*'

She swallows.

I hold her hands. 'We have to find a way to get my letters back.'

'But how?'

'Send John out again.'

'A houseboy can't just walk in there and take them! You've landed him in enough trouble making him deliver so many. And me. God, why did I accept that crinoline off him? Let the two of you have my room?' She groans.

'You've done more than that,' I say, quietly.

Christina nods at Janet, sitting in the corner, pale and still. 'And so has she.'

Blood sisters.

'I'll think of a way,' I say, just as John arrives, breathless, in the doorway.

'The master says to go up to the drawing room, Miss Madeleine,' he says.

'Tell him I'm too unwell,' I say.

'He said to take no excuses.'

'Come on,' says Christina, pulling me up by my elbow. 'Splash your face and tidy your hair. You've got one chance at this.'

They'll put you away.

You've got one chance at this.

Tap, tap, tap.

Upstairs I go, shaking on feeble legs. Outside, it's a cold March day, a blowing day, a biting day. Something inside the house nips at my heels; even my hair seems alive. I know Christina's watching me from the bottom of the stairs; if I turn round and she's still looking at me, she'll turn to stone.

So I twist to see, but she's not there, and light from the open drawing-room door is beckoning instead. I shake out my skirts, set my shoulders back, try not to tremble. I have one aim in mind: my letters.

'Papa,' I begin softly on entering, 'I've heard that—'

But another man's in the room with him, and one I recognise. The French consul, Monsieur de Mean, the friend of Emile's he used to lodge with sometimes in Helensburgh. We had met him once or twice on the few occasions that we went out walking together.

'Sit down, Madeleine,' Papa says. He's white-faced, and looks years older. 'Your Mama is in bed; she has informed me of – of what has occurred.'

Monsieur de Mean nods and I curtsey before taking a chair.

'I was visited today by Mr William Stevenson.' Monsieur de Mean directs his words to me. 'He is the employer of the late Monsieur L'Angelier – God rest his soul – at Huggins and Company.'

Monsieur de Mean is a very handsome Frenchman, with dashing black hair that shines, and a black beard, and a moustache that he fingers each time he stops speaking. I try to picture him in other circumstances, but the image won't come to my mind at all. He coughs.

'He bade me come today to Monsieur L'Angelier's apartments at Franklin Place. His body has been removed' – he directs this to my father, but Papa's staring out of the window and so he addresses me again – 'and his landlady, Mrs Jenkins, asked me to remove some of his belongings.'

His belongings. *My* letters. And my heart lifts. I want Papa gone so that I may take Monsieur de Mean into my confidence properly; my brain struggles to think of a reason.

'I found a letter in the pocket of his coat,' Monsieur de Mean is saying. 'It seems that Monsieur L'Angelier had gone to Bridge of Allan, and a note directed to him here in town was forwarded to him there. The delivery of that note called him back here, to town.'

I swallow softly.

'The note appears to have been written by you, Mam'selle Smith.'

I realise that Monsieur de Mean has already told Papa, whose head jolts back.

'Your father has requested that I recover any more such – *notes*,' Monsieur de Mean begins, but he's interrupted by Papa, who says to me, 'Are there more, Madeleine? How many more?'

I can't speak.

'Are there any more?' he barks.

'You would be better to let me know,' Monsieur de Mean says, softly. 'I will call tomorrow morning at Huggins and Company. Mr Stevenson has the key to his desk, and I will request it from him and retrieve anything inside—'

'You will?' I say. 'Oh, but that's good for—'

Papa seizes the poker and strikes the mantelpiece with it, making us both start. He hits it over and over, and one of Mama's favourite pieces, a Dresden shepherdess, is caught by it and smashes into tiny pieces.

Papa stops then. He has his back to me; his shoulders are shaking.

Monsieur de Mean bends towards me and whispers in my ear, 'How many letters might I expect to find?'

'I don't know,' I murmur, truthfully.

'A great many?'

'Possibly.'

'I forbade you *the summer before last* to have anything more to do with the man,' says Papa. He's staring at the mantelpiece, at the china crumbs of the shepherdess.

'I will do everything I can to keep this matter quiet, Mr Smith,' Monsieur de Mean says.

His words hang in the air; I stand and try to catch them, thinking to put them in my pocket, for if I take them and hide them, they'll not exist, and nothing that has happened today will be real. But when I take a step forward, the room spins and tips just like before, and once again, I lose my footing and tumble to the floor.

It's dark when I wake to *tap, tap, tap*, but it's only the clock striking three, for it's the middle of the night. Janet sleeps by my side, snoring softly. It might be any other night, only it's not, for everything has changed, and when the world wakes in a few hours, everything will have changed again. But for the better, this time, when Monsieur de Mean retrieves my letters.

I fall asleep; there's no more tapping in my head. Next time, when I wake, it's to Christina shaking me. It's almost nine in the morning; whatever she gave me last night – I remember something dimly – has done its work. So I eat quietly in the kitchen with Janet, restored enough to enjoy a little coffee and toast.

'Maybe we can walk out today,' I whisper to Janet. 'Go to the shops. Once Monsieur de Mean has been, of course.'

We spend the morning getting dressed, Janet and I, but as the minutes pass I grow more uneasy. Surely Monsieur de Mean would have gone first thing to get the key from Mr Stevenson at Huggins? At noon, the bell upstairs goes, and shortly afterwards, I'm ordered up to the drawing room.

I haven't seen Mama since I fainted in her bedroom, or Papa since I fainted in the drawing room. They both look at me oddly, as though I don't belong to them. I curtsey to them, and to Monsieur de Mean, who's just arrived. He's out of breath and seems anxious.

'Mr Stevenson would not hand over the key,' he says straightaway, dashing my hopes before I've even sat down. 'And – he has paid for a post-mortem, too, which has taken place this morning.'

'Will there be – an *inquest*?' asks my father. My mama grasps his hand, blinking, and I realise she's about to weep.

'Yes,' says Monsieur de Mean. 'Madeleine – Miss Smith. I must ask you – forgive me, but it is very important that you tell me – did you meet with Monsieur L'Angelier at any time in the hours before he died?'

A wave of nausea rolls through me and my legs wobble. I swoon a little, wait for the wave to wash over me completely and bring me down to the floor, but this time, it doesn't. I sit down, gulp and try to swallow, but my throat's too dry. Monsieur de Mean repeats his question.

'Of course not,' I whisper. 'No – no, I haven't seen him at all. Not for – a long, long time.'

'How long?'

'Months – weeks. I didn't even know he'd left the city until you told us yesterday.'

'The note from you—'

'Only to tell him – about my engagement to Mr Minnoch. I thought to explain it to his face – and to ask for my letters.'

My mother lets out a terrible groan and seems to fall; my father holds her up. Monsieur de Mean looks terrified for them both and lifts his hands. They're like actors in a play, and I wonder about the staging of it, this scene. I put my hand to my brow; perhaps, I think, if we all pretend enough—

'Did he ever call on you here?' Monsieur de Mean asks, breaking into my thoughts.

The look on his face says he knows the answer, so I sigh and say, 'Oh, no! Well, not inside the house. I sometimes spoke to him – at my window. Only to tell him to go away, Papa!'

My father's moving across the room towards me like a hunter retrieving his catch; I shrink back in my seat.

'He was so very distraught about my engagement,' I say. 'He was not – *right*. In his head, I mean. Monsieur de Mean, you were his friend; you know it, too. How wrong in his head he could be. How very persistent. I'm not the only one of my acquaintance, Mama, to have a persistent admirer. Someone who doesn't listen when you tell them to go away. He *terrified* me with his obsessions. I thought he would do me harm. I wrote only to tell him to stay away, over and over. But he was like a madman—'

I burst into tears; Mama murmurs something. Papa stops at my chair.

'Oh my dear, why did you not tell us?' Mama's saying now, to my great surprise. I lift my head. Her face is full of anguish. *This is not my fault.* 'Dearest Maddie, why did you never speak to us about it? My child, we would have *protected* you – we would have done something – James, we should have reported this man.'

She's out of her chair now, patting my father's arm in a reproving manner.

Papa looks abashed, ashamed suddenly.

'You're right,' he says, shaking his head. 'I'll never forgive myself for not chasing him away. You should have told us the truth, Maddie.' And just like that, it's back to me, so I must bat away this blame again.

'He threatened me, if I told anyone. I was so afraid. I thought he might hurt Janet, too. He commented once, how pretty she was – oh, I couldn't let him hurt her—'

Papa's face looks fit to burst; Mama gasps in horror. She runs to me, puts her arm around my shoulders.

'A monster!' she says. 'A monster of a man – James, James!'

'It's as well he's dead,' my father mutters. 'Or I'd have killed him myself.'

Mama gasps.

I say, quickly, 'I did just as you asked, Papa. I told him to leave me alone, over and over again, I promise you—'

Monsieur de Mean, who has been silent through this, coughs suddenly, and I turn to him.

'I must have any – *notes* – returned to me. They are my property!'

'Monsieur L'Angelier is being buried tomorrow,' Monsieur de Mean says. 'But the results of the post-mortem today mean that your – *notes* – are being handed over to the Procurator Fiscal. Probably at this very minute.'

My heart plunges again, and I moan in terror, grip Mama's hand.

'I don't understand,' Mama says. 'My daughter has been the object of a dreadful madman's harassment! James! Can you not stop this? The results of a post-mortem' – she shudders at the word – 'can hardly make a difference.'

'They must – in a case of suspicious death,' says Monsieur de Mean.

Suspicious death.

'Please, Mama,' I murmur. 'Please, Papa. He *was* mad enough for violence and not just to me – oh yes, for he threatened it many times, the harm he'd do *himself*. I couldn't *ignore* it.'

Papa looks as horrified as I've ever seen him. 'My wife is right, Monsieur de Mean,' he says. 'There must be a way to stop this, to get my daughter's notes returned. She shouldn't be connected to this. She has been the victim of a monster, a violent madman. Ah, these abominable foreigners!'

Monsieur de Mean raises an eyebrow but says nothing.

Papa continues, 'They come here to terrify innocent young women! So much that they're afraid even to tell their own families!'

He goes to Mama's side, lays his hand on her shoulder. I begin to weep softly.

'My daughter will not be the subject of gossip and slander,' he says.

Monsieur de Mean watches the three of us, united as a good family must be.

'Then perhaps you will want to engage a lawyer,' he says. 'According to the post-mortem, a great deal of poison was found in Emile's body. A great deal.'

Papa immediately sends out word to a friend of his, a legal counsel who might advise what best to do. That I once encouraged my 'persistent admirer' is forgotten by him, and by Mama, because of the horror of his threats to me, to Janet, to himself. Mama blames herself over and over for not protecting me more, and is terrified at the thought of Janet falling prey to a wicked foreign man, even at thirteen years of age. So she calls for Janet's things to be moved upstairs to her room, as though such men might sneak in and kidnap her from under her nose. But I cannot bear to be alone at night, I tell her, and after some persuasion, she relents.

As for me, I must pace my bedroom floor for hour after hour during the day, until I'm exhausted and it's time for the dinner party I'm due to attend with William at the home of Mr Middleton, our church minister. But I fidget all through the first course, enough to make William still my hands below the dining table. Snatches of conversation jab at my brain and the lights flicker oddly as the main course slowly progresses. The wine's too sweet and too warm, but I'm drinking it more quickly than the houseboy can fill my glass.

And then Mrs Middleton mentions something that catches my breath, mid-sup, and I lean forward to hear what she's saying.

'It was a hideous figurine, made of ivory,' she says. 'Left to me by an aunt in India whom I never met. The ugliest thing I ever saw, some temple goddess or some such.' She laughs, a light, mocking sound.

Her neighbour murmurs something. Everyone else is talking to one another. Then she says, a little more clearly, 'So tell me – did you hide it away somewhere? Where no one can be offended by the sight of it?'

I cut a piece of my fish, wait for her answer.

'At first I did – then the maids kept coming across it, and putting it on show!'

'Did you throw it out?'

'Well, one can hardly throw out *ivory* with the day's rubbish, and you cannot burn it. Nothing will *destroy* it.'

'Did you make a present of it elsewhere?'

'Ah, Mr Middleton would never permit that. So let me simply say that one fine afternoon last summer, we took a trip upriver,' Mrs Middleton replies softly, with a wink. 'A careless moment, and it fell overboard – gone, alas, for ever.'

Her neighbour tsks, and shakes her head as if in sorrow, smiling all the while.

When dawn breaks the next morning, I've made my decision, and dress quickly in the dim light, fastening my heavy cloak, the one with the deepest pockets. Silently, I make my way to Christina's little room and wake her to tell her of my plan, for she must hold the house still and quiet for as long as possible. Then I hurry out into a grey, misty early morning, and cross the square to Blythswood Street, to hurry down the hill past the grand, stately banks and the insurance buildings to James Watt Street, where the tobacco houses and customs warehouses stand.

When I arrive on the busy Broomielaw on the way to the docks, the gloomy light begins to brighten, making me blink and hold up my hand to shield my eyes, even as fishmongers and coal carriers and all sorts of tradesmen jostle and bump alongside.

The river beyond glints sharply between the storehouses and ships that cluster along the dockside.

There's plenty of time before the first boat leaves northwest for Greenock. Rowaleyn is upriver, on the opposite side of Greenock, past Helensburgh. In my purse is money for my ticket; there are very few respectable women about, though, so I stay close to the boat, and am relieved when it's time to board.

A train wouldn't do for my purpose; a boat, sailing on the water, is what I need. Back and forth along the deck I go, keeping a watch for anyone from the house, for I can't say when my disappearance will be noticed, even though Christina has promised to do her best. Janet was fast asleep when I left, and doesn't usually rise until eight.

At last the ship's horn sounds, and off we sail along the narrow tributary all the way to Bowling, before the river widens and we make our way towards Greenock. The air clears; the early morning mist has fully lifted, and the day promises to be a good one. I make no conversation with the few fellow passengers who pass by me on the deck, and receive a few strange looks, for there are mostly working people on the boat at this time. But I owe no explanations.

After a while, the deck is deserted. I stand at the railing, observe the waters, which are choppy and blue. The wind is fierce.

When I ease the wooden box up out of my deep pocket, I take a good look around, but nobody's in sight. Out it comes, that loathsome thing, that object I hate, snug inside its velvet folds.

And then, just like that, I let it go, let it tumble into the water.

At first, it floats, like a feather on a cloud, and I worry someone will see it, will call for it to be seized from the water, somehow. But no shouts rise up; the boat chugs on; and soon we are so far away that the sight of it has disappeared entirely, as the waves fold over and over and over.

And something dreadful and heavy eases from my shoulders then; I close my eyes, lift my face to the sun peeking out from a passing cloud, and breathe deeply. I stretch my arms up as far as possible; wave them gently, as if attracting someone. When I open my eyes, the day seems just as it was, as though nothing has changed, but I know a new sense of peace. A great sigh escapes me and is carried away by the breeze.

When a shout does go up some time later, it's to indicate that we've reached our destination, and the horn sounds. I'm still standing on deck by the same railing; in a few minutes I see the pier, and not long afterwards, the gangway clatters down. I take my time, not rushing, and wait on the dockside for the boat across to Helensburgh. It's a beautiful day indeed, and a short trip across the water, until I disembark a second time, the wide blue sky all around me and the welcoming water below.

I'm so delighted with the day, in fact, that I miss the shouting of my name at first.

'Madeleine! Madeleine!'

Then another voice. 'Maddie? Maddie, what are you doing here?'

It's William, and my brother, Jack. William seizes my arm before I can say a word.

'What on earth, Madeleine?' he says. 'What were you thinking, running off so early, and not a word to anyone? We have come to fetch you back, Jack and I.'

But Jack's too close by.

I whisper only, 'Let's speak of it later, not in front of – *others.*'

He doesn't say another word, but steers me towards a waiting carriage. The three of us climb in, but I cannot speak in front of Jack.

When we get home, Jack gets out of the carriage first. William turns to me as I sit, waiting. 'Tell me why you left your house so early this morning, Madeleine. Tell me now.'

'A gun for a wolf,' I say.

Shaking his head in puzzlement, he says, 'I was worried that you had taken the boat because I thought you meant to throw yourself over. You understand what my beliefs are, don't you? I would have your spirit haunt me, Madeleine, no matter what you did.'

I gaze into his eyes, trying to read something more there. 'I thought you might harm *him*,' I murmur. He starts; does he know who I mean? He must. 'How terrible it would be for you. I dreamt about him hurting you.'

'So you thought – what? To *murder yourself*?' He grips my hand and presses it to his mouth. 'You make no sense, Madeleine.'

But there's no more time to speak, for Papa appears and we must get out of the carriage. I say nothing more, and after William leaves, I explain to Papa that it was the thought of Emile's funeral that made me want to leave the city so urgently and so early.

All day, I flit about, unable to decide on anything, not even what to eat or when to go to bed. Waiting for that wolf's howl, or that *tap, tap, tap*.

The object may be gone, but my letters still exist.

I inch closer to the bedroom fire, as if the flames can burn what's not even there, and only when the edges of my hair begin to singe do I realise I'm too close. Janet enters, shrieking and throwing the water jug at me, which only makes me laugh, before I start to cry.

'Get a grip, Maddie,' mutters Christina in my ear as she heaves me up on to the bed, pulls over the quilt.

'They'll send me away,' I murmur. 'When they read my letters – they'll lock me up.'

My teeth chatter so much that she fetches a hot stone.

Mama looks in, fetched by Janet. 'My poor girl,' she says, and to my amazement, strokes my forehead. 'What that wicked man has done to you!'

My dreams at night are all dark cupboards and unlit passageways, where strange creatures lurk, their stench filling my nostrils and their hard laughter in my ears. I think I see a wolf's tail, and ears, and wake up, screaming, but in fact I'm voiceless, and Janet sleeps on peacefully beside me.

I'm too wretched to get up the next morning, but Christina forces me out of bed. 'Make a show,' she says. 'Don't hide away like a guilty thing.'

Later that day, William calls at the house to see how I am after my trip on the boat yesterday. Up in the drawing room, he won't stop pacing about, and it's irritating me, how he walks back and forth over the same piece of rug. I fancy worn patches already, and bite my lower lip, wonder what Papa will make of *that*.

'I have been thinking about our last conversation,' he says, at last. 'It has been bothering me, what you might have misunderstood about my spiritual beliefs – what you might have *done* on the boat.'

I'm running my forefinger along the mantelpiece; it catches dust. I'll have to tell Christina to get one of the maids up here; it must be clean before our wedding.

'That man you know, who has died – from poison. A great deal of poison,' William says. 'So much that they are asking why so much of it was in him, for a suicide needs only very little – Madeleine, please, will you stop that?'

I hadn't noticed what I was doing, tapping like that on the mantle. With Papa's meerschaum pipe – *tap, tap, tap*, over and over.

William approaches me, tries to take my hand, but I birl away.

'I think everyone is being very silly,' I say.

He says, 'Is there something else you want to tell me, Madeleine? The spirit of the deceased man – he will tell it.'

'Yes, you told me he would be reborn,' I say. 'That was what you said. You told me that "death is the greatest adventure". Isn't that the case? And now he is on that adventure.'

His face is white; it makes his pinkish lips smudge more. 'Did you – did *you* set him on this adventure?'

He is so very close to me, his whispering a tremble at my ear. I touch his lips with my finger. 'I think I hear him. They say there are no more wolves on these isles, but—'

He breaks away from me, horrified.

'You must never say a word about this!' he says. 'What I told you – you must never speak of it again. Not a word of it.'

I frown a little, for I have told him nothing, really. 'I don't know what you mean, William,' I say, a little cross, for so many men have been telling me what to do lately – Emile, Papa, Monsieur de Mean, William.

He says a few more things very quickly that I don't pay attention to, and then he is gone. I open the door to go back downstairs to see Christina and Janet, but then someone pulls the bell outside and suddenly, Christina appears in the hallway.

Mama arrives at the bottom of the staircase as a strange-looking man in a kind of uniform is ushered in through the front door. I wonder if this is perhaps a dream; it feels like one.

'*Madeleine Hamilton Smith?*' he asks abruptly. He looks comical in his beard and whiskers, and his hat and stiff coat.

'Yes,' I reply. 'How may I help you?'

The dream is odd, though; I blink and blink, but it doesn't go away. Mama's hand on my shoulder feels very real; the contours of the hallway are clear.

'My name is Archibald Smith,' he says. 'I am the Sheriff Substitute of Lanarkshire, and I am here to take you into custody concerning the death of Mr Pierre Emile L'Angelier.'

Mama's hand is over her mouth.

'I don't understand,' I say. My heart skips, so I press my palm over it to slow it down. 'Mama – what is—?'

But Mama's hand slips off my shoulder as she falls forward, to be caught by Christina.

I turn calmly to the sheriff, for this may be still a dream, and say, 'Might I fetch a coat downstairs?'

He nods. Mama is shouting; Christina, too.

I glide down to the bedroom, where Janet is. She's alarmed. 'What's all the noise?' she asks.

I explain about the sheriff, then whisper, 'Remember what you must do, yes?' She nods, and I kiss her. 'You promise?'

Blood sisters.

'I promise, Maddie,' she says, white-faced. I have no time to speak alone with Christina, alas, but Janet will do so. I have to hurry back upstairs to the sheriff, who is waiting for me in the hallway. He nods, and opens the front door to the square, and the black carriage waiting for me.

I go down the front steps, slowly. A sudden feeling of dread makes me take great care; a feeling that I will never set foot in this house, or on Blythswood Square, again.

V.

'Why, if you believe Christina Haggart, he did enter the house, and was a whole hour with her on one occasion. Whether then this is anything more than a mere denial to (the Dean of Faculty), whom she may have thought had no right to question her as he did, you will not pay much attention to it, especially if you believe the fact that she had at least one long interview with him.'

– The Lord Justice-Clerk charge to the jury in the trial of Madeleine Smith, 9 July 1857, Edinburgh

New York, 1927

At first I thought he was just teasing. Trying to fool me with that 'someone else knew' remark. Perhaps it was the revelation that he wasn't Teresa's grandson after all that had eased me into a false sense of security, for I still felt it, like a cooling balm on the fire of my anger at his lying.

So I refused to rise to the bait. 'I think you've threatened me for the last time,' I said, quietly.

Outside, the afternoon was warming up, and I wondered how Violet was doing, if maybe she'd called on me while I was out. Harry might not have family – who knew what loved ones he really had? – but I did. That was the main difference between us. I had people I loved, and who loved me.

'I think you must make up your mind what you're going to do, Harry. First, you accuse me of killing Emile along with Mr Minnoch. Now you say that "someone else knew". And this is after telling me you're not my friend's grandson after all, but his business partner – and that he doesn't even know you're here, doing this to me!

'No, Harry, I don't think I can believe a word you say about anything anymore. So don't you think it's better just to call a halt to this – *nonsense*.' I waved my hand in the direction of his equipment. 'Perhaps it's just as well you're not in front of the camera after all. Your own "pretending" could do with a little more work, I think.'

I wanted to goad him; wanted to push him as far as I could now, after all his false history, his vain theories. I was more of a match for him than I'd thought, now I knew more than he did.

'It doesn't bother you,' he said, suddenly, 'what he died of? I expected you'd deny it, sure. But it's an ugly death, arsenic poisoning. An agonising one, and messy, too. You don't seem too disturbed by that, though.'

'I'm the one who's had to remind you we're talking about someone who has died,' I said, bristling a little. 'I'm not the one trying to make money out of a tragedy.'

I'd forgotten I was in the process of leaving, and had sat down, but now I got to my feet again.

Harry seemed to be confused about what to do, in spite of his accusations. It seemed to me I'd really caught him on the hop, so I took my chance and made for the door. To my surprise, he didn't try and stop me. He wasn't done, though.

'You were rich and Emile was poor,' he said. 'He was balancing on that edge the whole time. You toyed with him – made him believe you'd marry him and he'd be secure the rest of his life.'

'Is that your quarrel with me now?' I said, opening the door to the grand but empty corridor of identical gold-framed doors. I couldn't remember which direction the elevator was in, and hesitated. 'You want to expose me because you resent my having had money once?' I turned round to him. 'Really, now – so many motives, so many theories you have, Harry.'

'The balls – the country home – the servants,' he said. He'd got up now, too, was coming out with me, as if to try and intimidate me. 'What chance did a poor man like Emile have? Of course he'd have been bowled over by you. Had his head turned.'

Out in the vestibule, I could scoff at that. 'You disapprove of the rich now, Harry?' I said, opening my arms. 'Look at all of this! You're in the most expensive hotel in the city, maybe the world. You drive a Chrysler. I live in a little apartment in the Bronx. I spent over twenty years in a tiny brownstone on Eighth Avenue. And I'd still take that over a country mansion and servants any day.' I was tired again. 'Now, I insist you take me home,' I said, and he gave that annoying mock-bow of his. To my relief, someone came out of the elevator further along the corridor, so I was able to make my way to it without asking for his help.

Once out in the open again, it was a relief to me to breathe even the dense, humid, city fumes. I exchanged very few words with him on the journey back to Park Avenue, and after he'd left me alone on the stoop and driven away, exhaustion overtook me, and a strange kind of shaking.

I'd had a victory of sorts, but I knew it was only temporary. The final battle was still to come, for Harry wasn't one to admit defeat and I didn't think he'd let me go, not without a fight.

What the outcome of our last battle would be I couldn't yet see, and I still hadn't figured how to stop Violet from discovering it all.

Perhaps that was why, that very night, I dreamt of Willy and of my mother. They were holding out their arms, urging me to them. *Hurry*, they seemed to say. *Hurry to us*. And I was running to them, my arms outstretched, too. But deep down as I was running, I knew it was wrong, what I was doing. I knew it meant eternal damnation if I did as they bade me; what else can you call it but damnation, when you force that journey on yourself before your time?

They wanted me with them because they loved me, they said. I ran to them because I loved them both, too. But I loved Violet as well, and Tom. And to take the easy way out, to put an end to one's self? I wasn't religious enough to attend church, but I did believe in a spirit that went on beyond us, and I did believe in Heaven and in Hell. So when I woke, I told myself they couldn't have been Willy or my mother after all, for they wouldn't have damned me, no matter how much they wanted me with them at that moment. They'd wait for me, however long it took.

I said a silent prayer that morning, after I'd washed and dressed and readied myself for Harry's next visit. The prayer wasn't enough, though. That was the trouble with ghosts; they knew your weak spots, especially the ones pretending to be loved ones calling. They knew the power of crazy suggestions in the night, suggestions that in the light of day didn't seem so crazy after all.

'I've been thinking about what you said yesterday,' Harry was saying, as he helped me out of the Chrysler and the doorman dipped his head towards us, just as he had the last couple of days.

'About the rich and the poor?' I said. 'I want a cup of strong tea first, Harry. Not a word until I get one.'

In the suite, the camera was whirring and the light was burning into my eyes as the record ran. A silver tray with teacups and a teapot arrived at the door. I sat sipping my tea, making it last as long as I could.

'I want to ask you more about what we were talking about yesterday,' Harry began.

'You mean your lying about who you were, Harry?' I said that clearly into the microphone, and he frowned.

'You said Emile was pretending to be something he wasn't. But what about you? Were you pretending, Lena?'

I was too aware of being recorded this time. Too aware of the camera watching me, and how this might all look on the screen. Until now, my main preoccupation had been Violet finding out, but it occurred to me as I sat there that perhaps that was the wrong focus. Perhaps the way out of this was to remember how it would look to folks in a movie theatre.

'I – I don't know – what – what you mean,' I stammered.

He frowned. 'You gotta speak up, Lena. I meant – you were pretending to be in love with him, that you were his wife. But you weren't. So it was all just a game to you, wasn't it?'

'I don't understand,' I said, shaking my head. 'Do you mean – *William Minnoch*?'

'I mean *Emile*.'

I acted surprised, put a look of wonderment on my face. Harry got annoyed.

'You know who *Emile* is.' Then he said, 'Oh, I get you. Pretending with me now, too – I get it. Well, it strikes me there was only one person in this whole sorry tale who wasn't pretending.'

I pursed my lips, did my best innocent-old-lady look. 'You're going too fast for me, Harry; I can't keep up,' I said.

'I think you can. And she's the only other person who knows the truth.'

We were back to that. The 'someone else knows'.

'No – no, I really don't follow,' I said, and wiggled my fingers a little, fluttered my eyes. If the audience ever got to see my performance, they would think I was just another dotty old lady.

'Let me explain it to you, then,' Harry said. 'But tell me first about Christina Haggart.'

'Christina Haggart? Well, she was one of our housemaids, but we had many servants.'

'Not all of them carried letters between you and Emile, though, did they?'

I didn't say anything.

He continued, 'You asked about the difference between the rich and the poor, Lena. Well, it strikes me that "the rich", such as they are, are always pretending – look at this place, like you said. But who's paying to stay here, and how? I'll tell you – credit. Most of these folk don't have a dime to their names, but they're pretending they do. Act the part of being rich and suddenly you are.'

I wondered again about his own financial state. About the idea of Shaw and *Pygmalion*, and making a fortune out of 'speakies'.

'You're staying here on credit, too,' I said.

But he just shook his head. 'Christina Haggart was the only one of the three of you – you, her, Emile – who wasn't pretending to be something else. You were lying to Emile about Minnoch, Emile was pretending he loved you – but Christina wasn't lying to anyone; she was just a housemaid. She had no ambitions, beyond marrying her fiancé, did she? She was poor; she didn't pretend to be anything else but that.'

'*Christina Haggart*,' I said, and gazed up at the ceiling as though she might be floating there to jolt my memory. 'I don't understand what her "ambitions" might or might not have to do with anything—'

'Because I like how she figures in your story,' he said, rubbing his chin. 'I like that she's carrying all those letters back and forth between the two of you. That she's lending you the use of her room to meet Emile in private. That Emile bought her that crinoline to keep her sweet. It's all in the book – you should read it, if you don't recall it well enough.'

He smirked a little at that.

'You asked what "her ambitions" have to do with anything. Well, she accepted a nice skirt from Emile; she was getting married; she wanted money, maybe a better position,' he said. 'But she was up to her neck in this, wasn't she? I think she knew exactly what took place that night before Emile died.'

I swallowed a little at that 'knew'. Was Christina dead now, after all these years? She could be. Or she could be alive, just as I was. His very next words confirmed that was his thinking, too.

'I don't know if she's still living – but she testified in your murder trial, and she can't testify again. You can't be tried for the same crime twice. But I'm not looking for another trial, Lena – you misunderstand me if you think that's what I'm after.'

I let out a breath. 'She had a hard life,' I said. 'A very hard life. The life of a servant isn't an easy one. So I very much doubt she's still alive after all this time, Harry. Another dead end, it would seem. How unlucky for you.'

I'd forgotten my confused-old-lady act in my surprise at his mention of Christina. It brought back a lot of memories, hearing her name. It brought back resentment, and fear – real, palpitating fear – and I felt those emotions crowding in, threatening me.

'I like,' he said, 'that she must have *hated* you. Yes, I like that. I think I'd have hated you, too, if I'd been her.'

'I don't know what – what a – a *housemaid* thought of me,' I stammered a little again, but this time it wasn't put on. 'It wasn't something I—'

'From what she said at your trial – you must remember that? Yeah, I think she hated you, all right.'

He'd caught me out. I raised my voice. 'My family treated everyone very well indeed. You cannot say that we did not. I will not have that. We were kind; we were thoughtful people. My mama was an angel, my papa was strict but fair. We had wonderful summers at Rowaleyn. We gave wonderful parties; everyone said so.'

'It became you well, didn't it?' he said, his voice low. 'You gave parties in London, too, when you married George Wardle. All that partying – all that fun. But someone has to clean up after, don't they? Someone has to get their hands dirty. That's what servants are for.'

I didn't want to say any more.

'Did she clean up after you, Lena?' he said, bringing his face close to mine. 'Did she clean up your mess, too? Is that why she said what she did at the trial?'

Suddenly I felt afraid. Christina, my God. If she was still alive . . . I was about to get to my feet, fear creeping up from my toes, through my bones, when suddenly the great mechanical light focused on my face made a loud fizzing noise, and the bulb exploded with a bang.

We both jumped; I let out a startled 'Oh!', and clutched my heart as though I'd been shot.

The room fell dark suddenly, for a thunderstorm was coming, and we hadn't noticed how dark the day outside had become.

Harry got up, cursing at the light. Then he said to me, 'You OK, Lena?'

I nodded, and reached for one of the teacups on the silver tray, the ones he had ordered just after we came in. A mix of the residue from the dark tea leaves sat in the bottom of both cups. I pursed my lips, which were so very dry, licked them once or twice.

'Bulb's well and truly gone,' he said, from behind the light, 'and I don't have another one.'

I poured myself a little cold tea, just to wet my mouth, try and calm my nerves.

'I'll have to scout around, see what I can pick up – but we're done here for now.'

I was never more thankful, and when he drove me home, I stumbled up the stoop and shut the front door behind me, my heart beating fast and hard.

Those ghosts in the night and their terrible allure.

But maybe they were Willy and my mother, after all.

Maybe they were right, pulling me to them, making me think how to get to them sooner.

Fear can do a great deal to a person. It can change a person's thinking, feelings, actions, from normal, everyday ones to something more monstrous. They say love is the strongest emotion, and once upon a time, I thought that was true.

But fear makes us take action just as much as love does; maybe even more so.

Christina and her hatred. I thought of Violet and Tom, of my love for them and their love for me. A pure, honest love.

Now, I thought, there was so much I could save them from, if I chose to. Perhaps that was what my dreams of Willy, and of my mother, had truly meant.

So I told myself, but I knew deep down that it was fear driving me on. Fear of Christina; of Harry; of that film of his, so exposing and crude.

Yes; I was afraid.

Tom had always known the truth about me; he and Willy were my main confidantes all the years I lived here. It was Tom who introduced me to Willy, through one of the working men's associations that had begun to spring up in the wake of the 'Red Scare'. They weren't Communists out to destroy their country, Tom and his friends. They were just working men who wanted a fairer deal, and what was ever wrong about that? I went along to a few of their meetings after I arrived here, and when a dance night was organised, I went to that, too – and there he was, looking so fine in his best suit and hat, and holding out his hand to me.

William Sheehy.

Another fiancé named William.

But now I lay in my single bed without him by my side, trying to find his ghost again, to hear him calling on me like before.

Not once that night did he appear.

The next morning, to my surprise, Harry didn't show, and he sent no word about why. I assumed he was having trouble getting another lightbulb. The break from him seemed significant in its timing. Perhaps the world was giving me an opportunity, and telling me to seize it, though my hands shook enough to stop me seizing anything for real, and that produced a grim kind of smile from me at least.

The storm hadn't cleared away the humidity, and when morning broke, it was hot and sticky, the worst kind of New York day. Newspapers had been busying themselves with more dreadful descriptions of the conditions at Sing Sing Prison, where Ruth Snyder was being held, and newsboys were shouting out more gruesome headlines as I passed, which lowered my mood, too.

I made for the nearest bakery first, for the rugelach I loved; the butcher, for some pastrami; the fruit and vegetable stall for some fine-tasting strawberries. I hoped it would all be enough. I'd made my decision, still telling myself it wasn't fear making me do it. No: Willy wasn't coming to me, so I would go to him. That's what I muttered, over and over again as I took my time along the sidewalk.

The hardware store was my final stop. I told the man that there were rats in the building. He sympathised, said, 'This is best for your trouble,' and showed me the package, 'ROUGH ON RATS', accompanied by a picture of a rat lying upside down, presumably after being poisoned.

'What's in it?' I said.

'Mainly arsenic,' he said, and I shuddered.

'I want something that causes them less pain,' I said. 'I don't like to think of something like that.'

'You could try red-squill powder – comes from the plant of the same name,' he said, showing me a tin of it. 'It's not so effective, though – you want rid of rats, arsenic's what you need.'

He made me take both packages, in case the red-squill didn't work, he said. So I did as he suggested, and then headed back to the apartment.

I made myself a cup of strong tea first, and thought of writing letters to Violet and Tom. But I wanted them to think what I'd done was an accident, that I'd mixed in something bad by mistake. I didn't drink cocoa often, but I had a can of it somewhere, so I laid it out. It didn't look like the red-squill at all, but who knew what a woman of my years might confuse.

In the parlour, I set a favourite song from last year on the gramophone. I'd go through to the kitchen, shake what I had to over my favourite food, and have a last meal. Yes, I told myself again; this was the only way now.

I liked to think later on that it was you, Willy, who came to me in that dark, dark moment. My great love, who lifted the arm of the gramophone and set down the needle for me.

When night-time comes stealing
I wonder how you're feeling
Are you lonesome and sorry,
the same, dear, as me?

I hadn't listened to Ruth Etting's voice in such a long time. I hummed along to 'Lonesome and Sorry', which had come out just as Willy was dying on me. Perhaps that was why I hadn't played it for so long; the words themselves were too close to the bone.

This time, though, I just wanted to hug the melody, let her voice fill the parlour and hold me safe.

I lay down on the daybed and closed my eyes tight. My breathing was shallow at first, then deeper, my arms wrapped around a pillow for comfort. This will be the night I meet with you again, Willy, I thought. 'Dear God, let it work and get me back to him,' I murmured.

As I lay there, I wondered how long the red-squill would take, once I'd mixed it with my rugelach, my pastrami on rye, my strawberries. I'd come back here after eating, I decided, and lie down just like this. I was rehearsing, it seemed, my own deathbed scene.

Our old time friends all ask for you in vain
I always say that you'll be back again

On sang Ruth Etting, in her sad, sad voice. So fitting for what I'd be doing shortly. Ruth Etting. Ruth Snyder. All the Ruths.

'Of course,' I murmured, realising something. 'Ruth "Etting". Of course.'

'Etting' was the singer's maiden name.

How funny it seemed to me in those terrible, last moments of my life. To be so preoccupied with Ruth Etting, of all people. She was married to a gangster called Moe the Gimp, whose surname was Snyder.

The coincidence had me almost smiling in the dark of the parlour. Ruth Etting was *also* 'a' Ruth Snyder, but no newspaper had remarked on it – at least none that I had seen. And it tickled me, as her voice filtered through the room, the macabre nature of the world.

Two Ruth Snyders in New York City at the same time. One due to be executed for the crime of murder, and the other releasing hit after hit.

What a macabre coincidence, indeed. I couldn't help wondering that no lazy reporter had mixed them up, confusing a famous singer with a convicted murderess. Well, of course, they wouldn't have, a little voice in my head said. It was only their names that linked them, not who they were or what they'd done.

Two completely different women, but sharing the same name.

I thought about Harry. How he'd feel if he thought he'd confused two different Lena Wardles, because they shared the same name. What an embarrassment for him. What a showing-up he'd get, if he released a film, telling the world he'd found the elusive Madeleine Smith and she turned out not to be the woman he thought, after all.

No; he'd never do it, not if he knew.

And finally, in the darkness, I smiled.

North Prison, Glasgow, to Edinburgh, 1857

'The back gate was usually snibbed; it was sometimes locked. Then a person from the inside could open the back door by the key which stood in the door, and then open the back gate by unsnibbing it?'

'Yes ... The back door makes a noise when opened, if locked.'

– Testimony of Christina Haggart or McKenzie, wife of Duncan McKenzie, joiner, examined by the Solicitor-General at the trial of Madeleine Smith, 3 July 1857, Edinburgh

It was my very last note to him that caused my removal to this place.

So Mr Wilkie, Papa's solicitor, has said. *Tomorrow night*, I wrote in that final note to Emile.

'But I meant Saturday, not Sunday,' I told Mr Wilkie, making my eyes wide as I could.

The difference between them is crucial, he says.

My purchases of arsenic are a cause for suspicion, too, of course.

But Christina had said it would look better to take Janet with me, or a friend like Mary Buchanan, so that was what I did, for it would look more innocent if anyone should ask. But who would go to the trouble of searching through the poison books of different apothecaries to see when and where and by whom arsenic was purchased, I had argued. Especially when Emile used it himself.

I haven't told Mr Wilkie any of that.

I was able to speak with Janet before they took me away, but not with Christina. In this place, they read any letters that come to me, and any that I send out. So how to get a word to her now that she's married her fiancé, Duncan McKenzie, so quickly, and left our household – and a word that the wardens wouldn't read – is a puzzle that's causing me terrible headaches. I have to know what she's thinking; what she might say. We are three, after all. Christina and Janet are the other two points of the triangle we made; they are the base, I am the tip. That was how I explained it to Janet before I left.

'You must hold hands with her, my dear, in your mind, and hold the line steady, so that I don't fall down,' I said, and she nodded and made me see that she understood.

But I didn't get to Christina before the sheriff substitute took me away, and now all I hear at night in bed is Christina's voice saying the same thing, over and over.

They'll put you away.

'Mr Wilkie's here,' says the warden, Mrs McLachlan, interrupting my thoughts. I have a desk here, and a comfortable bed, a dresser, a washstand and a soft armchair with cushions, all delivered from Blythswood Square while I wait, day after day, for my release. Papa pays extra for the food I struggle to eat; I've begun gnawing at my wrists again, scratching at my neck.

Devouring myself, but not from hunger this time. This time, it's the urge to a thinness that might let me slip through the bars at the window and drift back to everyone, to William, to Janet.

The window itself isn't very clean, of course, with the prison being so near the St Rollox chimney. Even if it was washed every day, by night-time it would be covered in soot and grime again. When I wipe it with a handkerchief and push it open for some air, those little black particles fly in with the breeze and settle on all my things, on my books and my hairbrush, my chair and my bedding. We don't have a maid to clean every day, though a girl takes away my chamber pot every morning.

I get up from the desk, where I've been writing a letter. 'Can we have some tea, please, Mrs McLachlan?' They are very kind to me here; Mrs McLachlan thinks it's a disgrace that I'm locked up like this.

She says, 'Of course, my dear,' and then Mr Wilkie rushes in, all flapping collars and unkempt whiskers. He's tall and thin, with a boyish face that makes me think he's not much older than I am, which doesn't give me confidence in his abilities, though Papa says he has a fine brain.

I settle myself on the chair, spread my skirts about me. Papa has promised I won't be long here. It seems that he and Mr Wilkie have both decided that the accusations against me will be dropped soon and no case will be brought to court. So perhaps today is the day I may go home.

'Ah, it's not good news, Madeleine,' Mr Wilkie says, panting, as he sits down on my little bed. 'I'm sorry to say – but there is going to be a trial after all.'

'No!' I cry. 'But Papa said there wasn't enough evidence, that I would be home soon—'

Just behind him is Papa; I'd had no word he was visiting today.

'What do they mean, Papa?' I say. He comes to my side, holds my elbow, for I think I might faint. I close my eyes, sway a little in the warm, clogged air of my room. Fragments of soot seem to settle on my lips, blown in with Mr Wilkie. I put a finger to my mouth but it comes away clean.

'You were meant to put a stop to this, Wilkie. You're the one who said it was most unlikely.' Papa is furious, but he's white-faced, too, and seems to have shrunk in stature in the days since I've been held here. '*Most* unlikely, when they have no evidence at all that my daughter even met this *reprobate* the night before he died.'

'I'm sorry – but they have ruled that Miss Smith's purchases of arsenic, on top of the letters she sent him, are enough.' Mr Wilkie blushes; his failure makes Papa whiten even more. Looking at both men makes me realise that I must be the strong one. They have both failed me. But Janet will not, and Christina – no, Christina loves me. She'll not fail me either.

'What is the charge?' I ask, my chin up, trying not to show fear.

'There are *three* charges—'

'Three!' thunders Papa, letting go of my elbow and going up to Mr Wilkie.

I think for a moment that he's going to strike him; I say, 'Papa, no!', but Mr Wilkie's not afraid. He doesn't cower or back away, and instead it's Papa, shorter and even thinner, who blinks first and shrinks even more before him.

'I'm sorry to say so, sir,' Mr Wilkie says. 'Two charges of attempted murder. One charge of murder.'

We all fall silent. Crows caw on the high window ledges outside, and I think of William's little tattoo.

They'll put you away.

'There's an excellent Queen's Counsel, John Inglis,' Mr Wilkie says to my papa. 'Expensive, of course, but he has the best experience of the courtroom. There's some roughness to his manner, but it is a fighter you will need to have in there. He is the best chance – maybe the only one – of your daughter escaping the noose—'

He stops when he sees my face.

The noose.

I don't remember what's said between them after that, because my head's pounding with such a noise it's hard to hear them, and they're huddled together in the darkest corner of the room anyway, only occasionally glancing my way. It's as though I'm quite detached from them, though they must be speaking about me, and the strangeness of their muttering sounds like a hundred waves battering a shoreline, and all I can see is the object, washed up on the sand, covered in soot. Why didn't I bury it, instead, I think, biting my fingernails. Why did I throw it into the water from a boat full of passengers, any of whom might have seen—

'Maddie!' says Papa, sharply, but he's too late, for I'm slipping.

When I open my eyes, Papa and Mr Wilkie have both gone, and it's Mrs McLachlan who's bending over me, her hand under my neck as I stretch out on my bed.

'You had a wee faint, dear, that's all. Take this and you'll be better soon.'

I swallow the mixture on her spoon, whatever it is, and that smooths me out, all the lines of worry that criss-cross in front of my eyes, and I sleep.

When I wake later, it's night, but I'm feeling well enough to light a candle and finish my letter, which is on my desk, secure under the pile of books sitting there.

You said, I write to William Minnoch, *that a soul can be reborn. So Emile is not really dead; he is simply born into another body. Not the body of a wolf after all, of course not that. A human body – but one that begins at birth all over again. Or can his soul settle into a body that is already adult? Forgive my ignorance,* I write, *but it is important that I know.*

Emile's body had so very much of it in him, Mr Wilkie said. Arsenic. Eighty-two grains, the post-mortem found, when four to six grains are enough to kill a person.

'It's absorbed into the blood, that's how it gets everywhere in the body so quickly,' Mr Wilkie had told me. 'And that was after excessive purging. A doctor I consulted told me at least four to five times that much must have been taken by him initially – over two hundred grains! But how on earth is such a dose to be administered without being noticed?'

I bit my lip when he said that; I'd not considered, of course, that such a large amount would raise questions. I'd thought only of stopping him. That was all. That was all. And on that last night with him, I still hadn't been sure there was enough . . .

'It is quite impossible for such an amount to be disguised in a cup of cocoa. And that is the key to your release, Miss Smith. Monsieur L'Angelier could not have taken in such an amount without knowing it was there, and being willing to do so. Which is why the only possibility is suicide.'

He's not a stupid man, Mr Wilkie.

'Might they not argue that I did try to poison Emile with arsenic in his cocoa, and he knew it and drank it anyway?' I said.

He had looked confused for a moment, and I thought I must be wrong, and he is a stupid man after all.

I wonder what answer the 'rough' Mr Inglis might fashion to that question, when I meet him at last. I was asked some questions by the sheriff substitute when I first arrived here.

Yes, I said, I would give Emile cocoa sometimes. Yes, I bought arsenic on some occasions, to use as a cosmetic, diluted with water, to apply to my face, neck and arms. I didn't want the druggist to know it was for that, so I said it was for rats.

So I told the sheriff substitute, and Mr Wilkie, and everybody who asks, and everybody has nodded – so why have they brought these charges against me? Three charges!

Could Emile have come back as some kind of wicked actor in this drama? I ask William. It strikes me that he might be returned as a man of the court, someone who will prosecute me, who knows exactly how such a dose might be administered—

I shake my head in the candlelight. Emile, reborn as a grown man with power to put my neck in a noose! *Tell me more of this theory so I may put my mind at rest, dearest William,* I write.

Mr Wilkie left behind a newspaper for me. It calls my arrest 'an event of the most painful character', and laments that 'the family will have suffered deeply by having one of their household even suspected of a crime so odious'. It wonders how someone like me could possibly come to be here, in this place. It doesn't mention my family's name, but that will all change now that we are to go to trial.

'The world's a cruel beast,' Mrs McLachlan murmured before

she left me earlier. 'And it's cruellest of all to young women who don't deserve it.'

They'll put you away.

Why didn't I have a better plan? Why didn't I talk with Christina about what we might do, if it all went wrong? But I trust her, I do. We are three. We are *blood sisters*. If one of us falls, so do we all.

It's early the next morning when I'm woken by Mrs McLachlan, barely past dawn.

'Mr Inglis has come already,' she says, shocked, 'and it's hardly even light!' She helps me with my dressing quickly, takes out the chamber pot herself. He's arrived without even Papa to escort him.

I'm still uncurling the paper from my hair when he strides into the room. 'Miss Smith!' he booms, 'John Inglis QC.' And he bows.

'Good morning,' I say, politely, and shake out my curls, with no time to tie them.

He has a thick head of hair and the face of a sailor, or what I imagine a sailor's face to be, with a blunt nose and square chin, and strong blue eyes. He's not handsome at all, but he's used to being heard, and that gives him a certain kind of bearing.

He's suspicious of my refusal to tell him any more than I have already told Mr Wilkie.

'The written statement you gave the sheriff substitute isn't enough,' he says. He takes to calling me 'Madeleine', which I don't like. My room seems very small as he paces about while I sit still, hands in my lap and head bowed, like a novice nun. I skipped supper last night and have left my breakfast of porridge untouched. All I can taste are dust particles from the St Rollox chimney, and I wish I was gone from here.

'You'll be transferred to the prison at Edinburgh tomorrow, Madeleine,' he says, as if I've spoken out loud. Perhaps I have; it's hard to tell when you're alone with your thoughts so much. 'No *homely items* will be allowed there for your comfort, alas.'

He seems oddly pleased by that.

Once he's gone, I write to Papa that I don't think he's the best man for the job at all; I don't like him, I say, he's coarse and pompous. Mrs McLachlan takes the letter to post for me, then returns to help me pack up my few belongings, ready for the journey to Edinburgh.

'I'm going to miss you,' she says with a sniff, 'but I'll pray for you, every day, my dear. You'd not harm a soul, they'll see that.'

It's enough to make me weep; instead, I give her a sudden hug. Her body's as hard as it is round, and her uniform's so thin that every muscle in her arms and her back pokes out like a stone and offers no comfort at all, but I cling nonetheless because it's too long since anyone embraced me or I them. I think of Janet waiting for me to come home to her, and suddenly that's too much; an unpleasant shaking takes over the whole of my body, and Mrs McLachlan must sit still with me awhile, and stroke my hair and pat my hands.

That night is long and I don't sleep, so I'm tired in the morning. But the carriage to the new prison at Edinburgh is well-sprung, for Papa has paid for that, too, and there are plenty of cushions, so I doze a little on the journey. The noise of gates creaking open lets me know when we've arrived, and when the carriage door opens to a dark night lit only by a few lamps held by a warden, I sniff hard. Sea air is what greets me first, not sooty smells from St Rollox. No gritty little particles rest on my lips; no grime settles in my eye. Just a little sea salt, white and pure.

As Mr Inglis said, my room in Edinburgh is nothing like the one I had in the North Prison, being very bare, with just a bed and a small table and chair, and my trunk with a few dresses, and a washstand for my jug and basin. I have my books, at least, and a letter from Janet. There's still no word from William Minnoch, and none from Papa or Mama. And I still have no idea how to reach Christina.

Mr Inglis arrives just after my porridge has been delivered, though for some reason, I couldn't keep it down, and retched into a chamber pot just before he came.

Miss Aitken, the warden here, covered the pan and took it away. She has instructions to examine my chamber pot every morning, apparently.

Mr Inglis doesn't mince his words. 'Let me set it out before you, Madeleine, in the plainest terms.

'You have been charged, firstly, with Intent to Murder on the nineteenth or the twentieth of February, which is when Monsieur L'Angelier's first illness is recorded. But as your first recorded purchase of arsenic at Murdoch Brothers takes place on the twenty-first, which is after his illness, we can be sure that charge will not hold.'

'Why would they accuse me—' I start to say, but he interrupts with a wave of his hand.

'Because they must go by the dates of his reported illnesses, not by the dates of your purchases of arsenic.'

I nod, but say nothing. He continues, 'The second charge

is Intent to Murder on the twenty-second or twenty-third of February. This is the date of the second illness that Monsieur L'Angelier reported to his landlady. That charge against you is harder to disprove, of course, as his illness comes almost directly *after* your purchase at Murdoch's on the twenty-first.'

My fingers twitch in my lap.

'You are recorded as purchasing arsenic from Currie's on the sixth of March, but Monsieur L'Angelier reported no illness after or near that date. Then' – he takes a theatrically deep breath and I picture how he'll be in court – 'you purchased arsenic a third time on the eighteenth of March, a day after you returned from Bridge of Allan. Monsieur L'Angelier dies of arsenic poisoning on the morning of the twenty-third of March. Hence, a charge of Murder on the twenty-second or twenty-third of March is made against you.

'Are you clear about it, Madeleine? Obviously, the third charge is the most grievous. I must ask you, too – did Emile ever ask you to buy arsenic for him?'

I shake my head, nip the inside of my mouth, which is so dry. The taste of vomit is in my throat. 'He did lodge on Great Western Road beside the Botanics,' I murmur. 'He said they used *it* there as a kind of fertiliser, I think. He got poppy seeds from there.'

It's the best I can do.

'The prosecution will want to know what happened to that second purchase of arsenic,' he says.

'I used it for cosmetic purposes,' I say. 'I used all three purchases for cosmetic purposes.'

'And that will be the argument we maintain throughout.'

'Will Christina be called to testify?' I ask. 'May I not speak with her before it? I'd like very much to, she might be able to help—'

He looks curiously at me. 'That is impossible, Madeleine,' he says. 'We thought at first she'd disappeared completely, for we had great trouble finding her – but no doubt she is frightened to death. What with her carrying your letters back and forth as she did, giving you both her room—'

I stare. 'Christina's not afraid of anything,' I say. 'Or anyone.'

'She'll be afraid of a noose – and so she should be.'

'But I'm the one on trial! I'm the one who is accused! I'm the one who purchased arsenic! Not her! She has nothing to fear, nothing at all.'

Which is how it's meant to be, I think later, after Mr Inglis calls for the warden and she administers a little laudanum to calm me, for I'm too agitated to listen to what he's saying. Only later, alone in the tiny room with a single window high up, do I think, *Was this how she meant it to be from the start?*

But I won't believe such a thing; 'Christina loves me,' I say out loud.

Does she love you enough to put her own neck in the noose to save you? asks a little voice in the dark, a question that prickles my skin and has me shivering uncontrollably.

That night I dream about her. Christina, laughing at me. She's married Emile, in my dream, and she's given birth to their child, a hideous creature. Then she points at me and, to my horror, my belly is swollen, too, and it swells as I stare at it, until I think I am about to burst open, guts and blood and all – and that's when Miss Aitken shakes me awake because I've been calling out in my sleep, she says. I try to eat some porridge, but once again, it won't stay down, and it's all I can do to sip a little boiled water.

When Mr Inglis arrives, he brings me a newspaper. There's a cartoon inside. In the drawing, a figure that is supposed to represent me is handing a cup of poisoned cocoa from a basement bedroom window up to Emile on the street, as he leans through the railings.

'But don't they know the gap between my bedroom window and the railings is too wide and high for me to stretch and reach anybody on the street?' I ask him, puzzled.

He says, 'That isn't the point, Madeleine. They all think you poisoned him with a cup of cocoa. We will show that's impossible, not without him knowing it was there all along.'

There's something else, though, that might be a further problem. 'A memorandum book written in Emile's own hand,' he says, 'but I will insist it may not be used as evidence.'

'I didn't know he kept such a thing.'

'Only for a certain period, which is odd enough in itself, don't you think? Almost as though he wanted—'

'To implicate me?'

'I'd prefer a jury not to see what he wrote: the dates he saw you, where, and how he was taken ill afterwards. At least he doesn't ever say that he drank any cocoa made by you.'

'I didn't give him cocoa the night before he died, I didn't!' I say, then stop, realising what it is that I've said. My hand flies to my mouth, too late.

Mr Inglis looks at me. 'But you met with him?'

'No,' I say. 'No – that was what I meant! Because I *didn't* see him, I didn't give him cocoa.'

He asks a few more questions, but I can tell he doesn't believe me. The next few days follow the same pattern – he goads me a little more each time, but I grow wiser to it and he cannot catch me.

In our final week before the trial begins, he hands me a box from Mama. Inside it is a brown silk gown, lavender gloves, and a very pretty white bonnet with a veil. There is another small package. 'Smelling salts,' he says. 'Should you feel faint at any time.'

I have been very sick all the mornings of this past week. The silk gown fits a little big; I have lost weight, it seems. I don't gnaw at myself now; I'm too sick to keep down anything, even my own fingernails.

It's the morning of the trial at last.

He's not really dead, he's not really dead, I think, as Miss Aitken pats the soft rings she's made of my hair, and sets down the collar of my dress. She accompanies me all the way in the prison carriage to the High Justiciary building, as we bump and jostle over the cobbles on the High Street. Only once do I catch a glimpse through the black curtains drawn over the carriage window at the rabble gathered outside St Giles cathedral. Working men and women; stalls of food; carriages; men in wigs and capes rub shoulders with one another. 'They are here for me?' I ask Miss Aitken, amazed.

We are to enter by a side entrance, unseen by the crowd, and once inside, I am escorted to a single cell, its door heavy with a lock and a bolt, and a small second room beside it for any ablutions. The corridor is very bright, though, with high windows, and the light makes me blink, for the July day is hot.

Miss Aitken waits with me in the cell, until Mr Inglis appears in all his finery. He looks quite different in his red robes, much more magisterial, and for the first time, I think I might have confidence in him. 'Madeleine,' he says, nodding, and I stand up, and follow him out into the corridor.

A flight of stone stairs is behind a door on the left. 'You go up to the very top,' he says, and then he disappears. There are other court officers behind me; I'm confused for a moment, then lift my skirts and take to the stairs, which are very steep and turn to the left at the top. I can hear voices ahead; a light shines, and suddenly a face comes into view. A man, also in robes, beckons me on, and suddenly I am up and through a kind of trap door, and in the middle of the vast courtroom.

It is like a beautiful gallery. I gasp at its grandeur, stare at the ceiling with its great white rose emblems, beneath which the packed viewing gallery rises, enormous arched windows on either side letting in the sunlight. A man of the court takes my arm to help me turn and sit on the bench, to face the judge, seated at the curved table ahead, beneath three arch windows.

Mr Inglis is on one side; the prosecution sits on the other. Both men have assistants who take up the rest of the table. There is some murmuring, before silence is called for. I close my eyes; mouth the Lord's Prayer, and then look up again through my veil, at Mr Moncrieff, the Chief Prosecutor. He looks a kindly man, which surprises me; indeed, he reminds me of our minister, Mr Middleton, and I almost smile at him.

I am the tip of the triangle, I tell myself. Christina won't let me down; Janet won't let me down. They'll not destroy me, because if they do, they destroy themselves, too.

They love me.

Then Mr Moncrieff begins, and with my last letter to Emile.

It's our greatest threat, Mr Inglis has said. But it's also proof of the greatest doubt.

> *Why, my beloved, did you not come to me? Oh, beloved, are you ill? Come to me. Sweet one.*
>
> *I waited and waited for you, but you came not. I shall wait again tomorrow night – same hour and arrangement.*
>
> *Do come, sweet love, my own dear love of a sweetheart. Come, beloved, and clasp me to your heart. Come, and we shall be happy.*
>
> *A kiss, fond love.*
>
> *Adieu, with tender embraces, ever believe me to be your own ever dear, fond MIMI.*

It's so strange to hear my own words read out like this, and by a man who resembles a church minister. I can hardly believe I wrote them.

It's the prosecution's most important piece of evidence, Mr Moncrieff says.

'Miss Smith insists that she wrote the letter on the *twentieth* of March, so "I shall wait again tomorrow night" was meant to be the twenty-first, so she claims,' he says. His voice is firm, not harsh. I cannot believe he wants me to be found guilty. I fidget a little in my seat. The room is very hot already, and we have only just begun. 'The letter itself is not dated. But the *envelope* is dated the twenty-first! And so I suggest it was *posted* on the twenty-first, and that the defendant *wrote* it on the twenty-first.

'Thus, when Monsieur L'Angelier received it, he naturally thought she meant that "tomorrow night" meant the night of the twenty-second of March, and so he made his way to Blythswood Square to meet her then.

'The twenty-second. The night he consumed poison, and died in the early hours of the twenty-third.'

There's a ringing in my ears that goes on and on, until Mrs Jenkins, Emile's landlady, is called by Mr Moncrieff. She seems a very simple woman, full of fear and easily confused. Her account of his last hours is horrible, though. She goes on about 'bowls of green bile', and I can't help dabbing at a few tears when she describes how he vomited, how very ill he was. I'd not thought it would be so painful, so sordid at the end.

We didn't want to hurt him, not any of us. Not even Janet, who hated him the most, I think. No; I didn't want him to suffer like that.

A few people who saw Emile on the day before he died are called to appear: then Mary Tweedle, a servant at Emile's friend's house, where he stopped on the evening of the twenty-second, says he seemed well enough to her.

It's not true, what she's saying, though. When he came to me later that night, he was rough and wild and ill-looking, but of course, I cannot challenge her account.

Indeed. I am not to say a word throughout. I can give no account of myself in my own words; it is not permitted. And so I sip water a few times, for the courtroom's so warm and my brown silk is heavy, and the lies they each tell seem to settle in the very air. Just when I think I might give out at any moment, we end for the day, and I am escorted back downstairs to the little cell, where Miss Aitken has been waiting for me. We are escorted out to the carriage, and I am driven back to my prison cell.

My first day is over. I tremble a little as I remove my veil and jacket, my boots. Miss Aitken hurries away to fetch me some food, and that is when Mr Inglis appears with one of the earliest editions of the day's newspaper.

'Eager crowds gather in the early morning at the gaol, and in Parliament Square, to catch a glimpse of the prisoner as she is taken to the court. In the evening, thousands gather in the streets to see the cab in which she is borne back from the courtroom to the prison.

'Hundreds are passed in for a few minutes by official friends to get a glimpse at the prisoner, and may be seen departing with the air of satisfied curiosity upon their anxious countenances.

'The newspapers in the second, third and fourth editions with which the town is deluged, stop the presses to tell how she looked at a particular hour ... and how for breakfast she had coffee, rolls and a mutton chop, which she ate with great apparent heartiness.'

Eager crowds? The town is deluged? 'Are they so interested, then?' I ask Mr Inglis, amazed once again as I was by the crowds that morning.

'Of course!' he says. 'You are the sensation of the year, Madeleine. Maybe even the decade.'

'But they only write about my dress, or my manner. Not what they have heard about the suffering Emile endured.'

'Be grateful they do not,' is all he says to that.

But it's all I can think about.

How can he not want revenge on me? I write another letter to my dear William, but the warden says she can't deliver any mail during the trial.

I spend the night wishing for Janet, hugging a jacket in

place of her. The next morning I'm sleepy but overwrought, too, as in court, Emile's fellow workers give an account of him. His employer, Mr Stevenson, and the French consul, Monsieur de Mean, say unflattering things about him, mentioning his fondness for poppy seeds and laudanum.

Then Miss Perry is called. She has on a heavy brown wool dress and a black bonnet, too warm for this July day. Her spectacles sit on the end of her beaky nose, which shines with sweat.

'Monsieur L'Angelier did not tell me he had seen Miss Smith on the nineteenth of February, but he did tell me of having had a cup of chocolate which had made him ill,' she says, eagerly, when the questions begin.

Then she says more.

'And on the ninth of March, when he took tea with me, he said, "I can't think why I was so unwell after getting that coffee or chocolate from her." He spoke of his attachment to Miss Smith as a *fascination*. He said, "It's a perfect fascination, my attachment to that girl. *If she were to poison me, I would forgive her.*"'

The court erupts. Mr Inglis is on his feet, shouting and waving something. The viewers' gallery behind me seems to shake with stamping.

Mr Moncrieff waits for the noise to subside, then nods at Miss Perry, who tweets in her murderous, birdlike voice: 'I said to him, "You ought not to allow such thoughts to pass through your mind. What motive could she have for giving you anything to injure you?"'

'And he replied?'

'He said, "I don't know, but perhaps she might not be sorry to be rid of me."'

'And what do you think he meant by that remark?'

'That he meant, to be rid of her engagement to him.'

I have never loathed another person so much in my life, I tell Mr Inglis afterwards in my room.

'It's not so clear-cut as it appears,' he says. 'Look at what *The Times* is saying.' He produces his early copy.

'She entered the court in her usual airy manner, and sat for some time unveiled; she appeared in excellent health and never during the day even slightly hung her head, except when reference was made to her love letters with the deceased.'

'You see how much they like you?' he says. 'They think you are very respectable, Madeleine. Very innocent and demure. That's good.'

I can't believe it, though. That night, I kneel by the side of my bed and close my eyes and pray. Not to God, but to Emile. *Forgive me*, I say, over and over.

The next day, a physician and a professor of chemistry, Dr Penny, testifies about the remains of arsenic in Emile's body. The question arises: *how did so much arsenic get into him?*

I couldn't face coffee or porridge this morning again, and my head feels lighter than the dust motes in the courtroom air. Dr Penny dismisses the possibility of disguising so much in a cup of cocoa as it would simply adhere into a single large lump, but says that boiling the chocolate and arsenic together might break that lump into smaller ones.

So I could still have done it.

The jurymen don't give me hostile looks, not even after this, or Miss Perry's evidence the day before. But it seems that it's all mounting up against me, even though later on, Mr Inglis says no.

The next day is William's turn.

He smiles prettily in the courtroom but doesn't acknowledge me at all, even though my veil is lifted and I try to catch his eye.

When he's asked about coming after me on the boat, he says only that I wouldn't tell him what it was about. And he says that he never heard the name Emile L'Angelier mentioned at all.

He doesn't look my way once as he lies to the court. A kind of coolness wafts over me like a breeze, though the courtroom is again so very stuffy that it's hard to get a breath. Perhaps it is really a kind of relief, that he has not told them the truth. Perhaps he even means to help me by doing so.

He hasn't answered a single letter of mine since my arrest.

When they call the next witness, the coolness returns.

It is Christina. At last! But she looks pale, her cheeks waxy. I judge she must be six months into her pregnancy by now but none of that is showing and I wonder if something has happened to the baby. I have so many questions for her but she doesn't even glance my way, for all she's so near where I sit.

We three, sings the blood in my veins. *Remember our pact? Our cut fingers?*

I wish that she might be cool as I am, with her white face. Then I remember what Mr Inglis said about her being afraid.

'Can you explain exactly the layout of the rooms in Blythswood Square?' Mr Moncrieff begins. 'For instance, where was Miss Smith's room?'

'It was downstairs, on the same floor as the kitchen,' Christina says. 'I slept in a back room near to the back door.'

'Please tell the court of an instance when Monsieur L'Angelier called on her.'

'Well, one night, I left the back gate and back door open and returned to the house. Miss Smith asked if I would leave the back door open and stay in the kitchen a little, for she was to see her friend. So I stayed in the kitchen. I didn't know where Miss Smith was. I didn't know she was in my bedroom. I had no doubt she was there, but I didn't *know* it.'

'You didn't *know* it?'

'Well, at night, you see, she could pass from her bedroom to the kitchen without being heard by me, if I was in my room. So I would not hear her in my room if I was in the kitchen.'

'What *could* you hear from your bedroom, or from the kitchen?'

'I could hear the back door – it makes a noise in opening.' She stops for a moment then says, louder, for emphasis: '*Unlocking the door makes a considerable noise, you see.*'

Mr Moncrieff raises his eyebrows and presses on. 'Is it always so noisy?'

'Not if someone inside the house has already unlocked the back door, and then unsnibbed the gate. It wouldn't be so noisy then.'

'And on the night of Monsieur L'Angelier's death? What did you hear?'

I stare and stare, mute as a statue.

'I wasn't well that day,' Christina says, her voice a little shaky. She looks down at her feet, mumbles. Her face is still flushed red. 'I kept my bed, and only got up between five and six. I saw my husband – Duncan McKenzie – that evening between seven and eight.

'I went back to bed at ten. I wasn't aware of anything taking place in the house during the night. I didn't hear anything, and wasn't aware of any stranger being inside.'

A tiny sigh escapes me. Then she says, 'When McKenzie went away just before ten, I saw him to the back door and the outer gate.

'I snibbed the gate, and I've got no reason to suppose I didn't lock the back door as usual.'

Mr Moncrieff looks delighted.

'You say "have no reason to suppose" you didn't lock the back door?' he says, and looks around the room, waves in the direction of the jury. 'But you cannot be fully sure that you *did* lock it?'

Christina's mouth falls open.

I stare at her, holding my breath, willing her on. Of course she will say that she remembers locking the door. Of course she will. She must! There must be no doubt of it at all.

But she does not. 'I've got no reason to suppose I did not,' she repeats, but she stutters over her words, and her eyes look only at the ground.

I'm too furious to sit still.

Later in my room I accost Mr Inglis. 'The jury will see her doubting her own actions,' I say. 'They will see it!' But my rage is cold; my fingers are icy on my cheeks.

Mr Inglis says, 'Doubt is not so bad for us – it means the jury cannot be sure.'

But my prosecutors want only to damn me, no matter what the newspapers say. I have read that the famous Pre-Raphaelite brotherhood have called me a 'stunner', after their famous models. 'They'd never hang a stunner!' says one report, quoting the painter, Mr Rossetti.

They'd never hang a stunner.

Today is the worst day, for my letters are read out in court. It takes up the full session.

So Mama and Papa know it all now, the lies I have told them. What Emile and I did together, all those many, many times, they know it all.

I wish for coldness now, but my head is so hot throughout the day, and at one point I have to cover my eyes. Mama; Papa; the newspapers, which will hate me. I can't look at anyone, my shame is too enormous. I want only to be back in my room, to crawl under the bed and hide there. But I cannot resist the evening reports that Mr Inglis brings me, even knowing how bad they will be, and I scour them just as I do every day. One reporter writes that 'I have seen complete copies of these epistles, and I pray God I may never see such again.'

According to the *Times of London*, I 'scarcely maintained' my 'jaunty, indifferent air during today's proceedings, but appeared to feel the exposure' which my letters made.

Of course I felt it! The *Times of London*. The Queen reads the *Times of London*. Lord Palmerston, the Prime Minister, reads the *Times of London*, too. They will know who I am. What I have done. What I wrote to Emile.

If someone had said to me that one day, the Queen herself would know about me, about my letters, would read the words I wrote—

My fingers grip the newspaper, and when the warden comes

in to check on me later, they are still gripping it. All through the night, my fingers curl in that same hold, as I lie awake, hour after hour.

In the morning, I retch up bile into my chamber pot yet again.

On Monday, Mr Inglis calls for Janet.

My dearest girl. She's trembling, and wants to smile at me; I lift my hand to wave before Mr Inglis frowns, so I nod only slightly, and Janet nods back.

Mr Inglis turns gently to the night of the twenty-second. I blink at her, as it's all I can do to remind her of what I told her so many months ago.

'We went downstairs together from the dining room that night,' she says, clearly and slowly.

'As usual?'

'Yes. I don't remember which one of us got into bed first, but we were both undressing at the same time and we both got into bed at nearly the same time.'

But Mr Inglis is hurrying her, getting her tongue-twisted in that way she does when she's nervous. I wish he'd let her speak at her own pace, but he doesn't.

'My sister was in bed with me before I was asleep. I don't know which one of us fell asleep first. It wasn't long after we went to bed.'

'And when you woke?'

She stumbles over her words, has to say them again.

'She was in bed with me – when I woke – about eight.'

My dear, dear girl. For I wouldn't have her stand here in this court with me for all the world. If I've done only one good thing in my life, it is that I refused her wish to lie for me, to say that she woke many times through the night and each time saw me lying there beside her. It was what she wanted to do, she said to me just before the sheriff substitute took me away from Blythswood Square.

But I wouldn't let her lie for me. Not like that. It was enough, what she had to do that night. Her knowledge of it was enough.

Mr Inglis is very pleased with himself but I don't know why, as it all sounds terrible to me. Tomorrow Mr Moncrieff will sum up his side of the case, and Mr Inglis the day after. The day after that, the Lord Chief Justice will give his opinion, and the jury will be sent out to consider its verdict.

'We have our useful quandaries,' he says. 'Did you see Emile the night before he died? Did Christina leave the back door unlocked? Neither can be *proven*.'

'And that is good?' I say, glumly.

'That is good,' he says.

When he speaks two days later, he tells the jury that 'no man probably can tell certainly at the present moment how L'Angelier met his death. Yet it is but fair that we should for a moment consider the character of this man: his origin, his previous history, the nature of his conversation, the numerous occasions upon which he spoke of suicide, naturally suggest *that* as one mode by which he may have departed this life.'

It is suicide, then, that will linger in the jury's minds. That, and the trial of one Eliza Fenning, who was accused of murder and hanged, only for the true perpetrator to come forward a long time after. Mr Inglis relishes this, licking his lips. *Do not make of her another Eliza!*

He thinks about the newspapers as much as I do. The reporters in the courtroom have pricked up their ears, for the case of Eliza Fenning was once as famous as my own is now. The Paris correspondent of the *Herald* even had to apologise to his readers, for thanks to the 'cause célèbre now going on in Edinburgh and which is creating so great an interest in Paris', he had no other news for them.

'Her case,' Mr Inglis says of Eliza Fenning, 'remains a flaming beacon to warn us against the sunken rocks of presumptuous arrogance ... it teaches us, by terrible example, *to avoid confounding suspicion with proof*... I pray God that neither you nor I may be implicated in the guilt of adding another name to that black and bloody catalogue.'

Do not make of her another Eliza.

They'd never hang a stunner.

Two reasons for them not to condemn and kill me.

But I may have a third reason, very soon. For I have another secret, but I won't tell it yet.

I wait in my cell below the court, my hands still in my lap. Miss Aitken waits with me, as does Mr Inglis.

I'm wondering not about death anymore, though. I'm wondering about life, and when life begins to show on a woman. When her belly will begin to protrude through her dress. How a crinoline is managed.

My menses should have come last week; they should have come five weeks ago.

They should have come months ago, but I forgot all about them, and then I didn't notice, of course, because of my worry over going to trial.

But now I know it. The douche I performed after that time with Emile wasn't good enough. And now *he* grows inside me. The essence of him.

Reborn.

A clerk from the court knocks on the door and nods at Mr Inglis.

'It's time, then, Madeleine,' Mr Inglis says.

'I didn't kill him,' I murmur. *For he is not dead.* How can he be, when he is *inside me*?

I go along the corridor to the door that leads to the stairs up into the courtroom, as I have done every morning these past few days. The jury has been out for barely thirty minutes. That's a good sign, Mr Inglis says, just before I ascend the stairs.

I reach the top, and into the courtroom I step once again.

I must remain standing for the verdicts, and my body is strangely still, I do not tremble at all. Mr Inglis nods at me, and the Lord Justice-Clerk is handed a note by an officer.

'On the first charge of Intent to Murder?'

Not guilty.

It seems as though the walls are shaking, such is the cheering and stamping outside on the High Street, as the first verdict is repeated.

We love you, Madeleine, someone shouts.

They love me? I look about; there's a rustling in the courtroom, as though some creature has been let loose to slither through and we must make way for it.

'On the second charge of Intent to Murder?'

Not proven!

The noise outside is so deafening I almost cover my ears. *Not proven?* I'm confused suddenly – it's not *not guilty*, which is what Mr Inglis has promised. What will it mean? Will I be imprisoned?

'On the third charge of Murder?'

They will kill me. They will condemn me and murder me.

Not proven!

The courtroom erupts. I still don't understand what it means. Am I free? I reach helplessly for Mr Inglis, but other men are surrounding him, clapping him on the back. Then suddenly a man leaps from the spectator's gallery down on to the court, right in front of me, and I scream. Cheers deafen the officers' cries as they apprehend him; Mr Inglis fights through his colleagues to reach me, as the judge bangs his gavel. It does nothing to deter anyone, for there's such cheering and whooping inside the court, and outside.

'What does it mean?' I say, desperately, to Mr Inglis.

But the judge announces it first. 'The prisoner is free to go,' he bellows.

Mr Inglis seizes my arm and shouts in my ear that I must go back downstairs, for the crowds will want to celebrate my release, and there's no controlling a crowd bent on celebration, he says.

I still don't understand – what is there to celebrate? *Not proven!* It means they think I killed him, but they can't prove it. I'm arguing about it with Mr Inglis as he bundles me back downstairs as though I'm returning to my cell, which cannot be right. But once I'm there, I find a young woman struggling out of her dress.

I am to change out of mine, Mr Inglis says. He has paid this young woman to be a decoy. As we wordlessly exchange dresses, my brother Jack calls from the corridor outside.

'Hurry, Maddie!' he says. 'You're to come with me.'

And then Mr Inglis rushes us both along another corridor to the back of the building. An unmarked carriage waits for us there.

'Get her to Rowaleyn as fast as you can,' he says – then he slams the carriage door shut.

VI.

'It is the letter of a girl rejoicing in what had passed, and alluding to it in one passage in particular in terms which I will not read, for perhaps they were never previously committed to paper as having passed between a man and a woman.'

– The Lord Justice-Clerk charge to the jury in the trial of Madeleine Smith, 9 July 1857, Edinburgh

New York, 1927

The following morning, Harry didn't show again. Perhaps he hadn't found the right bulb for his light. I poured myself a strong cup of tea, and sat in the window and watched the street for a while, patting my chest every so often, for I was still anxious.

But as the sun rose and set and the Chrysler never appeared, my anxiety eased a little. I prepared a small supper, played my records quietly. That night, I slept more easily.

The next day was just the same. A small hope began to grow in me that perhaps he had given up.

Perhaps he'd even gone back out west.

Perhaps he'd realised all by himself that something was wrong; that there was a reason I couldn't give him what he wanted. That a name, in the end, just wasn't enough.

On the third morning that he still didn't show, I felt that things had truly shifted, somehow. I could breathe better, and enjoyed taking my time washing and dressing, sipping my tea by the window, even waving to a child chasing a hoop along the sidewalk. I decided I might go and call on Violet. She'd sent a note the day before to say that Tom was much better, which was a great relief. She was still at his apartment taking care of him. I decided to surprise them both with a visit, and looked out my hat and gloves, my purse. The day was a little cooler, and I thought I'd walk a block or two before taking the trolley car.

I was humming to myself when the doorbell rang. I was just about to shut the parlour window when he shouted through the front door in that actor's voice of his, 'Mrs Sheehy!', and my heart sank.

'I have plans for the day!' I said, rudely, when I opened the door to him. 'And you're not one of them.'

But he wouldn't take no for an answer. He seemed very sombre, I thought, though, not his usual self, as he helped me down the steps and into his motor.

He knows it's our last day, I thought. Somehow he knows it, too.

The days without him hadn't weakened my plan. Now it came roaring back, building just as my courage did all through that journey, block after block after block. The moment I'd humiliate him, destroy his show.

So I was brisk, once we had reached the Waldorf and were upstairs in his grand suite. He looked at me in some surprise. 'Let's get to the point, Harry,' I said. 'Ask me your question. Go on.'

I readied myself on the chair in front of the dazzling light. The words were on the tip of my tongue. *I'm not who you think I am.* But he surprised me by shaking his head. 'Tell me about when you first came over here,' he said, quietly.

I blinked.

'You sailed on the *Arizona*, September 1893, is that right?'

'That's right,' I said, with a little shrug.

'You left behind in London your husband and your daughter. That was a strange thing to do.'

It was as though he was talking to himself, trying to work something out. It wasn't what I expected and it threw me off-course a little. 'Not really,' I said, momentarily forgetting my plan. 'I was just *visiting* Tom. I intended to go back, of course—'

'But you didn't go back. You've stayed here, almost thirty years. Why?'

'Because I met Willy.'

'Not right off the boat, you didn't.'

'I fell in love with the city,' I said.

'And out of love with your husband, George?' Harry sat back, thoughtful, watching me. 'You married him in 1861. Just four years after your trial. He was the drawing master in the town where you were living, Devonport, where you'd gone to live just a couple of years earlier. You got married in London, though, because George was taking up a post with William Morris, the designer.'

'My, you have been doing a lot of research,' I said.

'And you had two children together, Tom and Mary. You held parties for artists like Rossetti, who was a friend of Morris's. You joined Morris's Socialist League. You worked alongside the likes of George Bernard Shaw—'

'Yes, yes,' I said, impatiently. All this proof of who I was, when I wanted to establish something else, was testing me now.

'What was he like, Rossetti? I mean, what did *you* like about him?'

'I – I – well, he was a genius, of course.' But I didn't want to say this; I wanted to make a fool of him, not shore up his 'discovery'.

'It's a long life in London,' he said, steepling his fingers. 'You lived there almost thirty years, Lena. Had so many friends.

Gave all those parties, joined those societies. But here you live so quietly.'

My fingers twitched, as though they wanted to grasp hold of something.

'Why didn't you ever marry Willy, when you loved him?' he asked, suddenly.

'But I did!' I said.

'There are no documents saying you did so. Not in New York City, anyway. I've been checking.'

I fell silent. Was this my moment? Had it come at last? I opened my mouth, ready to astonish him, when he said, 'You never divorced George. But you could have married Willy after George's death in 1910. And yet, there's no record that you ever did.'

A kind of pleasing coolness bloomed over my chest.

'I went down to the Port Authorities yesterday,' he said. 'Oh, I was thinking I'd report you, see, for not being married to William Sheehy. Violet thinks you were. I figured, if you weren't married to Sheehy, then you could be deported – oh, I wasn't looking to do that, just to hold it out as a threat, make you give me what I wanted.

'So I went to the Port Authorities looking for information, and they looked you up for me, and it was just like I said – you came here on the *Arizona*, September 1893.'

My fingers found the sides of my chair. 'Yes,' I said. How to challenge him now, though? When he was so convinced I was truly who he'd always thought I was? He'd never believe me now. My chance seemed to be slipping away from me. I gripped harder.

'You even signed your name in the ship's books. "Lena Wardle, London."'

There was an odd light in his eyes.

'Thing is, though, you gave your year of birth as 1857. The year of the trial. Isn't that odd?'

That was news to me. I blinked. 'But I couldn't have—'

'It's right there in black and white. "Lena Wardle, London, 1857". Why'd you write that?'

My mouth dried.

'You want to know what I think?' he said. He leaned forward so that he was close enough for me to see the pores on his nose, the sweat on his upper lip. His eyes were a little too pink; the crows' feet were deeper than I'd first thought. It occurred to me he might not live a long time, a man like him. 'I think that maybe you were thinking about the trial year for some reason, and put down the wrong date. Simple as that.' He leaned away.

My shoulders sagged. 'Harry – it's not what you think—' I began to say, but he held up his hand.

'Maybe you saw it as the year you got a chance to live again, when you might have been hanging dead, and now you were heading to New York to start over. Was that it, Lena?'

The stubble on his chin was dotted with grey. I glanced at his hair, that smoothly creamed parting of his that was too black, and realised that he dyed it.

'Or maybe – and this is the crazy idea that's been bothering me. Maybe there's more than one Lena Wardle. There's the Lena Wardle who used to be Madeleine Smith, and there's the Lena Wardle who didn't, who has nothing to do with any of it. Whose birth year really is 1857.'

Two Ruth Snyders. Two Lena Wardles.

And I began to smile.

'You like that?' he said, bending forward to me again. 'But why pretend to be someone you're not? That's the question I can't answer. You *must* be the right Lena Wardle. Only that date, that date . . . It makes no sense. I just – how can I know if you are the right one? The right Lena Wardle? Because if you're *not*, then – ah, then I'm only making the biggest mistake of my life, and you're making the biggest fool out of me.'

He'd arrived there all by himself; I hadn't had to do a thing. What a triumphant moment it was for me. His confusion was writ across his face, the worry of humiliation ageing him ten years in a second. I allowed myself a small smirk.

'Perhaps I am, Harry,' I said. 'But you can never be sure, can you? What a great risk I've turned out to be for you.'

'Then tell me who you are, Lena! Once and for all. Tell me the truth. Who are you?'

I stood up and turned round, headed for the door. But just at that moment of victory, something stuck in my throat. My vision fogged and my heart leapt. No, I thought, no. *Not now I've won.*

In my panic, I stumbled, and my fingers grappled in the air for a hold that wasn't there. Harry reached out to catch me and save me from falling, but I wouldn't take hold of what he offered.

The 'truth' of a ship's logbook.

The 'truth' about myself.

And as I fell to the floor, the 'self' I'd been hiding so long took her chance, and my eyelids fluttered, and my voice shook, as I spoke the name I hadn't used in decades.

Emily.

Oh, it had been patient with me the last thirty years. My real name. Biding its time, holding its breath, as it became *her* name instead, and I buried myself deep within it.

For once upon a time, thirty-seven years ago, I had spent every day of three weeks standing on a corner of Bloomsbury in London, on Charlotte Street, opposite house number nine.

The street was always clattering and busy with carriages and callers, so nobody noticed or cared about a drably dressed young woman, staring and biting her lip and fretting with her purse for hours at a time. It was a mild autumn that year, with blooms flowering and the trees still in leaf; perhaps the gentleness of that October day gave me the courage I'd been lacking thus far, to take my first step over the road, and dodge between the carts and the carriages, the omnibuses that trundled over the earth.

Deliveries had been getting dropped off regularly all through those three weeks, for they did a lot of entertaining at number nine, and there were a lot of callers, too. Serious-looking young folk, most likely friends of the girlish-faced young woman whom I'd observed walking out with a baby in a perambulator every morning.

But *she* never appeared: the one I was waiting for. In rain or shine, she never showed. I looked for back entrances, for lanes and servants' doors, but she never showed there, either. It seemed she liked to be about early, and to walk out late. For no sinister reason; these were just the hours when she preferred the world, when she could think.

That day around noon, though, something pushed me on. The young woman had just left the house with her child as usual. There weren't usually callers until the afternoon; there were no delivery carts stationed outside.

My chance had finally come and, picking up my skirts and clenching my fists, I made for the painted black door. A surprise shower burst from the heavens just before I pressed the doorbell, one of those new electric ones, and I looked up at the sky, as though it was sending me a message, too.

It felt like for ever to me, standing in the pouring rain after ringing the bell. Finally, though, calls were uttered behind the door for a servant to answer, and that was who I expected to meet when it opened. I readied myself with my introduction. *I'm here to call on Mrs Wardle.* I never did think about what I'd say after that.

But, to my shock, it was the mistress of the house who greeted me, not a servant. I was still brushing raindrops from my skirts when she said, 'Can I help you?' in that light and cheerful voice of hers, in an accent that couldn't be easily placed. It was the kind of voice that said she'd be a good host of parties.

When I looked up though, it was her eyes that made the words catch in my throat, not her voice.

For her eyes were my eyes, too. My eyes, large and blue-green, and staring right back at me.

My life growing up in Devonport hadn't been a bad one. My adoptive parents, George and Ellen, had cared for me very much.

When my mama told me the truth about my origins just before she died, I scarcely heard the name of the unmarried stranger who had given birth to me.

'Peter is no less your brother for not being born to us either,' my mama said of the brother I adored, 'and I am always your mama.' But in that moment it was as if she had ripped my brother out of my arms, and exiled me from our home.

My papa, who'd been the curate at St Stephen's church nearby, had died a year before without a word about any of it, leaving it all for my mama to shoulder. The Home for Fallen Women that they'd founded together beside the church didn't last long after his demise; Mama was too bereft to carry it on, and I had no interest in it – nor did Peter. We moved, my mother and I, to a smaller house just a street away from the home where I'd done my growing and my grieving; at thirty years of age, I'd been engaged twice, but the Boers took my first love, and Burma my second, and I swore I'd never get engaged again.

So I stayed home, helping Mama direct the sorry young women who'd still come looking for Papa, asking to be saved by him even after he was gone, to another town, another sanctuary. After Mama's funeral, I sat in the church I'd known all my life, where my papa had given his weekly sermons, and though it had only shown me kindness thus far, I cursed it for keeping the truth about my origins from me all these years.

It was easier to blame the church than blame my mama. When she told me about my own birth in the very house that I'd forever called home, I'd asked, 'Did she fight to keep me, my birth mother?'

I knew what the answer would be, though; hardly any of the girls who came to the Home for Fallen Women fought to keep their babies. They knew it was set against them from the start, the world.

So I asked, too quickly, 'Why did you keep me for yourself?'

Mama, though she couldn't speak much in those last days because of her illness, said, 'I knew the moment I looked at you that I couldn't give you away to anyone. I loved you as though you were my own flesh and blood.'

It wasn't enough to make me forgive. Her body was fresh in the earth when I gathered up my most necessary things and made my way to the train station in the middle of the night. The streets of Devonport were quiet; I waited on a deserted station platform for the first train to London, watching the sunrise and refusing to weep, without any plan in my head beyond finding my birth mother.

Her name was Lena Smith; that was all I knew. I had no idea where she lived, except that my mama had let slip something about London being too big to find anything or anyone when I voiced my intention to go looking for her.

So, before my departure, I had gone raking through my mama's correspondence: every letter, every enquiry, every official-looking statement, and all my papa's correspondence, too. And I found a birth certificate marking the date of my birth, and my name, Emily Mason, with George and Ellen Mason listed as my parents.

A lie made official by the erasing of the woman who'd laboured to bring me into the world.

Lena Smith.

If she was married now, so many years after my birth, I couldn't yet know. She might even be dead. But I was going to look for her, just the same.

How to find a Lena Smith in London, without any more information beyond my own date of birth, turned out to be an impossible task, though, and I soon realised there was probably more truth back in Devonport. And so, six months after I'd left for London, I was back to stay with my brother Peter and his wife while I searched for more information.

It was by chance that one day I found myself in conversation with a woman who'd once run a boarding house in town on George Street, the same street on which I'd been born.

When I asked, half-heartedly and expecting very little, if she remembered anything about a 'Lena Smith' thirty-odd years ago, my shock that she did was almost greater than the news about the truth of my birth had been.

'Why, yes I do, for she was a young lady who married one of my boarders. The drawing master, he was,' she said. 'I'll never forget him – George Wardle was his name, and he was so very handsome. His art classes were full of all the young ladies for miles around. He moved to London with her, was what I heard.'

How simple it was. A chance meeting, a conversation, and then I was back on the train to London, searching parishes for marriage certificates and wedding notices. It took me almost six months, but I found it.

Madeleine Hamilton Smith and George Young Wardle, at St Paul's Church in Knightsbridge, 4 July 1861.

'Can I help you?'

That they were the first words she ever said to me seemed significant later, but at the time, as I stood on the doorstep, I was so unnerved I could barely reply at all, and so she repeated herself.

Then she said, 'Are you here for my daughter, Mary? Because she's just left.'

'No,' was all I said, at first. Then a tentative, 'I'm here – for *you*.'

She looked at me properly then; she told me afterwards that she knew, in that moment, exactly who I was. Her arms shifted by her sides, and her sea-wide blue-green eyes opened so it seemed her face was nothing but looking. We stared at one another as the world passed noisily by along Charlotte Street, and then she reached out for my sleeve and pulled me in over the threshold.

What I felt in that moment wasn't at all what I'd expected. I'd thought elation – or relief – would be my primary feeling, but instead apprehension flooded me. For the first time, it occurred to me she might not want me; strangely, it had never struck me before, not once in over a year of searching.

'George – my husband – is out,' she said, breathing a little hard, her fist curled at her neck. It was a gesture I recognised in myself. 'He'll be back soon – I have a party tonight, you see.'

The vestibule was long and narrow and rather shabby, and lined haphazardly with plants and mirrors and paintings. Boxes of all sorts and sizes were piled up against the walls, wherever there was space. 'It's a rather large party,' she said, and patted her forehead with her palm, as though it was too hot; she indicated the spattered apron she wore over a plain, charcoal dress.

'I've been in the kitchen all morning with Alice. Our cook. I think perhaps we might go' – she looked about her – 'upstairs.'

She bade me follow, and at the top of the stairs turned to the first door on her right. It was a bright room that faced the street, and was clearly her own, judging by the decoration and the framed portraits of two children, a girl and a boy. *Her* children, I assumed. I still hadn't spoken since standing in the doorway downstairs, but now I found my voice.

'I only wish to know—' I said, but she took me by surprise then, silencing me with a sudden hug, pulling me into her with real strength.

When we parted, I saw her face better, and noted the smoothness of her skin, the few wrinkles, the merry aspect to her eyes that my own lacked; she looked young for her age, and in that respect we differed, for I looked very much my thirty-three years. She seemed only a little older than me in attitude, as well as in looks.

It struck me that to an onlooker, we might more closely resemble sisters than mother and daughter.

Her hair was a deep, dark red, where mine was mousy brown, and there was a little rouge on her cheeks and on her lips, for all she had been baking or some such in the kitchen below. My glamorous older sister, the one who liked to party, I thought. And somehow, that felt easier to manage; the tide of emotion in me receded a little, for which I was thankful.

'I hoped – I knew – one day, you'd come,' she said. 'What did they name you?' Her eyes had filled; she dabbed at the corners with fingers short and stubby, like mine.

'Emily,' I said, looking down at my gloved hands. I pulled them off, as if to show her. 'I'm known as Em – for short.'

She laughed suddenly, a short burst of laughter. 'Oh my,' she said. 'Well, I'd never have chosen that. I wanted Charlotte. And here I am – on Charlotte Street! As though it was a sign.'

She beamed; I was still savouring my might-have-been name, Charlotte, on my tongue, when she said, 'Will you wait here? I'll go down and tell Alice I have a guest, and we need tea. If you hear something break, it'll just be her temper; we've so much to do, you see.'

I nodded, and she headed for the door.

'Oh – and sit down, please!' she said, turning to give me another devastating smile. 'I won't be long.'

My legs gave way, rather than let me sit, after she closed the door. I put my hand to my heart and tried to ease its bumping with slow breaths. The room itself might have been designed for calm, so easeful it was in the forest depictions on the walls and on the cushions, in the giant marigolds on the wallpaper, and the soft golds of the lampshades. I felt as though I were in some kind of prelapsarian wood; even the rugs at my feet depicted deer and rabbits, and the sofa itself was a deep olive colour, maintaining that sense of the natural world. There were three large vases of fading flowers that added to the cheerful messiness of the room, and two planters by the high window. Her husband, Mr Wardle, worked for the Arts and Craftsman, William Morris, of course. The evidence of his influence was everywhere.

But I couldn't relax, beautiful as it was. I took off my gloves, and unpinned my hat, but wouldn't remove my little jacket, not yet. My outfit was clean and my best one, but in this room it showed up poorly, as something old-fashioned and too plain. I never carried a mirror with me, for I'd never cared much about my looks. But now I wished I'd done something better with my hair that morning, and pinched my cheeks for a little colour. My complexion tended towards sallow and I wondered if I, too, could do with some rouge. I bit my lip to bring the blood to it, in compensation.

Already, after only a few minutes, I was meeting and matching her ways of looking. That would take on further and faster than I knew then, in that untidy but beautiful room. At this point, I wasn't so aware of it; I only knew that I wanted not to disappoint her.

When she came back, she'd dispensed with the apron, and seemed to have taken a sip of something, for I caught a whiff of alcohol – brandy, possibly – when she told me Alice would be up in a minute. I couldn't blame her; I'd have taken a sip of brandy myself if it was offered. Her dress was still the same one, but without the apron, it showed more of a loose style, tied at the waist, with a lower, wider neckline, and now long pearls and other little gem stones hung from her neck. Though her hair was still up, little strands tumbled from her forehead, and I was minded of those paintings by Rossetti of medieval princesses that I'd seen in a gallery in town.

'I always hoped you'd find me – one day,' she said, sitting beside me on the sofa. An aroma of lemons and roses engulfed me. 'Do you mind?' she said, stroking back a loose hair from my cheek, to tuck it behind my ear.

I wasn't untidy, quite the opposite, but she wanted to touch me, for then she put her hand under my chin before taking my whole face in her palms and giving me soft kisses on both my cheeks. My eyelids fluttered.

'My dearest, dearest baby girl.'

'Your eyes – they're so like mine.' The words spurted out of me in little starts, that sudden new fear of rejection still there. I longed for reassurance.

She nodded, eyes sparkling like blueish emeralds in a way that mine, however similar they were, never did. Perhaps they'd never had occasion to. 'The same shape, colour,' she said. 'Yes: that's how I knew almost as soon as I saw you.'

Just then, a tray banged against the door, and she got up and opened it to an aged crone of a woman. 'Alice, thank you! Alice, this young woman is—'

'Emily,' I said, hurriedly. 'Emily Mason.'

She looked puzzled for a moment; perhaps she'd really meant to announce me to her cook, or housemaid, or whoever Alice was, as her daughter, her first-born. But I wasn't ready for that yet. I wasn't ready to share my discovery – my 'mother' – with anyone yet.

She seemed to understand though, and nodded, saying, 'Emily. It is a pretty name,' as Alice scowled and turned away and shut the door behind her. She shrugged. 'Alice has been with us since I had Mary – she's part of the family.'

I took one of the sandwiches she offered, though I wasn't hungry at all; in fact, I wondered how I'd manage to keep it down, my stomach was in such a turmoil, but the cup of tea helped a little, although I only ever sipped at the edges of it.

'Where do we start? Oh, there's so much to say – you must have so much to tell me! Is it too much?' she said.

It was, suddenly, too much indeed, and to my surprise, and my shame, even, I started to cry.

She took the teacup from me without saying a word, holding my hands as I sobbed. Then she took a handkerchief from her skirts pocket and dabbed at my face, murmuring, 'There, there,' just like a mother would. 'My poor baby girl.'

That did produce a small laugh from me. 'I'm thirty-two!' I said. 'Thirty-three at the end of the year.'

She patted my shoulders and sighed. 'Of course. All those years! But tell me about yourself, I want to know – are you married? Do you have children of your own?'

I shook my head, gulping a little. 'I've never been married – "unlucky in love", so my mama – ah, I'm sorry—'

'No, no – she *is* your mama. Dearest Ellen – and how is she? Did she give you my details? I'm surprised she knew where, we lost touch—'

I shook my head. 'No – she died. Eighteen months ago. Papa died a year or so before that.'

'You've been alone all this time?'

Again, I laughed a little. 'I'm not a child,' I said, and smiled for the first time, if weakly. 'But I had to come when my mama – Ellen – told me about you. It was only when she was dying that she did.'

'You mean, you grew up thinking she was your mother?'

I nodded. Something strange came over her face then. A hint of betrayal, maybe – or perhaps I was imagining it.

'She wanted to protect you – me – yes, that was it,' she said, and clicked her tongue. 'People do what they think is best. George and Ellen are – were – such good people.'

I didn't ask how she first knew them, because at that moment we heard the door open downstairs and the wail of a baby.

'Oh my,' she said, jumping up. 'That's Mary back already.'

'Don't tell her yet,' I said, fixing my hat in my hurry to be gone. 'Please – I need to go; I just want a little more time.'

'Of course,' she said, pressing her hands on mine. Her hands were soft.

My mother's hands, I thought.

'But you'll come back? You're not staying far from here?' she asked.

I didn't know what to say.

'Come tonight,' she said. 'Come to my party – I'll introduce you as my friend. You can take as long as you like. But please come.'

I could hardly refuse. 'And Mr Wardle?' I said. 'What will he say?'

'Oh, you leave George to me,' she said, smiling. 'The party's for him – he's retiring. Oh my – and I have a cake to decorate! Seven o'clock – I will be expecting you!'

And with that, she hurried me downstairs and out the front door while Mary was in the kitchen with the baby, and somehow I made my way back to my rooms on the omnibus, rattling all the way.

I'd taken a room in a boarding house in Clapham, which was the best I could afford. I didn't know then that it would be one of my last nights there.

I returned from Charlotte Street, shaking and a little hysterical. I sat down on the little iron bed, where the springs poked through the thin mattress, and laughed a little, my hand over my mouth.

I'd arrived at my destination, but with no idea of what to do next. For a few minutes, I rocked back and forth, before a little bout of weeping took over. It was some time later that I washed my face, and, with shaking fingers, started to look out something to wear to the party.

I'd meet my half-sister, Mary, my mother had said. *My mother.* Mary had gone into the morning room with her baby by the time I'd come downstairs, and I hadn't been ready to meet her then anyway. Meeting my mother was enough. But I'd heard her talking to her baby, and it struck me suddenly that I had a whole new family to know.

I had no clothes suitable for London parties. My mother was so very stylish, and no doubt her friends would be, too. I had nothing to even brighten up my dull Sunday-best dresses. I went out to look for some ribbons for a more bohemian touch, but they made it worse. My only option was to play on my drabness, to let it be my disguise. I didn't want to draw attention to myself, after all, especially not at Mr Wardle's retirement party. It wouldn't be kind to do that, I told myself, though I knew it would be impossible for me to outshine the hostess or her husband.

The truth was, I was terrified. All the way on the omnibus back to Charlotte Street that evening, I wished for something to go terribly wrong, like a crash, or even a bomb set off by French anarchists. But it delivered me to my destination, and I made my way to number nine just as I had that morning.

'Emily Mason,' I said, when a maid, a young girl fresh out of school, opened the door. 'Guest of Mrs Wardle.'

'Emily!' she said, appearing in the hallway at that exact moment. The house was alive with folk; it thrummed with talk, and laughter, and the clinking of glasses. A piano was being played in another room – I recognised 'A Wandring Minstrel' – and some people were singing to it, with much laughter. 'Thank goodness you came!' she said in my ear, gripping my arm. 'I wasn't sure you would, after you left.'

'I nearly didn't,' I confessed. 'I'm not so good at parties.'

'My shy girl,' she murmured, before handing my coat to the maid. The door to the drawing room on the left was slightly ajar; I trembled at the noise behind it, the jollity, the strangers I was about to meet. 'But don't worry. And what a lovely brooch you're wearing. To enhance your eyes.'

It was the only piece of jewellery I owned: an emerald brooch of my mama's – of Ellen's – that she'd wanted me to have just after papa died. The only glitter I had, the only shine. She took my hand, then, and smiling, pushed open the door. I held my breath, half-expecting everyone to turn and look my way, but scarcely anybody did, and I found my shoulders easing as the same little maid offered me a glass of punch from a silver tray, and my mother – *my mother* – led me to a vibrant young woman holding court in the far corner.

My half-sister, Mary.

She didn't turn round; only when her mother tapped her on the shoulder did she notice me, and I said, hesitantly, 'My name's Emily Mason – I'm—'

'A convert to your cause, Mary. Aren't you, Emily?'

'Votes for women?' said Mary. She had a real look of her mother in every way except her eyes, and I panicked for a moment, thinking she'd see the resemblance between her mother and me. Certainly for a moment, she looked wonderingly, as though she couldn't understand what she was looking at, and then she smiled, broad and wide, and her mouth, her smile, was indeed her mother's. 'Why then, it's wonderful to meet you!'

I met so many folk that night. Mr Wardle wore a Spanish cloak and sported a long grey beard, which made him look like an elderly musketeer; he was surrounded all night by friends from his society, which looked after old buildings, and they were very passionate about them, too. His employer, William Morris, was a little frightening at first in his odd, jumpy way of speaking and gesturing, and his full figure took up the room. But his wife, Janey, a dreamy-looking woman in a flowing gown that resembled the rugs and paintings upstairs, and her daughter, May, who was similarly dressed, sat apart, observing quietly, and I was grateful I wasn't the only one at odds with parties.

The younger set was more fun and fiery, though; an Irish

theatre critic, George Bernard Shaw, teased me about my emerald brooch and urged me to join their Freedom Group, and not Mr Morris's Hammersmith Socialist Society; there were pamphlets all over the tables, which I'd never seen at a party before, all advocating *Freedom!* and *Revolution!* in dramatic lettering. Mr Shaw made me promise to call at a place in Cursitor Street, as he'd be giving a talk and wanted me to hear it. A dark, handsome Frenchman, Monsieur Coulon, urged me to come, too; so did a woman named Eleanor, but whom everyone called Tussy; she was the daughter of a man they all revered as a god, but I'd never heard his name before.

So much was new to me that night, and only later would I learn who was actually speaking to whom, and which faction of revolutionaries was on friendly terms with another, for they divided and made up as fast as children quarrelling, it seemed. But what might have been intimidating was the very opposite. Despite my buttoned-up dress and lack of style, I felt as though I glittered and dazzled along with everyone else; I laughed and chatted light as air about things I'd never even thought about before, never mind discussed, as the men teased me gently about my 'soft as buttercream' Devonport accent, and the women urged me to march for voting rights. When it was time to leave, my mother kissed me on the cheek and told me again that I was her dearest girl and that I'd done her proud.

I had no notion how soon it would all change for ever.

Two days later, I sat in a coffee house with my mother. She was telling me about the different factions in her political friendships, and I was running just to keep up.

'Does Mr Wardle know yet – about me?' I ventured to

change the subject; we were at a discreet distance from the other tables.

She had a fun air about her, a conspiratorial one; she loved games, I could see that already, and she loved secrets, too.

'Ah!' she said. 'Mr Wardle has always known about you. But no – in case you are wondering, George is not your father.'

We sat in silence for a moment or two. I drank my coffee while she seemed to ponder hard, frowning, not wanting to interrupt though I was bursting with more questions.

'All in good time,' she said at last. 'I will tell you about him – your father,' she added. 'Just – I want a little time, that's all.'

I was disappointed but understood. I could be patient a little longer. We left the coffee house and went on to Cursitor Street together, where Shaw was in a panic about what to do, as he had to cancel his speaking arrangement. My mother suggested finding someone else to read out his speech for him.

At this advice, he smacked his head in exasperation, saying, 'I should have thought of that!' and even asked if I would give the speech for him. Fortunately, another young man, by the name of Aveling, arrived and said he would do it.

I was still in a tizz, my head spinning, when we left some time later, so I didn't notice the raggedy, bony old woman covered in a shawl who must have followed us all the way to Charlotte Street.

I'd expected she was one of the raggle-taggle of folk that my mother's group were fighting for when I turned to her, but her hood had slipped to show a look of such malevolent intent on her face that it made me gasp out loud.

The crone laid a bony hand on my mother's shoulder before I

could stop her, and in a hoarse and chilling voice said, 'Maddie! Don't you remember me? Your old housemaid, Christina? Let me in, now, won't you? We've got something to talk about.'

And my mother's mouth fell open in shock.

Rowaleyn, 1857

I've never known Rowaleyn to be as silent as this. For there to be no parties given, no dinners. No friends of Mama and Papa calling, or staying with us. We have hardly any servants, either. No Christina, of course, and Mama is having trouble engaging folk from the village.

Because of me.

It is clear that L'Angelier exercised an influence of the most hateful kind . . . Her own character cannot be positively settled unless we go beyond the jury and confirm or reject the charge against her. Is she a Lucrezia Borgia, or is she only a boarding-school miss, led by a designing and theatrical Frenchman into a copy of a Parisian romance?

So one newspaper has written. I am either a Lucrezia Borgia or a boarding-school miss, and Mr Inglis said a choice between two was a good thing. But it became a choice between *three*, in my case: between guilty, not guilty and not proven.

A choice between three, which I did not deserve.

How little they understand anything, the newspapers. I don't know whether to be alarmed, or to laugh, at some of the things they've been writing about me since the verdict. Papa thinks to hide his newspapers and magazines away in his study, but I sneak in there at night and read them all. Why he keeps them, when they must give him so much pain, I don't know. Perhaps it's because they wonder, the newspapers, how many 'foreigners' might have been 'sneaking into the bedrooms' of the 'respectable daughters of Empire' through the length and breadth of the country all this time, and right under the noses of their 'noble, ignorant fathers'.

Perhaps Papa thinks of himself as 'noble' and 'ignorant', too. The father of a Lucrezia Borgia or a boarding-school miss. He doesn't understand, either. He thinks only that I lied to him, not about what Emile did to me.

Some newspapers remember his wickedness. The people certainly have. That's why they love me. Even if I am an *abnormal spirit*, as the Glasgow Sentinel says. The Examiner says I have *demeaned* myself; the London Morning Post that I am *a thoughtless girl and witless of the ways of the world*.

Of all of them though, one stands out to me.

A wolf had indeed stolen into the fold and entrapped one of its precious lambs; but what family might not suffer from such a disaster?

I wonder how the Glasgow Citizen has such an insight into it.

The wind is so very squally here, even in the middle of summer, what with our house being so high up on the hill. I fear the sound it makes sometimes, moaning as it does against the windows in the night, trying to get in. If I open the window, it will whistle through my room like a long-dead soul returning home.

Last night, though, the rain poured down and there wasn't a breath of wind. Washing it all away, I hoped. Washing away that *something* that waits outside for me now, pawing the grass, slinking through the woods. Howling with the wind.

When I go downstairs in the morning for breakfast, I tread carefully. Mama is complaining about draughts in the dining room, though the wind's gone now and it's damp and humid instead. A sticky August. My ringlets cling to my neck.

'Keep the windows shut, James,' Mama is saying to Papa.

He nods at her, which I notice he does much more often now. He wants to sell Rowaleyn, for all he loves it, and move away.

Because of me.

I take my seat beside Janet and open my mouth to say something about the heat, before catching sight of the morning's newspaper, still folded on the table. Papa would usually have read it by now. He takes it up, leaving the room as soon as I enter it, and without a word to me.

'Is anyone else waiting for post?' I ask, reaching for the coffee pot. It's almost empty and the toast rack has only a single slice left. I took too long with my hair and my skirts. We have no housemaid yet to help us dress, which is why Janet's wearing an old smock with stains on it. She takes the last slice of toast before I can reach it, then offers it to me, shame-faced.

'No matter,' I say, smiling at her. 'I'll ring for more.'

'There's only Susan,' Janet said, then glances at Mama, who's staring straight ahead of her.

'The new laundry maid?' I say. 'So she's arrived at last? Have we lost our cook, too?'

Janet crams the last piece of toast into her mouth as Mama stands up, pale and sweating, and swaying a little. She clearly has one of her headaches coming on. I move round the table to help steady her, but she has no need of my arm, reaching for Janet instead, and so together they leave the room and I am alone.

I open the window in spite of Mama's command, and take in deep breaths. The sky is cloudy grey, and the lawn, a little overgrown from our long absence, glistens from the rain the night before. Dark rhododendrons and the ancient oaks border the grass, and beyond them flows the great river.

I have a fancy to climb up to the top of one of the house turrets. What might I see from so high up, I wonder. We're far away from the St Rollox chimney, but a little of its sooty flotsam and jetsam, like tiny pieces of ash, has occasionally blown in and landed on our windowsills to coat them with a fine dusting. Perhaps I'll see the chimney from the turret, too.

Dust and treasure and new houses like castles.

The dining-room door opens; it's Janet, sneaking back in.

'How are you, Maddie?' she says, big blue eyes opening wide. 'Are you feeling better? Is the morning sickness easing?'

Her hair's in a dreadful tangle; I beckon her over to the window, and smooth down her curls.

'You're thirteen,' I say, 'you should be able to dress yourself better than this. I'm surprised Mama didn't send you back upstairs.'

'She didn't say a thing,' Janet says, wrapping her arms tightly around my waist, burying her face in my bosom. She shivers, weeping a little into my bodice. 'I kept thinking I'd say the wrong thing at the trial,' she mumbles, and for a moment my own eyes fill, too.

'But you didn't. You got it just right,' I say, and kiss the top of her head.

'But I could have said I woke up during the night, lots of times. And that you were there each time.'

'No, I didn't want you to, I told you that before they took me away. On no account—'

'But I could have – you wouldn't have had that verdict then.'

'All that matters is that I am here, and you are here, and Christina is . . .'

The less said about Christina the better. *We three.* Maybe she did mean all along, in her wicked, twisted way, to be rid of Emile. And even to be rid of me. I shiver.

'No more of this now, Janet.' I imitate Papa's voice and affect a stern look, to make her laugh.

She nods and smiles her baby smile.

'You didn't notice any post in the hall for me, did you?' I say, to change the subject.

'Is he coming to us after all – Mr Minnoch?' she says. 'Mama says he'll not. Mama says he's too ashamed.'

'Ah, who wants dull William Minnoch?' I say. 'But you should go upstairs and change out of that filthy smock. Have a bath!'

'Will you run it for me? We only have Susan to do anything.'

'Well, that won't do for very long, when there's more work to come. Mama must advertise straightaway. Or send a note to the village.'

'She says they won't want to, because of . . . But I can help out.'

'You and I together,' I say. But my stomach's rumbling, so I send Janet upstairs, tell her I'll be along shortly.

In our huge, silent kitchen I find the girl whom I assume to be Susan. She's all elbows and pale hair and sharp cheekbones and large hands. She's eating porridge like a veritable

Goldilocks, and doesn't get up when I enter but carries on eating, so I introduce myself.

'Miss Janet wants me to run her a bath. And we've run out of coffee,' I say. 'So I'm making myself some more before I do a thing.'

On the pantry shelf sits a biggin, a jar of coffee beans and a coffee mill. After I've ground a few beans just for myself, and boiled them until I'm happy with the result, I join Susan at the table.

'You'll have to get used to me being in the kitchen more often,' I say, 'until Mama can get more staff.' I like the idea of cooking, and say so. 'Here – I've made more than enough coffee for two. I always make too much. Have the rest with your porridge.'

She shakes her head and mumbles something about washing day before disappearing into the scullery. I'm not about to follow her in there, so I finish my coffee and go upstairs to Janet. Once she's in her bath, I decide to go out and pick some herbs from the garden – lavender is good for sore muscles, and so is rosemary. I could crush some in a mortar with a pestle and make a little poultice out of it.

'What will we do when they find it *all* out, though?' Mama is demanding.

We're in the drawing room, and it is after I disobeyed her by going out into the garden after all, and that group of men and women recognised me and tried to climb the gate. Only Papa shooting in the air made them stop. 'She'll be showing very soon, James. Dear God, but the shame of it. Does it never end?'

Papa mumbles something.

Mama says, 'I told her not to set a foot outside! Does she ever do what she's told?'

'How was I to know that people would follow us to Rowaleyn?' I say.

After Mr Inglis had bundled me and Jack into a carriage together, we drove to the station for the train for Greenock. I didn't get to speak to even one of my supporters, and there were so many hundreds of them outside the court, all of them waiting for me. For me!

'There is only one solution,' Mama says, still refusing to look at me, or acknowledge my presence. 'She must go away.'

I'm not wholly averse to this suggestion though. I like travelling; I think perhaps Baden-Baden, which is very fashionable now. I think Janet would like it, too, and say so.

Finally, Mama looks at me. 'I think you do not understand, Madeleine,' she says, slowly. 'Or you are being deliberately obtuse.'

She says something in Papa's ear that I cannot hear, then leaves the room, slamming the door behind her.

'I can take Janet with me very easily,' I say, eagerly. 'She'd benefit very much from going abroad. One of the spa towns, maybe, or—'

'Janet will be kept from you and your influence,' Papa says in a quiet voice. 'And for good.'

I can hardly believe my ears.

'Your mother is right. You'll be gone as soon as we can arrange it.' He follows Mama out of the room, stumbling a little.

Kept from me. My own sister, the person I love most in this world. My fists curl; I want to run after him, but the rumble in my belly turns into a kick, and I have to sit down.

It's all Christina's fault. Mr Inglis told me I'd be free, and I am. But he didn't say it would be with the shame of a 'not proven' verdict. Christina's unwillingness to confirm her locking of the back door is what introduced the doubt that saved me, Mr Inglis said. But it's also what condemned me to 'Not proven', and now Papa and Mama will never forgive me.

Yes. It's all Christina's fault. It was her idea, to do away with him in the first place. She urged me on. Brought Janet into it all.

Christina should have been in the dock, not me.

I sit in the drawing room, biting my lip. Perhaps Mama meant for me to go and stay somewhere closer, in the country perhaps, where Janet can still visit me, no matter what Papa says. For my 'lying-in', as Mama calls it in her old-fashioned way.

'I'll not help you bring up that *monster's* child,' she had said, after I told her the truth. I wonder sometimes that Mama doesn't see that there has been enough viciousness – and that she can't see her own part in any of it. If she and Papa had let me introduce Emile in the first place, none of this tragedy would have occurred.

But then I would have been married to him by now. A man who raised me up only to shame and degrade me; who would rather have let me die on the streets.

Christina, Mama, Papa, Emile. They all misused me. They are all to blame.

Papa writes to Mr Inglis, who suggests a place for me with a friend of his, a minister called Mr George Mason, and his wife Ellen, in the south of England. I am to go there for my lying-in, and to remain a few months after, to nurse the baby.

'And afterwards? Am I to bring the child home – to Rowaleyn?'

I demand to know, but Papa doesn't answer. Mama won't speak to me at all, but has taken to locking me in my room, and the window is fixed from outside, so I cannot escape that way, either.

The days are so dull that I agree to travel south out of desperation. Janet and I manage to pass little notes to one another under the door. She wants to come away with me, but it won't be possible; Mama and Papa will never allow it now. Susan is tasked with bringing me my meals, and taking away my hated chamber pot.

Then one night in bed, not long before my departure, I hear it. What sounds like a wolf howling. I light a candle and hold it up against the window pane.

I stare at the black woods beyond, where I used to meet with Emile. My hand rests on my belly. If Emile is anywhere, he is inside me, not out there in the world as William would have had it.

Suddenly it occurs to me that there are many kinds of prisons, and North Prison was only one of them.

They won't let me say goodbye to Janet, which is so unnecessarily cruel of them, I'm almost in tears about it as I pack my last items. I've written a note for her and hidden it where I hope she'll find it. I've told her I'll see her after the baby is born, no matter what Mama and Papa try to do.

She'll be disappointed that I won't be coming home with the baby. Mama and Papa have made that very clear, and though I'm often tearful these days, I'm not tearful at the thought of giving away *his* child. The feeling of being trapped, if only by his child rather than by him, has been growing by the day. Did

Emile intend that, I wonder, when he came at me that night in the kitchen and pushed me against the wall? The memory makes me shudder; what a creature he made of me.

Mimi.

I stopped being Mimi a long time ago. I believed I had become a new Madeleine. My hand settles against my belly. But who am I now?

Only once I'm settled alone in the carriage in the driveway, unhappy and alone, do I lean out to look up at the turret. Janet's face appears at its window. I'd told her to go there, in a brief moment when we were alone, so that we might wave at one another.

I stare up, as if she might have the answer. *Tell me who I am.*

She can only blow me a kiss; I blow one back. *I'll be home soon*, I mouth as I wave. She nods, then presses her face against the glass.

And a fear overwhelms me then, that I will never set eyes on her again.

VII.

'There could be no doubt of the state of degraded and unholy feeling into which she had sunk, probably not the less so if it was produced by his undermining and corrupting her principles.'

– The Lord Justice-Clerk charge to the jury in the trial of Madeleine Smith, 9 July 1857, Edinburgh

New York, 1927

I never did forget that moment I came face to face with Christina Haggart, though I didn't know at the time who she was, or what her relationship was to my mother.

But she opened the door to let in the old woman, and neither of them said another word to me, so I just followed them into the kitchen.

What a bloodless wraith she was. When she pushed the shawl back from her head, and all that wiry, grey hair flew in bundles about weather-lined, sallow skin that was oddly translucent, too, I was shocked by how huge and pale her eyes were. She had the look of a hungry person – or a consumptive, perhaps, and I fought the urge to cover my mouth and nose.

In silence, my mother set a kettle on the range for tea, but she was struggling to stay calm, for I saw her hand tremble when the whistle let out a shriek and she picked it up to pour the water into a teapot. Christina didn't seem interested in me at all. No: her eyes never once left my mother.

'I'm that starved,' Christina said, so I went, unbidden, to the pantry and brought back some bread and cheese, butter, a couple of plates. Christina tore the bread and hunks of cheese with her bare hands, which were dirty.

I sipped my tea, as did my mother, until she found a light, friendly tone.

'How are you, Christina? It's been so many years. What brings you here?'

The old woman finished chewing, then picked her teeth. The kitchen light was low, and at the back of the house, where a small garden spread out across the houses, a fox shrieked. Night had fallen fast while we were waiting for Christina to speak. It occurred to me that my mother might prefer to be alone with her, and I suggested I leave, but she put a hand over mine and muttered, 'No, I want you to stay.'

Christina answered my mother with, 'Oh, I've been here a long, long while now. Came down for work years ago.'

My mother whispered to me, 'Christina was our housemaid – when I was very young.'

Christina drew herself up a little. Her shawl slipped from her shoulders and revealed a threadbare dress that was more suited to a hot summer day, being thin cotton and pale in colour. It was stained, too, under her arms and at spots across the chest; she'd no doubt been sleeping in it. I sniffed, but she didn't smell of the street, or a tavern, or anything but the smoke and the city.

'Not so young as that, Maddie,' Christina said. She coughed, and it turned into a spitting-up into a filthy rag of a handkerchief. 'Not much younger than me, you were.'

'And how is – McKenzie, that was his name, wasn't it? Your husband.'

'Duncan. He died last year. And my son, too. This bloody town.'

My mother's eyebrows rose at the curse and she said, 'I'm so very sorry to hear that. You were all living here together?'

'Moved down for work, didn't we? But illness costs money,' Christina said, lifting her chin. She was proud, for all the tragedies that had befallen her. 'The money's gone now and I've got nothing left. Not a farthing.' She paused. 'You've done all right for yourself. 'Course you have. Ever the grand house for you, *Maddie*,' she said.

My mother grimaced a little at the use of that name.

Christina slapped her palm flat on the table suddenly, and said, 'You can afford to be generous. I can't get work; I'm ill, too ill for work. I need enough for a place to stay, and you owe me that. You owe me.'

My mother pushed back her chair and went out into the hallway for a moment, then returned with her purse. 'I can give you ten shillings,' she said, holding out the note.

Christina burst out laughing. Her teeth were yellow and uneven, and the bottom row was missing some. 'Ten shillings? I want a roof over my head for the rest of my days, and a good hot meal and new clothes. Fifty guineas a year and not a penny less.'

My mother gasped. 'What? Don't be silly. I don't have that kind of money—'

'Twenty, then,' Christina said. 'You can manage twenty. And don't call me silly.' She looked around the kitchen. 'And don't be lying to me, Maddie. You're rich enough.'

'You know I am *happy* to help. You are in need, and I am always happy to help folk in need.'

Christina sniggered, wiped her nose. 'What a liar you are. Ah, you're the same as ever.'

'I can help you get set up somewhere – help with lodgings, perhaps, or a job. I have friends who own factories—'

But Christina was busy rummaging about in the pocket of

her dress. She pulled out a bit of newspaper, crumpled and stained. This time a waft of body odour did indeed hit my nostrils, making me swallow. She flattened out the paper on the kitchen table.

I peered at it. It was from a month ago. A court case in Edinburgh, about some letters stolen from the archive of a trial which had taken place many years ago. The stolen letters had then been sold to a bookshop in Edinburgh for an undisclosed sum of money; the bookseller and the thief were both charged and found guilty, it said.

MADELEINE SMITH TRIAL OF THE CENTURY – SCANDALOUS LETTERS STOLEN – THIEF ARRESTED AND CHARGED

'I can't give you what you want,' my mother muttered.

'It's never going away, Maddie. See how they still talk about you. I know there's a law against a retrial, even for a not proven verdict, Maddie. But think what a new piece of evidence would be like for the papers! A new story from a witness!'

'Don't be silly,' my mother said. 'There's nothing—'

'Don't call me silly. Not when you know there is,' Christina said, getting to her feet. In the light from the hallway, her face showed more clearly. Life had not been kind to that face; it had seen things it should not have seen, been through bad times. I shivered for my mother. 'Just give me my money and nobody needs to know about the three of us. Remember, Janet was part of it, too.'

'The three of us – you'd ruin yourself into the bargain? You tried to destroy me well enough at the trial—'

My mother's voice broke. I gazed in amazement. My mother was on trial once? For what?

But Christina had more to say. 'I'll destroy a lot more than just you, if you don't give me the money.'

'What do you mean?'

'Your fancy friends, your parties, your children. They'd all disappear quick enough if they knew what you really did. So I'll wait till a week today. Landlord won't wait longer than that, and I'm not sleeping on park benches, not in that biting wind. You remember how cold it can get at night, don't you? Remember how it is, when a poor man might need a nice, warm kitchen fire to warm his feet at? Maybe even have a cup of cocoa.'

She gathered her shawl about her, flicking it over her head, then limped out of the door into the passageway. The front door slammed shut.

And then, in the dark of the kitchen, my mother quietly told me who my father had been, and that she'd once been accused of murdering him.

'It is a more – *complicated* story than most,' she said. She got up and went to the pantry, brought out a bottle of brandy and two glasses. 'I was very – *dazzled* by him. He was older, handsome, artistic, cultured. His parents were French, and he'd lived in Paris; he was experienced, worldly-wise. I was, needless to say, quite *in*experienced, a schoolgirl almost. But he was poor, only a clerk. I was rich – my father was an architect. Ah, but that part is dull, it's too common. If there was no poverty in the world – well, would impoverished clerks feel the need to exploit innocent girls who have money? You see my political interest – Mr Morris's beliefs are mine, too. "Have nothing in your home that is neither beautiful nor useful." For we should all be rich; we should all possess only the beautiful, or the useful.' She paused. 'Nobody should be punished for having less; nobody should be punished for *aspiring*.'

'But he was – aspiring? My father?' I asked.

She didn't answer straightaway, but poured us each a generous measure of brandy. I took a tiny sip – I rarely drank alcohol in those days – but my mother gulped it all back and poured herself another measure.

'*My* father was a very narrow-minded man, though,' she said. 'And very hot-tempered, too. He refused even to meet Emile, wouldn't entertain the notion of my walking out with him. To do such a thing to your daughter! He might as well have pushed me into Emile's arms himself. So we began to meet in secret. Ah, that was wrong, of course, but I was in love, so in love.'

She had loved my father. And he had loved her. How tragic that they should have been kept apart. I felt anger on their behalf, and on my own. How different my life might have been, had they been allowed to be together. My feelings tumbled about, and I followed my mother's example and took a deeper gulp of the brandy, which only made me cough. Once I was calm, she carried on.

'But after two years, it was clear that we'd never be allowed to marry. I had to face the truth of it, and accept the man my father had found for me, a man he *did* consider "good enough". And so, I broke with Emile. And in doing so, I broke his heart.

'Poor, poor Emile. He went out of his mind, you see. Which meant he began to threaten me, saying that he would tell my father all about us. His heart was broken, and his mind was, too. I tried to placate him but it was no use. One night, he took something – he always had a need for certain things, like poppy seeds, opium, even arsenic in tiny amounts. And on that night he took too much—'

She stopped as my hand covered my mouth. 'An accident – ?' I mumbled, horrified.

'I can never be sure, of course. He left no note. But I'm quite sure – I'm so sorry to say this – but I'm sure it was deliberate.'

'He – killed himself?'

She held my hands, looked right into my eyes. 'Rather than live without me. He told me so many times he couldn't live without me. It was always my greatest regret that I didn't believe him.'

'But you were – you must have been – pregnant with me. Did he know?'

Her mouth twisted a little. 'Ah, I had no idea I was carrying you when he died. Afterwards, when they found him, and found traces of the poison – well, I had bought some arsenic for my skin, you see. They used to believe it whitened the skin, in those days, and it was very near to my wedding. The police found letters I'd written to your father, so they knew he had threatened to expose me – and, well, they put two and two together and made five, not four. They even arrested me, as though I'd not been through enough. I was grieving – ah, how I grieved him! But a purchase or two of what he had taken himself – it was enough, they thought, to accuse me of murder and put me on trial.

'They had to punish me, you see. For loving a foreign man. For daring to break society's rules. How they wanted to make a spectacle of me! To teach me a lesson, as they do all young women.

'But in the end, I was set free. And the public adored me! You have to know, Emily – the public believed in me. They never left my side. They knew what was happening. They could see the injustice of it. The story was everywhere! I was famous! People didn't understand – they were very cruel about Emile, believing him to be so corrupting. One or two even wrote that he deserved what he'd got. People can be very – heartless. But yes, I was quite a "craze" for a while. They reported on it from here to India, you know.' She gave a small smile.

'What happened – afterwards?' I said.

'I'd have done anything to keep you, you must know that. But I had nothing without my family's support and they wouldn't hear of it. They sent me down south to a friend of my counsel – the man who represented me in court – who happened to be a Mr Mason. He and his wife had not yet started their special "home", but they wanted a child. I stayed with them, and when you were born, they persuaded me to hand you over to them.

'I *had* to leave you behind, do you see? Please tell me you understand, dearest Emily. There was so much publicity. If someone had discovered I'd had a child by the man I was accused of – it would have been—'

And then she closed her eyes, passed a hand over her forehead.

In all my life, I've never felt even the temptation of suicide. Why would I have? My father's decision to do such a terrible thing, when he could no longer have my mother, was a crime against nature, and more; it felt like a crime against *me*, the daughter he never even knew about.

So perhaps that was why I couldn't do it, after I bought the rat poison. Perhaps it wasn't Willy saving me so much as my mother, for we were so alike one another in so many ways.

Harry sat silent during my story. He knew it was the truth.

I'd asked my mother that night in the kitchen what aspects of my father – Emile – she could see in me.

'Your hair,' she'd said. 'And your smile. Your eyes are mine, as we know. You lack that terrible sadness he always carried with him, I am glad to say. His soul knew real darkness, I'm afraid. I can see in your face that you do not, and I'm glad of that.'

His hair. His smile. I liked to paint, but so did my mother. I liked poetry, and so did she. I reminded her of her little sister, Janet, she said, and I liked that.

'The photograph,' Harry said. 'I think I must have noticed it – your eyes.'

'She adored Janet,' I said. 'I don't know why she thought Christina would hurt Janet. She never did explain that. All I remember is that my mother didn't want Christina finding out about *me*. So we decided to take a little trip, to her in-laws in Leek.'

When Christina called at Charlotte Square a week after her appearance at the doorstep, she found that my mother had gone. Sir Thomas, my mother's brother-in-law, lived with his wife, Elizabeth, in a grand, three-storey red-brick house on St Edward Street in Leek, but it wasn't the grandeur that made me gasp when Sir Thomas's carriage stopped at the white, pedimented doorcase, after our train journey from London. No, it was what hung on the wall inside the entrance hall.

I recognised his painting style immediately, dark as the

interior was. Rossetti. His portrait was of a young man trying to pull a woman off her knees – a woman whose face is turned to a wall, such is her shamed refusal to look at him. It wasn't finished, which struck me as extraordinary, and when I gasped out loud and pointed at it, just as the housemaid headed off to fetch her master and mistress, my mother nudged me and whispered, 'I was the model for her, you know. Oh, it's not my face. That was Miss Cornforth. But she grew too large for him to work on later, and so he asked me to sit for it. Twisting round like that for hours on end wasn't comfortable, let me tell you! And the menagerie of his house! There was always something escaping. Once, an armadillo ran right over my feet while I was posing. I gave the biggest shriek you've ever heard.'

My astonishment only amused her. I approached the painting to peer at it more closely.

Both my mother, and *not* my mother.

By my side, she whispered, 'It is a great secret, that I stood in for her though, so you must never tell.'

'Sir Thomas doesn't know?'

'Oh yes, of course, *they* know.'

She was about to say more, but a grey-haired woman breezed into the hallway from a room at the back of the house. She wore a dark silk dress with a high neck, though it was early evening when we arrived and supper would be served soon.

'Lena!' she cried in an imposing way; the friendliness and warmth of Lady Elizabeth, who kissed my mother passionately on each cheek, made me shrink against my mother, who nevertheless pushed me forward like a reluctant little girl at a party. 'Ah, let me see the dear child!'

I didn't know whether to curtsey or bow or what, so I just

stammered, 'Please to meet you' or some such, like an uneducated urchin.

She seized my face in large, strong hands and peered right in my eyes. 'How extraordinary,' she murmured, as I stood, curling my hands into fists to stop myself from pulling away from her scrutiny in panic. I've never cared for strangers to touch me, not as a child, and not as a grown woman either. 'How extraordinary. Those eyes, those eyes.'

It made me so uncomfortable, that close peering of hers, and I thought I might be sick, right there in her grand entrance way. And that was probably the moment when I understood that my mother knew better than I did what I could support, and what I could not.

For it came to me during our stay in Leek that I wasn't of a temperament to endure exposure. The thought of Christina finding out about me, or even following us to Leek somehow, made me anxious. My birth story was mine alone; the tragedy of my father's suicide and the court case was still settling in my head those days, and I couldn't have borne someone discovering it. 'She'd sell you to the newspapers in a second,' my mother said of Christina. 'If she ever found out about you.' She would keep me away from London, she said. Away from Christina.

'We're just having a little holiday, my dear,' she would say whenever I fretted, but I felt fingers at my collar sometimes, creeping round my neck, trying to pull my face towards them, and I dreamt about them at night, too.

And then, one unusually balmy spring morning, after we'd been 'holidaying' in Leek long past Christmas, my mother and I were talking in the garden about the right time to return to

London, when the housemaid called my mother indoors to an urgent telephone call.

George had been in Italy since the New Year, and my mother had been contemplating us both joining him there after she'd been back to London. But now Mary had telephoned to say that Christina had stopped my mother's maid on the way to post some letters, knocking against her so that the post tumbled out of her hands on to the ground. Christina had lunged for them all, and had of course seen Mary's most recent letter to her mother here in Leek.

'Well, it's most annoying she knows where I am now,' my mother tsked, after taking the call. 'I did want to spend some time in London first, before travelling abroad. Ah well, it can't be helped – Christina *is* a pest.'

She made it sound like a small spoiling of her holiday plans, that was all. I was excited to be going to Italy sooner than I expected, though I never asked my mother what exactly Christina was threatening her with, beyond what she'd said that night in the kitchen. My mother's concern was always more for me; she wanted to protect me, she said, from the 'bad' and 'desperate' person that Christina was. 'Just like I'd protected Janet,' was all she would say, and I wouldn't damage our budding relationship by pushing further.

We departed for Dover the very next day and took a late passage to Calais, sitting up overnight, before the train to Paris and the Gare du Nord. After a further two days of travel, crossing the Italian border and on down to Florence, we pulled up in a rickety cart to the villa which George had rented in the hills of Antella, on the outskirts of the city.

At first, all was well. The summer weather was perfect, and we passed lazy days in the garden there, or viewing the sights of Florence. But in the winter, a letter came from Mary. A detective had come to the house in Charlotte Square. Christina had got talking to him one night in some tavern somewhere, and he wanted to know what my mother had to say about the 'accusations' Christina was making about her.

Too many of my mother's friends knew she was in Italy. It was only a matter of time before someone said something to someone, however innocently. I thought then that she might explain more; why a detective would take seriously whatever Christina had to say. But she never did. Only, for the first time since I had met her, did she look afraid.

I would have done anything to banish that fear from her face. George could only offer dismissals of Christina's threats but I could see that they didn't reach my mother, didn't banish whatever it was that was buried deep within her.

And deep within me, a tiny fear sprouted of something I might learn, that I wouldn't *care* to learn. I didn't doubt what my mother had told me, not one bit of it. But that there might be something overlooked, or unsaid, began to niggle at me. What might come out, with a detective looking?

I remembered, one late night, something about the trial, and it made me think. The next morning, I made my suggestion to my mother.

A decoy had been used to draw the attention of those waiting outside the court, after the verdict of Not Proven. A young woman had worn my mother's dress, her face hidden by a heavy veil. She'd been escorted from the court by two policemen. And while the crowds chased her carriage down the Royal Mile, my mother had headed away with her brother, Jack, to Rowaleyn.

She never knew the name, she said, of the young woman who was her 'decoy'. The crowds never caught up with her.

This time, I would be my mother's decoy.

We would tell all her friends that she had gone to New York to visit Tom, who was there with his wife Annita and their baby girl, Violet.

'But a detective will need proof,' I said. 'So someone must travel there who can be taken for you. Let me do it. I want to do it.'

It seemed so simple. Let this detective follow the trail of breadcrumbs I would leave him, in my guise as my mother, I said. 'Then, after a while, I can come back to London, and you can come back from Italy, and we can all be together again.'

I didn't say what we were all thinking: that Christina, wraith as she was, surely wouldn't survive too many years more. The possibility of it being a more permanent move was never voiced.

But nothing made me happier than to see the fear that had damaged her features in recent weeks, leave her face. It was agony to me to be leaving my mother after having found her so recently. But it made me happy, to protect her, just as she had wanted to protect *me*.

And so, every day, my mother fed me titbits of her life, like a blackbird feeding her chicks. Little pieces of information that would allow me to be her, to claim something of her history. And then, a few weeks later, I found myself on a Liverpool dockside, staring up at a ship the size of a street of the grandest houses.

'Remember who you are,' I muttered to myself. A rush of folk propelled me up the gangplank; maybe that was what caused my slip-up. That day was such a jumble of so many things; and in my thinking too much about what was to come and not about what was right in front of me, I made my mistake. Inevitable, perhaps.

I could still see it, in my mind's eye. My shaking fingers, my lack of breath. My first test, written in ink, as another person.

Writing down *Lena Wardle, born 1857* in the ship's logbook.

The year of my mother's trial.

But the year of *my* birth.

Not hers.

The hotel room was so very hot, and the day had been too long already. I was more than done with all of it.

'So you see,' I said, finally. 'I'm not her. But I am her daughter, and I'll not let you destroy those I love.'

Harry blinked; I insisted on tea, for my throat was so dry, and he rang down for a tray.

As we waited, he sat, shaking his head.

'It's too remarkable,' he kept saying. 'It's crazy; it's crazy.'

When the tea arrived, I said, 'You don't have a film, Harry – admit it. I'm not the draw she would have been. Ah, but she would have been perfect for movies! The sparkle she had! Photographs of her did her no justice at all. You had to see her in the flesh. How she lit up a room. I'm a poor substitute for her, believe me. And anyway, who cares about the daughter? Look at Ruth Snyder. Who cares about her daughter, who she is? Nobody – nobody wants to know about her. And nobody will want to know about me.'

He sat, frowning, not saying a word. It occurred to me suddenly that I had overplayed my hand. I had dispensed with the confusion – the threat of a showing-up, if Harry told the world he'd found Madeleine Smith. And in doing so, I had presented him with Madeleine Smith's daughter.

'I'm no draw,' I said again, a little more desperately.

'I think you might be wrong,' he said. 'I think they'll want to hear this, too.'

The record, the light, the camera, had all been rolling, of course. I'd forgotten all about them. He wasn't going to let up. I had made a terrible mistake.

Dizziness overwhelmed me. I stood up but fell back into my chair, breathing hard. Harry soaked a cloth in the bathroom to cool my head, but it was no use.

'I think I need – oh, a doctor. My heart,' I said, panting a little. 'Please – can you go down to the lobby and see if there's one in the hotel? Quickly—'

He nodded, and ran out of the room. In his panic, it didn't occur to him to just call down, which meant I had time.

I bent down and opened my purse. I'd brought it with me, of course. The package of arsenic I'd been forced to buy, along with the red-squill I'd meant for myself.

I took the teapot and poured out two cups of tea, one for him and one for me, then opened the package. Would he notice a few tiny grains in his cup? It took only four or five, after all. Could I do what I was sure my mother had never done, no matter what some said about her?

Just four or five grains to kill a man.

My hands shook as I peered into the packet. Inside it was all grey. 'Just a couple of grains,' I told myself.

I stared and stared at the package. 'Just do it, Lena,' I muttered to myself, and I sprinkled a couple of grains into one of the cups of tea.

Just do it, Lena.

Lena. How I'd lived her name all these years. For she was me and I was her; that was how I saw it. That was why, even after she'd died in Italy – suddenly, according to George – almost thirty years ago now, I still never came clean. It was why I never used my real name, Emily. I didn't want to be her.

No: I wanted to stay as Lena for ever; to be my bright, sparkling, enterprising mother, not dowdy, self-conscious, unsure Emily Mason. I wanted to be Lena, the woman who stood against a world that tried to break her. The woman who survived. Yes; I'd be her for as long as I drew breath.

And so I became a different person, and lived as that person long after I needed to. I wasn't the same woman who'd stepped off that ship in 1893. I'd become my mother; given birth, you might even say, to myself.

It was Harry who saved me, in the end. He arrived back in the suite to find me lying sprawled on the floor, clutching my stomach and groaning in pain. For I'd drunk that poisoned cup myself.

I was in a real state when he shouted out. I resisted his help at first; I wanted to die, or I'd have failed my mother, so I thought. But he took hold of me and made me vomit right there on the hotel suite floor, before heaving me into the bathroom. It was like the worst food poisoning imaginable, agonising stomach pains that had me retching into a bowl over and over.

I told him to leave me be and let me die, begged him at one point to finish me off, for the pain was so great. But he didn't pay attention to my pleadings. After I was done retching and vomiting up nothing but mucus, he ordered some hot, sweet tea, and that made me sick all over again.

Finally, it stopped. The pain eased; four or five grains weren't enough, as it turned out. I was still alive. Harry lifted me on to the bed, where I slept as he sat upright in a chair beside me through all the hours that followed.

When I eventually woke, surprised to find myself hungry, Harry was awake, too, watching me from his chair.

'What did you save me for?' I said, my throat nipping from all the bile I'd vomited up.

'I won't have a woman's death on my conscience,' he said. 'I'm many things, but I'm not a killer.'

Something inside me sighed then. For all that he was crude and mercenary and without scruples, he wasn't that low. He handed me a beaker of water to sip.

'I won't have you tell the world—' I started to say.

But he held up his hand to silence me. 'I won't. I give you my word. It's over.'

'I'll only do it again if you try—'

'There's no need. Ah – perhaps you're right. Who cares about the daughter?' He half-smiled. 'I'm not a monster,' he said quietly. 'Those newspapers at the time – they thought Emile – your father – was one, blackmailing your mother like that over her letters—'

'Like you blackmailed me,' I couldn't help saying.

He had the decency to look ashamed at last. 'The way they talked about him in court. How they saw him, what he did – well, maybe he *was* a monster. And maybe your mother did kill him. Hell, maybe Christina was a monster, too. But I'm not.'

I swallowed. 'And you won't say anything to Violet?' I said.

'No – but I think you should. You're not ninety-two, you're seventy. If you live another twenty years, how are you gonna explain being one hundred and twelve years old to her?'

'I'll cross that bridge when I come to it,' I said. It was what Willy had always said to me, too.

He shook his head. 'Do you think you can walk?' he said.

I nodded.

He handed me my shawl and hat. 'Let me take you home,' he said.

The shiny equipment in his suite looked ridiculous now.

'What will you do with it all?' I asked, nodding at the microphone, the camera.

'Shaw's still in town,' he said, and grinned a little.

We drove in silence back to the apartment. 'You promise not to use anything I told you?' I said again, as we halted.

Just then, a newspaper boy ran past with more headlines.

ALIENISTS EXAMINE SNYDER SLAYERS

'See?' he said. 'The mind doctors are on it now, wanting to know why she did it. They really don't care about the daughter.'

He shrugged then, and I knew I was safe. After he got out and helped me up the stoop, he tipped his hat in silence and I waited until he drove away, out of my life.

Only then did I go inside to the parlour. There was an Irving Berlin song I wanted to hear very much, and so I put it on and sat down on the daybed, to think about my mother, whose eyes were so like mine. Whose life I had protected with my own. I nodded at the photograph of Janet that her lawyers had sent to Tom when she died. Janet, with the same eyes.

The music got me swaying, humming along to the words.

I'll be loving you always,
With a love that's true always.
When the things you plan,
Need a helping hand,
I will understand,
Always,
Always.

Epilogue: Tuscany, 1901

How warm the evenings are here! I breathe in deeply and reach for George's hand. Our garden is full of scent, orange blossom and hyacinths, and other kinds of exotic blooms I could never grow in London.

'You're thinking about her, aren't you?' he says, and gives me a small smile, for he's very sad this evening, though my heart feels lighter, at last.

'We had so little time together,' I say. 'Oh, with all of them, of course. Tom, and Mary, and the children. But Emily – I will always be sorry for what we missed out on, all those years we might have had together—'

A little lump forms in my throat. A knot of regret and anger that I've never resolved, not in the almost ten years since I left London. Of course she had to come back, Christina, and ruin everything, that October night so long ago, when I had just found my daughter and she had just found me.

How it's been playing over and over in my mind. Perhaps because the time has come; the reckoning that's long been due to me.

'Will you not change your mind?' George says, squeezing my hand a little.

'No,' I say. 'I'm not going to change my mind. You know I can't.'

'Yes,' he says, sadly.

But my thoughts aren't of him. They're of my dear Emily, who'll soon be told that the time has come, and she can be herself again.

George gets up and goes inside the house. I have only a few moments left, but I want to see the sunset, for the last time.

My diagnosis has been so devastating for him. But I refuse to be a burden, I've said. The truth is, I fear the pain of a long, drawn-out illness.

This way is better. I watch the light in the bedroom go out, and I know he's leaving me to fulfil my own wishes. I get up, now it's dark, and make my way inside to the kitchen.

A tincture of poison stands in a dark little bottle that reminds me of the ones my mother had when she would take her illnesses. Those strange little bottles whose scents made me feel so ghostly.

Prussic acid. How ironic to have it in my possession now, so many years later! I sit down in the chair and remove the stopper. I sniff. A scent of almonds. I tilt my head back a little and pour it down my throat, every last drop.

I have no regrets about my life or about anything that I did. I never have regretted it, that act of mine that led to so much pain. Sometimes we have no choice in this world, but to survive, and I am glad that I did, and that *he* did not.

Perhaps I'll be reborn, for I did once believe in such things.

How would I like to come back? That is my last thought. Before an impossible sound reaches me – a wolf howling, far away in the forests beyond – and I laugh.

THE END

Author's Note

At the end of 2012, the writer Emma Tennant rang me. I had reviewed many of her later novels and interviewed her a couple of times for newspapers, and we'd even had lunch once in London when I was there meeting with an agent. She had a proposal for me: that we should write a novel together about Madeleine Smith.

About two years before this, I had reviewed *Murder and Morality in Victorian Britain: The Story of Madeleine Smith* by Eleanor Gordon and Gwyneth Nair for the *Herald* newspaper, so I knew something about her life. At the age of twenty-two, the granddaughter of one of Glasgow's most renowned architects, Madeleine Smith, had stood in the dock accused of poisoning her French lover, Pierre Emile L'Angelier, with arsenic. The case was shocking for several reasons: sex before marriage was considered a scandalous thing, especially amongst the middle classes; the love letters Madeleine had sent Emile were sexually candid; and the lovers were socially mismatched, as Emile was a clerk, while Madeleine was a wealthy heiress.

Even more scandalous than all of this, though, was the verdict: Scotland's infamous 'not proven', which, as everybody knew, meant 'we think you did it but we can't prove it.' The trial was reported from America to India, and was one of the greatest scandals of the Victorian age.

It was also one of the most 'unsolved' crimes of the age, and remains so to this day. Emma Tennant's opener was a question: how did Madeleine get so much poison into Emile? There was too much of it to go unnoticed in a cup of cocoa or coffee, as the trial noted at the time. Some had speculated that Emile knew the poison was there but drank it anyway, such was his distress at Madeleine's engagement to another man, William Minnoch.

Emma cited a different answer, one given by the journalist George R. Sims (and one which is referenced by Henry Blyth in his 1975 biography, *Madeleine Smith*).* Sims was a member of 'The Crimes Club', a group founded by Arthur Conan Doyle in 1903 that would meet at the Carlton Club in London to discuss

---

* 'There was a theory propounded by certain medical authorities at the time, and passed from ear to ear in horrified whispers, that Madeleine and Emile performed acts of oral sex. This led to the supposition that she might have poisoned Emile by using an arsenic paste or ointment on her vulva. This seems possible and indeed probable. This theory would explain why Madeleine never seemed to fear pregnancy, despite initial fears expressed after their love-making at Rowaleyn, and it would help to explain how they were able to make love without waking Janet. Above all, it would explain how Emile failed to detect the flavour of arsenic in the cocoa; for in this theory it is not suggested that all the poison was sexually administered, but that it was so administered first – with the cooperation of Emile, an addicted arsenic eater – and then, without his knowledge, in large doses in the cocoa. If Emile knew that he had acquired the poison sexually, this would explain the otherwise inexplicable fact that he did not tell his landlady how and where he had become ill.' pp.196–7, Blyth.

unsolved crimes. On one occasion, the case of Madeleine Smith came up, and Sims said he knew how Madeleine had done it. He cited the rumoured practice of prostitutes in Ancient Greece who wanted to avoid pregnancy; they would make a suppository containing arsenic, which they would then insert inside themselves. He believed Madeleine had done such a thing, and that a phrase she used in her letters of Emile 'loving her at the window' referred to cunnilingus. In short, she had poisoned Emile by means of a sexual act.

Emma wanted to use this theory for her part of the novel that we would write together; I had suggested that I write the 'older' Madeleine's narrative. After the 'not proven' verdict of her trial, Madeleine disappeared, almost certainly to her family's country estate, Rowaleyn. How long she stayed there for, we don't know. She kept out of sight for four years until 1861, when she married George Wardle in Knightsbridge. He was a drawing master who had been living in Devonport.

Gordon and Nair found evidence that Madeleine had also been living in a house in Devonport run by a couple, the Reverend George Mason and his wife Ellen, who happened to be in charge of a 'house for fallen women'. When exactly Madeleine moved in with them we can't be sure – Gordon and Nair suggest 1859, but it might have been before that. After her marriage to Wardle, Madeleine, now known as 'Lena', moved to Bloomsbury, had two children, and became a noted society hostess amongst the Pre-Raphaelites and their friends. Wardle became the foreman in William Morris's Arts and Crafts company, and Morris's wife, Jane Morris, became a good friend of Madeleine's. There are rumours that Madeleine once sat for Rossetti*, and when Morris formed the Socialist League, Madeleine was its treasurer and librarian.

She disappears from view in 1890, though – the 1891 census doesn't record her living in the UK at all, and we don't glimpse her again until 1893, when she boards a ship for America, ostensibly to visit her son Tom, in New York. As far as we know, she never returns to her husband, George, or sees her daughter Mary, ever again, and in April 1928, she dies at the age of ninety-three and is buried at Mount Hope Cemetery in the US.

The ship's register from her journey to New York throws up another mystery, however, for Madeleine gave her year of birth there as 1857. That is, of course, the year of her trial for murder, and not 1835, her real birth date. So did she lie about her age – and if so, why? Or did she simply make a mistake?

In New York, Madeleine would live with a man called William Sheehy, and it was thought that she married him after George Wardle's death in 1910. However, Gordon and Nair showed that no marriage ever actually took place – why not? They also cite the rumour that a film company from Hollywood approached Madeleine in 1927, the seventieth anniversary of her infamous

---

* Rossetti is famous for using his mistresses as models for his paintings, so they are all easily identifiable. However, his painting *Found*, which featured the head of Fanny Cornforth, was never finished – he started painting, then left off for several years, then went back to it again, then left it. When he returned to it, he had only painted the head of the model – it's Fanny Cornforth's face we see. But by this time, Cornforth was obese, and it made me wonder if Madeleine could have stood in as the model's body. The fact that one of the painting's earliest owners was Sir Thomas Wardle, Madeleine's brother-in-law, made that idea even more alluring.

case, and pressured her into performing on film for them. If she did so, there is currently no evidence that this film exists. But I found this suggestion intriguing, and wanted to imagine the elderly Madeleine being blackmailed once again by a man, and how she might have managed it.

When Emma and I met face to face a few years after this conversation, she was recovering from a severe illness and was unable to write her part of the novel. She asked me to complete both parts, and gifted me the twenty-six pages she had managed to write. I couldn't match her genius for that postmodern, Henry Jamesian style she had; instead, I had to write the narrative of Madeleine in 1857 in my own voice. But in my final version here, I have carried over some mementoes of her short extract, as a kind of homage to her – the mention of the St Rollox chimney, for example, is from Emma's pages, and she mentioned it because it was owned by her ancestor, Sir Charles Tennant. I also found a way to use the balloon ride she depicted Madeleine enjoying.

In May 2014, I was fortunate enough to win a month-long Writer's Residency at Gladstone's Library, and managed to complete a first draft of my novel there, but I had a long way to go before it was ready to send to an agent. Just under three years later, Emma sadly passed away. My manuscript went through many different stages and rewrites before it came to publication, not least because I couldn't agree with Sims' suggestion of how Madeleine had killed Emile, although I agreed with Emma that it might well have been through a sexual act. I also couldn't answer the question of why Madeleine had written 1857 as the year of her birth when she travelled to New York.

Two things changed that for me. As I went over the facts of

the case, I found myself questioning why Madeleine made a trip to Rowaleyn on the day of Emile's funeral. Biographers have never known why – her fiancé William Minnoch's 'explanation' is only a guess on his part as to why she left that morning, slipping out of the house before anyone was awake, and making a solitary boat trip from Glasgow's docks to Greenock, then taking another boat across the Clyde to Helensburgh. He also maintained in court that Madeleine had not told him why she made the journey, keeping tight-lipped on the carriage ride from Helensburgh to Glasgow, and telling him nothing.

This trip has always disturbed me, because the explanation he gave – that she wanted to get away from the city on the morning of Emile's funeral because it might upset her – never quite seemed enough. A novelist would need a better reason than that if they were to include it in a story! Then I realised the significance of the date might not be that it was the morning of Emile's funeral, but that it was the morning after the evening when the French consul had visited the Smith household and informed them that Madeleine's letters would be going to the Procurator Fiscal, who would be determining the date of the inquest into Emile's death.

To me, that was the significant moment. It's the moment Madeleine realises this will likely be a criminal case, and her letters won't be returned to her. William Minnoch was right when he said that Madeleine wasn't attempting to escape – he made a point of saying in court that she looked quite happy to see him when he arrived in Helensburgh to find her sitting, waiting. She wasn't trying to flee the country.

Why, then, had she decided to make this boat trip, and at such an early hour of the day, at dawn? The biographer doesn't have to provide an answer, but the novelist does, and to me, the only explanation was that she was getting rid of something that would incriminate her. And what would be more incriminating than the murder weapon?

That she chose to travel by boat, and not take, say, a train to Edinburgh, seemed highly significant to me. She was getting rid of incriminating evidence that she couldn't put in a fire because it was made of material that wouldn't burn; nor could it be thrown out with the day's rubbish, because it would be noticed. She couldn't throw it from a train window because someone might see her, and it would be left by the side of the track, possibly recoverable.

But thrown into water? It was a perfect solution, so I began to think about what that object could be. Following on from Emma's suggestion of a sexual act, I came across an article in April 2017 in the *Guardian* about an auction in County Meath, where a particular object was for sale, described as an 'antique carved ivory ladies' companion in scarlet lined leather upholstered carry box with inset bevelled glass panel'.* It was dated back to the 1840s, and belonged to a 'well-travelled man' who'd shot an elephant in India and had the ivory tusk shaped 'into something more useful' as a present for his wife. The auctioneer told the newspaper that this 'would have been a very loving gift from a husband to wife. You can see that because the level of detail is incredible, down to the folds of the skin . . .'

---

* Collins, Pádraig. 'Victorian-era ivory sex toy generates excitement at Irish auction'. *Guardian*, 22 April 2017.

Writers like Fern Riddell* have opened our eyes to sexual behaviour in the Victorian age, and it's now understood how popular sex 'toys' were during that era, especially among couples who might not see one another for months at a time†. It made me wonder if Emile, a sexually experienced man who had lived in Paris during the revolutions, could have provided Madeleine with such an object. There were long periods when the lovers were apart, given that Madeleine's relationship with Emile was a clandestine one. Although she tells Emile at the beginning that her father had forbidden the relationship, she later confesses to him that she lied about that, and that only her mother knew. (In my novel, for dramatic reasons, I have it that she does tell her father, as she initially told Emile she did. I'm not convinced she isn't lying to him later on, when she says that she never told her father.) It's not easy for forbidden lovers to meet, and when the Smith family were at Rowaleyn for six or seven months of the year, it would have been even more difficult for them to see one another often, as Emile was employed in Glasgow.

The second part of the puzzle was that date on the ship's passenger list in 1893, when Madeleine sailed to New York. Why did she give 1857, the year of the trial, as the year of her birth? Nobody has asked that question, as it was only recently discovered, first by Bill Greenwell, then cited in Gordon and

---

* Riddell, Fern. 'No, no, no! Victorians didn't invent the vibrator'. *Guardian*, 10 November 2014.

† Furman, Anna. 'Unmentionable review – the Victorian sex manual revisited'. *Guardian*, 1 November 2016.

Nair.* I had the opportunity to meet with Eleanor Gordon and ask her, and Gwyneth Nair very kindly sent me a link to the entry she found through an ancestor search.

It was my mother-in-law who suggested that Madeleine might simply have made a mistake if the case was on her mind for some reason, and my husband who suggested that it might not even have been her on the ship. That made me think: if it wasn't Madeleine, then who was it, and why were they pretending to be her? Eleanor Gordon said that she had looked for evidence that Madeleine had had a baby out of wedlock and that was why she was staying with the Masons in Devonport, although she was living in their house, not the 'home for fallen women' that they ran. Alas, she found nothing to suggest that Madeleine had given birth there, although there were many rumours after the trial that she was pregnant, when she was hidden away from public view by her family immediately after the verdict. The 'decoy' that her counsel employed to draw crowds away from her is a true story, and does suggest the family were keen to keep her away from the public's sight. Was it indeed because she was

---

* 'In 1893, at the age of 58, (Madeleine) determined to make another fresh start. She boarded the SS *Arizona* in Liverpool, and on 11th of September arrived in New York. Taking full advantage of the opportunities offered by such a departure, she declined to give her marital status and stated her age to be 36.' p. 184, Gordon and Nair. See also Bill Greenwell's notes on Madeleine, where he writes: 'She sliced twenty-two years from her age on the immigration documents – on the ship's manifest, she is shown as 36, when she was actually 58. Presumably this was done with Tom's connivance, since he was now technically "older" than his mother.' www.billgreenwell.com.

pregnant? Or just because she had caused them such scandal?

I have no proof that 'Emily Mason' ever existed, or that Madeleine had a child by Emile, or anyone else, in 1857. But the contrast between her life in New York, which was quiet and respectful, devoid of all the political and artistic connections that she had made in London, and her salon-hosting lifestyle in Bloomsbury, seems odd to me. It was reported that her own grandchildren knew nothing of her scandalous past. Gordon and Nair note that her sister, Janet, believed Madeleine was living in New York and mentions her in her will, although she doesn't know anything about William Sheehy.*

As I worked on the manuscript, I also became more and more convinced that Madeleine didn't act alone in her poisoning of Emile. I do believe today that we would see his psychological control of her as abuse, and that we would judge her mental state differently, too. Her actions are premeditated, but a great deal of work has been done to show that women, after a long period of abuse, and feeling themselves to be physically weaker, will plan beforehand, rather than act in a single moment of impulse.

At the time of Emile's murder, Madeleine was surrounded by people. There was her fiancé, William Minnoch, who saw her almost every evening at that time; her sister, Janet, who slept beside her every night; Christina the housemaid, who had carried letters between Madeleine and Emile, had accepted a skirt from him, had allowed the lovers to use her own room on

---

* 'The remainder of (Janet's) estate was left to "my sister Mrs Madeleine Smith or Wardle, widow, presently residing in the USA."' p.187, Gordon and Nair.

occasion, and who slept along the corridor from Madeleine. It always struck me as strange that Janet didn't provide an alibi for her sister, as she could easily have said that she woke up several times during the night of Emile's poisoning and her sister was beside her throughout. That Christina should emphasise in her testimony that she hadn't left the gate unlocked that night, but that anyone else inside the house might have, indicated to me a person who was terrified of being blamed somehow – as a servant, Christina wouldn't have had the resources to hire the best legal team that Madeleine had. That Janet left items to her sister in her will suggests that they remained on friendly terms throughout their lives.

Of Christina, there is no further mention in any biography that I could find, and my depiction of her returning to threaten Madeleine is an invention. I have no proof that Christina was even still alive at this point. But it is my belief that something – or someone – forced Madeleine to leave her husband and daughter, and baby grandson, in 1893. And it wasn't just her family, but also her close friends, her social connections, her standing in the community that she'd built up over almost thirty years – all of them were left behind suddenly, and without explanation.

Madeleine's last years in Italy with George are an invention on my part, as is her taking her own life. George Wardle did indeed leave London for Italy in 1890, and did not return until 1901. He died in 1910.

I have left Madeleine's sister Bessie out of my novel. Madeleine and Bessie do not seem to have been close, as Madeleine and Janet were, and although it's thought Bessie might have been present when Madeleine first met Emile, and

Bessie accompanied Madeleine on one of her trips to the apothecary for arsenic (in the book, I have changed her companion to Janet), it wasn't the sisterly relationship that I felt really had a part to play in the murder of Emile. I also omitted mention of her second brother, James. In real life, neither Bessie nor Janet ever married. Madeleine's father died in 1863, but her mother lived a long time, until 1894. I have also invented William Minnoch's interest and belief in reincarnation.

Harry Townsend is an invention, born from the rumour that a film company once blackmailed Madeleine into performing on screen for them in New York.* Violet is real, although I have portrayed her as a little younger than she would have been in 1927.

The 1927 timeline was the narrative that I promised Emma Tennant, of course – I don't know what she would have made of my final story here, but I hope she would have liked it. She gave me the cover quote for my very first novel, and I'll never forget that lunch we had in a restaurant just along from her flat in 2006. I was slightly starstruck, needless to say, and so that day is something of a wonderful blur to me now, even though certain moments will always stay with me. I think she was a true literary genius, and I'll always treasure those two meetings I had with her. I only wish there had been more.

One final note on the Christina Rossetti poem that I quote from at the beginning, 'Winter: My Secret', which she composed

---

* 'Once again, the newspapers carried stories that mixed fact and fiction ... she was exposed by "film people" angered by her refusal to play herself in a movie and threatened with deportation.' p. 188, Gordon and Nair.

late in 1857, and whose meaning has long puzzled readers. It includes the lines, 'Spring's an expansive time: yet I don't trust/March with its peck of dust . . .' The Pre-Raphaelites were obsessed with Madeleine's case – in later years, Dante Gabriel Rossetti wrote a little skit about Mrs Lena Wardle, slipping some poison into her husband's employer's cocoa. I like to think that 'Winter: My Secret' is actually about a murder.

– September 2024

Bibliography

A Complete Report of the Trial of Miss Madeline Smith: For The Alleged Poisoning of Pierre Emile L'Angelier (Edinburgh: Ballantyne and Co, 1858)

Anderson, Mark Lynn. *Twilight of the Idols: Hollywood and the Human Sciences of the 1920s* (Berkeley: University of California Press, 2011)

Blyth, Henry. *Madeleine Smith* (London: Duckworth, 1975)

Blum, Deborah. *The Poisoner's Handbook: Murder and the Birth of Forensic Medicine in Jazz Age New York* (New York: Penguin, 2010)

Bryson, Bill. *One Summer: America 1927* (London: Transworld, 2013)

Campbell, Jimmy. *A Scottish Murder: Rewriting the Madeleine Smith Story* (The History Press, 2003)

Colquhoun, Kate. *Did She Kill Him? A Victorian Tale of Deception, Adultery and Arsenic* (London: Little, Brown, 2014)

Dangerfield, George. *The Strange Death of Liberal England* (London: Granada Publishing, 1983)

Flanders, Judith. *The Victorian House* (London: Harper Collins, 2003)

Gordon, Eleanor and Nair, Gwyneth. *Murder and Morality in Victorian Britain: The Story of Madeleine Smith* (Manchester: Manchester University Press, 2009)

Hartman, Mary S. *Victorian Murderesses: A True History of Thirteen Respectable French and English Women Accused of Unspeakable Crimes* (London: Robson Books, 1977, 1985)

Hawksley, Lucinda. *Bitten By Witch Fever: Wallpaper and Arsenic in the Victorian House* (London: Thames and Hudson, 2016)

McGowan, Douglas. *The Strange Affair of Madeleine Smith* (Edinburgh: Mercat Press, 2007)

Rosenblum, Constance. *Boulevard of Dreams: Heady Times, Heartbreak, and Hope Along the Grand Concourse in the Bronx* (New York and London: New York University Press, 2009)

Simon, Kate. *Bronx Primitive: A Memoir* (London: Harrap Books, 1981)